As a child, **Julia Justiss** found he
her to create stories of her own. Sh
After university she served stint
an insurance company and edito
newsletter in Tunisia. She now t
Texas, where she lives with her
two dogs.

Don't miss these other Regency delights from Mills & Boon® Historical romance's bestselling authors!

REGENCY
Secrets

Julia Justiss

MILLS & BOON

All the characters in this book have no existence outside the imagination
of the author, and have no relation whatsoever to anyone bearing the same
name or names. They are not even distantly inspired by any individual
known or unknown to the author, and all the incidents are pure invention.

Harlequin Mills & Boon Limited, Eton House,
18-24 Paradise Road, Richmond, Surrey TW9 1SR

REGENCY SECRETS © Harlequin Books S.A. 2011

The publisher acknowledges the copyright holders of the individual works
as follows:

My Lady's Trust © Janet Justiss 2002
My Lady's Pleasure © Janet Justiss 2002

ISBN: 978 0 263 88732 7

052-0311

Harlequin Mills & Boon policy is to use papers that are natural,
renewable and recyclable products and made from wood grown in
sustainable forests. The logging and manufacturing processes conform to
the legal environmental regulations of the country of origin.

Printed in the UK
by CPI MacKays, Chatham, ME5 8TD

My Lady's Trust

In memory of fellow writer
Nancy Richards-Akers
Shot to death by her estranged husband
June 1999
And to all women caught in domestic abuse.
Get help. Get out.
Your children need you.

Prologue

Soundlessly Laura crept through the dark hall. Having rehearsed—and used—the route before, she knew every carpet, chair and cupboard in the passageway, each twist of the twenty-nine steps down the servants' stair to the back door. Even were their old butler Hobbins and his wife not snoring in their room just off the corridor, the winter storm howling through the chimneys and rattling the shutters would cover the slight rustle of her movements.

Just once she halted in her stealthy passage, outside the silent nursery. Leaning toward the door, she could almost catch a whiff of baby skin, feel the softness of flannel bunting, see the bright eyes and small waving hands. A bitter bleakness pierced her heart, beside whose chill the icy needles being hurled against the windows were mild as summer rain, and her step staggered.

She bent over, gripping for support the handle of the room where a baby's gurgle no longer sounded. Nor ever would again—not flesh of her flesh.

I promise you that, Jennie, she vowed. Making good on that vow could not ease the burden of guilt she carried, but it was the last thing she would do in this house. The only thing, now, she could do.

Marshaling her strength, she straightened and made her way down the stairs, halting once more to catch her breath before attempting to work the heavy lock of the kitchen door. She was stronger now. For the past month she'd practiced walking, at first quietly in her room, more openly this past week since most of the household had departed with its master for London. She could do this.

Cautiously she unlatched the lock, then fastened her heavy cloak and drew on her warmest gloves. At her firm push the door opened noiselessly on well-oiled hinges. Ignoring the sleet that pelted her face and the shrieking wind that tore the hood from her hair, she walked into the night.

Chapter One

The crisp fall breeze, mingling the scents of falling leaves and the sharp tang of herbs, brought to Laura Martin's ear the faint sound of barking interspersed with the crack of rifle shot. The party which had galloped by her cottage earlier this morning, the squire's son throwing her a jaunty wave as they passed, must be hunting duck in the marsh nearby, she surmised.

Having cut the supply of tansy she needed for drying, Laura turned to leave the herb bed. Misfit, the squire's failure of a rabbit hound who'd refused to leave her after she healed the leg he'd caught in a poacher's trap, bumped his head against her hand, demanding attention.

"Shameless beggar," she said, smiling as she scratched behind his ears.

The dog flapped his tail and leaned into her stroking fingers. A moment later, however, he stiffened and looked up, uttering a soft whine.

"What is it?" Almost before the words left her lips she heard the rapid staccato of approaching hoofbeats. Seconds later one of the squire's grooms, mounted on a lathered horse and leading another, flashed into view.

Foreboding tightening her chest, she strode to the garden fence.

"What's wrong, Peters?" she called to the young man bringing his mount to a plunging halt.

"Your pardon, Mrs. Martin, but I beg you come at once! There were an accident—a gun gone off..." The groom stopped and swallowed hard. "Please, ma'am!"

"How badly was the person injured?"

"I don't rightly know. The young gentleman took a shot to the shoulder and there be blood everywhere. He done swooned off immediate, and—"

Her foreboding deepened. "You'd best find Dr. Winthrop. I fear gunshots are beyond—"

"I already been by the doctor's, ma'am, and he—he can't help."

"I see." Their local physician's unfortunate obsession with strong spirits all too frequently left him incapable of caring for himself or anyone else. 'Twas how she'd gained much of her limited experience, stepping in when the doctor was incapacitated. But gunshot wounds? The stark knowledge of her own inadequacy chilled her.

Truly there was no one else. "I'll come at once."

"Young master said as how I was to bring you immediate, but I don't have no lady's saddle. 'Twill take half an hour 'n more to fetch the gig."

"No matter, Peters. I can manage astride. Under the circumstances, I don't imagine anyone will notice my dispensing with proprieties. Help me fetch my bag."

She tried to set worry aside and concentrate on gathering any extra supplies she might need to augment the store already in her traveling bag. The groom carried the heavy satchel to the waiting horses and gave her a hand up. Settling her skirts as decorously as possible, she waited for him to vault into the saddle, then turned her restive horse to follow his. Spurring their mounts, they galloped back in the direction of the marsh.

As they rode, she mentally reviewed the remedies she brought. During her year-long recovery from the illness that nearly killed her, she'd observed Aunt Mary treat a variety of agues, fevers and stomach complaints—but never a gunshot. To the assortment of medicaments she always carried she'd added a powder to slow bleeding, brandy to cleanse the wound and basilica powder. Had she thought of everything?

She had no further time to worry, for around the next bend the woods gave way to marsh. A knot of men gathered at the water's edge. As she slid from the saddle, she saw at their center a still, prone figure, the pallor of his face contrasting sharply with the scarlet of the blood soaking his coat. His clothing was drenched, his boots half submerged in water whose icy bite she could already feel through the thin leather of her half-boots. The squire's son Tom held a wadded-up cloth pressed against the boy's upper chest. A cloth whose pristine whiteness was rapidly staining red.

Her nervousness coalesced in firm purpose. She must first stop the bleeding, then get the young man back to Everett Hall.

"Peters, bring more bandages from my bag, please."

At her quiet command, Tom looked up. "Thank God you're here!" His face white beneath its sprinkling of freckles, he scooted over to let her kneel beside the victim. "He's bled so badly—and…and he won't answer me. Is…is he going to die?"

"Help me," she evaded. "Lean your full weight against him, hard. Keep that cloth in place while I bind it to his shoulder. Did the shot pass straight through?"

"I don't know, ma'am. I—I didn't think to look."
Tom's eyes were huge in his pale face. "It's my fault—
I wanted to hunt. If he dies—"

"Easy, now—keep the pressure firm." To steady
Tom—and herself—she said, "Tell me what happened."

"I'm not sure. The dogs raised a covey, and we both
fired. The next moment Kit clutched his chest, blood
pouring out between his fingers. Maybe—perhaps one
of our shots hit that bluff and ricocheted. He fell in the
water, as you see, and we dragged him to land but
feared to move him any further until help arrived."

Listening with half an ear, she worked as quickly as
she could, her worried eye on the unconscious victim's
gray face and blue-tinged lips. If the shot was still
lodged in his body, it must be removed, but at the moment she didn't dare explore the wound. Fortunately,
the chill that numbed him also slowed the bleeding. She
only hoped the effect would last through the jolting necessary to take him to shelter. And that his dousing in
frigid water wouldn't result in an inflammation of the
lungs.

"Is he...tell me he'll be all right!"

The desperate note in Tom's voice recalled her attention. Avoiding a direct answer, she looked up to give
him a brief smile. "We must get him out of the cold.
Have you sent to the hall?"

"Yes. My father should be along any moment."

Indeed, as Tom spoke they heard the welcome sound
of a coach approaching. Riding ahead was the squire, a
short, rotund man on a piebald gray. He took one long
look at the scene before him and blew out a gusty
breath.

"God have mercy! What's to be done, Mrs. Martin?"

"If you would help me bind this tightly, we can move him into the carriage and back to the hall."

After securing the bandage, she directed the grooms to carry the victim to the coach, the unconscious man groaning as they eased him against the padded squabs.

"Tom, ride on ahead and alert Mrs. Jenkins. We'll need boiling water and hot bricks and such." The squire shook his head, his nose red with cold and his eyes worried. "Go on, I'll settle with you later. There'll be a reckoning to pay for this day's work, make no mistake!"

Wordlessly his son nodded, then sprinted to his mount. After assisting Laura into the carriage beside her patient, the squire hesitated. "You'll tend him back at the hall?"

"Until more experienced help arrives, of course. But I recommend you send someone with strong coffee to sober up Dr. Winthrop, or over to the next county for their physician. I've no experience with gunshots, and to tell the truth, the young man looks very badly."

To her surprise, the squire seized her hands. "You must stay, Mrs. Martin, and do all you can! 'Tis no country doctor we'll be having! I've sent word to the lad's brother to come at once and bring his own physician. Please say you'll stay with the boy until he arrives!"

An instinctive prickle of fear skittered up from her toes and lodged at her throat. She glanced at the still figure beside her. Was there something familiar about that profile? "He is from a prominent family?" she ventured, already dreading the response.

"Younger brother of the Earl of Beaulieu."

For a moment her heart nearly stopped. "The Puzzlebreaker?'' she asked weakly. ''Friend to the prime minister, one of the wealthiest men in the realm?''

''Aye, he founded that daft Puzzlemaker's Club, but he's a sharp 'un, for all that. It's said Lord Riverton don't make a move without consulting him. Been visiting friends up north, with this cub set to join him next week.'' The squire sighed heavily. ''When I consider what Lord Beaulieu may think should his brother Kit die in my care... I do swear, I rue the day my Tom met him at Oxford.''

''Surely the earl could not hold you responsible.''

The squire shrugged, then raised pleading eyes to hers. ''I beg you to stay, Mrs. Martin. With any luck, my messenger will reach the earl within hours and bring his physician back, mayhap by nightfall. I'd not have the worthless Winthrop near him, drunk or sober, and Lord knows, my sister will be no help. Mistress Mary thought so highly of your skill—none better in the county, she swore. Will you not keep the lad alive until his kin arrive?''

And thereby encounter the Earl of Beaulieu? All her protective instincts screamed danger as the metallic taste of fear filled her mouth, seeming stronger than ever after its near two-year hiatus. Though her first impulse was to jump from the carriage, mount the borrowed horse and race back to the safe haven of her little cottage, she struggled to squelch her irrational panic.

She must fashion a measured reply. The squire would be expecting from her nothing more extreme than worry.

While she fumbled for appropriate words, the squire sat straighter. ''You cannot fear I'd allow the earl to take you to task should...the worst happen. My good madam, surely you realize your well-being is of great import to me!'' He leaned closer and kissed her hand awkwardly. ''I only seek to do all we can for the poor lad until his brother arrives.''

''I know you would ever safeguard me,'' she replied, and managed a smile. *You're being a nodcock,* the rational part of her brain argued. The great earl was hardly likely to recognize her as one of the unremarkable chits making her bow he'd met but twice a handful of Seasons ago. Though this task was clearly beyond her skill, she had more expertise than any other person within a day's ride, and the boy needed help now.

As she vacillated, torn between the safety of refusal and the peril of acceptance, she heard again Aunt Mary's last words *God spared you for a purpose, missy. He's given you skill—use it wisely.*

She glanced again at the boy, motionless and bloody beside her. Did not that innocent lad deserve the best possible chance to survive? Even if caring for him placed her in some risk.

But a risk much less serious than the young man's chances of dying if left untended.

''Have the coachman drive slowly. He must be jostled as little as possible,'' she said at last. ''If the wound begins bleeding again, there will be nothing I can do.''

The squire released a grateful sigh. ''Thank you, ma'am. I'll keep pace by the coach. Call if you need me.''

He stepped down and closed the door, leaving her in the shuttered semidarkness with a barely breathing boy whose powerful brother, Lord Beaulieu, would be upon her within hours, perhaps this very day.

What had she gotten herself into?

Hugh Mannington ''Beau'' Bradsleigh, Earl of Beaulieu, leaped from the saddle and tossed the reins of his spent steed to the servant who materialized out of the darkness. His bootsteps ringing out on the stone steps, he approached the flickering torches flanking the entry of Squire Everett's manor house. Before he reached the front portal, however, a tall, freckled lad he recognized as Kit's Oxford friend rushed out.

"Lord Beaulieu, thank God you're come. I'm so sorry—"

"Where is he?" At the stricken look coming over the young man's face, Beau briefly regretted his abruptness, but after a message designed to convince him Kit could die at any moment and the most exhausting gallop he'd endured in years, he had no patience for an exchange of courtesies.

A shorter, rotund man with a balding head darted into view. "This way, my lord. Squire Everett here, but we'll not stand on formality. Cook has a platter of victuals and strong ale waiting. I'll have them sent up at once."

Beau spared a brief smile for the older man who, though obviously anxious, made no attempt to delay him with excuses or explanations he at the moment had no interest in hearing. "You, sir, are both kind and perceptive." Taking a deep breath, as he followed the squire to the stairs he voiced the anxiety that had eaten at him every second of the arduous ride. "How goes it with Kit?"

The squire gave him a sidelong glance as they started up. "Not well, I'm afraid. We very nearly lost him this afternoon. When do you expect your physician?"

The tension in his chest tightened. Kit—laughing, sunny-tempered Kit, so full of the joy of life. He *could not* die—Beau would simply not permit it. "Morning at the earliest. Who tends him now? Have you a doctor here?''

''Only a jug-bitten fool I'd not trust with a lame dog. Mrs. Martin keeps vigil, a neighbor lady skilled with herbs who is often consulted by the local folk.''

The image of an old crone mixing love potions for the gullible flew into his head. ''An herb woman!'' he said, aghast. '''Od's blood, man, that's the best you could do?''

The squire paused at the landing and looked back in dignified reproach. '''Tis not in London we be, my lord. Mrs. Martin is widow to a military man and has much experience tending the sick. She, at least, I was confident could do young Kit no harm. Indeed, she's kept him from death several times already. In here, my lord.''

He should apologize to the squire later, Beau noted numbly as he paced into the chamber. But for now all his attention focused on the figure lying in the big canopied bed, his still, pale face illumined by the single candle on the bedside table.

Still and pale as a death mask. Fear like a rifle shot ricocheted through him as he half ran to his brother's side. ''Kit! Kit, it's Hugh. I'm here now.''

The boy on the bed made no response as Beau took his hand, rubbed it. The skin felt dry—and warm.

''He's turning feverish, I fear.''

The quiet, feminine voice came from the darkness on the far side of the bed. Beau looked over at a nondescript woman in a shapeless brown dress, her head covered by a large mobcap that shadowed her face. This was what passed for medical aid here? Fear flashed anew—and anger. ''What do you intend to do about it?''

"Keep him sponged down and spoon in willow bark tea. He was so chilled initially, I did not think it wise to begin cooling him from the first. I'm afraid the shot is still lodged in his chest, but I dared not remove it. When does your physician arrive?"

"Not before morning," he repeated, anxiety filling him at the echo. This kindly old biddy might do well for possets and potions, but was she to be all that stood between Kit and death until MacDonovan came?

No, he thought, setting his jaw. *He* was here, and he'd be damned if he'd let his brother die before his eyes. "Tell me what to do."

"You have ridden all day, my lord?"

"Since afternoon," he replied impatiently. "'Tis no matter."

The woman looked up at him then, the eyes of her shadowed face capturing a glow of reflected candlelight. Assessing him, he realized with a slight shock.

Before he could utter a set-down, she said, "You should rest. You'll do the young gentleman no good, once he regains consciousness, if you're bleary with fatigue."

He fixed on her the iron-eyed glare that had inspired more than one subordinate to back away in apologetic dismay. This little woman, however, simply held his gaze. Goaded, he replied, "My good madam, the boy on that bed is my brother, my blood. I assure you, had I ridden the length of England, I could do whatever is necessary."

After another audacious measuring moment, the woman nodded. "Very well. I've just mixed more willow bark tea. If you'll raise him—only slightly now, heed the shot in his chest—I'll spoon some in."

For the rest of what seemed an endless night, he followed the soft-spoken orders of the brown-garbed lady. She seemed competent enough, he supposed, ordering broths up from the kitchen, strewing acrid herbs into the water in which she had him wring out the cloths they placed on Kit's neck and brow, directing him to turn Kit periodically to keep fluid from settling in his lungs.

Certainly she was tireless. Although he'd never have admitted it, after a blur of hours his own back ached and his hands were raw from wringing cloths. Mrs. Martin, however, gave no sign of fatigue at all.

Their only altercation occurred early on, when he demanded she unwrap the bandages so he might inspect Kit's wound. The nurse adamantly refused. Such a course would engender so much movement his brother might begin bleeding again, a risk she did not wish to take. Unless his lordship had experience enough to remove the shot once the wound was bared—a highly delicate task she herself did not intend to attempt—she recommended the bindings be left intact until the physician arrived. So anxious was he to assess the damage, however, only her threat to wash her hands of all responsibility for her patient, should he insist on disturbing Kit, induced him, grudgingly, to refrain.

Despite their efforts, as the long night lightened to dawn, Kit grew increasingly restless, his dry skin hotter. When, just after sunrise, the squire ushered in Beau's physician, both he and Mrs. Martin sighed in relief.

"Thank you, Mac, for answering my call so quickly."

"Ach, and more a command than a call it was." His old schoolmate Dr. MacDonovan smiled at him. "But we'll frash over that later. Let me to the lad. The squire's told me what happened, and the sooner we get the shot out, the better. Mrs. Martin, is it? You'll assist, please.''

The nurse murmured assent, and Beau found himself shouldered aside. ''Go on with ye, ye great lown,'' his friend chided. ''Fetch yerself a wee dram—ye've the look of needin' one.''

''I'm staying, Mac. Let me help.''

His friend spared him a glance, then sighed. ''Open the drapes, laddie, and give us more light. Then bring my bag. I may be wanting it.''

By the time the gruesome procedures were over Beau was almost sorry he'd insisted on remaining. First came the shock of the jagged entry wound, the flesh angry red and swollen. Then he had to endure the torment of holding down his struggling, semiconscious brother while the physician probed the wound with long forceps to locate and remove the shot. His back was wet with sweat and his knees shaking when finally Dr. Mac-Donovan finished his ministrations and began to rebind his patient.

It wasn't until after that was complete, when the physician complimented Mrs. Martin on the efficacy of her previous treatment, that he remembered the woman who had silently assisted during the procedure. With the cap shadowing her lowered face, he couldn't read her expression, but her hands had remained steady, her occasional replies to the physician calm and quiet throughout. He had to appreciate her fortitude.

Having lowered his once-again mercifully unconscious brother back against the pillows, he followed as the physician led them all out of the room.

The squire waited in the hallway. ''Well, Sir Doctor, how does the patient fare?'' he asked anxiously.

''The shot was all of a piece, best I could tell, which

is a blessing. If I've not missed a bit, and if this lady's kind offices in tending the lad until I arrived stand us in good stead, my hopes are high of his making a full recovery. But mind ye, 'tis early days yet. He mustn't be moved, and the fever's like to get much worse afor it's agleaning. It's careful tending he'll be needing. Have ye a good nurse aboot?''

The squire glanced from the doctor to Mrs. Martin and back. "Well, there's my sister, but I'm afraid her nerves are rather delicate—''

"I shall be happy to assist until his lordship can find someone,'' Mrs. Martin inserted, her face downcast.

"Excellent. I recommend you accept the lady's offer, Beau. At least until ye can secure the services of another such reliable nurse.''

"I've already sent a message to Ellen. That is, if it will not be an inconvenience for you to house my sister and her daughter, squire?''

"An honor, my lord,'' the squire replied with a bow. "And yourself, as well, for as long as you wish to remain.''

"Then I should be most grateful to accept your help until my sister arrives, Mrs. Martin.''

After she murmured an assent, the squire turned to the physician. "If you tell me what I must do, Doctor, I'll sit with the lad while Mrs. Martin takes her rest. She's been at his side since morning yesterday and all night, too.'' The squire directed a pointed look at Beau, a reminder he owed the man an apology—and a humble thanks to the quiet woman who'd so skillfully nursed his brother. "Lord Beaulieu, you must be needing your rest, as well. I'll just see the lady on her way and then return to show you to your chamber.''

He bowed. With a nod and a curtsey, Mrs. Martin turned to follow the squire.

Delaying his apologies to pursue a more pressing matter, Beau lingered behind. "Was that report accurate, or are you merely trying to ease the squire's anxiety?" Beau demanded as soon as the pair were out of earshot.

Dr. MacDonovan smiled and patted his arm. "God's truth, Beau. 'Tis hard on you, I know, but there's little we can do now but give him good nursing. He's strong, though—and I do my job well. I canna promise there won't be worrisome times yet, but I believe he'll pull through."

Beau released a breath he didn't realize he'd been holding. "Thanks, Mac. For coming so quickly and—" he managed a grin "—being so good. Now, I'd best give the redoubtable Mrs. Martin a word of thanks. Probably should toss in an apology, as well—I've not been as...courteous as I suppose I might."

The doctor laughed. "Frash with her, did ye? And lost, I'll wager! A lady of much skill, Mrs. Martin. 'Tis she more than me you'd best be thanking for keeping yon Master Kit on this earth. Lay in the icy water of the marsh nigh on an hour, I'm told. The chill alone might have killed him, had he not been carefully watched." The doctor frowned. "Aye, and may catch him yet. We must have a care for those lungs. But away with ye. I can keep these weary eyes open a bit longer."

Beau gave his friend's hand a shake and started down the hall. Now that Kit was safe in Mac's care, he noticed anew the ache in his back and a bone-deep weariness dragged his steps.

He saw Mrs. Martin by the front door as he descended the last flight of stairs, apparently in some dispute with the squire, for she was shaking her head.

"Thank you, sir, but 'tis only a short walk. There's no need for a carriage."

Beau waited for the little courtesies to be observed, his eyes nearly drooping shut until he noticed the squire make Mrs. Martin an elegant leg, quite in the manner of the last century.

"No indeed, dear ma'am, you mustn't walk. I'm fair astonished such a gentle lady as yourself has not collapsed from fatigue ere now. What fortitude and skill you possess! Qualities, I might add, which nearly equal your beauty."

After that pretty speech, the squire took Mrs. Martin's hand and kissed it.

Surprise chased away his drowsiness until he remembered the squire had called Mrs. Martin a "lady," widow to a military man. An officer, apparently, since his host would hardly extend such marked gallantries to an inferior. Beau smiled, amused to discover the middle-aged squire apparently courting the nondescript nurse, and curious to watch her response.

"You honor me," said the lady in question as she gently but firmly drew back her hand.

Coy? Beau wondered. Or just not interested?

Then the nurse glanced up. Illumined as she was by the sunshine spilling into the hall, for the first time he got a clear look at her face—her young, pretty face.

In the same instant she saw him watching her. An expression almost of—alarm crossed her lovely features and she swiftly lowered her head, once again concealing her countenance behind a curtain of cap lace. What remark she made to the squire and whether or not she availed herself of the carriage, he did not hear. Before

he could move his stunned lips into the speech of gratitude he'd intended to deliver, she curtsied once more
and slipped out.

By the time the squire joined him on the landing his
foggy brain had resumed functioning. Mumbling something resembling an apology as the man escorted him
to his chamber, he let his mind play over the interesting
discovery that the skillful Mrs. Martin was not only a
lady, but a rather young one at that.

He recalled the brevity of her speech, even with the
squire, whom she apparently knew well, and the way
she skittered off when she found him watching her.
More curious still. Why, he wondered as he sank thankfully into the soft feather bed, would such an eminently
marriageable widow be so very retiring?

Having the widow tend his brother would give Beau
the opportunity to observe this odd conundrum more
closely. Which would be a blessing, for as his brother's
recovery—and Kit simply must recover—was likely to
be lengthy, Beau would need something to distract him
from worry. Luckily, nothing intrigued him as much as
a riddle.

Chapter Two

A few hours later Laura pulled herself reluctantly from bed and walked to the kitchen. A bright sun sparkled on the scrubbed table and Maggie, the maid of all work the squire sent over every morning to do her cleaning, had left her nuncheon and a pot of water simmering on the stove.

She'd remain just long enough for tea and to wash up before returning to her patient. The kindly Scots physician had ridden straight through, he'd told her, and would be needing relief.

She frowned as she poured water into the washbasin. It wasn't fatigue that caused the vague disquiet that nagged at her. She'd learned to survive on very little sleep while she cared for her dying "aunt Mary."

No, it was the lingering effects of working for so many hours in such close proximity to the Earl of Beaulieu—a man who exuded an almost palpable aura of power—that left her so uneasy.

He'd not recognized her, she was sure. Even when he looked her full in the face this morning, she'd read only surprise in his eyes—surprise, she assumed, that she was not the aged crone he had evidently taken her to be. An impression she, of course, had done her best to instill and one he might harbor yet if she'd not stupidly looked up.

A flash of irritation stabbed her. She'd grown too complacent of late, forgotten to keep her head demurely lowered whenever there might be strangers about.

'Twas too late to repair that lapse. However, despite discovering her to be younger than he'd expected, there was still no reason he should not, as everyone else around Merriville had done, accept her as exactly what she claimed to be, the widowed cousin of the retired governess whose cottage she had inherited.

She felt again a wave of grief for the woman who had been nurse, friend and savior. That gentle lady, sister of Laura's own governess, who had taken in a gravely ill fugitive and given her back not just life, but a new identity and the possibility of a future. Who'd become her mentor, training Laura to a skill which enabled her to support herself. And finally, the benefactor who'd willed her this cottage, safe haven in which to begin over again.

A safe haven still, she told herself firmly, squelching the swirl of unease in her stomach. She need only continue to act the woman everyone believed her to be. Young or not, a simple country gentlewoman could be of no more interest to the great earl than a pebble.

As long as she stayed in her role—no more jerking away in alarm if his eye chanced to fall upon her. She grimaced as she recalled that second blunder, more serious than the first. "The Puzzlebreaker," as the ton had dubbed him after he'd founded a gentleman's club devoted to witty repartee and clever aphorisms, was a gifted mathematician and intimate of the Prince's counselors. But as long as she said or did nothing to engage that keen intellect or pique his curiosity, she would be perfectly safe.

Be plain and dull, she told herself—dull as the dirt-brown hue she always wore, plain as the oversize and shapeless gowns she'd inherited from her benefactress.

And avoid the earl as much as possible.

Dull, dull, dull as the ache in her head from the pins that had contained her long braided locks for too many hours. With a sigh of relief, she loosed them and, tying on a long frayed apron, set about washing her hair.

Beau smiled as he surveyed the modest gig and the even more modest chestnut pulling it. How London's Four Horse Club would laugh to see him tooling such a rig.

But after a few hours' sleep took the edge off his fatigue, a deep-seated worry over Kit roused him irretrievably from slumber. A check on his brother, whose color had gone from unnatural pale to ominously flushed and whose rapid, shallow breathing was doubtless responsible for the frown now residing on Mac's tired face, had been enough to refuel his anxiety.

His physician friend looked exhausted after a ride doubtless as arduous as his own. Humbly acknowledging, at least to himself, that he'd feel better sending Mac off to bed with Mrs. Martin present to direct Kit's care, he'd offered to fetch the nurse. At least the drive in the pleasant early fall sunshine gave him something to distract himself from his gnawing anxiety.

As the squire's son promised, her cottage was easily located. He pulled the gig to a halt before it and waited, but as no one appeared to assist him, he clambered down and hunted for a post to which he could tie the chestnut. Finding none, he set off around the walled garden. Surely behind the cottage there would be some sort of barn.

Having found a shed, by its look of disuse no longer home to horse and tackle but still sturdy, he secured the rig and headed back to the cottage. A gate to the garden stood open, from which, as he started by, a black and white spotted dog trotted out, spied him, and stiffened.

Kneeling, he held out a hand. After a watchful moment, apparently deciding Beau posed no threat, the dog relaxed and ambled over. Beau scratched the canine behind his large ears, earning himself an enthusiastic lick in the process, after which the dog collapsed in a disgraceful heap and rolled over, offering his belly.

"Some watchdog. Where's your mistress, boy?"

The dog inclined his head. When the rubbing did not resume, with an air of resignation he hopped up and loped off into the garden. Amused, Beau followed.

Behind the walls he found cultivated beds, herbs interspersed with a charming array of asters and Michelmas daisies and alternating with chevrons of turnips, onions and cabbages. Inhaling the spicy air approvingly, he was halfway across the expanse of tilled ground when a slight movement near the cottage drew his attention and he halted.

Halted, caught his breath, and then ceased to breathe.

A young woman leaned back against a bench, eyes closed, her head tilted up to a gentle sun that painted a straight nose, arched brows, high cheekbones and full lips with golden highlights. The collar of her gown lay unfastened, revealing an alluring triangle of warm skin from her arched neck downward to the top of an old worn apron, whose blockage of the view that might otherwise have been revealed below he would have fiercely resented had not the garment redeemed itself by clinging snugly to its wearer's generous curves.

The lady's hair, which she was drying in the sun, swirled over the back of the bench and cascaded down beside her in a thick fall of burnished auburn curls.

Just then she reached up to comb her fingers through one long section, fluffing it as she progressed. The movement stretched the threadbare apron taut against her body, its thin white cloth silhouetting her breast against the dark bench, full rounded side to sun-kissed tip.

Beau's mouth grew dry, then dryer still as one curl tumbled from her shoulder, caught on the apron's edge and came to rest cupped, like a lover's hand, around the outline of that perfect breast.

She sighed, a slight exhale that parted her lips and made her look like a woman rousing to passion's whisper. His body tensed in automatic response, his mouth tingling to trace the outline of that arched throat, taste the honey promised by those lips, his fingers itching to tangle themselves in that cloud of copper silk and pull this arresting vision closer.

A vision that was, he realized with a shock that rippled all the way to his toes, the woman he'd hitherto identified as the mousy, nondescript Mrs. Martin.

He tingled in other places, as well. And had not yet regathered wits enough to decide what to do about it when the dog, whose presence he had totally forgotten, had the deplorable ill timing to seek out his mistress.

At a lick to her hand, Mrs. Martin sat up and opened eyes as piercingly blue as the clear autumn sky. Eyes that went in an instant from sleepy to shocked. With a small shriek, she leaped up and backed away.

Conscious of a sharp sense of loss, he nonetheless

endeavored to set her at ease. "Please, don't be alarmed, Mrs. Martin. It's Hugh Bradsleigh—Kit's brother. I'm sorry to have startled you."

As big a plumper as he'd ever told, he knew, realizing he'd never have been treated to this glimpse of heaven had the reclusive Mrs. Martin sensed his presence earlier. He still couldn't quite believe the silent woman who had toiled at his side all night and this enchanting siren were indeed one and the same.

"L-lord Beaulieu! You—you startled me. Misfit," she scolded the dog, who hung his head, tail drooping, "why did you not warn me we had visitors?"

Misfit. Beau grinned. Now there was an apt name. If he'd had the foresight to bring a bone, the wretched animal probably would have given him the run of the cottage.

Nonetheless, the pooch had led him to The Vision and thus Beau felt compelled to defend him. "He did inspect me rather thoroughly before he let me in."

He watched regretfully as with one hand Mrs. Martin fumbled to fasten the buttons at her collar and with the other gathered her glorious, sun-burnished hair into a knot. Though he was somewhat guilty at having startled her, he wasn't so conscience-stricken that he felt compelled to point out the dowager's cap for which, with sidelong glances as if she expected he might at any moment attack, she was quite obviously searching.

Instead he picked it up. "Your cap, Mrs. Martin." With a slow smile, he held it out, just far enough to be polite but not so close that she could reach it without approaching him.

And, ah, how he wanted her to approach. After a moment, skittish as a startled doe, she did. "Thank you, my lord. I'll take it now, if you please."

Come get it, he almost said. Biting back the words lest he frighten her off, he simply stood, waiting.

She took the few steps that separated them, then snatched at the cap. Her hand grazed his palm as she grabbed, and for a moment, their fingers caught.

He felt the flame of contact in every nerve. And so, he realized exultantly as he watched her, did she.

Her blue eyes widened in shock, her lips once again parting slightly in surprise—an unconscious invitation. She even forgot, for a moment, to take the bonnet.

All too soon she remembered. Murmuring a disjointed thanks, she jerked it away and jammed it down on her head.

"I'll...just gather a few supplies." With that, she swiftly retreated into the interior of the cottage.

Leaving Beau gazing after her, amazed.

He sat down on the bench she'd just vacated to pull together his disordered thoughts. The *young* Mrs. Martin—she could not be more than five-and-twenty—possessed not just a pretty face, but an alluring figure. Indeed, the rush of attraction to that lush body still thrummed in his blood. An attraction that, based on her reaction to their unexpected touch, experience told him was mutual.

With his typical methodical precision, he pondered the implications of these new discoveries.

The first question posed by his now-fully-piqued curiosity was why so lovely a lady would choose to mask her beauty beneath dowager caps and ill-fitting gowns.

His second thought was of Kit—reviving a burden of worry heavy enough to extinguish the lingering embers of lust. For the immediate future all he had need of was a skillful nurse. Attraction or no, until Kit was out of danger there'd be no time to pursue other matters.

Still, that the intriguing Mrs. Martin had twice managed to distract him from his pressing anxiety was mute
testament to the power of that attraction.

As he stirred restlessly, wondering how much longer
it would take for her to "gather supplies," it suddenly
occurred to him that having the most capable nurse in
the neighborhood take up residence at the squire's
manor would be much more convenient. Having that
nurse be a lovely and discreet young widow with whom
a mutual attraction had flared might, once his brother's
condition improved, afford enticing possibilities.

Despite his worry, a ghost of desire stirred at the
thought and he grinned, more cheered than he'd been
since he received the dire message of his brother's injury. Kit would survive—he was in Beau's care and he
must survive—but after this present crisis he would
doubtless require a long convalescence. Beau had detailed his men to wrap up the investigation in the north,
and must shortly return to London to assemble his report. The imperative to resolve his present case would
not permit him to linger here, but he would certainly
visit frequently to check on Kit.

Beau took another deep breath of herb-scented air.
Now this was a charming bower to which he'd happily
return.

But first, he'd have to win over the shy Mrs. Martin,
which would probably also require penetrating the puzzle of why she seemed to take such pains to remain
invisible.

How fortuitous, he thought, his grin widening. He did
so love solving puzzles.

He reconsidered the alarm that had crossed her face
when she'd seen him watching her in the squire's entry.
Since his name and title were rather well known, she'd

likely recognized who he was from the first, but in the sickroom she'd displayed no awe of his position or inclination to toady; indeed, rather the opposite. He smiled again at the memory of her stubbornness regarding Kit's treatment and her total lack of deference as she ordered him about.

So why the mistrustful look? Perhaps she'd been raised on warnings about the subtle seducing ways of the high nobility, and saw him as such. Though he was by no means a saint, he could recall no escapades scurrilous enough to have penetrated this deep into the hinterlands. Not in recent years, at any rate, he amended.

He must demonstrate that though the wealthy Earl of Beaulieu might sit at the councils of government and move in a society many country folk deemed immoral, he was also Hugh Bradsleigh, a man like any other, who would never lead farther than a lady would willingly follow. Somewhat to his surprise, he found the notion that the lovely Mrs. Martin might be that rare individual who could appreciate him for himself alone immensely appealing.

Disarming her wariness would be quite a challenge—the one thing, he thought, spirits rising in anticipation, he loved almost as much as solving puzzles.

Chapter Three

A few moments later Mrs. Martin returned with a large satchel. The care she took that their hands not touch as he relieved her of it reinforced his conviction that she was not indifferent to him—an encouraging sign.

Once the lady realized he meant her no harm, she would doubtless be less wary. And begin allowing herself to respond to the pull he felt crackling between them.

He paused to savor the small delight of taking Mrs. Martin's hand as he assisted her into the gig. Availing himself of this unexceptional excuse to lean close, he caught a whiff of soft perfume. Rose with a hint of lavender? Lovely, and it suited her.

How to set her at ease? he mused as he settled the satchel to one side of the seat and walked over to untie the chestnut. Questions about home and family, interspersed with teasing compliments, had usually relieved anxiety in the shier or more tongue-tied young ladies with whom he'd had occasion to converse, he recalled.

By the time he'd rounded the gig and hopped in, Mrs. Martin had repositioned the satchel between them and moved to the edge of the seat—as far from him as possible.

Suppressing a grin, he set the gig in motion. "Did you grow up in this area, Mrs. Martin?"

She slid him a sidelong glance. "No, my lord."

"It is home to your late husband's family?"

There was a minute pause. "No, my lord."

"Do you enjoy the country? Your garden is certainly lovely."

"Thank you, my lord."

"I must thank *you,* for your devoted care of my brother. We are both much in your debt."

"Not at all, my lord."

"I must apologize, as well," Beau persevered. "I fear I've not been entirely courteous. Kit and my sister are all the family I possess, and I'm very protective of them. It's distressing to know Kit was—still is—in danger."

"Naturally, my lord."

Beau stifled a rising exasperation. Could the woman not string together more than three words at a time? Even the most stuttering of young females managed better. Was she really as dull as she seemed?

He felt an irrational disappointment. *Idiot,* he chastised himself. Just because a woman possesses a certain skill—and a voluptuous body—does not mean she owns a mind of equal caliber. Besides, discretion is a more useful quality in a bedmate than conversation.

If he managed to persuade her there—an intention this one-sided conversation was doing little to strengthen. Until he recalled that sinuous fall of mahogany silk spilling about her sides and shoulders, one copper curl resting where he would wish to touch, to taste.

Interest stirred anew. Doubtless the effort would be

worth the prize. Experience taught him women valued baubles, time, attention—and marriage. All he need do is discover which combination of the first three this little brown sparrow desired, and the attraction to him she was taking such pains to suppress would win out.

For a moment he allowed himself to contemplate the gloriously satisfying interludes that might thereafter ensue. And when his brother was fully healed, when he left Merriville for good, he would, as usual, be most generous.

He frowned slightly. A generosity, it occurred to him as he recalled the necessity of tying up his own horse and the total absence of servants, of which she seemed to stand in definite need. Did she truly—she a lady of gentle birth—live entirely alone in the cottage with only that unreliable mutt to safeguard her?

A well-honed protective instinct sprang up to overlay a more base desire. He glanced at her silent figure, as far away from him on the narrow bench as she could manage without falling out of the gig altogether, and smiled, a stirring of fondness in his chest.

A mutually satisfying interlude would benefit them both. He need only persevere, gently but persuasively, until Mrs. Martin realized the truth of that herself.

Would this interminable drive never end? Laura's neck ached from keeping her head angled to the side, as if in rapt contemplation of the country scenery through which she walked nearly every day. Would such action not have looked extremely peculiar, she'd have been tempted to jump from the gig and finish the journey on foot.

At last it seemed Lord Beaulieu had, mercifully, abandoned his attempt to engage her in conversation.

Perhaps, if she were lucky, her monosyllabic answers to a nerve-racking series of personal questions had left an impression of such dullness that he would not choose to pursue her acquaintance any further.

She needn't find his queries alarming. Most likely the earl was merely attempting to make sure that the person he'd asked to care for his brother was entirely respectable. At least she hoped so, not daring to sneak a glance at his expression to verify that theory.

Her heart still beat a rapid tattoo, but that was to be expected after Lord Beaulieu had nearly scared her witless, suddenly appearing as if conjured out of air. Whatever had possessed Misfit to allow him to enter the garden unannounced? The animal was too shy of gunfire to make a hunting dog, for which reason the genial squire allowed the hound to stay with her, but he was usually an excellent watchman, greeting any approaching interloper, man or beast, with a volley of agitated barking.

Her cheeks warmed with embarrassment as she recalled how disheveled she must have appeared to him. She'd caught a speculative gleam in his eye at first, but sprawling like a wanton as she'd been, her hair all unpinned, she supposed she'd deserved that. Fortunately she'd also been wearing one of the oldest of Aunt Mary's gowns, possessed of no style whatever and overlarge to boot.

By the time she'd buttoned up properly and tidied her hair, that unnerving look had vanished, though she'd remained so rattled, she'd forgotten where she'd left her cap. He'd had to hand it to her, which he did politely but pointedly, as if to subtly underscore how unladylike her behavior had been.

Charleton would have been much less kind.

Then there'd been that odd rush of...fear?—when her fingers chanced to entangle his. So jolting had that touch been, she'd made sure to avoid it happening again.

To her enormous relief she spied the gateposts to Squire Everett's manor. A few more moments and she'd be delivered from his lordship's excruciating proximity.

They were nearly at the manor when Tom rode toward them. A single glance at his face, tears tracking down the dust of his cheeks, was enough to drive the discomfort of the earl's hovering presence from her mind.

"Oh, Tom! He's not—" she began.

"No. Not yet. But the doctor was sending me for you, Lord Beaulieu. He said you should s-see Kit n-now before..." Swallowing hard, Tom left the sentence unfinished.

With a muffled curse the earl pulled up the chestnut, tossed the reins to her and sprang from the gig. By the time she'd controlled the startled horse and guided him to a halt before the front entrance, the earl had vanished.

The squire's son was weeping openly as he helped her down from the gig. "I...I'm so sorry, ma'am. I should never... How can I ever forgive myself if—"

She patted his shoulder. "You mustn't blame yourself! If the shot that wounded him was a ricochet, it might just as well have been his own bullet that struck him as yours."

Shaking his head against her reassurance, Tom took the chestnut's reins and led both animals toward the barn. For a moment Laura just stood there before the entry.

Should she go in and offer what help she could? But

the earl's physician was there, and much more knowledgeable than she. If the boy were truly dying, his family and friends would not want an outsider hanging about. Perhaps she should just quietly return to her cottage.

She considered the tempting notion for a moment before rejecting it. As long as the boy lived, she must at least offer her help. Only if the earl refused that offer might she in good conscience return home.

When she entered the sickroom a few moments later she found Lord Beaulieu bending over the boy, lips moving as if in conversation with his brother, hands clasping Kit's limp arm. Though the earl seemed oblivious to her arrival, the doctor spied her immediately and walked over.

"There's an infection beginning in his lungs, just as we feared. I've given him syrup of poppy, but weak as he is, I daren't bleed him. If you've aught of remedies to try, I should be grateful of them."

Laura scanned her memory for the treatments Aunt Mary had used when one of the squire's tenants had contracted an inflammation of the lungs the winter previous. "We might set a pot of mint steeped in boiling water by his bedside," she whispered. "The vapor seems to make breathing easier. And wrap his neck with flannel soaked in camphor."

The doctor considered a moment. "It canna hurt. An herbalist had the teaching of you, the squire said? There's much they use that works, though we're not knowing the whys and wherefores. Let's try it, for God's truth, I've done all I can for the laddie."

After that she lost track of time. When she finally slipped from the room to find the necessary, night had fallen. On her way back the squire intercepted her, begging her to let him send Maggie to the cottage for her things so that she might remain at the hall to tend the patient. Taken aback, she fumbled for an answer.

"Both Lord Beaulieu and Dr. MacDonovan asked that I add their requests to my own," he said. "The doctor admires your skill, and his lordship wishes every experienced hand available be put to his brother's care."

Though logically she knew if she were to be of continuing assistance it made much more sense for her to stay at the hall, still she resisted the notion of quitting even briefly the cottage that meant safety and comfort. A stirring at the depths of her being still whispered danger.

Don't be ridiculous, she told herself crossly. The earl was fully occupied with his brother, whose survival remained in grave doubt. He had neither time nor interest to waste on his brother's nurse.

"You will stay, won't you, Mrs. Martin?"

Since refusing so sensible a request would appear both uncharitable and extremely odd, despite her forebodings Laura had little choice. "Of course, it would be much more convenient for me to remain. If my being here will not be an imposition on you or Lady Winters?"

"It will be a blessing," the squire returned with a sigh. "My sister is in a state, what with sickness and more noble visitors about, and I've all I can do to keep the house running. 'Twould be a great comfort to me to know you were watching over the boy."

"I must stay, then." She made herself smile. "Thank you for your hospitality."

He nodded and pressed her hand before releasing it. And so she returned to the sickroom, her concern over her patient's condition underlined by the disquieting knowledge that for the indefinite future she would be residing under the same roof as the unsettling Earl of Beaulieu.

Just after dawn a week later Laura roused herself from a light doze. She glanced up quickly and was re-assured to find her patient still sleeping deeply, brow free of perspiration and color pale but natural.

Another quick glance confirmed that the earl also slept, his tall form curled on a pallet beside his brother's bed where he'd had a cot installed at the start of the crisis.

Though Lord Beaulieu had helped as much as possible, the responsibility for Kit's care had still fallen primarily on Dr. MacDonovan and herself. She'd endured an exhausting and anxiety-ridden blur of time while Kit Bradsleigh teetered on the edge between living and dying, too preoccupied with nursing him to worry about the elder brother who seldom stirred from the boy's side.

Last evening, the lad's temperature had spiked and then, for the first time since the inflammation began, dropped to normal. After having hovered for days in a restless, semiconscious haze of pain and fever, Kit woke up clear-eyed, keen-witted—and ravenous.

Laura sent for as much chicken broth as she gauged her patient could tolerate, and Dr. MacDonovan. The physician, who'd been eating a late dinner with the earl, came at once, Kit's brother on his heels. After a swift examination, to everyone's great relief the doctor declared that, though Kit was still very weak and would need a long period of rest to fully recover, his lungs were clearing and he was probably out of danger.

The squire went off immediately to fetch a bottle of his best claret while Dr. MacDonovan laughingly admonished Kit, who demanded a glass of his own. As thrilled and relieved as the others, Laura uttered a quick prayer of thanks. And then shooed the men out, telling them that since her patient needed rest and their well-deserved celebration would likely be lengthy, they should take their bottle in the salon and she would keep watch alone. Abjuring her as a downy, kindhearted lass, Dr. MacDonovan shook her hand heartily and ushered the earl out.

She heard Lord Beaulieu come back in after midnight and gave him a nod of reassurance as he silently approached his brother's bed. He took Kit's fingers and held them a moment, as if to verify that the fever had really left, then looked back at her with a tired smile. "Thank you," he whispered, and took up his post on the cot.

The earl's valet would see to Kit's needs when he woke, and both the doctor and Lord Beaulieu would keep the boy occupied during the day. Her work here would soon be done—perhaps for good, as Lady Elspeth, sister to Kit and his lordship, was expected soon.

She could return to the safety of her cottage before the household reverted to a normal routine—and the earl had leisure to become curious about his brother's nurse.

She paused a moment by the doorway. In the hazy pastel light of dawn, the earl's stern features were relaxed, his handsome face more approachable. She felt again that inexplicable pull, as if his commanding personality called out to her even in sleep. A tiny sigh escaped her.

If events had not transpired as they had, she might

risk lingering here, responding to the wordless, urgent imperative that somehow drew her to this man. And then shook her head at her own foolishness.

If events had not transpired as they had, she would never have landed in this remote rural corner of England.

Fatigue must be making her whimsical. Straightening her weary shoulders, Laura slipped from the room.

Two paces down the hallway, a touch to her back made her jump.

"Don't be alarmed, Mrs. Martin!"

She turned to see the earl behind her. "My lord?"

"I've not had the opportunity before, with you so occupied tending Kit, but I didn't want another day to go by without thanking you for your efforts. Though at times I may have appeared...less than appreciative—" he gave her a rueful grin "—I want you to know mere words cannot convey the depth of my gratitude."

She felt a flush of pleasure at his praise even as she set about denying it. "Not at all, my lord. I did only what any person trained in the healing arts would have."

"You've done a great deal more, as we both know. Left the familiar comfort of your own home, devoted nearly every waking hour and worked yourself nigh to exhaustion in Kit's care. Indeed, the squire's since told me were it not for your prompt and skillful action immediately after his wounding, Kit would never have survived the journey back to the hall. And before you deny it, that assessment was confirmed by Dr. MacDonovan himself."

Since she had, as he predicted, already opened her lips to demur, she was left with nothing to say.

"I owe you debt I can never repay. I won't insult

you by offering money, but were it in my power, I'd go to the ends of the earth to grant you your heart's desire.''

The quiet conviction of those words somehow compelled her to raise her downcast eyes. She found his gaze fixed on her with such intensity, her heart gave an odd lurch.

He smiled, his face lightening. ''Now what, I wonder, would such a calm and quiet lady desire most in the world?''

Freedom from fear. The thought flashed into her head on a stab of longing. She struggled to stem it, to summon up a reply blithe enough to match his teasing question. ''M-my needs are few, my lord. I'm quite content.''

The earl chuckled. ''A lady with no demands? What an extraordinary creature!''

''Not at all. Alas, I'm entirely ordinary.''

The wryness of her rejoinder faded, replaced by a curious mingling of alarm and anticipation as the earl stepped closer. While she stood motionless, breath suspended, his expression once again turned so fiercely intent she could not make herself look away.

''No, my lady,'' he said after a long moment. ''Though you may be many things, 'ordinary' is certainly not one of them. But you'll be needing your rest.'' He stepped back, breaking the invisible hold. ''Suffice it to say you have my eternal friendship and support. If I can ever be of service to you in any way, you have but to ask.''

He made her a bow. When she continued to stand motionless, he gave her shoulder a gentle shove. ''Go on now. If you expire from fatigue in the squire's hallway, Kit will never forgive me.''

The unexpected contact sizzled through her. "My lord," she said faintly, and curtsied. All the way down the hall she felt his lingering gaze on her back, while the imprint of his fingers smoldered on her shoulder.

Leaving Kit Bradsleigh in the physician's charge, the next day at first light, Laura slipped from her patient's room. She turned toward the stairs to her chamber, then hesitated.

Though she was tired after her long night, a vague restlessness haunted her. Accustomed to daily exercise tending her garden, walking out to gather supplies of wild herbs or to let Misfit ramble, she felt stifled after having been confined to the squire's manor for nearly a week.

She considered taking the air in the garden, but unsure of the earl's schedule, reluctantly dismissed that notion. The intricate arrangement of alleys and shrub-shrouded pathways would make it difficult to spot someone far enough away to avoid them, and should she chance to encounter the earl, he would doubtless feel compelled to invite her to stroll with him. Though she might simply refuse, with brutal honesty she had to admit the draw of Lord Beaulieu's stimulating presence and the beauty of the fall flowers would likely prove a combination beyond her power to resist.

Why not visit the library instead? She'd become acquainted with its rich treasures two years ago when the squire had offered her a book to beguile the tedium of her long recovery. Given free rein thereafter, she'd been delighted to explore the excellent collection it contained. That decided, she headed for the front stairway.

Though Kit Bradsleigh was out of immediate danger, he remained seriously ill, and Dr. MacDonovan thought it prudent he still have care both night and day. Quite cleverly, she thought with a touch of smugness as she descended, she'd arranged with the physician to take the night watch while the doctor and Lord Beaulieu provided medical treatment and diversion during the day. She had further requested, since she would be eating at odd hours, that her meals be served in her room.

Yesterday when she'd returned to her patient, she'd discovered that Lord Beaulieu's cot had been removed from the sickroom. Naturally, with his brother on the road to recovery, the earl would resume sleeping in his own chamber. So it appeared she would not see him again during his stay, since she'd neither meet him at mealtime nor encounter him in the sickroom during her night vigil.

Her relief at avoiding his too-perceptive eye mingled with a touch of what might almost be...regret. He affected her so strangely, setting her skin tingling with a sort of prickly awareness, as if some vital essence about him telegraphed itself to her whenever he was near. She found that entirely involuntary reaction both exhilarating and frightening.

Like that touch to her shoulder, the morning he thanked her for saving his brother's life. Close her eyes, and she could almost feel it still, his fingers' imprint branded into the sensitive skin of her collarbone.

How...peculiar. And a warning to her to be doubly on her guard.

After peeping ahead to ascertain no one was in the front hallway, she scurried to the library. Safely over the threshold, she paused to breathe in the comforting, familiar scents of beeswax and leather bindings before walking to the bookcase that shelved the complete Milan set of the *Iliad* and *Odyssey*. Her self-imposed confinement would seem much more tolerable if, after her rest, she could look forward to an afternoon among the heroic cadences of Homer's poetry.

Impatient to inspect the treasure, she selected a volume and carefully smoothed open the manuscript. Just a few pages, she promised herself, and she would slip back to her room.

Within moments she was completely entranced. Eyes avidly scanning the verses, she drifted across the parquet floor, shouldered open the library door—and stepped smack into the tall, solid body of the Earl of Beaulieu.

Chapter Four

Beau was striding briskly down the hall, invigorated by his dawn ride, when a figure popped out the library door and slammed into him. The slight form rebounded backward, a book spinning from her hands.

Swiftly recovering his balance, he grabbed the maid's shoulders to keep her from falling. His automatic irritation over the girl's inattention evaporated instantly as first his fingers, then his brain registered the identity of the lady in his grip.

"Excuse me, Mrs. Martin! Are you all right?" Delighted with this excuse to touch her, he let his hands linger longer than absolutely necessary to steady her, reveling in the rose scent of her perfume.

As soon as she regained her footing, she pulled away. "Fine, thank you, my lord. And 'tis I who must apologize, for not watching where I was walking."

With regret he let her go. "Are you sure you're uninjured? I'm a rather large obstacle to collide with."

"Quite all right."

"Let me restore your book to you." As she murmured some inarticulate protest, he bent to scoop up the volume.

And froze for another instant when he read the title. The first volume of Homer's *Illiad. In Greek.*

Slowly he straightened. "*You* are reading this book?"

Something like consternation flickered in her eyes as she looked up at him. She opened her lips, then hesitated, as if she found it difficult to frame an answer to that simple question. "Y-yes, my lord," she admitted finally, and held out her hands for the volume.

He returned it. "You must be quite a scholar."

For a moment she was silent. "My father was," she said at last.

He waited, but when she didn't elaborate, he continued, "And you, also, to be reading it in Greek. As I asserted earlier, not at all an ordinary lady."

"But a tired one, so if you will excuse me—"

"Another moment, please, Mrs. Martin." He couldn't let her go, not yet, not when the only communication they'd shared for days previous or were likely, given her nursing schedule, to have in the days ahead were terse directives uttered in the sickroom. "You are looking pale. I fear you've been too long cooped up in the house. Do you ride?"

She shot him a glance before quickly lowering her gaze. "N-no, my lord."

"You must stroll in the garden this afternoon, then. The day promises to be fair and warm. No excuses, now! I shall call for you myself after your rest to ensure it. We can't have you endangering your own health."

Again, that darting glance of alarm. "That...that is exceedingly kind, my lord, but I wouldn't dream of inconveniencing you."

How could he ever disarm the wary caution so evident in those glances if she persisted in avoiding him? Determined not to let her wriggle away, he continued,

"Walking with a lovely lady an 'inconvenience?' Nonsense! 'Twould be my pleasure."

"Your offer is most kind, but I—I really should return and tend my garden. Weeds grow alarmingly in a week, and I must restock my supplies."

"I should be delighted to drive you there. Perhaps you can explain something of your treatments. Dr. MacDonovan tells me Kit is likely to have a weakness in his lungs for some time, and may have continuing need of them."

"Possibly, but I could not allow you to abandon your work for so tedious an errand."

"I have no pressing business at the moment," Beau replied, dismissing without a qualm the two satchels of dispatches his secretary had sent from London by courier just last evening. "What time should you like to go?"

She tightened her grip on the book and inhaled sharply. His concentration faltered as he watched her dart the tip of her tongue over the pouting plumpness of her lower lip. A unexpected bolt of lust exploded deep in his gut, recalling in sharp focus that vision of her in the garden that lingered always at the edges of his consciousness—arched white throat and pebbled breasts and wild tresses calling for his touch.

Heart hammering, he wrenched his thoughts back to the present. Mrs. Martin stood a handspan away, gaze lowered, cheeks pinking, her breathing as erratic as his own. She felt it, too, this primal beat pulsing between them in the deserted hallway. And as surely as he knew his own name he *knew* eventually she must succumb to it. To him. Already he could sense in her the fluttering anxiety between acceptance and flight.

"N-no, really, I... To be frank, my lord, I should be

most uncomfortable to receive such marked attention from one so far above my station.''

She was trembling. He could feel the delicious vibrations thrum through him. How long and hard would she fight their attraction?

He did not wish to push her—too much—but he'd eagerly meet her, could she but persuade herself to advance a part of the way.

Would she? Caution said 'twas too early to rush his fences, but he couldn't seem to help himself.

''Your service to my brother makes us equals, Mrs. Martin. But given your obvious reluctance to bear me company, I fear I must have alarmed or offended you in some way. If so, I most sincerely apologize. I stand already so deeply in your debt, surely you know I would never do anything to injure you.''

She looked up then, as he'd hoped. For a fraught moment she studied him, her puzzled, questing gaze meeting his while he stayed silent, scarcely able to breathe, knowing the whole matter might be decided here and now.

Slowly she nodded. ''Yes, I do know it.''

Elation filled him, urged him to press the advantage. ''What time shall I bring the gig 'round, then?''

Energy seemed to drain from her and she sighed, as if too weary to withstand his persistence any longer. ''Four of the clock?''

''I shall be there.'' He reached toward her cheek. She stood her ground, permitting the slight glancing touch of his fingers. ''Sleep, Mrs. Martin. Until four, then.''

She nodded again and, holding the volume to her chest like a shield, turned and walked swiftly to the stairs.

Beau stood staring after her, waiting for his heartbeat to slow. He'd been attracted to her from the first, but this…compulsion—he couldn't think what in truth to call it—to claim the fair Mrs. Martin far exceeded anything he'd anticipated or previously experienced.

He shook his head, still amazed by it. Until a few days ago he'd believed that his current mistress, a lovely dancer as skilled as she was avaricious, had been more than meeting his physical needs.

Mrs. Martin roused in him a similarly intense response that was at the same time entirely different. Oh, he wanted her as he'd seen her in the garden—warm, eager, ardent—but he wanted just as fiercely to discover the story behind those skilled hands, the quiet voice that soothed his delirious brother's agitation, to penetrate within the lowered head and engage the questing mind that read Homer.

He laughed out loud. *Greek,* no less! How could he have thought her intellect dull, even for a moment?

Maybe it was the shock of Kit's close brush with death that heightened all his senses to so keen an edge. Normally he was the most analytical of men—the successful performance of his job depended upon it—but the power of whatever arced between them this morning defied analysis. This was alchemy, elemental substances bonding through some force buried deep within their respective natures, a force not to analyze, but to experience.

He intended to do so. Once Kit was out of danger, he wanted to experience every thrilling facet the unprecedented power of this mutual attraction promised.

That decided, he switched directions and headed for the breakfast room. The more he knew of Mrs. Martin, the more tools he'd possess to lure her to him—and turn his molten imaginings into reality.

Time to prime the voluble squire's conversational pump.

He was pleased to find Squire Everett already at breakfast. "Come in, come in, my lord. Fine morning for a ride, eh?"

"A wonderful morning indeed."

"M'sister won't be down this morning—female palpitations or some such, so don't stand on ceremony. Please, fill your plate. Marsden will pour your tea."

"Have you had a dish sent up to Mrs. Martin yet?" he asked casually.

"Cook will take care of that. Must see that she gets her nourishment. Thin as a wraith anyway—can't have her going into a decline."

"Indeed not. What an invaluable member of the community! Has she resided here all her life?"

"No, the last few years only. Her late aunt, Mrs. Hastings—a most genteel lady, God rest her soul—owned the cottage first. Mrs. Hastings helped her husband, a botanist he was, in his studies of herbal plants, and became something of an expert herself." The squire paused to take a bite of kidney pie and waved a finger at Beau. "So you see, my lord, 'tis no crone of a medicine woman who had the teaching of Mrs. Martin, but the wife of an Oxford don! Anyways, once the folk hereabouts learned of Mrs. Hastings's skill, they took to consulting her. And when Mrs. Martin contracted a puerile fever, her family sent her to her aunt. Nearly died, Mrs. Martin did, and took the better part of a year to recover."

"I'm sure her neighbors are most grateful she did."

"God's truth, that!" The squire motioned the footman to pour him another cup. "Given the, ah, weakness of the local sawbones, there's a number of folk who'd be in bad frame indeed, were it not for Mrs. Martin."

"My own brother included."

The squire nodded. "Glad to know you realize that!"

"Her husband was a military man, you said. In what regiment?"

The squire stopped buttering his toast and looked up. "Can't say as I know. Does it matter?"

Back off, Beau. "Not really. I'm trying to ascertain how I might best reimburse her for the time and skill she's expended for my family. She would not accept payment in coin, I expect, but I should like to offer some gesture of appreciation. Is she perchance a reader?"

The squire chuckled. "My, yes! Quite a little bluestocking. Why, when she was laid up recuperating from her illness, I swear she must have read every musty tome in my library twice through. Not that I grudged her the loan of them, of course. Nay, I was glad to see them off the shelf for better reason than to make way for Hattie's feather duster." The squire put down his fork, suddenly serious. "Mustn't think she's one of them annoying, opinionated females who are always trying to tell a body what to do. Not a bit of it! Our Mrs. Martin's quiet and deferential, a real lady."

"So she has shown herself, under the most trying circumstances," Beau agreed, noting the squire's slight stress on the possessive "our." "The rest of her family is not from this county?"

"No. Now that I think on it, I'm not sure where her parents live—nor her husband's people." The squire shrugged. "Never seemed important. She's quality, as one can tell by looking at her, and that's all that matters."

"Of course." Beau paused, choosing his words with care. "It does seem to me somewhat—odd, though, that she should be living alone, without any relations to accompany her. I must confess I was shocked when I went to fetch her and found not a single servant. I cannot help but think she stands in need of better protection."

"Protection?" The squire stiffened and threw him a suspicious glance. "She's well protected now, sir. I'd have a servant at the cottage full-time, if that's what you're hinting, but she'll not hear of it. And my grooms have standing orders to keep a close eye on the place."

Beau returned a bland smile. "That's not the same as having her safe within one's household. Perhaps I should speak to my sister—"

"No need for that!" the squire interrupted, his glance turning frostier. "She'd not stir from Merriville—likes to feel useful, she tells me. In any event, I've plans for her eventual protection—quite legitimate plans! No need to disturb your lady sister—Mrs. Martin will be well cared for, I assure you." Pushing his chair back, the squire rose. "I'll just go check on that breakfast plate."

Giving Beau another sharp look, the squire paced out.

Beau savored the rich scent of his tea and smiled. So, as he'd suspected, the squire had "legitimate" plans in regard to Mrs. Martin. But though a match of such unequal age would not be unusual, often resulting in affection on both sides, he was certain the lady did not in any way reciprocate the squire's tender regard.

Thanks be to God.

To his eye, Mrs. Martin's reaction to the squire's gallantry indicated disinterest cloaked in polite avoidance rather than coquetry. Nor, given the care she took to mask her beauty, did it appear she sought to attract any of the eligible gentlemen hereabouts.

Twofold thanks to heaven.

Why a vulnerable lady in such a precarious financial position would not wish to ensnare the affections of a potential suitor puzzled him. Solving that mystery was the key, he suspected, to unfettering the attraction between himself and Mrs. Martin.

Fortunately, uncovering people's emotions and intent was a skill he'd perfected when still a lad, fascinated by puzzles of all sorts. While mastering chess, he'd discovered to his amusement that he could often learn as much about his adversary's strategy from watching the reactions of face and body as by following the play. A sudden widening of the eyes, a quick indrawn breath, the alerting of the body and tensing of shoulders might indicate an opportunity discovered, or a check about to be set. Intrigued, Beau began to actively track such reactions. By the time he left Eton for Oxford he was able to pick up much more subtle signs.

Which allowed him to enjoy a quite profitable career at cards while at university. In addition, his ability to sense out which of two boxers would triumph, which jockey would bring home the winning horse, or which of two gentlemen would win a bet had led friends—and opponents—to wait on his choices and seldom wager against him.

And later led him to the secret career he now pursued, assisting Lord Riverton, an older Oxford classmate and now a cabinet member, in rooting out governmental corruption.

Given the strength of his need to disarm the wariness of Mrs. Martin, he gave thanks both for his skill and the invaluable contacts he'd accumulated over the years.

The news of Kit's accident had pulled Beau from a house party, where the number of congenial friends present had sweetened the business of observing a high-ranking government official suspected of embezzlement. His agents were at work amassing invoices and shipping figures—hence the satchels arriving daily by courier. The accumulating evidence, observation and instinct all told him the suspect he'd been watching was indeed the architect of the scheme.

Though he'd put all thought of miscreants aside while Kit's life hung in the balance, once he was assured his brother was truly out of danger and Ellie arrived to oversee Kit's care, duty compelled him to return to London and finish his assignment. Still, he could spare a few more days to recover from the shock of nearly losing a sibling—and to figure out how best to win the trust of the cautious Mrs. Martin. For when he returned to check on his convalescing brother, he intended for her to welcome him back with all the fire he knew she possessed.

As he drained his cup and took the stairs to Kit's room, Beau considered various explanations for Mrs. Martin's atypical behavior. Perhaps the lady avoided gentlemen and garbed herself in gowns that camouflaged her beauty because her heart still belonged to her late husband. If she didn't avoid men out of heartache, she might do so from distaste, though he'd not noticed in her interactions with Mac, the squire, or his brother anything to indicate a dislike for men in general. Or perhaps she brooded over some disappointment in love.

The powerful physical connection that flared between them did not support any of those theories. Besides, he sensed in her not aversion, disdain, or the despair of lingering grief, but…a wary watchfulness.

The hallmark of someone with secrets to hide.

He stopped dead, arrested by the conclusion. He might be wrong—occasionally he was—but he didn't think so.

He continued his analysis, excitement accelerating the pace. Mrs. Martin apparently moved easily among—indeed, was sought out by—the community in and around Merriville, so she didn't avoid all society.

Mrs. Martin the widowed healer met society, he amended. Mrs. Martin the woman hid behind shapeless gowns and voluminous caps. What could a lovely lady of gentle birth feel so obliged to conceal that she tried to make her person virtually invisible?

Beau couldn't imagine. But with urgency thrumming in his blood and the goad of an imminent departure, he intended to bend every effort to find out.

Chapter Five

Her palms damp with nervousness on the wicker basket she carried, at precisely four o'clock Laura Martin walked into the entrance hallway to meet the Earl of Beaulieu.

Despite her exhaustion this morning, she'd lain awake wondering if there might have been some way she could have avoided this excursion. Before falling into a leaden sleep, she'd concluded there was none, save a blunt refusal that would have been as ungracious, given the concern the earl expressed about her well-being, as it was insulting.

She'd blundered badly again, being caught with that volume of Homer. No chance now of Lord Beaulieu believing her to be dull-witted. But a scholarly lady could still be a recluse of little social skill—indeed, before her marriage had she not been just such a girl? As long as she kept conversation to minimum and behaved with an awkwardness that, given the state of her nerves, she would not have to feign, the outing might pass off well enough.

But as she stepped out under the entry archway to await the approaching gig, Laura couldn't help but feel a surge of gladness. The afternoon was as fair as the earl had promised, gilded with the special light that only occurs in late autumn when balmy breezes, teasing reminders of the summer just past, seduce the mind into forgetting the cold threat of winter to come. The sun-warmed herbs in her garden would greet her with a bouquet of piquant scents, the beds of mums and asters with a painter's palette of russets, oranges, golds, lavenders and pinks.

After having been trapped indoors for nearly a week, she simply would not let the exasperating, unnerving seesaw of reaction the earl seemed always to evoke in her spoil her enjoyment of this perfect afternoon.

Given the paucity of her experience with men, it had taken her time to realize, with some chagrin, that at least part of the uneasy mix was an entirely carnal attraction. Once long ago, when young Lord Andrew Harper took her walking in her mother's garden, she'd experienced the same quivery awareness and agitation. Acutely conscious of the muscled masculine form beneath Lord Andrew's tight-fitting coat and buff breeches, she'd both longed for and been terrified that he might kiss her.

He hadn't, though he'd looked into her eyes with the same searing intensity as the earl. Soon after that walk, her father informed her he'd accepted the distinguished and much older Lord Charleton's offer for her hand, putting an end to titillating interludes in the garden.

Could the earl desire her, too? A flattering thought, though ludicrous. If the Earl of Beaulieu did find his brother's dowdy nurse attractive, it would only be because gentlemen, as she knew well, were not particularly discriminating in their passions. Any minimally satisfactory female would do until a more appealing prospect happened along, and there were surely few prospects in Merriville.

She was still smiling at the notion of the Lord Beaulieu ogling the village baker's buxom daughter when the earl pulled up in the gig.

Sunlight glistened in the burnished ebony of his dark hair and warmed the brown eyes to amber flame. *Apollo cast in bronze,* she thought, as a now-familiar slash of awareness stabbed her belly and quivered down her legs. She didn't realize she was standing motionless, simply staring at him, until the earl addressed her.

"Should I call someone to assist you up? I'm afraid the horse is so fresh, I cannot leave him."

"No, I can manage," she replied, cheeks warming. *The cat looking at the king,* pathetic as the old nursery rhyme.

Transferring the reins to one hand but keeping his eyes on the restive chestnut, Lord Beaulieu leaned over to steady her elbow as she climbed in, his touch light and impersonal. Nonetheless, tension simmered between them as she took her seat.

"Is the day not truly as splendid as I promised?" he asked, and turned to give her a brilliant smile so full of comradely enjoyment she had to smile back.

"Indeed it is. Thank you for offering to drive me."

"Let's be off, then. Do you need to gather wild herbs as we go, or just those in your garden?"

"I need only garden-grown medicinals."

"Nonetheless, if you spy anything on the way that you can use, let me know. This fine animal isn't capable of blazing speed, so it will be no trouble to bring him to a halt. Squire Everett told me your uncle was a botanist, and you came to Merriville to be treated by your aunt. Had you worked with herbs before then?"

Laura tensed. "No."

But his tone was easy, almost teasing as he continued. "I understand you were quite ill. A lady whose mind is active enough to acquire Greek must have found the forced inactivity of convalescence irksome. Learning about herbs would have blunted the frustration, I should guess."

She glanced at him, surprised at his perspicacity. "Yes, it did."

"A fascinating art, the business of healing. From time immemorial men have attempted to understand it, sometimes with appalling results. Imagine, recommending the ingestion of black powder and lead to relieve stomach distress!"

She laughed. "Barbarous indeed."

"Did your aunt start treating illness at your uncle's behest? Or out of her own concern?"

Laura paused, uncertain how to frame a monosyllabic answer—or whether, in truth, she needed to do so. Unlike the unnervingly probing inquiry he'd subjected her about her family the last time he drove her, these questions were less personal.

Perhaps, given his brother's illness, Lord Beaulieu had developed a genuine interest in the practical use of herbs. What harm if she replied at more length on this relatively safe topic?

Cautiously, tracking his reaction with quick, cautious glances, she began, "My uncle studied the makeup of plants and how the elements in them affect healing. He believed, and my aunt practiced, that only natural materials, especially such long-utilized botanicals as willow bark, foxglove, rosemary, and the like be used to treat the sick, and then in small doses. 'Tis best to intervene as little as possible, let the body's natural strength heal itself.''

''That sounds wise. Do we pass any beneficial wild herbs on our route?''

''Several, though they are not at the peak moment for harvesting now.''

''Point them out, if you would.''

And so during the remainder of the drive, she indicated stands of willow and horehound, pockets of tansy, goldenseal and echinacea. At his prompting, she added details of the teas, infusions and poultices one could make from them.

Having the earl's intense, probing mind focused on treatments rather than the individual describing them was an immense relief. Though a strong awareness of him as a man still bubbled at the edges of consciousness, by the time they reached her cottage Laura had relaxed to a degree she wouldn't previously have believed possible in his lordship's company.

As soon as Lord Beaulieu handed her down from the gig, which he did with business-like efficiency that further reassured her, Misfit bounded up. Whining with joy, tail wagging at manic speed, he blocked her path and insinuated his head under her fingers. Perforce halted, Laura laughed and scratched hard along the knobby bones at his tail while the dog groaned with delight.

The earl laughed, as well. ''I believe he missed you.''

''He becomes distressed if I'm away for long.''

''Don't like being left alone, do you, old boy?'' Lord Beaulieu reached over to rub his long fingers behind the dog's ears. ''Misses his fellows, too, I'll wager. Why doesn't the squire take him out with his pack?''

''Having been caught in a poacher's trap as a pup,

he shies so at the sound of gunfire he's useless as a hunting dog. After I healed him, the squire let me keep him.''

"As your guardian?" the earl guessed.

She shrugged. "Something like, I suppose. Please, do go in. I'm afraid I haven't much to offer, but there will be cool water in the kitchen."

"Knowing you'd likely not have anything in the house, I had the squire's cook prepare us a basket of refreshments. I'll fetch it when you're ready."

That so wealthy a gentleman, who doubtless had his every need anticipated by a small army of servants at every one of his numerous establishments, should have noted and planned for that small detail impressed her. "Thank you. Should you like to wait in the parlor while I tend the garden? I have a set of the studies my uncle published. You might find them interesting."

"I'm sure I should, but I can't imagine remaining indoors on so glorious a day. Let me help you."

The idea of the impeccable earl down on his knees pulling weeds was too ludicrous to resist. Stifling a grin, she recommended that if he preferred to stay outside, he might seat himself on the old willow bench on the porch.

The same one, she recalled with a jolting flash of memory, on which he'd discovered her drying her hair that afternoon.

If he remembered the incident, too, he gave no sign. Thanking her, he inclined his long form on the bench and sat watching her.

At bit uncomfortable under his scrutiny, she donned her faded apron and a tattered straw bonnet. But after a few moments she fell into the familiar, satisfying routine, wholly absorbed in freeing the beds of weeds and snipping the leaves, stems and branches she needed.

A short time later he materialized at her side, startling her. To her surprise and amusement, there he remained, questioning her about each plant she weeded out or clipped to save, holding the trug for her to deposit the harvested bounty, and twice, over her laughing protests, carrying off a load of weeds.

After she'd finished, the earl fetched the picnic basket. Once more claiming it was too lovely to go indoors, he insisted on seating her beside him on the willow bench and unpacking the refreshments there.

Having abandoned them during the dull weeding process to sniff out rabbits or other pernicious vermin, at the first scent of food Misfit ambled back, waiting at Laura's feet with polite, rapt attention for the occasional tidbit.

The golden afternoon dimmed to the gray of approaching dusk and the mild air sharpened. As if sensing his mistress would soon depart, Misfit trotted off and brought back a fallen tree limb, then looked up at Laura with tail wagging, an irresistible appeal in his eyes.

"All right, but only for a few moments," Laura told him. With a joyful bark, Misfit dropped the limb and danced on his paws, awaiting her throw.

She lobbed it to the far wall, watching with a smile as the dog raced after, a dark streak of motion in the fading daylight. He bounded back, did a little pirouette before her, and dropped the stick once more.

Lord Beaulieu snatched it before she could, and after a grimace at its condition, threw it again, clear over the fence and into the brush beyond. The hound rushed to the wooden barrier and then out the gate.

"He'll love that," Laura said. "'Tis a shame he cannot hunt, for he dearly loves to retrieve. Keeps my vegetables safe, and provides hares for the stew pot several times a week."

The earl gave his slimy hands a rueful glance. "He makes a rather messy business of it."

"So he does. Thank heavens you were not wearing your gloves—they'd be ruined!" Laura rummaged in her basket for a rag. "Here, let me wipe them."

He held out his hands. Without thinking, Laura grasped his wrist. Which, she immediately realized, was a mistake.

The warm touch of his skin sent a shock through her, while below the cuff of his shirt she felt his pulse beat strongly against her fingertips. Without conscious volition she raised her eyes to his.

He stared back. The air seemed suddenly sucked out of the afternoon sky, and she had trouble breathing.

She should look down, wipe his hands, step away. But she didn't seem able to move, her body invaded by a heated connectedness that seem to bind her to him by far more than the simple grasp of his wrist.

Finally, with a ragged intake of breath she tore her gaze free and wiped his dog-slobbered hands with quick jerky motions. After achieving the barest minimum of cleanliness, she released his wrist and shoved it away.

Still shaky, she stepped back—and tripped over Misfit, who chose that moment to bound up to her, stick in mouth. Not wanting to step on the dog, she hopped sideways and lost her balance altogether.

An instant later she hit the ground in an undignified tangle of skirt and limbs, face up to the startled earl and the star-dusted sky. Her cheeks flamed with humiliation, but before she could speak, Misfit, delighted she'd apparently decided to join him at his level, put both paws on her chest and leaned over to lick her face.

"Stop…Misfit…down!" she attempted to command between swipes by his long pink tongue, all the while trying unsuccessfully to wriggle out from under his weight. After a moment the absurdity of her position overwhelmed embarrassment. Leaning her head back under a continuing assault of doggy kisses, she dissolved into laughter.

He ought to shoo the dog away, help her up. Instead Beau stood frozen, watching the arched column of long white throat, the chest quivering with amusement. All afternoon he'd been haunted by memories of her on the bench where he'd surprised her sun-drying her hair, where today she'd invited him to linger, where, separated only by a picnic basket, they'd eaten the cold meat and cheese and bread, sipped the wine the squire's cook had packed. Which he'd eaten and drunk without tasting anything because it was her slender body, her wine-sweet lips he wanted to devour.

And now, while that ungrateful mutt dribbled slobber on her face, all he could think of was brushing the dog aside so he might kiss that throat, cup his hands over the breasts now prisoned by muddy paws, move over her and into her. It required another full minute and all the strength of mind he could muster to beat back the pulsing desire to gather her in his arms and carry her into the cottage.

But he was master of his appetites, and she was not ready for that. He called once more on the iron self-discipline upon which he prided himself, under whose guiding check he'd operated all afternoon, keeping the conversation carefully neutral, masking the desire she aroused in him with every small movement—the way she touched the tip of her tongue to her top lip when in contemplation, the subtle sway of her hips as she walked, even the tilt of her head as she gazed up at him inquiringly, like a little brown sparrow.

How unobservant people were, he marveled as he watched her tussle with her dog. How could any man look at Mrs. Martin, really look at her, and see only the drab exterior, miss the translucence of skin, the smoky fire of her hair beneath the ubiquitous cap, the sparkling brilliance of mind so evident once he finally got her into conversation. Dismissing the sparrow as dull and familiar without noting the intricacy and subtle shadings of color and pattern. Even the squire, though he'd not been totally blind, had perceived but little of her subtle allure, else she'd not still be a widow.

He was fiercely glad of that blindness, however. For she was his sparrow—*his*. The strength of that sudden conviction startled him, but it emanated from somewhere so deep within him he didn't bother to question it.

It would be a novel experience, using his skills to entice a lady. He'd not previously done so, being too circumspect to dally with married women of his own class and too protective of his bachelor state to pay singular attention to a maiden. The strength of his wealth and title alone, he considered cynically, had always been more than enough to garner him the favor of any lesser-born female who caught his eye.

But he would use them now, his vaunted skills, to lure this little brown sparrow and tame her to his hand.

Mrs. Martin, with her long white throat and deliciously heaving chest and frothy petticoats thrown back to reveal shapely ankles, represented temptation strong enough to break the resolve of a saint. Not being one, he'd best bring to an end the torturous pleasure of watching her. Thank heavens she was too modest to let her glances stray below his waistcoat, else she'd have clearly defined evidence of his desire the sternest of will could not conceal.

Ruthlessly he disciplined his thoughts, reassuring himself of the intimacy to come by recalling that timeless, breathless interval when she captured his wrist and his gaze. So strong was the sense of connection that he knew, he *knew,* she sensed and reciprocated the same powerful emotions that were roiling through him. However, though her agitation immediately after spoke of the depth of her attraction, her care to quickly move away told him she wasn't ready quite yet to succumb to the force that sparked so readily between them.

But she would be. Soon. And having made such progress today in setting her at ease, he'd not jeopardize her willing acquiescence by rushing his fences now, like an untried schoolboy.

"Misfit, heel!" he commanded. When, with a droop of tail, the dog reluctantly complied, Beau held out a hand. "Mrs. Martin, shall we retrieve you from Misfit's pack?"

At his teasing comment, she froze. The unselfconscious delight drained from her face and, ignoring his outstretched hand, she scrambled to her feet, brushing at the mud the dog had left on her apron.

"L-lord Beaulieu, excuse me! That was undignified."

"What need has one of dignity on so lovely a day?"

Her glance shot to his face and probed it, as if looking for evidence of mockery or disapproval. He held her gaze, his amusement fading.

Abruptly she lowered her chin, took a step away and grabbed her basket. "We've lingered far too long.

'Twill take but a moment to pack up the herbs. If you would be so kind, my lord, would you make sure the gig is ready?''

Somehow in an instant, the easy mood that had gilded the golden afternoon had shattered, leaving in its place a chill that had nothing to do with the evening's approach. Beau was at a loss to explain why it happened, or to figure out how to recapture their warm intimacy. Dismay and anger and heated frustration seized him.

He knew instinctively that pressing her to stay, teasing her further, would only deepen her wariness.

After a moment in which, his mind still a swirl of protest, he could summon no logical reason to stall their departure, he replied, "Of course, madam." And bowed, though she'd already turned away, retreated to her workbench, putting even more distance between them.

After watching her for another moment, Beau headed for the shed. Analyze, analyze, he told himself as, teeth gritted, he stalked over to prepare the gig. He hadn't even touched her hand to help her up, so it couldn't have been his barely repressed desire that frightened her off. What was it she had apologized for—a loss of dignity?

Dignity—a stifling word, that. Had some repressive individual—a stern governess, a cold mama, a disapproving father—or husband—stolen from her the ability to express joy openly? So that the keen zest for life, the unfettered laughter he'd just witnessed, emerged only in unguarded moments and was viewed as a lapse of propriety to be immediately regretted?

His anger shifted, redirecting itself against whomever had required his Sparrow to restrain her innocent delight in life. He'd like to teach the fellow the propriety to be found at the end of a clenched fist.

He felt again that surge of fierce protectiveness. Mrs. Martin had an enchanting laugh, and he meant to hear it, often. He'd have her indulging—and sharing with him—all the passionate responses she so diligently suppressed.

I'll make it so good for you, for us, he vowed as he speedily checked over the chestnut. *I'll give you freedom from want and restraint, cherish your body, revel in that questing, active mind. You need only let me.*

But his frustration revived on the drive back, which mirrored in unwelcome parallel the first time he'd driven her from the cottage to the hall. Mrs. Martin perched on the edge of the seat, as far from him as possible, replying to his every conversational opening an unvarying series of "yeses," "nos" or "I don't know, my lords."

How could she sit there so composed and distant, virtually ignoring him, when his body hummed with suppressed desire, his mind with the fervent need to probe her thoughts, know and explore and nurture her?

By the time he drew rein before the squire's entry hall, irritation at the unexpected setback drove him to be just a bit less cautious.

And so, after a groom came to the chestnut's head and Mrs. Martin turned to climb down from the carriage, he stayed her with a touch to the shoulder. Enough of impersonal, nonthreatening courtesy.

Beau took her hand and slowly, deliberately, raised it. "I enjoyed this afternoon very much, Mrs. Martin."

He moved his mouth across her knuckles, the barest touch of lip and warm breath. Then, while her eyes flared open and her gaze jerked up, he turned her hand over and applied the glancing, shock-spitting caress of his lips down her slender fingers to her callused palm. He had to call once again on his famous self-control to stifle the near-overwhelming impulse to sink his teeth into the tempting plumpness beneath her thumb where the palm narrowed to the soft, rose-scented skin of her wrist.

He released her then, pulses hammering, astounded that a simple brush with his lips could instantly rekindle desire to urgent fever pitch. He glanced down at her.

Lips slightly parted, eyes locked on him, she stood motionless, oblivious of the footman waiting to hand her down, looking awestruck as if she, too, could not credit the strength of what just passed between them. Her hand was still outstretched where he'd released it, fingers splayed and trembling.

Oh, yes, she felt *that*. Satisfaction surged through him, his only compensation for being forced to restrain himself from claiming her on the spot.

No, Mrs. Martin, he told her silently as he bowed in farewell. *This unnameable force between us cannot be ignored, try you ever so coolly to deny it. Sooner or later, all the secrets and passion you are at such pains to hide will be mine.*

Chapter Six

Her body and mind still spellbound by the earl's simple gesture, not until the squire offered a bluff greeting did Laura notice her host striding out.

"Come in, come in, my lord, Mrs. Martin! We've guests for you to meet. Lady Elspeth and her daughter, Lady Catherine, have just arrived."

Another stranger. Rattled as she felt at the moment, Laura was tempted to avoid the introduction. However, she swiftly realized that if she excused herself now, she might be pressed to join the party in the drawing room later. Better to brush through this quickly and avoid a more protracted conversation over biscuits and tea.

The arrival of his lordship's sister, however, meant she would soon be able to return home. An unexpected ambivalence dampened the surge of relief she'd anticipated at that reprieve.

Swallowing her protests over windblown hair and grubby gown, she followed the squire to the south parlor.

She refused to glance at Lord Beaulieu during the short walk. Drat, how the man unsettled her! Just when she'd thought they'd developed a comfortable rapport, nurse to patient's elder brother, he had to intrude again upon her senses with his tantalizing, dangerous appeal.

That so small a gesture as his lips brushing her palm could evoke so agitated a response only underscored she was a fool to believe she could remain a detached acquaintance. His very presence stirred both memories she'd rather suppress and longings she could scarcely put a name to.

She'd do better to follow her original plan of avoiding him.

By the time she reached that conclusion, the squire had ushered them into the parlor. A beautiful, raven-haired lady with the earl's dark eyes rose as they entered.

"Beau!" She held out her arms.

The earl strode over to envelop his sister in a hug. "How glad I am to see you, Ellie! But you're so pale. A difficult journey? Or did this scamp worry you to death?"

He turned to catch a child who hurtled into the room at him. "Uncle Beau! Do not tease Mama! She's been sick, so I've been ever so good. Did Uncle Kit really get his arm—eeh!" The rest of her sentence ended in a squeal as Beau tossed her into the air.

Laura looked at the small face, rosy-cheeked with excitement, the plump arms clasped about Lord Beaulieu's neck, and a painful contraction squeezed her chest. *My Jennie,* she thought, helpless to stop the wave of grief that swept over her.

By the time Lord Beaulieu deposited the girl on the sofa, she'd managed to form her lips into a smile.

"Stay still, imp!" his lordship ordered, and turned to the ladies. "Ellie, I have the honor to present Mrs. Martin, the lady whose skillful hands kept our graceless brother from a premature demise. Mrs. Martin, this is my sister, Lady Elspeth, and her daughter, Lady Catherine."

Laura rose from her curtsey to find his lordship's sister gesturing to her. "Come, Mrs. Martin, sit beside me. How can I ever thank you for saving Kit?"

"His lordship's physician deserves the credit, my lady. I merely kept watch," Laura said, reluctantly taking the seat indicated.

"'Twas much more than that, I'm told! But I must apologize for taking so long to arrive. As Catherine mentioned, I haven't been…well, and was forced to take the journey in much shorter stages than I should have liked."

The earl's face clouded. "What is it, Ellie?"

She patted his hand. "Nothing alarming, so you may lose that worried look! Though I fear I shall not be as much help to you as I'd hoped. I'm…I'm breeding again, you see." A smile of rapturous delight lit her face.

Lord Beaulieu leaned over to kiss her. "I know how happy that makes you. But after the difficulties you've had since Catherine's birth, was it wise to travel? I'm delighted to see you, of course, but I'm also astounded, given your condition, that Wentworth allowed you to come."

Lady Elspeth's smile turned impish. "He didn't. He was in London preparing for another tiresome diplomatic mission when your message arrived. I expect he'll be furious when he gets my note, but…oh, Beau, useless as I may be, I couldn't bear to remain away with Kit so ill!"

She turned appealing eyes to Laura. "We're hopelessly clannish, Mrs. Martin. And so, having barely met

you, I must beg a favor. I've suffered two...
disappointments since Catherine, and much as I want to
care for Kit I know I must rest and conserve my
strength. Can I prevail upon you to remain until Dr.
Mac feels he no longer needs constant nursing?''

A whirlwind of surprise, consternation, fear—and a
guilty gladness disordered Laura's thoughts. From the
confusion, only one conclusion surfaced clearly. As a
healer, she could not abandon her patient until her services were no longer needed. *She would not be leaving.*

She curtsied once more. ''My hearty congratulations
at your good news, my lady. Of course, if Dr. Mac-
Donovan, his lordship, and you all think it best, I shall
remain.''

''I'm sure the doctor will add his pleas to Ellie's,''
Lord Beaulieu said. ''You know how much I myself
value your skill, Mrs. Martin.''

The warmth of his tone, the compelling gaze he focused briefly on her before turning to the child pulling
impatiently at his coat sleeve, left her stomach churning
even as the protective part of her brain warned that remaining was a very bad idea.

''I want to see Uncle Kit! I want to see his shotted
arm. You have the bullet?''

''Catherine, please!'' the child's mother protested,
but Lord Beaulieu merely laughed. ''Bloodthirsty chit.
If the doctor says Kit is up to the visit, you may see
him. But no probing his wounds! It will hurt him too
much, poppet.''

The girl's bright eyes dimmed briefly, but she nodded. ''I won't hurt Uncle Kit. Take me now?''

''If you'll permit, I should withdraw and rest,'' Laura
inserted quickly and rose to her feet. ''Lady Elspeth,

Lady Catherine, a pleasure to meet you. My lord.'' She curtsied, eager to quit the room before he could protest.

''I must rest, as well,'' Lady Elspeth said. ''Indeed, I only returned to the parlor after our arrival because I wished to meet you, Mrs. Martin, at the first possible instant. Shall you be down for tea? I should very much like to become better acquainted.''

Not if I can help it, Laura thought. ''I'm afraid not, ma'am. I must rest if I am to watch through the night.''

''Of course. Perhaps you can visit with me tomorrow? I have not yet begun to thank you! And as my brothers will warn you, once I determine upon something, I'm most horribly persistent.'' The engaging smile which accompanied those dire words belied their threat.

''As you wish, my lady. Good day. And thank you again, my lord, for driving me to the garden.''

That summary of their afternoon together should put the interlude in proper perspective, Laura thought as she escaped from the salon.

''Beau, escort me to my chamber, please?''

''Ride me on your shoulder, Uncle Beau!''

Grinning, Beau bowed. ''As my ladies command.'' After inducing a series of giggles by throwing Catherine up to her post, he offered Ellie an arm. ''Are you truly 'fine'? Wentworth would never forgive me were something to happen to you while under my care. Nor should I forgive myself.''

''You know I want this too badly to take any risks. It nearly drove me mad to progress so slowly, but I forced myself to call a halt as soon as I tired or,'' she added with a rueful grimace, ''when the motion of the carriage overcame me.''

"Mama casts up her accounts," Catherine informed him. "Mostly every day. It's nasty." She wrinkled her small straight nose.

"Nasty indeed," her mama agreed with a sigh. "I shall be just as comfortable here as at home, and easier of mind, since I can see myself how Kit progresses. So if…something should happen, you cannot be blaming yourself."

Beau grimaced. "Is it so obvious?"

Lady Elspeth squeezed the arm she held. "Mac told me you had a cot placed so near Kit's bed, his every restless breath woke you. And that you scarcely slept or left his side the whole first week, as if you would hold him to life by strength of will alone." She paused, then added softly, "You cannot keep us from all harm, Beau."

The sound of a horse's scream, the smash of impact and shriek of shattering wood echoed out of memory. Forcefully he shut them out. "You are my charge, Ellie."

"I pray daily that all will go well, but what happens is in other hands. You might do well to remember that."

Beau nodded at the rebuke. "I shall, Madam Confessor. Now, scamp—" he eased his niece down "—here's Mary to take you to the nursery."

The girl clung to his arm. "Please, don't make me go! I want to ride with you!"

"It's too late today for a ride, poppet. But if you're a good girl and go without teasing your mama, I'll come up later and have tea with you."

The small hands at his shirt cuff stilled. "With rasp'ry jam and macaroons?"

He nodded solemnly. "Devon cream, too."

Lady Catherine sighed deeply. "And a ride tomorrow?"

"If the weather is fine."

"And I get to see Uncle Kit?"

"If the doctor says you may."

The pointed chin nodded agreement. With quaint dignity she dipped him a perfect curtsey, back straight, skirts spread gracefully. "As you wish, Uncle Beau. Good day, Mama. I shall go with you now, Mary."

Hiding a smile, the maid took the hand Lady Catherine offered. "Very good, miss."

Her mother stood looking after her, affection and despair mingled in her face. "She's such a scamp! One moment she's climbing trees, her petticoats in tatters, and the next she makes a curtsey that would not cause a blush at the queen's drawing room."

"Ah, the hearts she will break," Beau said with a chuckle. "I shall have to have all my unmarried friends transported the year she debuts."

"Thank heavens that won't be for a decade! Now, come sit with me a moment."

"Should you not better rest?"

Elspeth slanted him a knowing look. "As the lady managed to slip away, you must come in yourself and tell me all about Mrs. Martin."

Since his sister possessed an intuition superior to his own and powers of observation only scarcely less acute, Beau knew he'd not be able to avoid her questions without raising suspicion. Better to answer directly—but with care. He wanted no well-meaning "assistance" in the delicate matter of Mrs. Martin.

"She's been a godsend," he admitted as they took their seats. "Her quick action saved Kit's life the day he was wounded, as I'm sure Mac's informed you.

She's been the mainstay of caring for him through this difficult first week. Her remedies were most effective with fever, and the infusions seemed to calm Kit's restlessness.''

"She's a widow, the squire told me."

"Yes."

"And lives here alone, without other family?"

"Her aunt, who bequeathed her their cottage, died only recently, I understand."

"She's not nearly the old crone I was imagining."

Beau smiled. "No."

"In her mid-twenties, I would say. Hideous gown, which totally disguises her form, but her complexion is lovely and that auburn hair, what little I could see beneath that awful cap, is striking." She paused.

Grinning inwardly, Beau schooled his face to polite interest. "Yes, I agree. She is rather younger than I'd expected and quite attractive. As you'll doubtless see, our host has strong proclivities in that direction."

"Indeed!"

"It would not be so unusual a match."

Elspeth studied him a long moment. He maintained a face of bland innocence. "Perhaps he would do, if there are no younger contenders to hand. Or perhaps—she is of gentle birth, the squire said—I shall take her to London with me next season. So young and lovely a widow should have more choice in settling her future than is available in this country outpost."

"Is it so essential that she remarry?"

Elspeth gave him an exasperated look. "Certainly! What else is a woman to do? If what you say is true, she has no family to assist her. Who is to protect her if she falls ill or someone threatens her? Besides, she has no children, and she's certainly young enough to hope for some. No woman would wish to be deprived of that joy.''

The bittersweetness in her voice made his chest ache. Poor Ellie had suffered much for her babes. To lighten her mood he replied, ''Does Mrs. Martin have any say in this?''

Elspeth blushed. ''Of course. But our family owes her an enormous debt, you must allow. I'm merely considering how we might best go about repaying it.''

''Perhaps Mrs. Martin has plans of her own which will obviate your needing to intervene on her behalf.'' *Or mayhap someone else does,* he added mentally.

''Perhaps. But if not…I shall certainly do my possible. Now I really must rest. Don't let my minx of a daughter tire you out. She can be exhausting!''

Beau leaned to kiss his sister's cheek. ''I'm glad you're here, Ellie. I've missed you.''

She gave him a quick hug. ''And I you, big brother.''

Beau's smile faded as soon as he exited his sister's chamber. Having the determined Elspeth play matchmaker for Mrs. Martin was a complication he certainly didn't need. The mere idea of that lady giving herself to any other man, even in marriage, roused in him immediate and violent objections, though he would hardly voice them to Ellie.

For one, Mrs. Martin responded to *him* as she did to no other man in Merriville. True, he was hardly a disinterested observer any longer, but in his most professional assessment she'd displayed no such attraction to the squire, nor had her behavior indicated she harbored marital intentions.

Remarriage was certainly one remedy to her current insecurity, the most conventional remedy, but not the only one. He had the power and resources to make her permanently safer and more comfortable than any prospective husband Ellie could bring up to snuff, particularly the aging and only modestly well-to-do squire.

And Beau would make her happier. As lovers, partners and friends, they would please each other. He would stake his last shilling on it.

When—if—eventually they parted, Mrs. Martin would still have the option of remarriage. Only by then, their liaison would have left her socially and financially secure enough to take such a step out of desire, not necessity.

The vague discomfort occasioned by the very idea of Ellie marrying off Mrs. Martin faded, and Beau's mood brightened. He *was* delighted to have his sister here— he much preferred having all his family about. Especially since—a double blessing—Ellie's condition meant that her arrival no longer signaled the departure of Mrs. Martin.

Ellie would certainly attempt to befriend the widow, who was more likely to confide in his sister than in him. Through cautious questioning of his sibling, he'd probably discover more of Mrs. Martin's circumstances. Even better, Ellie might be able to coax her to join them at dinner or for tea. His spirits quickened at the thought of spending more time with her, even in company.

Of course, if Ellie did get her matrimonial plans in train, it would be the lady's choice whether she preferred a discrete and long-term liaison with Beau, or marriage to some beau of Ellie's choosing.

He'd just have to make sure her choice fell on him.

Later that evening another caller joined them. The vicar, Reverend Eric Blackthorne, had stopped by daily with prayers and encouragement during the crisis. Upon learning Lady Elspeth had arrived, he felt obliged to come by at once and pay his regards, he informed Beau's sister as they sipped tea, his own mama having been a good friend of her mother, the late Lady Beaulieu.

In virtually the next breath, Mr. Blackthorne requested that Mrs. Martin be bid to join them. Perhaps prompted by his recent conversation with Ellie, Beau was suddenly struck by suspicions he had not previously entertained concerning the reverend.

Beau's initial satisfaction when the footman returned to report Mrs. Martin begged their pardon for declining the invitation, as she was already on her way to relieve Dr. MacDonovan, turned to irritation when the reverend announced he would visit them both in Kit's chamber.

Best to determine the nature of this unexpected complication immediately, Beau decided. With brisk efficiency he eluded the squire and Ellie in the salon and insinuated himself into the sickroom call.

"Your mother, Mrs. Blackthorne, was a friend of my mama's?" Beau asked as the two men took the stairs.

"My mother, Lady Islington, was her friend," the vicar corrected. "My father is Viscount Islington."

Blackthorne of Islington. Of course. Annoyed with himself for not picking up the family connection upon their first introduction, Beau continued, "Richard, Baron Islington, is your brother? We were college mates."

The reverend slanted him a glance. "My *eldest* brother, yes."

Netted at that dig about his age, Beau nodded. So the vicar wasn't a country nobody, but scion of an important family. A detail that would surely be noted by his scheming sister.

"Do you intend to stay much longer, my lord?" the vicar asked. "I understand Kit is quite improved."

Beau's instinctive wariness deepened. Wanted him out of the way, did the vicar?

"That depends on Kit. Of course, I have pressing business in London, but I cannot depart until I am sure my brother is well and truly out of danger."

The vicar nodded in turn and the two men continued to the sickroom without further conversation, frosty awareness settling between them. During their previous meetings Beau had been too preoccupied by worry over Kit to take much notice of the vicar. It now appeared the man cherished as little enthusiasm for his presence here as Beau felt at this moment for the clergyman. An unsettling realization.

The frostiness, on Beau's part, grew chillier as he analyzed the vicar's behavior toward Mrs. Martin. The reverend was too well bred to single her out, instead conversing easily with Mac, encouraging Kit, and exchanging no more than a few polite sentences with Mrs. Martin.

Even so, Beau had no trouble determining from the warmth of the vicar's tone toward her, the glances that periodically strayed to the lady's downcast face even as he conversed with the doctor and Kit, that the reverend held Mrs. Martin in more than a pastoral regard.

Mac left to seek his dinner, the other two men walking with him. But when the vicar halted at the doorway, Beau stopped, as well. With Kit having dozed off again, Beau would be damned if he'd give the insolent fellow the opportunity for a private chat with Mrs. Martin.

Clearly as irritated by Beau's persistent presence as Beau was by his, the vicar said, "You'll wish to dine with the doctor. Please, my lord, feel free to do so.

There is no impropriety in *my* remaining here with Mrs. Martin.''

Was that a subtle rebuke? Beau's temper stirred. ''I know you would never overstep the bounds of your calling,'' he replied. ''But having lived for a week in constant anxiety over Kit, it still soothes me to be near him.''

Counter that, he thought, watching the vicar struggle for another argument to urge Beau's departure. Obviously failing, Mr. Blackthorne replied, ''As you wish, my lord.'' Walking to the chair where the widow sat beside her dozing patient, he said in low tones, ''How are you, Mrs. Martin? I trust you are watching after your own health.''

She did not look up, nor was there a shade of flirtatiousness in her tone. ''I am well, thank you, sir.''

''In any case, with Lady Elspeth here, you should now be able to return home.''

Before she could reply, Beau intruded into the conversation. ''My sister is in a delicate condition and must conserve her strength. Mrs. Martin has consented to remain here and continue to nurse Kit in her stead.''

Barely concealed annoyance colored the brief glance the vicar shot to the earl. ''Indeed.''

''A true compassionate, Christian lady is our Mrs. Martin,'' Beau said, nodding to her. ''All of us at Everett Hall value her highly, Reverend Blackthorne.''

''So I should hope. Though I must confess, having you remain under such...crowded conditions does trouble me, Mrs. Martin. Should you choose to return to your cottage, I would be happy to insure that you are escorted to the hall as required.''

''A kind offer, Mr. Blackthorne, but unnecessary,'' Beau again answered. ''Mrs. Martin would never slight the squire by inferring that his hospitality is less than adequate. And it is more convenient having her close.''

The vicar looked him full in the face. ''I'm sure it is—for you. 'Tis the *lady's* well-being that concerns me.''

''The squire's accommodations are quite satisfactory, Mr. Blackthorne, though you are kind to be concerned,'' Mrs. Martin broke in at last, a hint of exasperation in her tone. ''If I require assistance, I shall certainly let you know. But now, gentlemen, your discussion seems to be disturbing Mr. Bradsleigh. Why don't you continue it elsewhere and visit him again later.''

''As you wish, Mrs. Martin,'' Beau replied, amused and impressed. She'd just managed to banish the vicar—and himself, as well, unfortunately—with both tact and dispatch. ''Mr. Blackthorne, I believe we've been dismissed.''

His only consolation was that the lady seemed no more encouraging of the vicar than she was of the squire.

After the obligatory exchange of compliments, the two men left. Falling into step beside the vicar, Beau said, ''You need not worry about Mrs. Martin. I shall personally insure she takes proper care of herself.''

''That is precisely what worries me, my lord.''

Beau halted and pinned the vicar with an icy glare that had daunted many a subordinate. ''You will explain that remark, please.''

The vicar, to Beau's grudgingly accorded credit, did not flinch. ''I am concerned with the welfare of all my parishioners, Lord Beaulieu. You are a stranger, and may not understand the...harm you could do Mrs. Martin, however unintentionally, if it becomes known she is much in your company. Folk here do not approve of loose London ways.''

By gad, was the vicar maligning his honor by suggesting he'd give Mrs. Martin a slip on the shoulder under the very nose of the injured brother whose life she'd just saved? Had it been anyone other than a man of the cloth, Beau would have called him out on the spot.

Instead, controlling his outrage with an effort, Beau replied, ''You overstep yourself, sir. I am fully conscious of the magnitude of the service Mrs. Martin has done my family. I would never cause her harm.''

The vicar held his ground. ''I should hope not. But you should be aware, sir, that Mrs. Martin is not as defenseless as she might appear.''

''No, she is not,'' Beau shot back. ''She has the full protection of the Bradsleigh family. See that you remember that.'' Having reached the entry landing, Beau made a stiff bow. ''I will rejoin them now. Your servant, sir.''

''My lord.'' Face impassive, the vicar nodded and walked back toward the entry.

Beau watched him depart, struggling to master his anger. As if Beau would force his attentions on any lady, much less one to whom he owed such a debt of gratitude! Still, he noted, the vicar could have done nothing more revealing of his feelings toward Mrs. Martin than practically accuse Beau of intending to seduce her.

Given the judgment-impairing effects of such partiality—effects Beau had suffered himself—he would attempt to excuse the vicar's insulting innuendo.

That Beau entertained hopes of winning the lady's favor he would not deny. And though those hopes might not veer toward matrimony, Mrs. Martin was not a young virgin whose reputation could be ruined by a discreet affair.

Except…the vicar might be correct in asserting the rural folk of this neighborhood might take a less enlightened view of such a relationship. Perhaps Elspeth's idea of relocating Mrs. Martin had merit.

A circumspect liaison conducted elsewhere would, if anything, enhance her stature. In addition to the financial protection he was eager to offer, she'd meet prominent individuals whose influence could ease her way the rest of her life, as well as becoming acquainted with all the gentlemen of birth and status Ellie could hope for.

Should they later part company, most of these gentlemen would not consider her relationship with Beau disqualified her as a possible wife. Indeed, though her birth seemed merely respectable and her current position was less than modest, he wouldn't rule out the possibility of wedding Laura Martin himself. Especially since he found the notion of her going to any other man extremely distasteful.

The spark of an idea caught fire in his heart and head. Beau had already absented himself from his work about as long as he could afford. Returning to visit Mrs. Martin at this remote area on a regular basis might well be difficult. Having her established somewhere close enough for daily visits would be much more satisfactory—so satisfying, in fact, that Beau could almost forgive the vicar his temerity in broaching the issue.

That decided it. As soon as Kit had sufficiently recovered, Beau would have to persuade her to come to London.

Chapter Seven

By the next afternoon Beau was once again out of charity with the vicar. Apparently the reverend had spread word of Ellie's arrival and Kit's improvement throughout the county, for beginning that morning they'd had a steady stream of callers. Having been interrupted three times already while trying to assimilate the contents of the satchel his courier had delivered at dawn, Beau nearly told the apologetic footman who'd just appeared once again to convey his regrets.

Then, knowing his kindhearted sister would never be so uncivil as to refuse to receive the local gentry, and realizing the task of entertaining the curious would fall on her delicate shoulders should he shirk a duty he was finding particularly irksome today, he relented.

With a sigh he set his papers aside and followed the footman to the parlor. The striking blonde seated beside his sister surprised him out of his irritation.

The lady rose and followed him to the window where, after bowing a greeting, he'd gone to join the squire. "Lord Beaulieu, what a pleasure to see you again!"

She held out her hand. Compelled by courtesy, he

accepted it, his initial appreciation of her striking beauty dimming. *Forward baggage.*

"You'll remember me from Lord Greave's house party last fall at Wimberley. Lady Ardith Asquith."

As usual, the business reasons behind his attendance at that event had limited his time among the female guests. He scoured his memory, finally coming up with a flashy blonde accompanying an elderly peer.

His eyes narrowed as he swiftly assessed the daringly low-cut gown, the guinea-bright curls, the perfect skin, pouting lips—and bright, hard eyes. *A self-absorbed beauty.*

"Yes, I remember, Lady Ardith," he said, bringing her fingers to his lips for the obligatory salute. "And how is your husband, Lord Asquith?"

She flapped long painted lashes and gave him an overly familiar smile whose hint of shared intimacy he immediately resented. "Preoccupied as usual, my lord. Poor me—I so often have to find my own... amusements."

He knew he wasn't imagining the barely veiled innuendo, and his assessment of her character dropped lower. So Lady Ardith enjoyed collecting titled lover pelts, did she? He determined on the instant to discourage the connection.

But when he tried to reclaim his hand, she clutched it, causing him to automatically glance at his fingers—straight at the lavish breasts just below them, revealed to any downward-gazing eye all the way to the taunting pink edge of the nipples. A quick sideways glance confirmed the squire's gaze was riveted on the view.

He looked back up to catch his sister's amused but sympathetic eye. "Lady Ardith tells me her husband owns property in the neighborhood," Elspeth said, "and they often spend a few weeks here when not occupied in London."

"On those occasions when Lady Ardith—and Lord Asquith, of course—choose to honor us, their company is always a valued addition to our society," the squire said.

Lady Ardith leaned further forward as she squeezed the squire's hand. "Dear Squire Everett! How could I not attend your gatherings as often as possible when I know such a gallant gentleman awaits me?"

The squire paused, apparently too distracted for speech while he struggled between the propriety of raising his eyes to her face and the titillation of visually fondling the display beneath his nose.

Beau watched a knowing smile curve the corners of Lady Ardith's lips and his disdain increased. He'd bet the price of her elegant gown that, even bored to flinders in what she no doubt considered a rustic outpost, Lady Ardith would never consider adding the middle-aged, balding squire to her list of indoor sportsmen. Yet she seemed driven, as beautiful females often were, to captivate every male who crossed her path, whether she valued his regard or not.

Attracting a man of Beau's wealth and rank likely *would* interest her, he thought cynically. Since he had no desire whatsoever to help Lady Ardith beguile the tedium of her country sojourn, he'd end this game at once.

While she toyed with the squire, Beau crossed the room and usurped her seat beside his sister. Lady Ardith's self-satisfied smile wavered briefly when she discovered his move, but brightened again after the squire led her by the hand to a chair beside his own.

"Squire Everett, you must give a ball in honor of

Lord Beaulieu and Lady Elspeth!'' the lady exclaimed. ''I should do so myself, but since we open the house here for such short periods, we do not maintain sufficient staff.''

A pinch-penny, as well, Beau thought, disgusted. ''With my brother's health so uncertain, I do not believe we could consider a ball. And at present, Lady Elspeth's health is too...delicate for dancing,'' he replied.

''His lordship's got the right of it,'' the squire agreed. ''With young master Kit still so ill, 'twould not be fitting to disport ourselves at a ball.''

''You are right of course, my lord. A dinner, then,'' Lady Ardith persisted. ''Something rather more quiet, with just the first families of the neighborhood in attendance. That would not tax Lady Elspeth's strength, for she could retire early. I should be happy to preside over the tea tray for you, Squire Everett.''

''His sister, Lady Winters, could do so,'' Beau said.

His repressive tone didn't seem to dampen the lady's pretensions a bit. ''Ah, dear Lady Winters? Is she visiting you currently? I thought she'd removed to Bath.''

''No, surely you remember, Lady Ardith, she returned here when her husband died two years ago,'' the squire said.

Lady Ardith trilled a laugh. ''Oh, yes, how silly of me.'' She waved a hand, dismissing Lady Winters. ''I fear I have no head at all for dates and figures.''

''A dinner would be lovely,'' Elspeth intervened, wary of the growing irritation she no doubt perceived in Beau's expression. ''Assuming Kit continues to improve, Dr. MacDonovan will want to depart by the week's end. Before he goes, we should like to do something to honor him. And Mrs. Martin, of course.''

"Aye, it could be a tribute to both our angels of mercy," the squire concurred.

Beau opened his lips to squash the idea. He had no intention of providing both the forum and the target for Lady Ardith's next hunt.

But then he reconsidered. With a little arranging he could pawn that lady off on Mac and the vicar—and arrange to have himself seated near Mrs. Martin.

Mrs. Martin, her auburn hair freed from the ubiquitous cap, her form garbed in something more becoming than the awful brown sacks she habitually wore. His Sparrow in evening dress.

To savor that vision would be worth fending off a dozen Lady Ardiths.

"A capital idea, Squire Everett," he said. "The doctor and Mrs. Martin deserve our most warmest gratitude."

Lady Ardith's look of triumph faded. "Mrs. Martin? That local—*herb woman*—was allowed to tend your brother!"

"She saved his life, as the doctor will testify," Beau said, "and deserves the highest commendation."

"Your desire to acknowledge her is most kind, my lord, but...at a dinner?" Lady Ardith interjected. "Such a lowly personage would doubtless be most uncomfortable to be seated at a social gathering among her betters."

"Nonsense," the squire returned. "Mrs. Martin's gentry-born—her late husband was an army officer— and has dined with us on several occasions."

Better and better, Beau thought, his enthusiasm for the dinner party growing. Since Mrs. Martin had apparently already appeared at neighborhood social gatherings, she would not be able to escape with that excuse.

"It's settled then," Beau said. "On Friday, shall we say? Dr. MacDonovan told me this morning he hopes by then to declare Kit finally out of danger."

"Squire Everett, will arranging a dinner party on such short notice be too much for your sister?" Elspeth asked.

"Not a bit," Squire Everett replied cheerfully, obviously taken with the idea. "If she falls prey to the vapors, Mrs. Martin can help out. She's assisted Emily before. A lady of many talents, our Mrs. Martin."

"So it appears," Beau murmured.

Lady Ardith continued to haggle over the wisdom of including an unattached lady in the gathering, but convinced the squire would go through with the plan whether Lady Ardith chose to attend or not, Beau let the conversation fade to a babble while he set about reviewing the pleasing implications.

This dinner might be just the thing to breach Mrs. Martin's reserve for good. If she appeared at the party to receive the admiration and respect he knew her loveliness would generate, perhaps that acclaim would cause some of her nervous reticence to fade. Even better, he'd be able to pay her gentle, persistent attention in a forum where such behavior was entirely appropriate, nothing to inspire alarm. Once she grew less wary and more comfortable around him, he'd finally be able to get close enough to demonstrate his genuine respect and concern.

Surely then she would come to trust him—and heed the call that impelled her to come to him.

The next afternoon, in a pretty note begging her pardon for the inconvenience, Lord Beaulieu's sister asked Laura to join her in the sitting room attached to her chamber, as she found herself too weary after her journey to come downstairs. Bowing to the inevitable, Laura steeled herself for the interview.

As Lady Elspeth was several years older, she had already come out, married, and left London to raise a family by the time Laura made her debut. So there was no chance whatsoever, Laura told herself, trying to squelch her ever-present anxiety, that Lord Beaulieu's sister might recognize her.

Deliberately garbing herself in the ugliest of Aunt Mary's gowns and the most voluminous of the lace dowager caps, Laura forced her face into a mask of serenity and knocked at the door of Lady Elspeth's sitting room.

But as she entered, a small figure bounded up. "Did you nurse Uncle Kit and keep the angels from taking him to heaven?" she demanded.

"Catherine!" her mother protested from her reclining position upon the sofa. "You mustn't pounce upon people like that. Greet Mrs. Martin properly, if you please."

With a sigh the girl straightened, then dipped a curtsey. "Good day, Mrs. Martin. I trust you are well?"

The speech was so clearly parroted—and practiced—Laura had to smile. "Good day to you, Lady Catherine. I am quite well, thank you. And you?"

"Very well, but Mama's not. That's why she's so cross. Uncle Beau said you kept the angels from taking Uncle Kit. I'm so glad! He's ever so much fun, and I'm not finished with him yet."

The vision of angels tussling over Kit Bradsleigh's bed tickled Laura's whimsy, and some of her nervousness fled. She took the hand Lady Catherine held out and walked with her to the sofa.

"Perhaps God wasn't ready for him yet," Laura said. *Unlike my Jennie.* A dull ache permeated her at the unbidden thought, and wearily she suppressed it. "But Dr. MacDonovan did most of the work, you know."

The little girl looked thoughtful, then nodded. "Angels would surely leave Dr. Mac alone. He talks too loud and he makes you drink nasty medicine." She gestured to Lady Elspeth. "I think that's why mama is sick."

"Don't be impertinent, Catherine," her mama reproved with a frown. "If you cannot confine your conversation to more proper subjects I shall send you back to the nursery."

The small face grew instantly contrite. "I'll be good, Mama. Please let me stay. Uncle Beau said we can't ride for hours yet and Mary doesn't know any games, and the books Uncle Beau left are full of big words."

Lady Elspeth, looking in truth very pale and weary, sighed and leaned over to ruffle her daughter's hair. "I'm sorry, pet. Mrs. Martin, I'm afraid Catherine's nurse came down with a putrid sore throat this morning and has taken to her bed. I can't seem to summon the energy to go out, which leaves poor Catherine stranded in the nursery with only Mary for company. She's a kind girl, but not at all used to dealing with children."

Laura felt an instant sympathy for the spirited, active little girl forced to remain cooped up indoors. "Should you like to take a walk, Lady Catherine? The gardens are still pretty with the late roses blooming. That is, if you would permit, Lady Elspeth."

Lady Catherine's face lit. "Oh please, Mama, may I?"

"Are you sure, Mrs. Martin? I wouldn't like her to tease you, and she can be quite—energetic."

"I would love to! I used to tend my older sister's girls when their governess was—" Alarmed, Laura caught herself before she blundered into revealing more details. "Occupied," she finished, hoping Lady Elspeth hadn't noticed her sudden dismay. "I do enjoy children."

"Then I should be grateful. Mind, Catherine, that you let us drink our tea in peace."

"Yes, Mama." Lady Catherine looked up to give Laura a beaming smile. "You're nice, just like Uncle Beau said. I like you, even if you do wear such ugly gowns."

Lady Elspeth's eyes widened and she straightened, as if to make a grab for her lamentably plain-spoken child. But as she leaned forward, her face grew paler still. Clutching a handkerchief to her mouth, she struggled from her seat and seized a nearby chamberpot.

"Ugh," Catherine said over the ensuing sound of her mother's retching. "I hate Mama being sick. Uncle Beau says soon she'll be better, but she's been sick ever so long." The small chin wavered. "It scares me," she admitted, tears forming in her eyes.

Laura had intended to keep this meeting as brief as possible. But she couldn't bring herself to leave a frightened little girl in need of comfort, or depart without attempting to help alleviate the distress of her suffering mother.

She hugged Catherine, who came into her arms with no resistance, her body trembling. "Your uncle Beau is right, Catherine. Your mama won't be sick for too much longer." Not knowing what the child had been told, she decided not to explain further. "I've nursed lots of people, and I can tell when someone is very ill and when they're about to get better. Your mama will get better."

"You're sure?" The child looked up at her, anxious eyes huge in her troubled face.

"Cross my heart," Laura promised.

The girl sighed. "If you could keep the angels from taking Uncle Kit, I suppose you can keep them from Mama."

"Why don't you go back to the nursery and find your cloak and some heavy shoes. Then you'll be ready to walk when your mama and I finish tea."

The child nodded. "She won't drink any, though. She doesn't drink anything at tea now, and we don't have the pretty pink cakes anymore 'cause she says the smell makes her ill."

"How disappointing," Laura said. "You know, if we meet Squire Everett on our walk and you ask him nicely, I wager he'd have his cook bake some pretty pink cakes. You could share them with your uncle Beau in the nursery, where the smell wouldn't bother your mama."

The small face brightened. "He would? I shall ask today!" The child leaped up and hugged her. "You must have some cakes, too. Oh, I do like you! I'm sorry I said your gown was ugly. Though truly it is."

Grinning, Laura bent down until her lips were close to the girl's ear. "I know," she whispered, and winked.

With a giggle, the little girl skipped out. Laura turned to the mother, who was now wiping her face and trying to gather the remnants of her dignity.

"M-Mrs. Martin, I do apolo—"

"Please, Lady Elspeth, there's no need! I'm a nurse, you will recall. Come, sit down and try to get comfortable. Has your physician given you any remedies to help alleviate the sickness?"

Wearily Lady Elspeth settled against the cushions.

"He said an overheating of the blood causes it, and ordered Nurse to mix up some vile concoction that was supposed to cool the humors, but I couldn't keep it down. Nor would I let him bleed me, as he urged and Wentworth pleaded. I—I'm already so weak, I cannot see how bleeding would help."

Laura nodded. "My uncle found, after much study, that bleeding does tend to weaken the patient. He recommended more gentle means—teas blended with chamomile and peppermint to soothe the stomach, and lozenges composed of sugar, ginger root, and lavender to suck on when the queasy feeling strikes. I—I have a stock made up and could obtain some for you, if you should like to try."

"Just now I'm willing to try anything short of a pistol bullet to the head," Lady Elspeth replied grimly.

"I shall make up a tea at once. Here, recline with this pillow to your back. A cloth dipped in cooled rosewater applied to your temples may help, as well. I'll fetch one. Try it while I brew the tea."

"You truly *are* an angel of mercy, Mrs. Martin," Lady Elspeth sighed as she settled back. "But I did so want to chat with you."

"Later. First, you must rest and rally your strength." Laura paused. "By the way, does your daughter know the nature of your illness?"

Lady Elspeth opened one eye. "No. I thought it best not to tell her. For years she's begged me for a baby brother or sister. I feared if…if this ended as the previous two have, she'd be disappointed—and upset. When her dog died last summer, she was distraught for days."

"She's upset now, worrying about her mama," Laura said gently. "'Tis your choice, my lady, but if it were me I'd tell her what afflicts you is normal and shall soon pass. Children that young do not understand how babies arrive. If you tell her only that a new sibling is a happy possibility, she would probably be no more than mildly disappointed should your hopes…not be realized.''

"She worries?" Lady Elspeth said. "Ah, my poor babe. I suppose I've been too ill and cross to notice. Perhaps you are right, Mrs. Martin." She forced a tired smile. "A wise angel as well as a guardian one."

"Rest now and I'll fetch your tea. We'll talk later." *Much later, if I have any say in it,* Laura thought.

She'd brushed through that well enough, and the idea of walking in the garden with Lady Catherine—someone with whom she needn't be always on her guard—was enormously appealing. Perhaps she'd slip invisibly through the last few days of tending Kit Bradsleigh and reach home safely after all.

Chapter Eight

Feet clothed in sturdy walking boots and hands encumbered by a linen cloth filled with jam tarts fresh from the oven, two days later Laura entered the garden.

Though she still spent much of her time alone, keeping vigil over Kit Bradsleigh at night and dining in her room, she now had these afternoon outings with Lady Catherine to look forward to. Dr. MacDonovan had informed her this morning that, unless their patient took a sudden turn for the worse, he expected to leave at week's end. By then, Kit Bradsleigh would no longer need round-the-clock care.

Which meant surely Kit's older brother would be leaving soon, as well. A departure which she viewed with increasingly mixed feelings.

Removed from his too perceptive scrutiny, she'd be safe once more. And if life without the surge of mingled elation and alarm he sparked in her whenever he appeared would be less energizing, she'd do well to remember why she'd previously rejoiced at a life of dull monotony.

She'd also be able to return home, though she'd still

spend much time at Everett Hall tending the recuperating invalid. And visiting her new friend Lady Elspeth.

Laura shook her head ruefully. Lady Elspeth insisted Laura called her "Ellie," claiming she could not remain on formal terms with the woman who'd saved her brother's life and the practitioner whose treatments had considerably eased her own misery. She treated Laura with such beguiling warmth that, having been so long deprived of the companionship of a woman her own age, Laura had great trouble maintaining any reserve.

Catching sight of Lady Catherine, whose nurse, though recovered from her ailment, was happy to let Laura walk her energetic charge about the garden, Laura waved.

She loved spending time with Catherine, despite the ever-present ache of regret for what might have been and now would never be. She'd grown up the youngest child of a large family. When her elder siblings returned to visit with their offspring, it was only natural that the aunt, hardly older than her nieces and nephews, should join them in the nursery. Only natural, as well, that with only adult companions most of her days, she reveled in their company.

Better even than the warm memories Catherine's chatty escort revived, or Laura's freedom when with the child to relax the constant guard she otherwise maintained, was the precious ability to wander the grounds as long as she liked, protected by Catherine's small hand in hers from having to worry about encountering the earl alone.

In fact, Laura and her charge had met "Uncle Beau" every single afternoon. Always delighted to see the earl—who seemed to take equal delight in his niece, Laura noted with approval—Catherine had no qualms about monopolizing Lord Beaulieu's time and attention. Laura was able to observe him and indulge in the heady thrill of his company, freed of the stomach-clenching anxiety that normally afflicted her in his presence.

Since Catherine had confided her uncle planned to meet her after their walk to take her riding, Laura was not surprised when, soon after she and Catherine seated themselves on their favorite bench beside a fragrant hedge of late-blooming damask roses, Lord Beaulieu approached.

Awareness of him flashed over her nerves like a wind-driven ripple across a lake's calm surface.

"I saved you a tart!" Catherine cried, running over to offer him the crumbling remains of a pastry.

Ignoring the grubbiness of the jam-stained fingers, the earl accepted the treat. "Kind of you, princess. And I must thank the little wizard who coaxes the squire's cook to come up with these delicacies for tea every day."

"Not me," Catherine pointed out with scrupulous fairness, munching the last bit of her tart. "Laura does. Cook likes her. I do, too. Don't you, Uncle Beau?"

The earl turned his smiling face toward Laura—and caught her staring. She felt the warmth of embarrassment flood her cheeks and tried to look away, but his smile fading to something deeper, more intimate, he held her gaze…one minute, two. "Very much indeed," he said softly before turning his attention back to his niece.

While her cheeks burned hotter and fluttery wings beat within her stomach, Catherine continued, "Uncle Beau, I have a secret! Only Mama said I could tell you and Laura, so it's all right to share, isn't it?"

"If she said you could, poppet." The earl flashed

Laura a brief but oddly intense look. "I love secrets, and I *never* tell anyone."

Lady Catherine's eyes gleamed with excitement as she grabbed her uncle's coat sleeves. "It's wonderful, and you'll never guess. Mama said next Easter, I might get a new brother or sister!"

So Lady Elspeth had confessed, Laura thought, pleased.

"That's indeed wonderful news," Lord Beaulieu said. "Which should you prefer—a sister or a brother?"

"I don't suppose it matters. I'm ever so much older, it shall have to mind me. Mama says getting a baby is a curious sort of game. Playing it makes her sick sometimes, but if she wins, she gets to keep a baby. But not everyone wins, so I should not be disappointed if we don't get a baby after all." Lady Catherine wrinkled her brow. "It's a very odd sort of game, don't you think?"

Lord Beaulieu laughed. "I wonder what your papa would say to that?"

"Well, I much prefer ball and spillikins, but Mama says I can't play the game anyway until I'm a lady, and married. If we should get a boy, he can ride and play catch with me. And if it's a girl, I shall give her my old dolls and my dresses when I outgrow them. But only pretty ones. Not ugly ones like Laura's aunt Mary gave her."

Laura stifled a gasp, and Lord Beaulieu caught his breath. "That was very rude, brat!" he said after a moment. "Apologize to Mrs. Martin at once!"

A little daunted, Catherine raised pleading eyes to her uncle. "It's all right, Uncle Beau. Laura knows they're ugly—she told me so herself, didn't you, Laura?"

Her cheeks pinking, Laura merely nodded, carefully avoiding the earl's gaze.

"See?" Catherine turned back to her uncle. "Laura told me she wears the dresses even though they're ugly because her aunt Mary gave them to her, and she loved Aunt Mary. But I shall give my sister only pretty ones, so she'll love me even better."

"How could she resist?" Lord Beaulieu said, with a rueful glance at Laura.

Focusing her attention on Lady Catherine, Laura said, "I expect your uncle came to tell you the horses are ready. Since we've finished our snack, you'd best be off before it's too late to ride."

"Can you not ride with us?" the child asked.

Laura hesitated. "I—I have no horse."

"Uncle Beau can get you one. He knows all about horses. He brought me the wonderfulest pony."

"Another time, perhaps. You mustn't keep your mounts waiting, so off with you now."

"Go to the stables, and make sure Manson had your pony ready," Lord Beaulieu said. "I'll be right along."

"Can we race today?"

The earl rolled his eyes. "Perhaps—it depends on how wet the fields are. I make no promises!"

Lady Catherine angled her chin up and grinned at him, a mixture of precocious coquette and childish charm. "Bet I'll beat you." Evading the earl's mock punch with a giggle, she scurried off down the path.

The earl sighed and turned to Laura. Knowing their chaperone was even this moment racing out of sight, all her nerves alerted.

"I must apologize once again for my niece. She has a deplorable tendency to say exactly what she thinks."

"I'm not offended, truly." She attempted a smile, a

difficult matter when her lips wanted to tremble and her heart was beating so hard she felt dizzy. "Children usually do speak the truth as they see it, even when it might be better sugar-coated."

At that he turned his face to once again snare her with a searing gaze that would not allow her to look away. "'Tis always wise to tell the truth. Especially when those who hear it are friends who seek only our good."

Laura's breath caught in her throat and her lips went dry. He was speaking of much more than hand-me-down gowns, and they both knew it.

Trust him, a small voice deep within her whispered. *He will be that sort of friend.*

But the legacy of fear and a now-ingrained compulsion for concealment drowned out the voice. "No, my lord," she said, her voice barely louder than a whisper. "'Tis not always wise. Enjoy your ride."

Pivoting on her heel, she made herself walk back to the house, calm and unhurried. Feeling with every step the weight of his thoughtful gaze heavy upon her back.

Chest tight and mind seething with frustration, Beau watched Mrs. Martin escape to the house. In her expressive face, her guileless eyes, he'd read how very close he'd come to breaking through that wall of silent reserve. So close he could feel the acquiescence trembling on her lips, and now tasted the bitter sense of loss.

Still, the very fact that he had come so close was cause to hope that very soon the remnants of her reserve would crumble.

He could assemble all the small clues she'd let drop, add them to the information he'd extracted from the squire, set his team to work on it, and probably within a fortnight be able to reconstruct the whole of her life up to now. He could, but he didn't want to.

With a determination that grew daily more intense, he wanted Mrs. Martin to come to *him,* confide in him, trust him of her own free will.

He really ought to be making plans to leave. The information in the latest dispatches confirmed the careful theories he'd previously constructed, and if events continued in the same manner, he'd soon have enough evidence to complete the dossier and turn it over to Lord Riverton. Perhaps he ought to do that immediately and then return, free to devote as much time as necessary to finish winning over his Sparrow. He could then leave Merriville for good—with Laura Martin.

Still, the dinner party Friday night might allow him close enough to finally gain her trust. Tonight before Mrs. Martin went in to tend Kit, the squire would tender the invitation. Beau had primed both his sister and his brother Kit to press her to accept. He wasn't above enlisting Catherine, as well, if necessary.

He already had his niece to thank for one piece of information that, if handled correctly—and he was a master of handling information—should insure Mrs. Martin appeared at the party garbed in evening attire far more attractive than the hideous gowns she normally wore.

Yes, his niece—who was doubtless at this moment bedeviling the grooms while she waited impatiently for her uncle to arrive.

Beau took one more look at the door through which Mrs. Martin, with a calm belied by the agitation he'd read in those stark blue eyes, had just disappeared. *Soon we will be together,* he promised himself and her. *Soon.*

* * *

"Dinner on Friday?" Laura echoed the words in dismay. "That's very kind of you, Squire Everett, but I thought we agreed my uncertain schedule made it wiser that I not dine in company." With a nervous glance she surveyed the group who'd greeted her in the small salon when she returned from her walk with Lady Catherine.

"But 'tis my farewell party, ma'am," Dr. MacDonovan argued. "Sure, and you'd not be sending me off with a wave of a bandage roll across our sleeping Kit's bed?"

"You're to leave Saturday?"

"Aye. I've just examined the lad's lungs again, and it's clearer still they be. Under your competent care, I've little doubt of his eventual recovery, and it's needed I am back home."

"Yes, you must attend, Laura," Lady Elspeth urged. "I've felt so much better the last two days, I can finally envision dining without revulsion. Since I owe that improvement solely to you, you must help me celebrate."

"At the risk of putting you off entirely, I confess the party is as much in your honor as the good doctor's, ma'am," the squire said. "We owe both of you a great debt, and would like to publicly acknowledge it."

"Publicly?" Laura repeated in automatic anxiety.

"We've had the whole neighborhood asking after young Kit and praying with us for his recovery. 'Tis only fitting that all have the chance to help our distinguished visitors celebrate the good news before their departure."

"If 'tis to be a large party, then you'll surely not need me. It will make the numbers wrong," Laura offered.

"Pish-tosh, Mrs. Martin." The squire waved away the suggestion. "'Tis not some fancy London party, all standing on precedence. And you need not feel shy.

Excepting the earl, Lady Elspeth and the good doctor, 'twill be only neighbors you've dined with on several occasions. Oh, and Lady Ardith and Lord Asquith.''

Laura looked at the smiling faces—the squire, the doctor, Lady Elspeth. Some inner imperative told her to accept would be dangerous, possibly the most dangerous thing she'd done since coming to the aid of the earl's wounded brother. But as she had no reason to fear any of her neighbors—even the conceited London beauty Lady Ardith, who scarcely acknowledged her existence—Laura could dredge up no excuse to avoid the party that would not either cause offense or give rise to speculation.

Surely the earl would be present, too. The thought shimmered through her, adding to both her longing and dismay. Still, she didn't see how she could avoid this. ''You are vastly kind. I shall accept with pleasure.''

''Oh—m'sister may call upon you to write out the invitations. Her failing eyesight, you know. If that won't be too much of an imposition?''

Laura had to smile. Lady Winters, an indolent damsel of some seventy summers, had previously called on Laura to assist her after suffering palpitations at the mere prospect of the work entailed by an evening party. ''You may assure your sister I shall be happy to assist her.''

''Good, good.'' The squire patted her hand. ''Knew we could count on you. Want to send the doctor off with a good proper party, and with you overseeing the arrangements, I know 'twill be top of the trees.''

Though Lady Elspeth, bless her, objected it was not quite right that Laura toil on a party given partly in her own honor, she desisted when Laura assured her that she didn't mind in the least. Thanking the group again, Laura returned to her room.

It was only ingrained caution that made her so uneasy. All the guests would be well known to her. Besides, if she handled the arrangements for Lady Winters, she could arrange the dinner partners to suit herself, make a brief appearance in the parlor after the meal, then excuse herself before tea.

Thinking of the guest list again, she had to laugh at her apprehensions. With Lady Ardith promised to appear, no one would give the dowdy Mrs. Martin a second glance.

Late the following afternoon, Laura was returning to her room after going over the party lists with Lady Emily when Lady Elspeth hailed her in the hallway. "Please, could you join me for some tea in my sitting room before you rest for tonight? Being reduced to the company of the squire, Lady Winters and my brother at dinner, I sorely miss the conversation of a rational lady."

Having on occasion been constrained to be the rambling Lady Emily's dinner partner, Laura could sympathize. And after a few day's acquaintance, Laura had largely lost her reserve around Lady Elspeth. Here was a friend in truth, one who, even should she learn of Laura's deception—not that she ever intended to reveal it—would not, Laura felt sure, betray her. And she sincerely enjoyed the company of the earl's charming, cheerful sister.

"I should be delighted."

Laura entered to take the seat indicated on the brocade flowered sofa while Lady Elspeth poured tea. After handing her a cup, her friend gave her a measuring glance.

"I happened to notice that, though you agreed to help Lady Winters, you didn't seem particularly pleased to accept the squire's invitation to dine."

Laura sighed. "I'm afraid I'm painfully shy in company, a fault I've never managed to overcome."

"Please don't be offended, but do you hesitate for fear that, with the very fashionable Lady Ardith attending, you feel you do not possess a suitable gown?"

Laura laughed. "I certainly possess nothing cut up— or should we say 'down'—to Lady Ardith's standards."

"I should hope not," Lady Elspeth agreed with a chuckle. "But I wanted to ask a favor. I brought with me a new dinner gown just received from the mantua-maker that I've never worn, and now I find I cannot. If God wills, and I carry this child, by the time I visit London again fashions will have changed. Though I hope I'm not as vain as Lady Ardith, I doubt I'd wear it then. The color is a lovely green, and would suit you. Would you accept it?

"Please, now—" she held up a hand to forestall Laura's protest "—don't refuse outright. You know I won't insult you by offering payment for the care you gave Kit. Indeed, were I the richest woman in the universe, how could I ever pay you the worth of my baby brother's life? Beside that, a gown is the merest trifle. Still, it is too lovely to waste, and it would please me to have you wear it."

Though she didn't doubt Lady Elspeth's sincerity or kindness, Laura wasn't naive enough to believe this offer a coincidence. With a rueful grimace, she wondered who had whispered in her friend's ear. Lady Catherine, wanting "beautiful dresses" for her friend? Or Lord Beaulieu?

As she hesitated, Lady Elspeth misinterpreted her silence. "What a widget! Of course you can't decide until you see the gown. I'll have Jane bring it immediately!"

Laura tried to protest, but Lady Elspeth had already rung for her maid. Instructions were given, and by the time they finished their tea, the maid reappeared, bearing the dress. The demurral Laura intended to voice died in an inarticulate cry of wonder.

It was simply the most delicate, wondrous, lovely gown she'd ever beheld, a simple sheath of pale green silk whose wispy sleeves and long train were covered with a fairy's cobweb of fine lace. Not even in her debut season had she, limited to the whites and pastels prescribed for unmarried maidens, possessed such a dress.

Before she could muster her scattered thoughts to protest, Lady Elspeth had her on her feet, the maid holding the dress up to her as her friend gave instructions on where to pin, tuck or adjust.

"Ah, Ellie—it's marvelous! But I simply couldn't!"

"Since it's rather obvious you like the gown—" Elspeth paused in her instructions to grin at Laura "—and it becomes you wonderfully, I shall be most hurt if you refuse it."

The sober, responsible, cautious side of her urged that she do just that. But the woman in her slid the sensuous length of silk through her fingers, felt the sigh of lace against her arms, and knew she could never bring herself to turn this down. For one evening, like Cinderella in the fairy tale, plain, dowdy, shy little Laura Martin would be dressed like a princess.

And her Prince Charming, whom she might covertly watch and desire but never possess, would see her in it.

Even in a small gathering, wearing such a beautifully made gown would be sure to draw to her the universal attention of every lady present, and probably that of the gentlemen, as well. Inviting precisely the sort of widespread scrutiny she'd spent nearly three years carefully avoiding. Attending in that gown would be foolish, vain and most unwise.

And she would do it. If her benefactress were present, of course.

"You're sure you will be feeling well enough to attend the party?" Laura asked, grasping at straws.

Lady Elspeth's smile widened. "I wouldn't miss it for the world."

Chapter Nine

"Thank you, Jane. I can manage from here."

"Aye, ma'am. A right treasure you look, and so I'll tell her ladyship!" With a nod of professional approval, Lady Elspeth's maid curtsied and left the chamber.

Lips curving into a smile of pleasure, Laura closed her eyes, enjoying the pure sensual caress of the silk gown against her skin. Not until this moment, the smoky-green fabric swirling about her, did she realize just how much she'd missed what Lady Catherine would call "pretty dresses." After the door shut behind the departing maid, with a giddy laugh, Laura lifted her arms and waltzed around her narrow chamber, dipping and turning in the embrace of her invisible partner.

Cinderella in truth, for the dress was no more substantial than moondust and starlight. After months of wearing the stiff, heavy brown bombazine favored by Aunt Mary, so sheer and weightless did the garment feel Laura could scarcely believe she was clothed at all.

She stopped dancing and cast a worried glance down at her chest. Though fashioned with a décolletage nowhere near as deep as the style favored by Lady Ardith, the dress was still much lower cut than any she'd worn

during her brief Season. Perhaps she should have protested more strongly when Lady Elspeth absolutely forbade Jane to sew a lace tucker into the bodice.

Nonsense, she reassured herself. With Lady Ardith
present in all her scandalous finery, who would spare a
look for little Laura Martin?

Nonetheless, her disquiet increased after she left the
secure cocoon of her chamber. Since her near-
miraculous recovery from the fever that had almost
killed her, she'd worn naught but the mud-brown cam-
ouflage of her new identity. Daring to appear in public
without it made her feel even more unclothed than the
gossamer gown.

Still, if she meant to put off for an evening garments
guaranteeing obscurity, nowhere in England could she
do so in more safety than in Squire Everett's drawing
room. The only guests present would be neighbors
who'd long ago accepted Laura Martin, or relatives of
the boy whose life she'd help to preserve. None of
those, she believed, would consciously seek to do her
harm.

Honesty forced her to admit that her unease at descending to the drawing room was directly related to
the tall, commanding earl about to gather there with the
assembling dinner party. A man who inspired in her this
perilous swing of emotion from attraction to avoidance,
the man she'd felt impelled to give, for one brief evening, a glimpse of the woman behind the mask.

A man who, should he decide to tempt her out of
sanity into temporary dalliance, would tryst with her
and forget her the moment his carriage passed beyond
the gateposts of Everett Hall. In truth, no matter how
glorious such an interlude would prove—and every inexperienced but acutely sensitive nerve shouted that it

would be glorious indeed—she could not afford for him to remember her longer.

Laura Martin, you're an idiot, she concluded as she reached the floor on which the main bedchambers were located. As she started past the door to her patient's room, she paused. Perhaps she should check on Kit.

Glad to have a responsible reason to indulge her cowardly desire to dawdle, she knocked on the door. When Kit's valet, Peters, answered it, instead of standing aside to let her enter, he simply stood for a moment, jaw dropped, staring. "Cor, ma'am," he breathed, finally remembering to step back, "but you do look fine."

"T-thank you," she stuttered, not sure whether to be alarmed or flattered.

"Who is it, Peters?"

"Mrs. Martin, master—I think."

Kit Bradsleigh lay propped against his pillows, face pale and drawn. Only in the past two days had her patient been conscious and coherent enough to converse, though his lung ailment perforce limited speech. Still, she'd already come to appreciate the young man's unpretentious charm.

As she approached, his pain-shadowed eyes brightened with interest. "Fine indeed! Excuse my bad manners…not rising…to kiss the hand…of a lovely lady."

She smiled. "After all the hours Dr. MacDonovan and I have expended the last week to bring you to this evening, should you attempt so reckless a feat I'd be more tempted to bash you with the hand than let you kiss it."

"Then I am safe." He gave her a rueful grin. "Already attempted it…when Ellie stopped by. Found movement…most unwise. Must lie here…and admire from afar."

"It is a lovely gown and I do thank her for it. Shall you fare well here? I feel somewhat guilty going down to join the company, leaving you alone but for Peter's care."

He waved a hand. "If anyone deserves…an evening off…'tis you, ma'am! Afraid I've not…been in right frame…to express appreciation…but I want—"

"None of that," she interrupted. "Just praise heaven, as I do, that Dr. MacDonovan's skill and your own strong constitution were sufficient to bring you through."

He nodded, his thin face serious. "No more, then. But an evening…of Peter's company…is small recompense…for my debt…" His words trailed off, lost in a fit of coughing. Concerned, Laura leaned to press firmly against his bandaged shoulder, trying to immobilize the wound until the coughing subsided.

"Hush, now," she said when at last he took a gasping, cough-free breath. "Enough pretty speeches, though I do thank you for them. Peters, make sure he finishes the broth I send up, and no more conversation! You will call me on the instant if you feel I'm needed?"

"Aye, ma'am."

"Good. I'll bring up an herbal tea later." She squeezed Kit's hand. "'Twill ease your breathing and help you sleep." After he nodded acknowledgment, she looked with reluctance to the door. "I suppose I must go down."

She'd moved several steps away when his voice halted her. "Mustn't…be afraid."

Startled, she stopped short and turned back to him.

He managed an encouraging smile. "Beau intimidating…but kind. Never…hurt anyone good." He paused to put a hand to his chest, grimacing through another short cough. "Smile. You have...a lovely smile." He fluttered his fingers at her in a gesture of farewell and then closed his eyes, slumping back against his pillows.

Laura descended the stairs, more pensive still. Was her agitation when around Lord Beaulieu so obvious? Or had Kit, knowing the reaction normally evoked in underlings by his lofty brother, merely been trying to encourage her?

Too late now to debate the wisdom of coming tonight. Taking a deep breath, she pushed open the parlor door.

A din of massed voices rolled over her. Startled by the noise after years of self-imposed social isolation, Laura halted, alarm skittering across her nerves. Forestalling the butler from announcing her arrival with a short, negative shake of her head, she slipped in, her eyes scanning the room to identify the company.

Lady Winters sat in her customary spot, several neighborhood ladies gathered around her, Lady Elspeth and another guest on the sofa opposite. The squire and his son held forth by the sideboard, glasses of spirits in hand. By the window, surrounded by most of the men of the company, Lady Ardith sparkled in low-cut golden splendor.

A shiver passed through her as she recognized the tall figure toward which Lady Ardith was leaning her impressively bared bosom. The shiver magnified to a tremor as Lord Beaulieu, as if cued by some invisible prompter, turned toward the doorway and saw her.

His look of mild annoyance vanished and his body tensed. While she waited, unable to breathe, his gaze swiftly inspected her—his frankly admiring gaze. And then he smiled, a warm, intimate message of welcome, as if she were the one person for whom all evening he'd been waiting.

He thought she looked pretty. She tried to stifle her guilty pleasure at the realization and swiftly bent her head before he could see the answering smile that automatically sprang to her lips. Both gratified and alarmed, she hurried to Lady Elspeth's comforting presence.

Beau shifted restlessly, a polite smile in place while he tuned out the drone of Lady Ardith's speech as effectively as he blocked out the quite attractive but entirely untempting display of cleavage she insisted on continually thrusting beneath his nose. Blast, did the woman think him blind?

Had this whole evening been for naught? Despite his sister's assurances and Kit's offer to help if necessary, would Laura Martin fail to appear?

Just as, reining in his raveling temper with an effort, he was about to come to that conclusion, he felt a change in the room, a rush of cool air.

He turned toward the door—and saw her. For a moment he quite literally forgot to breathe.

Her thick auburn hair, twisted at the top of her head into a mass of ringlets, was obscured from his awed glance by only the smallest of lace caps. And to his enthralled eyes, Ellie's luscious green gown revealed with vivid clarity every curve and even more of the glorious ivory skin he recalled from lovingly tended memory of the Vision.

Her restive glance finally collided with his in a connection that was almost palpable. For a timeless moment they simply stared at each other, oblivious to the other occupants of the room.

He wanted her at his side, where she belonged. At the last moment sanity returned and he stopped himself from calling out to her. Instead he smiled, trying to imbue in that silent gesture all his unspoken urgency. *Come to me.*

But though her eyes widened and her lips responded with a smile she quickly bent to hide, she turned to walk not to him, but to his sister.

Beau gritted his teeth to keep from gnashing them in frustration. *Go easy,* he cautioned himself. He must not crowd her in front of this crowd of people. Not make her nervous by singling her out, or conspicuous by drawing down on her the rancor Lady Ardith would surely display if that calculating lightskirt decided the richest potential lover present was taking undue notice of some other lady.

He must wait, in short. And so he would. But sometime, somehow, he vowed, before this evening ended he would find a way to steal her to himself. After the other guests had departed, for a walk in the garden, perhaps. Just the two of them, alone under an embrace of moonlight.

Mollified by that pleasant thought, he was able to tear his eyes from the fetching silhouette of her slender form before Lady Ardith, presently toying with a portly knight who was Sir Everett's nearest neighbor, noticed his lapse in attention. Fortunately, that lady had so monopolized the other male guests that it seemed none but himself had noticed Mrs. Martin enter.

Just as well. Let them gape at the high flyer—and leave the refined elegance of Mrs. Martin to him.

The dinner gong sounded. Despite her change of attire, Beau noted with an inner smile, Mrs. Martin still managed to remain reclusive, slipping away from his sister as the guests rose from their seats, retreating toward the Squire and Tom before Beau reached her.

As they caught sight of Mrs. Martin, both men uttered exclamations of surprise and delight. Beau gritted his teeth once more as the squire's tone abruptly changed from bluff to coyly gallant. Squire Everett and Tom would not be the only gentlemen captivated tonight by the widow's swanlike transformation, he realized with irritated resignation. However, he promised himself again, regardless of how many gentlemen fell under the spell of her charm throughout dinner, the widow would end her evening in his company alone.

He was less pleased once they arrived in the dining chamber to discover that Mrs. Martin, whom he'd instructed the butler to seat near him at the head of the table, was instead positioned at its foot. He turned to his hostess.

"Lady Winters, this will not do! We're gathered here to honor Dr. MacDonovan and Mrs. Martin, the two individuals responsible for saving my brother's life. We cannot have one of them banished to the end of the table."

His hostess gave him a startled look, but before she could stutter an answer, Mrs. Martin said, "Marsden told me you'd requested that, my lord, but not considering it fitting that I be seated above the more distinguished guests, I had him change the cards, as I knew Lady Winters would wish." She fixed her gaze carefully on the fluttering figure beside him. "Though I am, of course, much flattered by his lordship's kindness."

Her reply attracted to her for the first time the general notice of the entire party. Beau watched with ironic amusement as the faces around the table reflected, first interest in the newcomer in their midst, then puzzle-

ment, then varying decrees of shock, astonishment—
and admiration as they finally identified the speaker.

By the time she finished her explanation, all other
conversation had ceased and the attention of everyone
present was riveted on Mrs. Martin. Finding herself suddenly the focus of every eye, the lady swiftly dropped
her gaze to her lap, her cheeks pinking.

A gasp sounded in the silence, followed by a "By
Jove!" The vicar, across the table from Mrs. Martin,
sat with mouth agape, while the knight seated next to
her exclaimed, "Mrs. Martin, what a capital rig. Capital!"

Lady Ardith stared at the widow with a look of
shocked indignation, as if one of the stone spaniels that
flanked Squire Everett's drive had just turned and bitten
her. Nonetheless, she was first of the ladies to recover.

"What an...interesting gown, Mrs. Martin. A hand-
me-down from the family of a grateful patient, no
doubt. When one is forced to earn one's crust, I suppose
one must accept all manner of payments."

Ellie gasped, indignation flashing in her eyes, and
though a matching anger flared in Beau, he reached out
swiftly to put a warning hand on her elbow.

The high color in Mrs. Martin's face paled. Before
Beau could intervene, she raised her gaze to Lady Ardith. Her coolly amused gaze. "Indeed, my lady."

Bravo, Beau thought.

"I hope," Ardith continued, sublimely oblivious,
"you've expressed your humble thanks to the squire
and his lordship for permitting you to be included in
this gathering. I daresay you've never dined in quite this
sort of company before."

Did he observe an instant's quiver in her lip? Before
he could decide, Mrs. Martin, her expression blandly

meek, replied, "You're quite right, my lady." Her eyes dipped briefly to Lady Ardith's jutting bosom before she continued, "I've never dined in such company before."

Beau choked back a laugh, then shot a glance at Ellie. His sister gave him a tiny nod, her eyes full of mirth.

"I do thank his lordship, Squire Everett and Lady Winters for including me tonight," Mrs. Martin concluded.

The vicar gave Lady Ardith a sharp look. "'Tis not so unusual for us to dine with Mrs. Martin. We have on several occasions been blessed with her excellent company."

"Country parties, of course," Lady Ardith replied. "Given the unfortunate lack of numbers often obtaining in country society, 'tis quite amazing the odd parties one is occasionally forced to make up." Noting the vicar still frowning, Lady Ardith leaned toward him, gifting the reverend with a full view of her generous endowments. "Though you, of course, Mr. Blackthorne, would be welcome at any party. And how is your mama, the viscountess?"

Being human, the vicar did gaze for a moment at the display beneath his eyes, but to Beau's grudgingly accorded credit, almost immediately raised his glance back to the lady's face. His closed expression hinted he'd already assessed Lady Ardith's character and found it, unlike her chest, to be somewhat lacking. "Quite well, Lady Ardith," he said shortly, refraining from adding a comment that might prolong the conversation.

Lady Ardith eyed the vicar for a moment, then shrugged at the subtle rebuff. Apparently considering the man not worth the effort—or perhaps writing him off as unattachable—Lady Ardith turned once more to the squire, and conversation became general again.

Beau was too far away to be able to overhear Mrs. Martin's comments to her dinner partners, but as she was seated on the opposite side of the table, at least he could turn occasionally and gaze at her. She sat quietly, speaking little, her head inclined in smiling deference.

Unlike Lady Ardith, who seemed unable to let her neighbors dine in peace. Scarcely had he taken a mouthful before, in a minor breach of etiquette, she waved across the table at him.

"Do you find the fish agreeable, Lord Beaulieu?"

To reply, he was forced to dispense with the bite in one swallow. "Very."

"Alphonse, our London chef, prepares a similar dish—much more elaborate, of course, as one would expect of a French *artiste*. You must stop by and try pot luck with us some evening when you are in town, mustn't he, Asquith?"

Her husband, mouth full and focus fixed on the wine glass the footman was refilling, uttered a grunt that might be taken as assent. Scarcely waiting for her spouse's reply, the lady turned to the squire with a flirtatious sweep of lashes. "How clever of you to procure so excellent a cook here in the country." She leaned forward and stroked one finger slowly down his hand. "I so *enjoy* a clever gentleman."

Having reduced the squire to goggling incoherence, Lady Ardith took another small bite and turned to Dr. MacDonovan. "Ah, delicious!" She slowly ran the tip of her tongue over her lips before saying in a husky voice, "Dr. MacDonovan, do they enjoy such delights in Edinburgh?"

After a sympathetic wink at Beau, Mac grinned at the

lady. "To be sure, Lady Ardith. Such treats should be devoured wherever they are offered."

She arched a brow at Mac and gave a soft, throaty laugh. "Naughty man! Though I believe you are correct, Doctor. Lady Elspeth, is he always such a rogue?"

"Always."

"You must excuse me for neglecting you, Lady Elspeth," Ardith continued. "I know the mama of so lovely and clever a daughter as Lady Catherine must want to be speaking of nothing but her offspring and alas, I fear I know little of children, his lordship and I not being so blessed. I try to console myself with the reflection that infants are quite ruinous to the figure. But then I am a silly, frivolous creature, as my lord is ever telling me. Ah, Lord Beaulieu, how do you like the shrimp velouté?"

And so, effectively shutting out the vacant Lady Winters, who seldom exerted herself to converse, and Elspeth, who was too polite to wrench the conversation back in her own direction, Lady Ardith continued to chatter through the meal, punctuating her running commentary with flirtatious glances and suggestive touches to the hands of the gentlemen closest to her, as if to keep them ever mindful of her physical allure.

Beau glanced from Lord Asquith, food-stained cravat askew, to where Lady Ardith was preening coquettishly before Mac, the knight Sir Ramsdale and his bedazzled son. He felt an unexpected flash of sympathy for the lady.

With her glittering blond beauty and siren's body, she'd doubtless been the diamond of her come-out Season, accustomed to being the focus of masculine attention since the day she left the schoolroom. Shackled now to a prominent, wealthy peer who apparently no

longer indulged appetites beyond the table, with no children to occupy her time, it was small wonder she felt
compelled to practice her wiles on any reasonably attractive male within reach.

Especially since, he had to acknowledge, the majority
of his sex would encourage her efforts. Given the lady's
alluring assets, few men would deny themselves the
pleasure of seizing the several hours of harmless, mindless, full-body amusement her enticing glances promised. Brutal honesty compelled him to admit he might
have been tempted to respond himself, had he not first
encountered the more intelligent, complex and subtly
attractive Mrs. Martin.

Certainly the gentlemen at table with Lady Ardith
now were competing to claim that prize. Although her
husband persisted in ignoring her, occupying himself
solely with the replenishment and emptying of his plate
and wineglass, the other men vied for Lady Ardith's
attention, responding eagerly to her suggestive banter.
The knight's adolescent son, to the neglect of his dinner
partners, chewed his meal while staring at Lady Ardith
in cow-eyed adoration.

In contrast, Mrs. Martin ate sparingly and spoke but
little, though her soft-voiced replies to her neighbors'
statements seemed to foster a continuous and lively discussion at her end of the table. Not was she entirely
lacking in admirers, Beau noted.

Despite the distracting presence of Lady Ardith at his
elbow, the squire nonetheless occasionally sent an appreciative glance toward the lady at the far end of his
table. And, Beau realized with an unpleasant shock, the
vicar, who sat in privileged proximity just opposite Mrs.
Martin, seldom took his eyes off her.

A man of the cloth, Beau thought with an immediate

surge of indignation, should not be entertaining thoughts that, to judge by the heated intensity of the vicar's expression, were obviously both covetous and carnal.

Beau turned to find Lady Ardith staring in the direction of his gaze, her eyes frosty as they rested on Mrs. Martin. With a glittering smile, she abruptly angled her head toward the squire's sister, who sat absently picking at her food.

"Lady Winters, you had Mrs. Martin write out your invitation cards, didn't you? Kind of you to offer her employment, which she badly needs, I imagine."

Belatedly realizing she'd been addressed, Lady Winters focused out of her haze. "Employed?" she repeated, looking confused. "No, I don't pay Mrs. Martin."

"Nay, of course not, 'tis as a friend of the family she does it," the squire clarified.

"Well, I knew the moment I received the invitation that someone other than dear Lady Winters had copied out the cards. I vow, one can always distinguish the hand of a true lady. My own *écriture* is so precise, I cannot address more than a handful of cards at a sitting. Before a ball, I must spend the veriest week at it."

That speech evaporated whatever tepid sympathy Beau had previously summoned for the acidic blond beauty. Squelching a strong desire to deal Lady Ardith a sharp set-down, Beau forced himself to remain discreetly silent.

"Quite a pretty hand she has, we think," the squire said with a nod toward Mrs. Martin.

"Indeed?" Lady Ardith raised penciled brows. "Mrs. Martin is fortunate you and Lady Winters are so obliging. I was quite shocked when first I heard that a woman, of supposedly gentle birth, chose to live alone without even the vestige of a chaperone. Did you not, in your good nature, continue to recognize her, I daresay she might not be received by any good family in the neighborhood.''

While Beau choked back his outraged response, Lady Ardith leaned confidentially closer to the squire. ''Though you might warn her to be more discreet. Appearing in such a—well, coming—gown, and living alone as she does, who knows what sort of thoughts she might inspire in some of the local men? Even the vicar looks quite…taken. Though perhaps that's her intent.'' Lady Ardith smiled slyly. ''Still, she'd best take care. *Exposed* as she is, a very little gossip deeming her 'fast' would be enough to ruin her reputation. Where would she be if the common folk no longer sought her out for their pills and potions?''

Her ''confidential'' advice, uttered in a tone that must have carried halfway down the table, if not all the way to the ears of the lady it derided, was the final straw. Deciding to end the conversation before he lost control and strangled Lady Ardith, Beau abruptly turned to his hostess. ''Lady Winters, is it not time for you to withdraw?''

Again looking startled, Lady Winters goggled at him. After fussing to find her handkerchief and reticule, she rose. ''Brother, gentlemen, if you will excuse us?''

Looking forward to the freedom of the drawing room where at last he could approach his lady, and knowing she would probably seek an excuse to leave the party early, Beau maneuvered the gentlemen out of the dining room after a single glass of brandy. Though Lord Asquith grumbled about being separated from his cigars, the rest of the men, doubtless relishing thoughts of a closer view down the bodice of his wife's dress, greeted Beau's suggestion with approval.

As he followed his host to the drawing room, Beau rapidly developed a plan that, with a little help from Mac, would ensure Mrs. Martin wasn't allowed to flee before the other guests departed. Short of storming her bedchamber—and he wasn't completely sure he'd not resort to that extremity if pressed—he was prepared to do whatever it took to get her alone.

Chapter Ten

It was, Laura decided, the nicest dinner party she'd ever attended. Despite the sparkling gown that had initially drawn her to the attention of the company, the far-more-glittering presence of Lady Ardith guaranteed that she was soon able to return to her preferred role as a quiet observer. And so, wearing a dress that made her feel like a princess, being treated with kindness and even a touch of deference by her neighbors, she could relax and with perfect propriety let her gaze stray down the table to Lord Beaulieu.

Who was without question the most impressive gentleman in the room. The midnight-black of evening dress suited his raven hair and dark eyes, and the stark simplicity of the color and cut of his garments merely emphasized his breadth of shoulder, litheness of body and aura of power. Though she could not make out his words, even at a distance she could tell how, despite the impediment of Lady Ardith, whose rapid, laughter-punctuated banter scarcely paused long enough to allow her to draw breath or consume a morsel, he skillfully handled his end of the table, managing to coax even the normally silent Lady Winters into the conversation.

Occasionally he glanced in her direction. When he caught her eye, his mouth would curve in that compelling, intimate smile, and she would again be seized with the absurd notion that despite being surrounded by a tableful of people, one of whom was an accredited beauty, he was interested in her alone.

Absurd, but on this magical night when like Cinderella she'd appeared in borrowed finery and caught the eye of a prince, she'd ignore the prosaic voice of common sense.

Giddy delight, like champagne bubbles rising, swelled in her breast, and she could not help smiling. How different this evening was from the mostly wretched dinner parties she'd attended as a shy and nervous debutante, then as an inexperienced young bride.

The smile faded. She'd come to hate social functions, knowing her hawk-eyed husband would observe her every gesture and remark, and after the guests departed subject her to a scathing critique. She was too forward or too timid; she spoke too little or too much, played cards badly, danced too frequently or too seldom.

Even after she'd stopped caring about his good opinion, realizing it impossible to obtain, she so dreaded those post-party diatribes she could scarcely eat during dinner. Especially since as Charleton seemed to sense her will to please him diminishing, over the passing months he became increasingly angry, demeaning—and violent.

An involuntary shudder passed through her. With an effort, she shook her thoughts free. She mustn't spoil a moment of this perfectly lovely gathering—the only occasion she would ever appear outside her dull brown persona—fretting over demons who were, she reassured herself again, safely consigned to the past.

"Is something the matter? You look...disturbed."

The vicar's question startled her. "N-nothing!" she replied, damping down an automatic alarm. "I was woolgathering, which was terribly rude. Please excuse me."

"No forgiveness necessary. I must simply redouble my efforts to entertain you. 'Twould be a crushing blow to my self-esteem to know the loveliest lady in the room found my dinner conversation dull."

She dutifully smiled at the compliment, though in truth the only mild distress she'd experienced since coming to the table was generated by rather too solicitous attention of Reverend Mr. Blackthorne. It seemed, as the courses were brought and removed in turn, that every time she glanced in his direction, she found his admiring and uncomfortably intense gaze resting on her.

"It is the excellence of your address, I fear, that condemned you to this end of the table, so far away from the belle of the evening," she replied, gesturing toward Lady Ardith. "For that I must truly apologize. Knowing how skillfully you converse with every member of society—" with a nod she indicated the querulous dowager to one side of him and the shy spinster on the other "—I'm afraid 'tis I who placed you here."

Mr. Blackthorne glanced at Lady Ardith, currently laughing as she plied her lashes at Dr. MacDonovan. "It cannot be lost on any gentleman present—" he leaned forward to murmur in a voice pitched for her ears alone "—who the true belle of the evening is. A lady whose beauty of countenance is matched by gentility of manner."

Unsure how to politely discourage his ardency, Laura blessed Lady Winters, who rose at that moment, signaling the ladies to withdraw. "You will excuse me, sir?"

"If I must," he said. "Until later, then."

I certainly hope not, Laura thought as she followed her hostess from the room.

'Twas time for Cinderella to depart, and not just to evade the attentions of the unexpectedly solicitous Mr. Blackthorne. Protected by the length of a dinner table, she'd been able to indulge her frivolous fantasies about Lord Beaulieu. But once the gentleman returned, there would be no barrier to his approaching her. Better to leave now, before Lord Beaulieu brushed away the fragile cobweb of her silly dream by ignoring her completely.

Or worse, made it all too real by approaching her.

In the parlor, the ladies took seats by age and inclination, save for Lady Ardith who, denied any other masculine attention, stood by the door dazzling a young footman. After the lad sprang away to fetch the wine she commanded, the lady drifted over to the window and stared out over the moonlit garden, one slippered foot tapping rhythmically against the floor.

Laura approached Lady Winters, intending to present her compliments and withdraw. But before she could utter a word, Lady Elspeth called to her.

"Please, Mrs. Martin, come sit by me." Lord Beaulieu's sister indicated the place beside her. "I've not had a chance to speak with you all evening."

Much as Laura would prefer to leave forthwith, she could not do so without being rude to the lady who'd befriended her. Forcing a smile, she walked to the sofa.

"How fortunate you are, Lady Winters, to have such a charming, intelligent neighbor as Mrs. Martin. No, my dear, you must not blush!" Lady Elspeth patted Laura's hand. "Dr. MacDonovan has sung your praises since the moment I arrived, and he is not a man to offer idle compliments. Indeed, have I not witnessed your skill for myself? I'm breeding, you see," she informed the others, "and have been most horridly ill. Mrs. Martin prescribed a tea that has eased the discomfort."

The neighborhood ladies all nodded. "'Tis a rare blessing she is to the whole county, just like her dear aunt, Mrs. Hastings," the knight's wife said. "Especially since one never knows whether or not Dr. Winthrop will be...available."

"All the more rare to find such skill in a lady of gentle birth," Lady Elspeth continued. "How comforting it is to be able to discuss intimate matters with an *equal.*" She cast a glance toward Lady Ardith as she emphasized the word.

As if pricked by the remark, that lady looked back toward the company, her disdainful gaze coming to rest on Laura. It seemed she would speak, but apparently deciding that without a masculine audience to exploit she'd not bother, she turned back once again to the window.

"With me feeling so peevish, Mrs. Martin has kindly stepped in to take my daughter for her walks," Lady Elspeth continued. "What a champion you have there, Mrs. Martin! Catherine can scarcely be contained until it is time for her outing, and comes back chattering of the clever things you've shown or said or read to her."

"Ah, children," said Lady Ardith from her window. "Charming creatures! So inexperienced, they possess no discrimination whatsoever."

"The intelligent ones do, from quite an early age," Lady Elspeth replied. "A shame you've apparently never encountered the like among your own family and friends.''

Lady Ardith pivoted to face Lord Beaulieu's sister, a martial light sparking in her cold blue eyes. Fortunately for Laura's peace of mind, at that moment the parlor door opened. In a rush of conversation flavored with the lingering odor of cigar, the gentlemen entered.

With a smile as glittering as her gown, Lady Ardith at once made for Lord Beaulieu. ''Ah, my lord, thank you for joining us so speedily!'' she cried, latching onto his arm. ''Deprived of your company, we women are such dull creatures. Babies and potions...I declare—'' she swept a dagger glance at Lady Elspeth ''—Squire Everett's winter garden is more interesting than the conversation we summon up.''

Dr. MacDonovan halted beside them. Was it Laura's imagination, or did a subtle glance pass between the two men? ''Ah, lass, I canna believe the lips of such an exquisite creature could pass on anything less than...delicious. Come,'' he urged, taking the hand the lady had pressed on Lord Beaulieu's arm, ''let us find some wine. Then ye must speak to me and prove the yea or nay of it.''

It appeared that the lady might refuse, until the doctor leaned closer and murmured something that brought a satisfied smile to her face even as she laughed and batted his arm. ''La, but you're wicked,'' she reproved, allowing Dr. MacDonovan to lead her to the sideboard.

Before Laura could look away, Lord Beaulieu's gaze met hers. He rolled his eyes briefly, a gesture so indicative of relief she almost laughed out loud. Then he smiled again, a slight curve of lip and fire of glance that once again ignited every nerve and set the champagne bubbles dancing through her veins. His eyes holding hers, she sensed more than saw him approach.

"Thank you, brother, for the rescue," Lady Elspeth murmured. "I was in dire danger of becoming... unladylike."

Lord Beaulieu bent to kiss his sister's cheek. "That, I could never believe," he said with a grin.

With Lord Beaulieu a mere forearm's length away, Laura could feel the heat emanating from his body, catch the faint scent of shaving soap and brandy. Almost, she could feel his hand once more resting on *her* shoulder, those lips dipping to brush *her* cheek. A shiver swept over her skin.

He turned to her, his grin fading as his imperious eyes found and commanded hers. Scraps of conversation, the popping of the fire, the clink of glasses faded, until she heard only the rapid beat of her pulse. While they both remained motionless, staring, she forgot even to breathe.

"Mrs. Martin," he said at last. "How very beautiful you look tonight."

"Th-thank you, my lord."

"I had hoped we might—"

"Excuse me, my lord," Squire Everett's hearty voice startled her. "The card tables are set, and Lady Ardith is demanding we choose partners now and begin play."

"Play," the earl repeated, and shook his head as if to clear his thoughts. "Yes, of course. If you'll excuse me, ladies." He made them a quick bow.

Almost dizzy with happiness, Laura watched him walk away. *He thought her beautiful.* As she'd dreamed all evening, he'd come to her, stood by her, gifted her with that special smile that transported her to a magical realm where nothing existed but the two of them alone.

Better to leave now, before anything occurred to mar

the perfection of an evening she would recall with wonder the rest of her days. Cinderella, mirrored in the eyes of her prince as "beautiful."

In a daze, she murmured thanks to Lady Winters and Lady Elspeth and floated toward the door.

Before she reached it, Lord Beaulieu called out, "No, Mrs. Martin, we cannot have you departing so early! Squire Everett needs a fourth at his table."

"Aye, madam, ye've had evenings enough of sick lads and laudanum," Dr. MacDonovan said. "Having kept vigil late these past days, ye canna be weary yet."

"You must stay, Mrs. Martin," Squire Everett said. "My sister declares she will not play unless you join us."

Desperately as she wished to break free, to tuck away this fragile gem of an evening in a protective tissue wrap of memory so she might preserve it forever, once again civility dictated she remain.

And so she let the squire lead her to the table, knowing in truth that the reticent Lady Winters, an indifferent card player, would be wretchedly uncomfortable unless matched with a forgiving partner.

And besides, depending on where Lady Ardith maneuvered Lord Beaulieu, she might be able to observe the earl a bit longer, add a few more gilded treasures to the trove that must warm her through the long lonely days after he departed. As soon he must.

A surprisingly bitter regret spiraled through her. Damping it down, she took her place.

Laura gamely played through several rubbers, though her modest skill was not sufficient to outweigh some of Lady Winters's disastrous discards. Their team ended by being solidly trounced, much to the delight of the squire and his partner Sir Ramsdale.

Naturally, Lady Ardith had snared the earl and Dr. MacDonovan for her table, with Lady Elspeth making up the fourth. The beauty seated the gentlemen—deliberately?—so that Laura could view only the back of his lordship's head, but from the frequency of Dr. Mac-Donovan's hearty laugh and the coos and squeals emanating from Lady Ardith, Laura surmised their table was enjoying a rousing good game.

The other tables were finishing up. Repressing the desire to linger, Laura turned to the squire.

"Thank you and Lady Winters both for such a delightful evening. I must go check on our patient now."

"Nonsense," Lord Beaulieu said, surprising her by appearing behind her chair. "Kit's valet will summon help if the need arises. Lady Winters, shall we not have some dancing? This handsome chamber seems designed for it."

"D-dancing?" Lady Winters repeated faintly.

"Capital idea!" Squire Everett said. "We've numbers enough for a respectable set. You can play for us, Emily."

Lady Ardith walked over then to put an entreating hand on the earl's arm. "Oh, yes, you must dance with me! Do say you will play for us, dear Lady Winters."

"Nay," Lord Beaulieu said, slipping his arm from under Lady Ardith's grasping fingers in one smooth movement. "I insist on leading my charming hostess into the first set. I've heard, Lady Winters, you were such a belle at your debut Season the gentlemen called each other out over the privilege of escorting you."

"Aye, a regular diamond our Emily was," the squire confirmed proudly. "Winters was smitten the moment he saw her. Weren't the only one, neither—even the old Duke of Clarendon came calling on her."

"I'll wager she can outdance us all still," Lord Beaulieu said. "If you would do me the honor, my lady?" He made her the exaggerated leg of a Georgian courtier.

"Oh, la," Lady Winters said, her face pinking with a mingling of pleasure and alarm. "I—I…"

"Excellent," the earl said. "Squire, Dr. MacDonovan approaches, so you'd best be quick if you wish to capture Lady Ardith for the first set." Ignoring the dagger glance that lady shot him, he turned to the rest of the company. "Ladies, gentlemen, choose your partners."

He turned back to Laura. "You will play for us, Mrs. Martin? I understand you are quite skilled." Without awaiting a reply, he offered his arm to the blushing Lady Winters and led her to where the couples were assembling.

Laura made her way to the piano, trying not to feel so…deflated. What had she expected—that the earl would ask lowly Mrs. Martin to dance? A woman who, whatever her origins, now occupied a position less elevated than a governess. A woman who, as Lady Ardith had cogently reminded the company earlier, had to earn her own bread.

She should focus on that fact and forget the seductive magic so briefly evoked by a borrowed gown.

"Let me help you find some music."

Mr. Blackthorne stood beside the piano, distracting her out of her dispiriting reflections.

"A country dance, perhaps?" he suggested.

She nodded, as perversely comforted now by his attention as she had been unsettled by it earlier. After selecting a piece, she began to play.

Within a few moments, joy at the mellow chords produced by the squire's fine instrument succeeded in dis-

sipating her melancholy. She glanced up to the dancers—and found the reverend's eyes focused on her with
alarming warmth. A smile leaped to his face as their
eyes met and he winked. Then, as he bent to turn the
page of music, he placed a hand on her bared shoulder.

She jumped, missing the next chord. The earl
whipped a glance over to them and frowned. Removing
his hand, Mr. Blackthorne stepped back, but she had to
struggle to recapture the beat, her quiet enjoyment shattered. Though he did not touch her again for the remainder of the piece, Laura remained uncomfortably
conscious of his presence beside her.

After the music ended, Laura looked up to find the
earl regarding them frostily. ''Mr. Blackthorne, we have
ladies in need of partners. I'm sure Mrs. Martin can
keep her place in the music without assistance. Lady
Ramsdale, did you not request the reverend's escort?''

''If you please, sir,'' the knight's wife said. ''You're
ever so fine a dancer.''

Laura thought for a moment Reverend Blackthorne
would refuse. Then with a sigh, he murmured, ''You
will excuse me?'' and walked to the dancers.

Waiting for a cue to begin the next piece, Laura
watched the earl bow over the hand of Lady Winters
who, flushed and laughing, shook her head in demurral.
Whatever he said in those deep, even tones must have
been persuasive, for after a moment, still shaking her
head, she let him lead her once again into place beside
him.

To her horror, Laura felt a shaft of bitter envy pierce
her.

If she were reduced to resenting the gentle, silly Lady
Winters, it was long past time to depart. The minute the
dancers tired of their sport, she would take her leave.

Laura tried, but was unable to recapture her previous delight in the music itself. After the current dance ended and the earl, insisting Lady Winters dance now with Dr. MacDonovan, turned to claim a waiting Lady Ardith, what tepid enthusiasm she had mustered dissipated completely.

She tried to ignore the girlish giggles and arch tones that disrupted her concentration whenever the movements of the dance brought the earl and Lady Ardith nearby. When, after the last chord faded, the beauty immediately implored Lord Beaulieu to partner her again, Laura had to fight to keep from grinding her teeth.

She should have escaped earlier. Now her lovely memories of the party would be soured by the sound of Lady Ardith's breathy voice and high-pitched titters.

Which is exactly what she ought to recall, argued the wiser, more cautious part of her. She'd been given a lovely gown and treated with deference by the company, which was everything and more than a woman in her position could expect or desire. She should banish once and for all every other moonstruck fancy.

"Yes, my lord, one more dance," Lady Ardith cooed. "And we simply must make it a waltz!" She looked over at Laura, her expression a mixture of triumph and disdain. *How dare you try to garner any attention at my party,* it said. "You do know how to play a waltz, Mrs. Martin?"

Ignoble but instinctive fury shook Laura. But before she could mendaciously deny she knew anything about the waltz, Lord Beaulieu intervened. "A treat we shall have to postpone, my lady. Our hostess is looking fatigued."

Lady Ardith's smile faded to a moue of annoyance,

but the earl had already relinquished her hand to stride toward the small group gathered around Lady Winters. Their hostess did in fact look ill, swaying on her feet as her brother supported her and Lady Ramsdale fanned her rapidly.

"Lady Winters, are you all right?" the earl demanded.

"A bit overcome by the heat," the squire replied. "I think I'd best take her up to bed. I've instructed the staff to bring in the tea tray. Mrs. Martin, would you kindly pour for us?"

With a flare of irritation, Laura nearly refused performing this additional service. If she did so, however, she knew the hostess's task would fall to Lady Elspeth, who ought to be delivered a cup and allowed to rest. "Of course, Squire Everett."

"She'll be as right as a trivet once her woman gets her tucked up in bed," the squire assured the rest of the company. "Come, my dear, and wave your goodbyes to our guests. I'll have you upstairs in a hound pup's lick."

"Please allow me to assist," the earl said, "and selfishly steal a few minutes longer with the most graceful dancer of the evening." Having received a weak smile from Lady Winters, he motioned in the servants who stood at the doorway, heavily loaded trays in hand. "Mrs. Martin will serve." Taking Lady Winter's other arm, he helped the squire lead her from the room.

My lord of Beaulieu was certainly good at ordering people about, Laura thought resentfully as she took her place behind the tea tray. But the small civilities of serving tea and the friendliness of Lady Elspeth, who insisted on installing herself at Laura's elbow, gradually soothed her irritation. By the time the squire and the earl returned to the parlor, Laura was able to prepare their cups with a fair measure of her usual calm.

Don't meet his eye. Don't listen for his voice. Pour the tea, smile politely, leave. Now that, at long last, she was finally about to depart, she felt an irrational sadness that the evening was truly going to end. Cinderella, returning to sackcloth and ashes.

"Another round of cards?" Reverend Blackthorne suggested. "I've not yet had the pleasure of partnering Mrs. Martin."

"Not for me, I'm afraid," Lady Elspeth said, smothering a yawn. "My daughter has me up betimes. My warmest regards to all, but I shall have to retire."

"I expect we should leave, as well," Sir Ramsdale said. "A capital party, though, squire! Be sure to convey our warmest thanks to Lady Winters."

Amid murmurs of agreement among the other guests, the squire motioned the butler to summon the carriages.

"I'm past needing to check on our patient. Please excuse me," Laura said with a curtsey to the company.

"I should like to look on him, as well," the earl said. "Squire, my lords and ladies, a delightful evening. If I might escort you, Mrs. Martin?"

Beau climbed the stairs beside Mrs. Martin in a silence that was both edgy with awareness and paradoxically, companionable. After Peters answered their soft knock, Mrs. Martin walked to the side of his sleeping brother's bed. "Has he been resting comfortably?" she asked the valet.

"Aye, ma'am. He argufied some, but I got 'em to drink all his broth."

"Good." She reached out to touch Kit's forehead, ran her fingers down to his temple, then moved them to the pulse at the base of his jaw and let them rest there. Beau felt a sharp, involuntary pang of envy.

"Fever is not much elevated, and his pulse is quiet," she observed. "Has he been coughing?"

"A bit. But not what's you might call excessive."

She nodded, then carefully laid her head against his brother's chest. Beau sucked in a breath, thinking it might be worth getting shot to be in Kit's place. Especially with a tad fewer witnesses and a lot fewer garments.

"Just a bit of a whistle in his lungs, and his breathing is easier," she said. "I expect he should do fine tonight, although perhaps it would be best if I—"

"There's no need, Mrs. Martin," Beau interrupted hastily. "Dr. MacDonovan would not have turned Kit over to Peters if he had any doubts about his well-being."

"You get some rest, ma'am," Peters said. "Young master will be fine."

Kit murmured and stirred. Beau took that opportunity to place a hand under Mrs. Martin's elbow. "Come, we don't wish to disturb his slumber."

She hesitated a moment before nodding. "Very well. Good night, Peters."

"Good night, ma'am, your lordship."

His hand still at her elbow, Beau urged her toward the door. He paused at the threshold to glance back—and caught Kit watching them. His brother flashed him a wink before snapping his eyes shut. Suppressing a chuckle, Beau led Mrs. Martin from the room.

At last he would have her to himself. Anticipation surged through his veins.

"You missed your walk with Lady Catherine this afternoon," he said, willing his voice to calm. "Or so she informed me during our ride, with no little indignation. You mustn't neglect your exercise, though, and so unless you are fatigued, I suggest you take that walk now. The evening is clear with no trace of wind, the garden near bright as day under a full moon, and with a wool wrap you should be perfectly warm.''

"What an appealing thought! I believe I will.'' She smiled. ''I've always wondered if roses smell as sweetly at night.''

"Shall we find out?''

Her smile dissolved, her eyes widening. ''W-we?''

"I can hardly allow you to walk about the grounds after dark without an escort. And since 'tis I who urged you to it, 'tis only fitting that I do the honors.''

"Oh, but my lord, you said you had work...I could not—''

"My papers will wait. Lady Winters's white garden was designed to be seen in moonlight, she told me. I should like very much to inspect it with you.'' His touch feather-light, he put a finger to her chin, tilting it up so her eyes were forced to meet his. *Come with me,* his gaze implored. ''Please, Mrs. Martin.''

He held his breath, frantic with impatience as he awaited her response. She had no guile; he could read on her face the distress, uncertainty—and longing his invitation evoked. All his energy concentrated in wordless imperative, he willed her to yield to the desire that warred with caution in her eyes.

Each moment she did not flee brought her closer to consent. Acquiescence trembled on her lips, and he sought to help it find voice. ''Does a white rose truly smell as sweet at midnight? I, too, should like to know.'' His eyes never leaving hers, he offered his arm. ''Let us see.''

Say yes, say yes, say yes. The refrain beat so loudly in his head he might have spoken it aloud. If she demurred now he wasn't at all sure he could make himself leave her.

The briefest flicker of a smile creased her lips. "It would be much wiser if we did not. But..." She uttered a small sigh, as if having won—or lost—some great struggle. "Let me fetch my shawl."

Relief, excitement and gladness shot through him like an exploding Congreve rocket. Knowing he was grinning like an infatuated schoolboy but unable to help himself, he said, "My cloak is in the library. 'Twill be warmer."

Before she could change her mind and bolt, he clasped her arm and led her downstairs, across the deserted entryway where the case clock ticked loudly in the stillness, and into the library. Snatching up the cloak he'd left there after his late ride, he fastened it beneath her chin with care, the deliberate avoidance of contact with the soft skin so tantalizingly near his fingers a delicious game of heightening awareness.

"Come," he whispered. Taking the gloved hand she offered, he led them out the French doors onto the terrace. As they descended to the garden, Mrs. Martin gave a gasp.

"It is a fairyland!"

Illumined by moonlight, each urn, bench and planting stood in its usual place, yet the silvered light and the odd, amorphous shadows it cast gave everything a strange, otherworldly aspect.

His senses seemed uncommonly acute, as well. He heard the plaintive call of an owl, the scurrying of some small animal in the bushes, the crunch of the gravel under their feet, the silken rustle of her skirts. Her subtle scent carried on the chill night air, teasing his nose with the warmth and fragrance of her. Moonlight painted her dark hair, silhouetted her small straight nose and delicate lips with a crystalline line. Each time she took a step the opaque darkness of his cloak parted to reveal a sparkling flash of gown, as magically luminescent as phosphorus in the wake of a ship.

In awed silence they walked down the center allée, then turned toward the west wing into the white garden.

Ghostly roses glowed against a shadowed trellis on the stone wall opposite them. The silver leaves of artemesia and curry drifted onto the pathway, a splash of stardust at their feet, while tiny white brushheads of asters stood out like dots of exclamation against a dark mass of greenery.

"It's beautiful," Mrs. Martin whispered.

He lifted her hands to his lips, exulting when she did not pull them away. "You are beautiful," he said as he kissed them, his voice husky. "Not a lady in the room tonight could compare."

She laughed, her voice unsteady. "With your sister and Lady Ardith present? Mendacious flattery, my lord."

"Absolute truth."

She made a scornful noise. "I am to Lady Ardith as a candle flame to a Yule log's blaze."

"You are to her as fine gold to dross. And so I would have told you earlier, but your having endured enough of her spiteful tongue at dinner, I did not wish to single you out and attract more sweetly acid commentary."

She tilted her head and gazed up at him with that inquisitive look he found so endearing. "It would not have been fitting in any event."

"Is propriety so important, Sparrow?"

"You must not call me that." The quiver of a chuckle belied the stern tone of her reproof. "Nor am I sure I like being called a plain brown sparrow, even were it proper."

"But you *are* a sparrow—quiet, observant, intelligent. Endlessly fascinating and entirely overlooked. Although tonight you were transformed into a swan, glittering and graceful." He held up a hand to forestall her protest. "And now I'll revert to observing the proprieties. I shall call you 'Sparrow' only when we are alone."

He heard her choke of stifled laughter and grinned. She'd caught his little joke, clever Sparrow that she was.

"As if our being alone together were not much more improper," she replied. "I should not have allowed you to accompany me."

It was too soon to ask, but the urgent need to know overrode caution. "But you wanted my company?"

For a long, anxiety-ridden moment she remained silent. "Yes," she said finally, her voice a low whisper. "Having admitted that, now *I* shall observe the proprieties, and leave you."

"Wait!" He caught her shoulder as she turned. "I've a question I've not yet asked you."

She lifted one hand, and for an instant he thought she meant to place it over his, strengthening his hold on her. Instead, she let it flutter back to her side. "One question, then."

"Will you dance with me?"

Her eyes registered surprise. "Dance?"

"Here, now." He gestured to the sky above them. "Accompanied by a symphony of stars, to the music of the wind's rustle."

"You want to dance with me here?" She repeated, her tone still incredulous.

"I didn't dare ask you in the drawing room, fearing my proper Sparrow would probably refuse. But there are no prying eyes now to criticize or condemn. So, my lady beautiful, dance with me." Beau held out a hand.

For a moment she simply stared at him. "This is madness," she murmured at last. And slipped her fingers in his.

He eased her into waltz position, shocks jolting through him as they touched at shoulder, waist, hip. How well she fit against him, he thought; how absolutely right and natural it seemed to have her in his arms. Tucking the silk of her hair under his chin, he moved her into rhythm.

Under the spangle of stars they dipped and twirled while Beau hummed a tune in her ear. The racing of his heart owed little to the exertion of the dance, everything to the feel of Laura Martin's hands clutching his shoulders as he swung her in ever-faster spirals, the press of her torso against his through the maddening thickness of his cloak, the warmth of her rapid breaths floating up to caress his face. Not until she gasped an inarticulate appeal did he slow, then halt, though he could not bring himself to let her go.

He didn't want her to leave the dance or his side, he realized suddenly. No, he wanted her solemn eyes and incisive mind and wood sprite's charm beside him for the rest of this night. Perhaps for always.

Still clasping her waist, he raised his other hand to trace her trembling lips. "I've been waiting all night to have you in my arms," he murmured.

But he lied. He wanted much more than that. He hungered to arouse the vision he'd glimpsed in her cottage garden, the siren with tumbled hair and passion-languid eyes and soft mouth tilted temptingly to his own.

Beyond strategy and caution, he bent his head toward her lips. To his joy, with a murmur she clutched his shoulder and strained up to meet his kiss.

He retained enough sanity not to plunder her mouth with the urgent need that pulsed in him, luring her instead with quick, glancing touches meant to tantalize, entrance. Not until she twined fingers in his hair, tugged his head closer did he deepen the kiss, licking and sucking at the fullness of her lips until on a moan they parted.

A tremor shook her, shook him when their tongues met, before she darted hers away. An unexpected tenderness welled up—amazingly, his Sparrow did not even know how to kiss. Holding in ruthless check the desire to swiftly conquer and possess, he made himself slow, his tongue once more teasing within the softness of her mouth, letting her accustom herself to the feel of him. After a moment, she rewarded his patience as, tentative, uncertain, her tongue sought his.

He returned that guarded tap, the oblique contact like the sparing blades of cautious fencers. And when she met him again, lingering this time, he boldly stroked her tongue's full length in a hot velvet slide that struck sparks to every atom of his body.

A strangled moan escaped her throat and he felt the bite of her fingers at his shoulder, her other hand delving into his coat, nails scratching at the buttons of his shirtfront as if seeking entry.

In some dim corner of his mind he knew control was eroding, that he was rapidly approaching the point where not even the October chill of the moonlit garden could rein in his desire. But before sense was lost in a mindless search for a bench, a terrace, even a softly yielding patch of grass, she abruptly wrenched her mouth from his.

In automatic response he tried to pull her back. She fended him off with one hand, her eyes focused on something behind him.

And then he heard it. A woman's high-pitched, provocative laughter, emanating from the chamber just beyond the garden.

He turned. Through the mullioned window, he saw Lady Ardith standing with her bodice undone, candlelight and moonlight illuminating the bareness of her breasts. Mac leaned toward her, sliding up her skirts as he bent to capture one shadowed nipple in his teeth, while Lady Ardith fumbled with the straining buttons of his trouser flap.

The consternation he felt was reflected in Laura Martin's horrified stare. Before he could utter a word, she shoved him away and fled down the path toward the library.

Chapter Eleven

Heart drumming against her ribs, gasping from her headlong flight across the garden and up the stairs, Laura closed the door to her room and sagged against it.

Moonsick madness. That's all it had been, enchantment spun from her silly dreams and a touch of moonlight.

Sensible Laura Martin would never behave so again.

But even as she tried to excuse the episode, shame flooded her chest, thick and stifling.

She could not blame the magic of the garden, her foolish fancies or even Lord Beaulieu's overpowering presence.

'Twas her own folly alone that had brought her to this near catastrophe. Her weakness in accepting an escort she should have refused at the outset, her fault in underestimating the strength of her own greedy desire that had almost led her to commit the same wantonness she'd witnessed through the west wing windows.

How could she be disgusted by Lady Ardith's lechery when she'd felt the same imperative pulsing in her blood?

Lord Beaulieu had enticed her, certainly, but 'twas she who'd eagerly responded. Heat burned her face as she remembered the shivering shock of his lips against hers, the rasp of his tongue releasing a scalding flood of sensation that seemed to melt her bones, turning her fluid in his arms, starving for something she could not name but frantically sought. Craving the touch of his hands, his mouth, closer, deeper, as man desperate with thirst craves water.

And she craved it still. What she'd felt for her young suitor in her mother's garden years ago was but a feeble precursor to the raging desire she'd discovered within herself tonight, like the tepid sunlight of an early spring morning that precedes a blazing July noon.

What she might have done, have allowed Lord Beaulieu to do, had that graphic vision of lust not shocked her into recognizing her own, she could only imagine.

And what must Lord Beaulieu think of her now? A woman who'd mouthed propriety, then shown herself as ready for a mindless tumble as the most amoral society matron. Regardless of the tangle of her own wildly contradictory feelings toward his lordship, in light of her behavior tonight his opinion of her must be humiliatingly clear.

A lonely woman, ready for the price of a few compliments to become his convenient during the short time he remained in the country.

Tears burned her eyes as she stumbled to the bed and struggled to strip off the beautiful, never-to-be-worn-again gown.

Cinderella, home at last among the shattered fragments of her dream.

Frustrated and furious, Beau paced the moonlit paths. Damn Mac and the randy Lady Ardith for choosing that particular chamber for their blatant display. He wanted to pursue his Sparrow, comfort her, recapture the magic shattered by that unintentional glimpse of mindless coupling, but some inner sense warned him she was too upset now for him to attempt it.

Tenderness softened the edge of anger. For all her mature calm, she was such an innocent, 'twas little wonder she'd been shocked. He'd been dismayed, as well, and he had far more experience than she.

Though brutal honesty compelled him to admit, had that unfortunate episode not occurred, he'd have been driven as urgently as Mac to unbind the spangled cloth veiling the lady he wanted so badly, to gently tutor her through every nuance of pleasuring and being pleasured. Even now, the desire to do so still thrummed in his veins.

But only when she was ready, only as far, as fast as she would willingly follow. Unlike the meaningless tryst they'd stumbled into viewing, their eventual joining would contain a joy and tenderness that fired lust into something purer and more lasting. A single night would not be nearly sufficient to satisfy his craving. No, he wanted all of her—heart, mind, as well as body— for the indefinite future.

She knew that—didn't she? A niggle of doubt troubled him. Surely she didn't think he'd lured her to the garden only to use her body with the sort of casual carnality they'd inadvertently observed?

The doubt occurred only to be dismissed. They had shared the burden and worry of Kit's illness, chatted of books and herbs and philosophy, touched each other's thoughts and emotions in countless small, significant ways before ever their bodies touched. She couldn't possibly think he viewed her as an object of temporary dalliance.

No, she'd been startled, repulsed, a reaction he treasured for the modesty and discretion it displayed. Nonetheless, just to be sure, he'd proceed carefully tomorrow, treat her with a special gentleness that, combined with a night's sleep and the prosaic perspective of daylight, would erase from her mind the event that had caused so abrupt and dissatisfying an ending to their walk.

She would leave today, Laura decided as she looked out through the raindrops slipping down her windowpane. Clouds enveloped the garden in a mist-shrouded drizzle, changing the silver walkways, urns and plantings of last night into soggy brick and sodden earth utterly devoid of magic.

As her life must be. She walked to the wardrobe and pulled out the plain brown bombazine. The gown seemed heavier than she remembered, its muddy hue uglier compared to the frosted emerald of the dinner dress. A little brown sparrow, Lord Beaulieu had called her, unnoticed and insignificant.

So she was. So she must be. And if desire could so blind her to that fact, if her protective instincts had eroded so badly that she could stray as far from that role as she had last night, then she must depart at once.

For the truth was, scold herself ever so severely in the fastness of her chamber, she knew if the earl were to walk in the room this minute, her hands would still itch to resume tracing the contours of his body, her mouth yearn to meld with his and see what new delights he could teach her. It shamed and horrified her to discover within herself such a deep vein of carnality, but in the stark light of morning, she was too honest to deny its presence or power.

Intensified by admiration and affection, such a force would be nearly impossible to resist. And if fully satisfied in a connection both physical and emotional, it would create a bond that would shatter her soul to sever.

She'd likely given him her heart already, a gift he'd never sought and surely wouldn't appreciate. At least if she prudently fled now, she might avoid completing the disaster by bonding with him in body, as well.

A leaden despair settled in her gut. Even if they both wished it, there could never be anything legal or permanent between them, nothing beyond a fleeting, temporary liaison. Besides, she had only her girlish fancies to suggest that the earl even desired her for more than assuaging the same need for which Lady Ardith had met Dr. MacDonovan.

She had more self-respect than to stoop to that.

Kit Bradsleigh no longer required her round-the-clock presence. Her garden needed tending, her dog craved companionship, and she ought to seek the solitude necessary to reconstruct the boundaries that protected her.

That isolated her.

She reached out to stroke the silky lightness of the dinner gown, still draped on a chair where she'd abandoned it last night. She closed her eyes, allowing herself for a moment to relive the feel of Lord Beaulieu's arms around her, the taste and touch of his tongue. A ragged sigh born of pain and loss slipped from her throat.

Then with quick, efficient moves she donned the brown gown, hung the spangled emerald dress back in the wardrobe, and left the room.

* * *

After handing Peters the chessboard, Laura turned back to Kit Bradsleigh. "I'll be coming by daily to check on you and follow any orders Dr. MacDonovan leaves for your care." Written ones, she hoped. After last night, she'd rather not meet the doctor again in person.

Kit eased himself painfully back against the pillows. "Both of you...deserting me at once."

"Dr. MacDonovan has sicker patients to tend. And I'm close by. Soon you'll be able to get downstairs to dine and receive callers, so I daresay you'll not be so bored." She smiled. "Most of them probably won't beat you at chess."

He grinned back. "Like a challenge. Besides, I'm not...quite myself yet. I demand a rematch."

"Soon," she promised.

As she rose to depart, though, he caught her hand. "Can't begin to thank you—"

"Nonsense!" she interrupted. "I thought we'd settled this long since."

He shook his head. "With you so stubborn and me so incapable, we just...stopped discussing it. But you must know...our family considers your service an unredeemable debt. Beau especially." He paused, stifling a cough. "No, let me finish. We're a small family...just Beau, Ellie and me. Parents killed in a carriage accident...I was too young to remember. But Beau was there...in the carriage. He seems to think it his duty now...to protect us from all harm. And after this, you, too. Should you ever need us, need anything, you have only to ask." He paused, unsuccessfully trying to keep the gasp from turning to a cough.

Laura took his hand. "There is no obligation."

Gripping his shoulder to damp down the cough's vibration, Kit once more shook his head. "Lifelong vow," he said when he could breathe again. "Word of a Bradsleigh." He squeezed the hand she held.

Protect her from all harm. Oh, that the Bradsleighs or anyone else could do that! But despite his influence, even the mighty Earl of Beaulieu was not above the law. Whatever safety she found must come, as it had since she'd chosen this course, solely from her own efforts.

"Rest now," she urged, gently withdrawing her hand. "I'll stop to bid you goodbye before I leave."

He squeezed her hand again and closed his eyes. With a nod to Peters, she left the room.

She'd snatched a hasty breakfast this morning, not wishing to encounter the earl, and now hoped he'd be occupied with his London satchels long enough for her to slip in a visit to Lady Elspeth and explain that she was returning home. After that, 'twould take little time to pack her few possessions. While the family was at luncheon she could pay her last call on Kit and depart.

Back to the safety of her cottage. Her books, her garden, her life of loneliness.

Before she indulged in greensick moping, she'd best remember on just how thin a thread that life still hung.

At her knock, Lady Elspeth bid her enter. To her delight, Lady Catherine was there, too.

"Miss Laura, come see! John Stableman gave me kittens!"

"Your mama lets you keep them here? I should think they'd rather be living in the stables."

"Oh, no," the child assured her. "They want to be here with me and Mama."

Over the girl's curly head, Laura looked up to see Lady Elspeth roll her eyes.

"You must thank your mama and the squire for letting them remain in your rooms, then. And be gentle with them," she cautioned as the girl reached to pluck one small furry body from the basket she'd fetched.

"Uncle Beau showed me how to hold them. He said they can break, just like my doll." She offered Laura a squirming, hairy handful. "Isn't he beautiful?"

Laura accepted the small creature, which mewed reproachfully at being removed from its cozy basket and regarded her with indignant blue eyes. "Handsome indeed. I'm glad you have some new friends to play with. Soon, your uncle Kit will be well enough to play with you, too. In fact, he's so much better I'm returning to my own home today. I'll stop by daily to check him, of course, but—"

"No!" Lady Catherine wailed. "You cannot leave!"

Laura deposited the kitten back in its basket and took the little girl's hands. "I shall not forget my friends."

"Catherine," her mother remonstrated, "Mrs. Martin has a house of her own which she must be missing. She's been kind enough to stay here to help Uncle Kit, but of course now that he is better she wants to return home."

The child patted Laura's dress and frowned. "If we gave you more dresses, would you stay? Uncle Beau will buy them! He told me he loves buying ladies pretty things."

While the girl's mother tried to explain to her why that would not be proper, Laura briefly wondered how many "pretty ladies" the earl had bought gowns for. A fair number, she imagined. Never her, she vowed.

Catherine's blue eyes filled with tears. Clearly unable to comprehend why anyone she'd befriended would wish to leave her, she turned from her mother back to

Laura. "But who will take me for my walk? Silly Mary doesn't know anything. And you tell the bestest stories!"

Laura bit her lip. For as long as the earl remained in residence, she wished to keep her visits to Everett Hall as brief as possible. But knowing how little there was to occupy a lively child—and recognizing poor Mary really was dull-witted—she couldn't withstand the appeal on Lady Catherine's face.

"I will walk with you every day, after I've checked your uncle," Laura conceded.

"But you will not stay?" the girl said, her lip still quivering.

"I'm sorry, poppet. I really cannot."

"Catherine, you must not tease." Lady Elspeth tried to soothe her unhappy daughter. "Miss Laura has already done so much for us. She's promised to visit you—and me, too. After all—" she smiled at Laura "—we have plans to make."

Before Laura could inquire what sort of plans Lady Elspeth had in mind, a quick knock at the door was followed by the entry of the one person Laura had most hoped to avoid—Lord Beaulieu.

While Lady Catherine threw herself at her uncle, chattering about kittens, Laura retreated to the window seat, disgusted to note her heartbeat accelerating merely because the earl had entered the room. She'd take no part in the conversation, avoid his eye, and make her escape at the earliest possible moment.

But she'd reckoned without her champion. Laura edged to the door while the earl duly inspected the kittens, but before she could slip out, Lady Catherine pointed at her.

"Uncle Beau, Miss Laura says she must go home

today, and I don't want her to. Please make her stay!''
The little girl gazed up to give her uncle a melting
smile. ''She'll stay if you ask her. Everyone does what
you wish.''

The earl's smiling face sobered abruptly. He looked
over at Laura, brows creasing in a frown. ''Going home
today? You made no mention of it to me.''

His eyes impaled her, almost—accusing. Laura
forced herself to look away, shaking her head to clear
a sudden light-headedness. ''Mr. Bradsleigh is recovering nicely, so there's no need for me to remain in
residence.''

''But with Dr. MacDonovan departing, it would be
wise to have someone of skill standing by, at least for
the first several days. Surely you'll not abandon your
charge now, Mrs. Martin.''

She couldn't let him make her weaken. Moistening
her lips, she replied, ''I'm not abandoning him. Dr.
MacDonovan assures me Kit no longer needs care
through the night. I shall check him every day and faith-
fully administer any treatments the doctor believes necessary. But I do have a household of my own that needs
tending.''

''A household which could manage without your
presence for a bit longer, I should think.''

''Perhaps. But I should be more *comfortable* returning there,'' she said pointedly. Damn him! He would
have her close to bewitch at his leisure. Well, she'd not
allow it.

His belligerent manner softened suddenly. ''I had
hoped to offer you every comfort here,'' he said quietly.

She felt the insidious longing invade her again. What
could a few more days hurt? She could be strong.

Liar.

She shook her head. "I—I appreciate all you have done. But I really must go."

"Even should I beg you to stay?"

She forced herself to resist the intensity of his gaze. "Even then."

After a long moment he gave her a stiff nod. "Very well. Go, then."

Lady Catherine had been watching the exchange with a smile, evidently entirely certain of her uncle's powers of persuasion. At that, however, she jumped up. "No, Uncle Beau! You cannot let her go!"

Lady Catherine ran to Laura and seized her hands. "Please, can you not stay? The kittens will miss you too."

Laura knelt down and gave the girl a quick hug. "Friends can still be friends even when they're not living in the same house. I shall walk with you every day, I promise. And if your mama permits, you can visit me. I have a dog who would love to have you throw sticks for him, and there's a walk by the river we could explore."

The girl looked up at Laura. "A friendly dog?"

"Very friendly. I've also got a big tabby cat and a pond full of frogs."

After a moment, Lady Catherine nodded. "I suppose you have to go home. Your dog and cat and frogs must be lonely."

Laura rose. Lord Beaulieu stood watching her, arms crossed over his chest, looking angry and—surely it wasn't hurt she read on his face. She jerked her glance away and walked toward the door.

"Return to your little household, Mrs. Martin," the earl said, a bitter edge to his voice. "Your very small household. Given how clever you are with children, 'tis a great shame your late husband didn't bless you with any.''

The pain was instantaneous, automatic, and even after more than two years, devastating. Without thinking she whirled to face him. ''How true, my lord,'' she snapped. ''Especially considering that I buried one.'' Dipping a curtsey, she fled the room.

Chapter Twelve

The slam of the door echoed in the sudden silence.

After giving him a speculative look, Ellie walked over to her daughter. "Let me ring for Mary, sweeting. She can help you take your kittens out for some air. Beau, if you would please wait, I'd like to speak with you."

While his sister took her daughter away, Beau tried to master his anger and make sense of his disordered thoughts.

How could Mrs. Martin leave now, when he had so little time left? He understood why the events of last evening might have upset her, but why flee from him, as if he were the perpetrator of that scene? It shocked—and he had to admit, hurt—him that she apparently had so little trust in his honor. When had he ever attempted to push or coerce her into doing something she didn't desire?

It hurt, too, that she seemed so willing to give up the little bit of time they had left together—time that had become increasingly precious to him.

But if Mrs. Martin wanted to ignore the connection between them and return home, so be it. Given a few moments to accustom himself to this unexpected development, he'd be able to deal with it. 'Twas only natural, having had his self-esteem unexpectedly bashed, that he'd succumbed to that rare fit of temper.

An uncomfortable tweak of conscience jabbed him. He'd have to pen her an apology after that gibe about her being childless. The idea of reaching out to her, even via the impersonal medium of a letter, suddenly lightened the sense of...dismay he'd experienced when she'd refused to be dissuaded from leaving.

Perhaps he'd call on her and deliver the apology in person. As that thought warmed him even further, the fact finally registered, too glaring and inescapable for him to evade the truth any longer.

He couldn't lose Laura Martin. The idea of going through a day without experiencing her smile, her wide-eyed sparrow look of inquiry, the jolt of pleasure that excited his nerves just to be near her, was simply unthinkable. Beyond the ever-present physical pull, she had become that rare friend who challenged his opinions and resisted his commands even as her wit invited his laughter and her quick intelligence piqued his mind.

He'd been looking forward with impatient anticipation to becoming more than friends. Exactly what form their long-term relationship should take, he hadn't yet figured out, but there would be time enough later for them to determine that together. First he had to ascertain what had so upset her, and coax her back.

Beau paced the room, trying to make sense of her behavior. Given the strength of the connection between them, despite her innocence he simply couldn't believe a mere display of lust would have horrified her into retreat. He'd given her no reason to suddenly fear he'd try to coerce her into similar behavior.

A radical thought popped into mind, a theory that would settle all the jumbled pieces into place so neatly, he halted in midstride.

What if Laura Martin wasn't what she claimed? What if she was not Lieutenant Martin's *wife*—but rather his cast-off mistress? A gently born girl who'd been seduced, disgraced and abandoned to bear alone a bastard child who later died?

Having forfeited through indiscretion the life of comfort and the respect that had been her birthright, estranged from everyone in her family save a kindly aunt, naturally she would wish to live quietly, zealously guarding the tiny niche she'd carved out in this rural society. Betrayed by a man she loved, with neither family nor dowry to protect her, she might well distrust the motives of men, and deliberately seek to discourage their interest.

And certainly she would flee if tempted to commit once again the folly that had led to her ruin. Seeing the writhing couple last night might have shocked her into remembering all she risked by allowing Beau too close.

There'd been too much raw pain in her tone for him to doubt that she'd lost a child. But what of the rest of what she'd revealed about herself in Merriville?

His analytical mind already speeding, Beau determined to send word by return pouch today to have his secretary launch an immediate inquiry into the family background of Lieutenant Winnfield Martin of the Thirty-third Innisford Greys, the man the squire told him had been her late husband.

Whether or not Laura Martin had suffered such a disgrace mattered not a groat to him. The woman who enthralled him had honor, intelligence and character written into her bones. Nothing that had occurred in her past could dissuade him from wanting her by his side.

Whatever the truth of her story—and well-honed instinct told him there was much more than she'd yet revealed—he must somehow persuade her she had nothing to fear and everything to gain by confiding in him, a man who regarded his family and close friends as both gift and sacred trust. He must seize another chance to convince her he would never betray her, that he wished instead to hold, protect and care for her the rest of her days.

He was still trying to decide the best way to approach Mrs. Martin when Ellie reentered the room. With his return to London imminent, he couldn't afford to wait for answers to an inquiry.

"An illuminating conversation, brother dear," Ellie said as she walked to his side. "And don't pretend you don't understand. You were very severe with Mrs. Martin."

He gave her a rueful grin. "You are right. I was... surprised. I shall have to apologize."

"I should think so." She pointed a reproving finger at him. "You do so hate it when someone within your purview makes a move without your consent."

"A despot, am I?"

"Absolutely." She kissed his cheek. "A benign one, but a despot nonetheless. Still, in this instance I think Mrs. Martin is being wise."

"And why is that?" he demanded, surprised and more than a little affronted.

"I've seen the...attraction between you. Not knowing you well, she might be fearful of what you mean to do about it. After all, Laura Martin is a woman living all alone, without family or defenders. Unlike that demirep of a sharp-spoken bitch, Lady Ardith, she's not the sort to indulge in idle bedsport. If you've dalliance in mind, brother dear, I recommend you confine your attentions to that one. She's eager enough.''

"Such language, sister mine," Beau replied with a quiver of amusement. "And thank you for kindly advising me to take myself off to someone you've just pronounced to be an acid-tongued witch.''

"She's beautiful enough, I'll grant. And quite suited for the casual interludes you men seem to enjoy.''

"Is that what you think I seek?'' Beau clapped a hand to his heart. "How wounding that my own sister holds my sex in such low esteem. I assure you, idle dalliance is of little interest to me.''

"Then your intentions toward Mrs. Martin are more...serious?''

Careful, Beau cautioned himself. Being not quite sure yet just what form his long-term intentions for Mrs. Martin might take, he had no intention of revealing anything to his deceptively disinterested sister. "Minx!'' he said, tapping her on the nose. "Suffice it to say that I would never allow the lady to come to harm.''

Ellie's air of detachment dissolved. "You value her that much? Oh, splendid, Beau!'' She took her brother's hand and kissed it. "I cannot tell you how relieved that makes me. Serene and competent as Mrs. Martin appears, there's about her an air of such...fragility. I worry about her future, alone in that little cottage with no kin to assist her. But if you, dear brother, have decided to watch over her, I can rest easy. Who knows better than Kit and I how safe and comfortable you make those lucky few you commit to your protection!''

"You like her very much, don't you?''

"Yes. And Catherine adores her.'' At his grin, she

added severely, "You'll say a mama would dote on the devil, were he sufficiently attentive to her child, but I assure you, children are fine judges of character. Laura is so good with Catherine. How tragic that she lost a babe!"

Ellie paused, sighing. "What a sad life she's had. No surviving family, apparently, and widowed so young." She shook her head. "From time to time I've made reference to Arthur, how I miss him when we're parted. Not once has she ever volunteered a word about her late husband."

"Prying, dear sister?"

"Certainly not," she retorted with some heat. "You men are close as monks about your feelings, but women often speak to each other of such things. That Mrs. Martin does not, leads me to believe her union cannot have been a happy one. As far as it lies within my power, I intend to see that her future holds the promise of better. You'll assist me in convincing her to come to London next Season?"

Beau laughed. "If you can persuade the very independent Mrs. Martin to accompany you to London," he offered, sure her future would have been decided in much different fashion by then, "you may tell your husband I'll frank the expense."

"We shall see her settled for certain." Ellie gave him an impish grin. "But given the interest hereabouts, if you refrain from appearing to dally with her, I may well not need a London Season to achieve that goal."

Did his sister mean the vicar? Instantaneous irritation ignited at the thought. Having Laura Martin wed the well-connected reverend was certainly not in his plans. Suppressing the sharp remark that vision engendered, he replied instead, "No matchmaking schemes, Ellie.

Let the lady choose her own way.'' *Our way,* he added mentally.

"Yes, brother," she replied with deceptive meekness.

Best to depart before Ellie tried to tease any more reactions from him. "Tell Catherine I'll ride with her before dinner." After kissing her cheek, he escaped to his room.

It being absolutely unavoidable, he'd work through the day on his papers, he decided, pulling out the first of several document satchels. Though he had a strong desire to confront Mrs. Martin again before she left, prudence said it might be better to let her depart unopposed. Allow her to regain the tranquility of her safe haven—and carefully prepare his approach before seeing her again.

Despite that resolve he paused, paper in hand, a bleakness invading him as he envisioned the long expanse of afternoon and evening which, for the first time in more than two weeks, would not be brightened by the sight and voice of Laura Martin.

As soon as he'd processed this stack of documents, he'd set about figuring out how to change that. *If you think me easily discouraged, you are mistaken, Sparrow.*

Figure it out and act upon it. Tomorrow, he promised himself as he sorted the papers on his desk, as early as he could reasonably expect her to be up and about, he'd pay a call on the newly resettled Mrs. Martin.

Wiping her muddy hands on a rag, Laura sat back on her heels and surveyed the weed-free herb bed. Misfit dozed in an early morning sunbeam nearby, a hot pot of tea and a fresh loaf of bread waited her in the kitchen, and she ought to be quite pleased with the results of her first morning home in over a se'ennight.

But she'd found upon arriving yesterday that the snug cottage she'd regarded for two years as a welcoming haven had somehow lost its power to comfort. Though she could still sense the presence of her beloved Aunt Mary, the small rooms echoed with emptiness. The conviction that her guardian angel watched over her yet had as little effect in raising her sagging spirits as the sputtering fire had in driving two weeks of chill from the room.

Another voice whispered through her dreams now, bringing her to wakefulness time and again awash in poignant longing. Another face appeared before her eyes as, weary of attempting sleep, she rose early to busy herself with weeding, gathering and replenishing her supply of herbs.

She missed the earl, missed even more sharply the energizing possibility that she might at any moment encounter him—at breakfast or tea or out walking with Catherine. 'Twas the height of foolishness to mourn the loss of a friendship which had never really been hers, yet she could not seem to banish the deep sadness that dogged her. Nor could she, to her mingled chagrin and shame, deny that the one spark of pleasure in this gloomy day was the knowledge that she would return to Everett Hall this afternoon to check Kit Bradsleigh, walk with Lady Catherine—and perhaps catch a glimpse of the child's uncle.

Soon Lord Beaulieu must return to London, beyond the possibility of a chance encounter. Her foolish partiality, she assured herself, would then wither and die, as it must. She should be proud she'd had the sense to tear herself away before she committed some irretrievable folly.

She wasn't.

A lick on her hand startled her back to the present.

Tail wagging hopefully, Misfit nudged her. With a short bark, he bent to pick up the stick he'd dropped at her feet.

Laura sighed. "Since you were the only one to enthusiastically welcome me home last night—even the cat having deserted me—I suppose I owe you a game."

Prancing in agreement, Misfit released the branch, then stood eyeing it avidly. He tensed as Laura held it aloft and swung it behind her back.

The instant she released it the dog tore off. She laughed, thinking ruefully how simple a dog's needs were: food, affection, an occasional game of fetch. Why could human vessels not be equally reasonable?

When after several moments Misfit did not return, she frowned, certain he could not yet have tired of the game. Then she heard his bark—the short, sharp one that meant he'd discovered something. Fervently hopeful that it wasn't another from a litter of skunk babies he'd tracked several weeks previous, she set off in pursuit.

She rounded the corner of the cottage—and stopped short. Smiling down at the prancing dog, who offered him up a stick, stood Lord Beaulieu.

Beau looked up to find Laura Martin staring at him from behind the gate that separated her herb garden from the country lane. Though she wore another worn gown faded to nondescript gray, the strengthening sunlight transformed that prosaic garment, outlining her slender figure in a halo of light and turning the stray curls that escaped the confines of her shapeless mobcap to copper fire.

Even with a smudge on her nose and mud on her apron, she looked beautiful, he thought, his heart swelling with gladness at the sight of her.

Were those shadows under her solemn eyes? Had she slept as little as he, tossing with impatience for the day that would bring him back to her?

He realized suddenly they'd both been standing, silently gazing at each other for some moments. Evidently she did, too, for she jerked her glance from his.

But not before he'd seen the surge of gladness in her face turn to wariness.

"Don't!" he cried, brushing past the dog to approach her. "Don't be afraid of me."

For a moment he thought she'd retreat back into the garden without even permitting him to speak, but at the last moment she stood her ground. She even managed a tremulous smile.

"Good morning, my lord. And—I'm not afraid of you."

He offered his hand. After a small delay, she extended hers. He savored the small courtesy of bringing it to his lips. "Are you sure? I've been much dismayed, worrying that somehow I drove you away."

"Not you. Prudence. Did...did you need something?" Sudden alarm crossed her face. "Kit has not suffered—"

"No, Kit is fine. Awaiting a rematch at chess this afternoon, he bade me tell you."

Her face relaxed. "Good. Did Dr. MacDonovan send you for supplies?" She tilted her head up, giving him that inquiring Sparrow look he'd come to treasure.

How fiercely he'd missed her after just one day. "No. I came to apologize."

A blush stained her cheeks. "There is no need—"

"There is. But I should do a better job of it seated. If we might?" He gestured toward the cottage.

He held his breath as alarm, indecision—and longing played across her expressive face.

Yes, she still cared for him. Exultation mingled with restraint and a fierce desire to embrace her, kiss away the caution in her eyes, seize the opportunity here, far from prying eyes, where they might recapture and deepen the wordless intimacy they'd found in the moon-lit garden.

Too soon yet, he told himself, stilling fingers already curled with anxiety to hold her again. "You are too kind to deny me that opportunity, aren't you?"

Before she could reply, the sound of galloping hooves approached. Beau looked up to see Lady Ardith, resplendent in a fur-trimmed riding habit, bearing down upon them, and cursed under his breath.

The lady drew rein and smiled down at him. "Lord Beaulieu, good day to you! Is it not a brilliant morning for a ride?"

Did a grin flit briefly across Mrs. Martin's lips? Before he could be sure, she curtsied. "Lady Ardith."

The blonde regally inclined her head. "Mrs. Martin." Her horse danced sideways and she tightened the reins, her trim posterior bouncing against the sidesaddle.

A deliberate move? Beau wondered cynically. With Mac departing this morning, was the wench already trolling for a replacement?

It won't be me. "Fine indeed, Lady Ardith. Do not let us keep you from your ride. Mrs. Martin, shall we?" Beau gestured to the cottage.

"If you should wish me to delay a few moments until you finish your business with Mrs. Martin—" Lady Ardith plied her long lashes and gave him a smoky glance "—I could be persuaded. 'Tis so enjoyable to ride with a partner."

Mrs. Martin made a choking sound, which she turned into a cough. "I can bring any necessary supplies with me when I call on your brother," she volunteered.

"No need for you to tarry then, my lord," Lady Ardith said. "Have you ridden the trail by the river? 'Tis wonderous scenic once you reach our land. My husband had several little grottos constructed that are charming and quite...private. Shall we race?" She inclined her head to the stallion he'd secured to the fence. "Your beast looks quite fresh, and my mare—" she sidled him a glance "—is nearly the best mount in the county."

"Do go, my lord," Mrs. Martin said, her innocent tone at odds with her suspiciously twitching lips. "I shouldn't wish to you to miss Lady Ardith's kind offer."

He shot her a sardonic glance. The grin she returned looked entirely unrepentant.

"Another day, perhaps," he told the horsewoman.

"Come now, I dare swear you've time for a little sport," Lady Ardith persisted. "I promise you'll not regret it."

Beau had no desire to conduct his business with Laura Martin while this lightskirt lay in wait for him outside the cottage. Giving Mrs. Martin an indignant glance that caused her to choke down another gurgle of laughter, he turned his attention to the necessity of getting rid of the annoying Lady Ardith.

"A short ride," he said.

"Excellent."

Ignoring the lady on the sidesaddle, he turned back to Laura Martin. "I shall see you later, ma'am."

A devilish twinkle lighting her eyes, she dipped a demure curtsey. "My lord, Lady Ardith."

Not bothering to acknowledge Mrs. Martin, Lady Ardith brought her horse closer. "Can that stallion of yours perform as well as my mare? Let's see!" With that, she spurred her mount.

"Soon," he warned Mrs. Martin, and set off.

Half an hour later Beau brought his stallion to a halt at the shed behind Laura Martin's cottage. He was not, he thought smugly as he dismounted and tied the horse to a post, the only person who could fob off an unwanted escort.

Leaving his mount hidden back here, where no passer-by could see it and decide to interrupt his visit, Beau stealthily traversed the garden, intending to enter by the back porch door.

Memories of the vision he'd stumbled upon the last time he'd silently approached down these herb-lined pathways kindled a flicker of heat in his stomach. Unbidden, the feel of her waltzing in his arms under the spangled stars, the taste of her lips meeting his eagerly, welled up in him, fanning the flicker.

Not yet, he told himself, curbing the memories. He'd not have the wit to calm her fears and win her trust if he walked in with his body aflame.

He paused by the door and raised his hand to knock.

And heard something—Mrs. Martin's high clear voice interspersed with deeper tones.

Not again. Frustration humming through his veins, he paused on the threshold, debating whether to wait out the annoyance of a second visitor or to slip away and return later.

He'd first determine who her caller was, he decided. Silently he eased the back door open and crept down the hallway until he could see into the front parlor.

The scene he spied there paralyzed both thought and movement. In front of Mrs. Martin, who sat on the sofa by the window, he saw Reverend Blackthorne down on one knee.

Chapter Thirteen

Disengaging her hand, Mrs. Martin backed away from the vicar—straight toward Beau. Recovering his frozen wits in an instant, he leaped aside to flatten himself against the staircase wall, knowing it imperative he remain hidden until he'd sorted out what to do about this extremely disagreeable development.

His first furious reaction—to stalk into the parlor, seize Reverend Blackthorne by his shirt collar and haul him bodily out of the cottage—he quickly discarded as impolitic, if eminently satisfying. His second thought was a throat-drying fear that in his self-absorbed concentration on maneuvering Mrs. Martin into the sort of relationship that would best satisfy *his* desires, he'd let this underestimated rival steal a perhaps insurmountable advantage over him.

If Blackthorne did in fact assuage Mrs. Martin's distrust of men by offering marriage, and she accepted him, how was Beau to counter that? He might lose her before he'd barely had a chance to press his own claims.

Cold purpose focused him, let him shake his mind free of angry dismay. *There had to be some way to stop this*. Without a particle of remorse, he focused on over-hearing as much as possible of the conversation.

"Please, Mr. Blackthorne, I beg you proceed no further," said Mrs. Martin, distress in her cool voice.

That reassuring request was followed by the soft pad of Mrs. Martin's footsteps, but in his current position Beau could not see where the occupants of the parlor now stood. *Move away from him,* he silently urged.

"Surely my feelings cannot come as a surprise," Blackthorne said, a bit of reproach in his tone. "I've long held you in esteem, as our dealings with each other must have shown."

"I felt you esteemed me as a member of the community who attempted to assist those in need, as I esteem you," she replied. "Nothing more."

"Perhaps I was not as…forthcoming as I should have been," he conceded. "A man of my position must naturally be circumspect to avoid becoming fodder for the local gossips. But I regret that restraint, if it left you in ignorance of the steadily increasing warmth of my regard. So much that I must beg you let me continue!"

Beau heard heavier footfalls, and grimly concluded the reverend must have pursued Mrs. Martin. "Please, sir—"

"No, dear lady, you must allow me voice! Granted, had certain…events not transpired I should not have chosen to approach you in so precipitous a manner, but at this critical moment both personal desire and my duty as your spiritual advisor demand that I address you now."

Beau heard Mrs. Martin's ragged sigh. "Continue then, if you must."

"I beg you will acquit me of conceit if I state what I see are the advantages to you of this match. At this moment I occupy a position which might appear to offer little worldly gain, but I have an income independent of this living and the ear of my father, who is, I assure you, a most influential man. My wife and children will want for nothing. For months I've been increasingly drawn by your modesty, excellence and nobility of character, a beauty of soul surely the equal of your lovely countenance. I think we could pursue a common purpose. While I cannot claim to be without flaws, I hope I bear no more than my human share. Should you do me the honor of becoming my wife, I should earnestly strive to make you happy.''

Though Beau could hardly have hoped the vicar would offer a lady of his parish carte blanche, still the formal proposal shook him to his boots. A widow in Mrs. Martin's tenuous position, unless she held her suitor in absolute abhorrence, would be a fool to refuse such an offer.

Torn between dismay and hopeless anger, Beau waited in wretched silence for the inevitable acceptance.

"Mr. Blackthorne, please understand I am fully cognizant of the brilliance of your offer. A woman who occupies as humble a position as I could not help but be honored that a man of your birth and position would consider her for his wife, but—"

"You are a lady born, as any *gentleman* could see, quite worthy to be offered a man's hand and name," Blackthorne said with some heat.

"Thank you, sir. But flattering as it is, I—I must decline your proposal."

Beau sagged back against the wall, shock and gladness weakening his knees. He could not imagine why she would reject so clearly advantageous an offer, but at this moment, having little doubt that Reverend Blackthorne would probably attempt to persuade her otherwise, he focused all his thoughts on willing her to persist in refusing it.

"You...find me disagreeable?" Despite himself, Beau felt a grudging sympathy at the mingled pain and humility in the reverend's voice.

"No, of course not. It's just..." Beau heard her soft, quick step, as if she were pacing the room. "I...can only tell you that my...experiences with the wedded state were such that I cannot envision ever entering it again. Pray, do not press me further."

So Ellie was right—her marriage had not been happy. Apparently the vicar had not been aware of it, for several moments of silence followed her declaration.

"My dear lady, I deeply regret any unhappiness you may have suffered," he began again, apparently taken aback but undaunted. "Still, I vow that if you will but entrust your future to me, I will do all in my power—"

"Sir, I beg you say no more! My resolve on this matter is unshakable."

"If you forbid me speak, I must honor that request, but you cannot silence me on a matter of even graver import. No, madam—" Beau heard the soft tones of her protesting voice under the vicar's more strident ones "—this must be said. It has not escaped me that recently you have become the object of interest to...a man of great position. Indeed, he has singled you out to a degree that has already begun to cause speculation in the neighborhood. I must warn you that I seriously question this nobleman's intentions toward you."

"Indeed, sir, I am sure you are mistaken!" Mrs. Martin's gratifying prompt response mitigated Beau's immediate desire to spring from his hiding place and plant the disparaging reverend a facer. "I am much too far beneath that person's notice," she continued, "for him to have any designs upon my person whatever. I agree that both he and his sister have singled me out to an extraordinary degree, but that is only because of the service I've rendered their kinsman."

"Dear Mrs. Martin, it does honor to the purity of your character that you view Lord Beaulieu's actions in that light, but in this you must bow to my superior knowledge of the world. I have closely observed the manner in which his lordship looks at and treats you. I wasn't called to the church until after I'd been some years on the town, and speaking as a fellow aristocrat who knows how such men's minds work, I assure you in the strongest possible terms that you do indeed stand in danger."

Another fraught silence followed that impassioned speech. Hands itching for the feel of the vicar's throat under his thumbs, once again Beau had to exercise supreme discipline to keep from bursting into the room. Damn the man's effrontery in so viciously maligning Beau's interest in Mrs. Martin! As if he desired only some hasty, meaningless backstairs coupling. Surely Mrs. Martin knew better than that. He might truly murder the vicar if the man weakened the fragile trust Beau had been working so hard to build.

"Y-you cannot believe that *I* encouraged—"

"Of course not! I'm sure I know your character better than that. But others will be less discerning and more judgmental. Believe me, Lord Beaulieu's very particular attentions, if they continue much longer unchecked, will create enough speculation that your character *will* be impugned and your standing in this community *will* suffer, be you innocent or not."

"I would stand condemned even if innocent?" A note of outrage colored the distress in her voice.

"Such is the world. Which is why I felt strongly that I must make now an offer that, I assure you, I have been contemplating for some time. Your becoming a married lady would put a halt to any untoward advances as well as preserve the purity of your reputation."

"I am to marry you solely to preserve my reputation?"

"For much more than that, I trust! I hope I do not err in believing that you cherish for me at least a modicum of affection—affection that two like-minded individuals committed to a life together could enrich and deepen. As my own emotions are already considerably engaged, I cannot stand by and see you harmed by one grown so accustomed to having his every wish and whim deferred to by others that he neither sees nor cares what harm he may do!"

"Mr. Blackthorne, having, as you've noted, spent much time with Lord Beaulieu, I must protest that harsh assessment. Whatever his intentions—and I still take leave to doubt he has any toward me at all—I cannot believe he would knowingly harm me."

Bless you, sweet lady, Beau thought, both gratified and humbled by her avowal.

"Given my own aspirations, perhaps I am too harsh," the vicar allowed. "But the danger to your reputation, even should his lordship's interest be as fraternal as you assert, is nonetheless grave, and grows daily more acute. Please, my lady, I beg you to let me take your hand, offer you the protection of my name and my heart."

"Sir, you will please release my hand."

"Not until you've given me the assurance that you

will carefully consider what I've said. I cannot leave
until you guarantee me at least that.''

"M-Mr. B-Blackthorne, you are d-distressing me.
P-please let go my hand now!''

"You will consider my words? You'll promise me
that?''

"Y-yes—no, oh, I don't know! J-just go, I b-beg
you!''

That ragged speech, followed by a choked sound suspiciously like a sob, had Beau poised on the balls of
his feet in murderous rage, ready once more to burst
into the room and drag the persistent clergyman away.

Before he could proceed, Mr. Blackthorne said, "I'll
withdraw now, ma'am, as you request. I am heartily
sorry to have distressed you by speaking so forcefully,
but I reiterate, the matter is grave. Rest assured I shall
keep an eye on the cottage. We will speak further when
you are calmer. Your servant, Mrs. Martin.''

Much as he'd like to go a few rounds with the vicar,
Beau had no desire to have the man catch him hiding
in the shadows like a petty thief. Quickly he slipped
back down the hall and out the porch door.

Where he stood, irresolute. Standing out most clearly
in the confused swirl of violent emotions racking him
were a total incomprehension of why Mrs. Martin
would refuse Blackthorne's proposal and an immense
relief that she had. Fear of the vicar's repetition of his
offer warred with a buoyant hope that it was not too
late for Beau after all, humility at her trust in his honor,
and the fervent need to prove himself worthy of it. A
renewed imperative to claim her for his own fired up,
fueled in part by anguish at the thought of her trapped
in a distasteful marriage. How could any man not have
cherished so gentle a heart, so sterling a character?

It seemed his careful theory lay in tatters. Apparently she *had* been wife rather than mistress to her lieutenant. Not only had her flat statement about marriage been utterly convincing, but a woman anxious to redeem her character should have leaped at, rather than refused, an honorable offer.

Unless her emotions were already elsewhere engaged. A rush of elation followed the thought. Dare he hope she might have refused the vicar at least in part because of the connection calling them together?

He'd find out—right now. Be she widow or wayward miss mattered naught—only their future together was important. He turned back toward the door, took two strides, and halted once more.

The vicar had been right in at least one assertion— Mrs. Martin was too distraught to receive anyone. Strongly as instinct called him to her side, prudence counseled him to give her time to recover from the turmoil created by the vicar's visit. He should call again later.

But as he reluctantly turned toward the garden, the sound of a shuddering sob stopped him.

The first was followed by another, then another. He stood paralyzed as a series of deep, gasping sobs flayed his already raw emotions, wrenching from him both the desire to flee the premises immediately and the need to return and comfort her.

Mama, Mama, don't cry! I'll help you.

Can't help...darling. Too...late.

Sweat broke out all over his body as he jerked his mind from the echo of his nightmare of that long-ago accident. He hadn't been able to help then, his mama and the unborn child she carried dying even as the frantic six-year-old jerked and tugged at the skyward-staring door of their shattered carriage. But much as the sound of Mrs. Martin's sobs ignited a revulsion that shuddered through him, he knew he couldn't walk away and leave her alone in her anguish.

He forced himself back down the hallway into the parlor. She still stood in the center of the room, face buried in her hands while sobs convulsed her frame. Neglected wife? Abandoned mistress? Whatever had befallen her, the agony shaking that slender body said the experience had been unendurably painful.

The remaining shreds of nightmare dissolved beneath an overwhelming need to help her. "Mrs. Martin," he called softly, not wishing to startle her.

In a gasp of breath, the sobs halted. Before he could take a step, she jerked upright, eyes wide, face contorted.

With fear, he realized. "Don't be alarmed—it's Beau Bradsleigh."

It took a long moment for the words to penetrate, before the alarm faded from her eyes. "M-my lord?"

"I—I was passing by and...and chanced to hear you. What has happened to so overset you? Please, let me help."

At first she stared at him as if his words had no meaning. An expression of infinite weariness gradually overtook the misery in her eyes. "T-thank you, my lord. But 'tis nothing that can be helped."

"Everything can be helped."

Her tear-stained eyes examined his face. *Tell me*, he silently willed her. She opened her lips, hesitated. Closed them again with a sigh.

And then, almost as visibly as if a curtain had descended, her face changed to a mask of distant politeness. "D-did you require something, my lord?"

He could not let it go, not now when he knew—*he knew*—she had come so close to telling him the truth. "I rather thought you might."

Alertness leaped back to her face. "My lord?"

"I could be of greater assistance if you would but answer me one thing. Who are you, Laura Martin?"

Chapter Fourteen

It was her worst nightmare come to life. Discovery.

Sheer panic blinded her. As the first shockwave receded, leaving behind a fear that seeped into every pore, her vision cleared and she saw Lord Beaulieu standing before her. Staring, his face intent and questioning.

In that moment she realized with bitter certainty that her overlong hesitation had just given her away. 'Twas too late now to summon up some glib remark, to feign bafflement. Even had she the inner resources left after her interview with the vicar to find the appropriate words.

Wearily she closed her eyes and stumbled to the window, leaning her forehead against the cool glass. She sensed Lord Beaulieu follow her. Like the vicar, who would not take her polite refusal and go away, who had pursued her, cornered her, seized her hand in a move so reminiscent of Charleton she'd almost become physically ill.

A faint spark of anger flickered and caught. No, she had not endured all she had suffered to live to this moment, managed day by painstaking day the recreation of her whole being, to let it end now.

Before she could decide how best to counter him, she heard Lord Beaulieu's soft voice behind her. "Whatever troubles you, know I only want to assist. Please, let me help you."

She felt a touch to her shoulder and whirled to face him, the reaction too ingrained to suppress. "Help? And just how do you intend to do that? By hinting to the community that I am not what I seem? Destroying my name, my reputation? Seeing me cast from the meager niche I've carved out for myself here, as a king would crush a bothersome insect?"

"Of course not! How could you think that of me? Who you were—who you are, does not matter to me as much as solving what causes you such distress. Will you let me?"

She stared at him with ferocious intensity, evaluating the angle of his body, the set of his expression, every remembered nuance of his voice. Her heart, her mind, her instincts all told her he was telling the truth.

He would not betray her.

Relief washed through her in a dizzying wave. "Y-you will say nothing?"

She must have swayed, for he reached out a hand as if to steady her. Drew it back as instinctively she stiffened. "I will say nothing without your leave." In his eyes she could read only a warm concern. "But that does not touch the heart of the matter. Tell me, sweet lady, how can I help you?"

The dregs of panic drained away in an upwash of emotion. How she loved him, this principled man devoted to his family who wanted only to ease her suffering, as she had eased his brother's. Who had power that nearly rivaled the king's, yet would not hold her against her will. Who coupled strength with gentleness, as her father had.

Not until the vicar's warning had she fully realized the depth of her desire to be with the earl, talk with him, touch him, become his lover for however short or long a time he would grant her. Not until then had she fully realized how impossible of fulfillment that desire truly was.

The vicar spoke the truth, however unpalatable. Now that Kit Bradsleigh was healing, to remain on any terms of intimacy with a man so superior to her in rank and fortune would be interpreted by the world in only one fashion. To be thought the earl's *chère amie* in the so-phisticated, amoral world of the London ton would be unremarkable—probably even elevate her status. In the more rigid, moralistic society of rural England, such a perception would ruin her reputation, make her an out-cast from local society and very likely destroy her live-lihood.

Being with the earl was but a foolish, impossible dream, and had been so from the very beginning. Strange that having to destroy it hurt so much.

She turned her face from the earl's too penetrating gaze. "If you truly desire to help, stop calling upon me. Do not speak with me except in greeting. Do not be seen with me outside in your brother's sickroom."

"That is what you want?"

She hesitated. "That is what must be."

"It need *not* be. Not if you want, as I do, so much more for us both. Would you throw away all that we could mean to each other without even trying to find another way? You know I would never allow anything to harm you! Please, can you not trust me?"

Oh, how she wanted to trust him. But with her livelihood, perhaps her very life, hanging in the balance, she dare not.

Unsure she could resist if the plea in his eyes matched the urgency of his voice, she walked away to once more gaze out the windows. "You will soon leave here. I must stay, live among my neighbors. If you agree to say nothing about me, I will be secure. That is the best thing you can do for me, the only thing I desire."

"I don't believe that. Look at me, Laura! Look me in the eye and swear you want me to walk away."

Back in a past she tried to forget, she'd managed to face up to Charleton and lie, even knowing her life might be forfeit if he caught her out. She could lie now if she must.

Laura took a trembling breath and, blanking her face of all expression, slowly raised her gaze to meet the earl's. "Please go, my lord, and do not come back." She paused, forcing herself to add with a touch of scorn, "I hope you will not insist on haranguing me to tears before you're convinced to comply?"

Something sparked in his eyes—anger, perhaps hurt. Ruthlessly she suppressed the pang of guilt, the need to explain. After a silent moment during which her cold mask did not melt under his fevered stare, he made her a curt bow.

"As you wish then, madam. I bid you goodbye."

Laura held herself unmoving while his footsteps retreated down the hallway, through the porch door's slam. Not until the jingle of harness and clip-clop of iron-shod hooves on the lane outside faded, signaling Lord Beaulieu's final departure, did she stagger from the center of the room to the sofa.

She collapsed upon the soft padded surface, unable

to move or think, conscious only of a bone-deep weariness made weightier by piercing sadness.

It was over. Over, really, before it ever began. Lord Beaulieu, accustomed to giving orders rather than taking them, summoning ladies of his choice rather than being dismissed by them, would not be back.

She was still safe, though. Surely some days or weeks or months later, when she could bring herself to truly acknowledge that fact, her heart would agree his loss was worth that gain.

Spurred on by fury and frustration, Beau drove his mount at a flat gallop through the woods back to Everett Hall. Damn and blast, the woman was stubborn! He could almost feel a kindred sympathy with the rejected reverend.

But perhaps, his normal clear thinking obscured by the unaccustomed depth of the emotions Mrs. Martin roused in him, he'd misconstrued Mrs. Martin's reactions over the past few weeks. Perhaps she had not responded to him to the degree he'd thought. In any event, her icy dismissal clearly indicated that she did not harbor the same intensity of feeling for him that he did for her.

Perhaps she had no wish to wed the vicar and disdained the whole institution of marriage because she abhorred men in general. Such women existed, he knew.

Whatever her reasons for refusing the vicar, the fact that she had also rejected both Beau and his offer of help was gallingly unambiguous. *Scornfully* rejected, he recalled with a renewal of ire, as if he were an impotent, bumbling schoolboy.

Well, he certainly had enough other problems to solve. Now that Kit was on the mend, easing his anxiety about his immediate family, he should apply himself to the weighty matters demanding his attention. He'd pack up and return to London tomorrow at first light.

Righteous indignation carried him through the swift disposition of the papers brought him by today's courier, a short afternoon interview with Ellie and Catherine and dinner with the assorted company. During that interminable affair, Lady Winters seemed more than usually vacuous, Ellie tried his patience by several oblique references to Mrs. Martin and the squire chatted on about trivialities with thick-headed obliviousness. With a little difficulty, he managed to squelch the nasty but entirely understandable desire, when Ellie brought Mrs. Martin's name into the conversation for the fourth time, to drop a tiny hint that the lady might not be who she seemed.

Regardless of how little others might esteem it, his sense of honor was unbreachable, he told himself when, after the brandy, he was at last able to escape back to his room. He *was* a man worthy of the highest trust— had not even kings and cabinet ministers deferred to his ingenuity and discretion? And he certainly was *not* suffering pique at having his desires thwarted, overlayed by more than a little hurt that his regard had been so ignominiously spurned. He was merely…disappointed.

By the time he'd finished packing his bags, however, the smoldering fury that had carried him through the day had burned itself out. In the cold void left after the heat of anger evaporated, the dispassionate logic upon which he prided himself belatedly resurfaced.

Mrs. Martin's wholly unexpected rejection of his overtures had shaken his certitude, but now that he calmly reconsidered the evidence, he was once again convinced he had not misinterpreted her reaction to him.

The desire, both physical and emotional, that bound them together was strong and mutual. Why would she then send him away with such cold finality?

The subtle signals she'd sent during that interview, nagging all day at the edges of consciousness, suddenly combined with everything else he'd observed these past few weeks to coalesce in a conclusion. One in which the apparently disjointed pieces of the puzzle that was Laura Martin fell perfectly into place. The utter certainty of it swept through him with the force of a gale wind.

Of course she had refused the vicar. Of course she lived quietly, deliberately discouraging the notice of society in general and men in particular. Of course she begged him to leave her in obscurity, proclaiming there was no remedy for the malady that distressed her.

Laura Martin was neither an abandoned mistress nor a widow. She was a wife. Some powerful man's runaway wife.

His heartbeat sped as he tried to grasp all the implications. Laura "Martin" had lived in this small community for nearly two years. If she feared her husband enough to remain in hiding that long—a fear, he realized now, he'd often been puzzled to see lurking in her eyes—the villain must be both a man of far-reaching influence—and dangerous.

"'Tis nothing that can be helped," she'd said. Under ordinary circumstances, she'd be right. The law gave a husband absolute ownership of his wife's property and person, a power neither her family nor any legal authority could contravene, regardless of circumstance. A husband could not be legally convicted of rape or assault if the victim of those crimes was his wife.

That the sole legal redress would not be easy and

would probably damage his own prestige irreparably, Beau dismissed without a qualm. He had considerable influence in the House of Lords and he would use it. Difficult though it be, he would force the loathsome coward who'd called himself Laura's husband to petition parliament for a bill of divorcement.

Perhaps deep within he'd known the truth of it even before the vicar's unexpected proposal shocked him to awareness, but regardless of when the realization struck, he knew it now. Laura Martin was the companion for whom he'd been waiting all his adult life. In order to keep her by his side, however, he must first free her from the man who had dishonored his husband's vows and abused her trust. Once she was free, Beau could then beg for her hand and the right to guard and protect her forever.

His most immediate task, however, would be to move her out of that vulnerable cottage, where there was naught but one disreputable mutt to safeguard her. He'd transport her to some location where he could watch over her while the legal proceedings moved forward. He blessed the fact that in his job he'd accumulated contacts who could help with that, as well.

The disappointment, anguish, hurt of the previous hours dissolved in an upsurge of joyous excitement. Over the past several years he'd perfected his calling, pursuing the enemies of the state with methodical precision, quietly content to have rendered valuable, if unheralded, service to his nation. Now he would use the skills honed in that service to rescue the woman he loved and fashion a place for them to be together for a lifetime.

He remembered then her stark avowal—that she would never again consider entering the state of wedlock—and some of his ardor dimmed. Would he be able to persuade her to once again trust in a man's vows to love, cherish and protect?

He refused to consider now the bleakness his life would become if he could not. But regardless of whether he was eventually successful in winning her hand, he pledged on his sacred honor that he would see her freed of her sham of a marriage, freed of fear, free to live once again in the open.

When he left for London at dawn tomorrow, Laura Martin must go with him. Now all he needed to do was to convince her.

The midnight air was cold and clear, the moon full enough that its light cast shadows across the cottage porch as thirty minutes later, Misfit gamboling joyfully at his heels, Beau stood at Laura Martin's door.

He fisted his hand to knock and then hesitated. Would an unexpected pounding on her door at midnight terrify her with fears of her husband's pursuit? Or had she been a healer long enough that she would merely think some individual sought emergency aid?

He decided on a single sharp rap. "Mrs. Martin, it's Beau Bradsleigh!" he called through the night stillness. "Please, I must see you at once!" Apparently deciding to add voice to the summons, Misfit began to bark.

By the time he'd quelled the dog's enthusiasm, he saw a light approaching. Her body obscured by a voluminous dark wrapper, the ubiquitous cap on her head, Mrs. Martin cautiously moved to the door.

Her eyes glanced off him into the empty darkness beyond. "My lord? Pray, what is wrong? Your brother—"

"No, Kit is well. Please, may I come in?"

She stood a moment, eyes examining his face, as if struggling between acceptance and refusal. Then, with a slight smile, she nodded. "This is certainly not wise, so it had best be brief." She gestured him inside.

He followed her into the parlor, dark and chill with no fire in the grate. After setting her candle upon the table, she sat and invited him to do the same.

He hesitated, searching for the most convincing words. "Forgive me for intruding upon you so late, but I leave for London in the morning and there is something we must settle before I go."

"Excuse me, but I thought we had already said everything that was needful." Sudden alarm flashed across her features. "Unless you've changed your mind—"

"I mean you no harm, as I assured you this morning. Quite the opposite, Mrs.—it isn't 'Martin,' is it?"

Her eyes fell. "No," she said softly.

"Nor is it the 'widowed' Mrs. Martin?"

She jerked her head upright, dismay in her eyes. She opened her lips. Closed them again.

"You're still married, aren't you? That's what—who you're hiding from. That's the matter that 'cannot be fixed.' Isn't it?"

She sighed. "Why could you not accept the surface appearance of things, as everyone else does?" She smiled, her expression half rueful, half self-mocking. "All of England, and I must take refuge in the one small community whose squire's son is friend to the Puzzle-breaker's brother. So now you've guessed the whole of my secret. But as long as you honor your pledge not to betray me—and I think you will—what is there to discuss?"

"You believe yourself in danger, do you not?"

Her smile faded. "Yes."

"Then you must come with me."

That startled an incredulous laugh from her. "Go with you! To London where the chance of Ch—of discovery would be so much greater? You must be mad! Why do you think I chose so obscure a location?"

"Obscure or not, you just admitted that, should your husband discover your whereabouts, you would not be safe here. I can keep you safe."

"I beg to differ, but you cannot! Clever though you be, you are not above the law. Should my husband find me, no one has the right to keep me from him."

"You think I would let him find you? A man who has used you so badly you felt it necessary to go into hiding to escape him? Think, Laura! I've many more contacts than you. I can see you settled secretly, somewhere safe. Where you can stay while I persuade him to pursue a bill of divorcement."

"Divorce?" She uttered a short, scornful noise. "Now I know you're mad! He's...an important man, fiercely proud of his family and his lineage. He'd never tarnish it with the stain of divorce. He'd see me dead first."

Beau shrugged. "If he is proud of his family, he'll want sons to carry on his name—which I trust you've not yet provided?" When she said nothing, he continued, "He'll not get heirs without a willing wife. 'Tis in his own interest to divorce you and find another. And should he refuse to proceed, he'll be made to do so. A man who causes his wife to flee cannot be a saint. There must be some stain on his honor he would not want revealed, something that would be more damaging to his name than divorce. If necessary, I'll guarantee him it *will* be revealed." Beau smiled slightly. "As you know, I'm rather good at ferreting out secrets."

Laura shook her head. "He will not be coerced. Only remember—society, law, custom are all on his side! Alerting him to my presence would only encourage him to arrange the one thing that truly would make him free…" Her fervent voice faded to a whisper. "My death."

"Do you think me so poor a champion?" Beau asked, appalled, frustrated and more than a little stung by her lack of faith.

She looked up, her eyes lit with tenderness. "You are a wonderful caretaker to those who depend on you—your sister and brother and niece. But you cannot protect me. Even if I had some valid claim to your protection."

"Do you not, Laura, my sweet?" He reached for her hand, and she let him take it, bring it to his lips. "Your fierce spirit laid claim to my heart that first long night we toiled together at Kit's side. Every day that passes, each moment we share deepens that claim. A bond and obligation quite apart from what my family owes you, a link between you and I alone. Surely you feel it, too."

A statement, not a question. Her lips trembling, she squeezed his hand. "Y-yes. But it cannot—"

"It *can!* We *can* be together, if you will only believe in me, trust me. I want you with me, Laura. I want to protect you and care for you and love you. I'll pledge my life to prevent any harm coming to you. And I will do whatever is necessary to set you free."

Tears welled in her eyes, the candlelight reflected in their watery sheen. "I believe you. But you do not know him. You don't know what he's…capable of. I promise you, he would never consent to a divorce. Soon I'll be…safer, as safe as I shall ever be in this life. But only if I stay here, if you promise to take no action that might bring to his notice some hint of my where-abouts.''

"Laura, that's nonsense! Only a divorce will truly make you safe. Won't you tell me the whole, help me set the process in motion?''

"I cannot!''

Damn, but the woman was stubborn. Fighting exasperation and fatigue, Beau tried again. "Laura, I must leave tomorrow. How can I go, knowing you are alone and unprotected? I realize you've built a life here, and it's only natural that you are reluctant to abandon it. But if I managed to piece together the truth, someone else might as well. Or what if, one day as you passed the village posting inn on your way to tend a patient, the door of a private carriage opened and your husband stepped out? What then?''

If Beau had harbored any vestige of doubt about the depth of Laura's fear, the stark look of panic that widened her eyes and paled her skin at that possibility would have erased them.

The urgency of persuading her goading him ever more acutely, Beau pressed his argument. "It could happen, Laura. Please, come with me! I swear on my family's honor to keep you safe and to see you freed.''

Pressing her lips together as if to still them, she pulled her hand free and backed away from him, stumbling as she encountered the wall behind her. Swaying with the force of her agitation, she remained there, eyes riveted on his face, while doubt, confusion and dismay played across her expressive face.

He let her retreat. "Trust your heart, Laura,'' he urged her softly. "Trust me.''

Knowing there was nothing more he could say or do,

Beau simply stood, willing her with all his strength to agree.

Finally, as he watched in consternation, a distant, shuttered look descended on her features, as it had this morning. She gave her head a small, negative shake. "I'm sorry, but I must stay. Please, do not urge me further."

Beau grit his teeth and resisted the urge to shake her like a disobedient child. How could she not admit the superior logic of his plan? He took a deep, calming breath. "Laura, I know you are afraid, but—"

"Lord Beaulieu, must we part in anger? I will not go, and nothing you can say will change my mind. If you intend to depart at dawn, I suggest you return to the squire's and get some rest before your journey."

As if they'd just finished some innocuous social chat over tea, she turned away, apparently intending to lead him to the door.

Irritation and the daunting knowledge that he hadn't succeeded in convincing her roughened his voice. "Damn it, Laura, I can't just abandon you here!" As she tried to bypass him, he seized her by the shoulder.

With an inarticulate cry she wrenched out of his grasp, scuttled sideways and whirled to face him, arms raised protectively over her head.

As if to ward off a blow. The realization exploded in his brain and radiated in shock waves through his body.

He'd known, intellectually, that her husband must have abused her. But not until this moment, as she half crouched before him, her breath coming in gasps, her eyes dilated and feral as a cornered animal's, had the reality of what she must have lived with, fled from, truly registered.

While he stood there staring at her, incredulous and

horrified, she slowly straightened, lowered her arms back to her sides. Her wide, watchful eyes never left him.

Blind rage filled him, a sick revulsion at the indignity she must have suffered. Though given the evidence he'd just witnessed there was little need to ask, he couldn't seem to stop himself from voicing the awful truth.

"He hurt you."

She nodded, a quick jerk of the chin.

"Often. Badly."

She pressed her trembling lips together and squeezed her eyes shut, displacing a single tear that tracked down her cheek, a glaze of liquid diamond in the moonlight.

"Ah, Sparrow," he whispered against the ache in his throat. "I'm so sorry." And walked over to gather her against his chest.

She trembled within the circle of his arms, trying not to weep. He'd guessed her most shameful secret, and yet he'd not turned from her in disgust after she cowered before him like some sort of brute beast. Instead, he sheltered her in his embrace, offering her refuge while she regathered the few tattered shreds of dignity Charleton had left her. For that mercy alone, did she not already love him, she would surely have given him her heart.

Not for more than a year, since Aunt Mary had entered her final illness, had Laura been embraced by another human soul. How she had missed the sweet peace conveyed by simple physical closeness. For long moments after she'd recovered her composure, she could not make herself move away. But when finally she did force herself to push against his chest, he released her instantly.

"How long?" he asked quietly.

Even now, 'twas best not to be too specific. "A number of years."

"And he...misused you from the first?"

She sighed. "Nearly."

"Did your family not suspect?"

"I ran back to them the first time. But he came after me, so charming and regretful, that he convinced them—and me—'twas all a silly misunderstanding, that I was young and overreacted. I believed him—until the next time. And then it was too late. I was watched too closely."

"Until one day you felt you could stand it no more?"

He cannot be a saint...there must be some stain on his honor he would not want revealed... But no, Charleton was too clever. Even if she told Beau what had happened, it would end up her word against her husband's—and which was the court likely to believe? Better, still better to say nothing. "Until I could stand no more," she agreed.

He took her hand and kissed it. "Were these medieval days, I would find him and kill him, but we are supposed to be more civilized now. Won't you leave with me, let us fight this together?"

So he might protect her from Charleton. Her champion. Another tear escaped her. "N-no. I'm sorry, but I cannot. I've suffered much to construct a haven here. Please, please do nothing to jeopardize it."

"Only legal action can prevent that," he repeated, and then smiled, his voice softening. "Though I truly believe it best, I'd never force you. You know that, don't you?"

Gentleness with strength. Not sure she could reply without her voice breaking, she merely nodded.

"I'll be back for you, Laura. Soon. With plans to win your freedom so foolproof and irrefutable you shall have to agree to them."

He wouldn't be back, of course. There was no safe haven for her beyond this place—and in any event, once Lord Beaulieu returned to London and the press of his business there, he would soon forget the dowdy, troublesome little nurse who'd dared oppose his authority. During his rare moments of leisure, he'd doubtless have any number of lovely ladies eager to distract him from remembering.

An upsurge of longing swelled in her, and a bitter regret for the closeness they'd almost attained. Swallowing hard, she nodded.

"You are right, my sparrow, I must get some sleep, else I'm likely to fall asleep in the saddle tomorrow. But before I go, would you grant me one favor?"

"If I can."

Slowly, as if to ensure he did not alarm her, the earl reached over to caress her cheek with one knuckle. "Would you take down your hair for me?" he asked. "Let me see the moonlight cast shadows on that lovely auburn hair, as the sun did that first morning in your garden?"

His reverent touch, as if she were a precious object to be handled with awe and respect, melted any remaining caution. When he started to move his hand back, Laura caught it, held his palm against her temple. With her other hand, she stripped off the nightcap, splayed her fingers to comb out the braiding, then shook the tumbling plaits free to cascade over her shoulders, down the back and sides of her worn woolen wrapper.

"Like this?"

Moonlight silvered his sliver of smile. "Like that."

Emboldened, she sought his other hand, brought it up to twine in her rippled locks, arched her neck and bent her head back, thrilling to the feel of his fingers against her scalp, the delicious shivery pull of his hand through her hair.

He caught her chin, steadying her. And bent his head toward hers.

He was going to kiss her, as he had the garden. A rush of memory awakened every sense, and a greedy exultation filled her.

She'd never be the mistress he'd hinted she become, never have days or weeks or months to delight in his company. But perhaps, if she could entice him to it, she might have tonight, just one night in which the coming together of man and woman held all the joy and tenderness that most intimate coupling should contain. A joy she had never yet experienced, and once he left her, likely never would.

Please, her mind whispered like a prayer as she raised her mouth to his. *Give me one perfect night.*

Chapter Fifteen

She opened her mouth to allow him entry. Encouraged by his moan of response, the sudden tightening of the fingers cupping her face, she tentatively moved her tongue to stroke his. She felt his body shudder, and in one swift move he slid his hand from her face to wrap his arm about her shoulders, binding her closer.

Yes, she wanted closer, wanted the plush of his tongue probing, exploring, igniting shivers of sensation that tingled all the way to her toes. She reached up to tangle her fingers in his dark hair, pull him nearer so she might launch her own exploration into the delicious peaks and valleys of his mouth.

The warmth of him heated her despite the barriers of greatcoat and wrapper, but she craved more contact, yearned to feel the bone and muscle of his body against hers. Impatient, she pulled loose her robe, tugged at the buttons of his coat.

With a shuddering gasp he broke away, pushed her back. "Ah, Sparrow, I want you too much. I must leave now, while I still can."

"No!" she cried, catching his hand. "Please…don't go. Not yet."

He went entirely still, turning the full force of his gaze upon her. She stared back, desperate with hope and yearning.

"Are you sure?" he asked. "If I stay, I cannot promise to stop."

"I know," she said. "Please, stay."

For another long moment he studied her. "So be it," he said hoarsely, and kissed her hand.

Trembling at her unaccustomed boldness, she tugged him into motion and led him down the shadowy hall to her small bedchamber.

Through years of marriage she'd endured the invasion of her body, from the painful initiation on her wedding night until the last time Charleton had taken her, barely recovered from childbed. Each time, she'd accepted but never welcomed the forcible joining of a man's flesh to her own. But now she wanted it, wanted the heavy weight of the earl's flanks across her thighs, tautness of his belly against the roundness of her own, her breasts crushed under the muscle of his chest. Something feverish and urgent pulsed within her at the thought of that vital, thrusting part of him buried deep within her. She wanted the sound of his breathing gone crazed and ragged as he approached the peak, his cry of fulfillment as he surmounted it. And she wanted the sweet peace of his head pressed to her bosom as, sated and spent, he collapsed against her.

If she were fortunate, perhaps instead of springing up immediately afterward, he would be content to lie beside her, gifting her with the music of his breathing as it slowed. And if she were exceptionally lucky, perhaps he might doze while she held him close, daring to lightly trace the lines of his body, storing in her memory the contours of the strength and vitality she'd once been privileged to briefly hold to her breast.

While the earl closed the door behind her and deposited the candle on the bedside table, Laura stood, suddenly uncertain. Was the earl ready? Sometimes before the act, Charleton had required her to...stimulate him.

She turned to see the earl regarding her gravely. "Second thoughts?"

"Never."

His eyes lit. Smiling widely, he shed his greatcoat and pulled loose his cravat. "Then come to me, Sparrow."

Pulling off her wrapper as she went, she ran to his arms. He caught her, lifted her, laughing softly. Set her back on her feet and bent his head.

He kissed her gently this time, light, teasing, touches like the brush of rose petals against her lips, her chin, her cheeks. She murmured a protest, wanting more, and he obliged, tracing the outline of her mouth, sucking softly. The blade of his tongue found hers, the clash setting off shudders deep in her belly.

She swayed on her feet and he caught her against him. She shuddered again at the evidence of his readiness, surprisingly large and hard against her belly. Fire sparking at the center of her, instinctively she rubbed herself against it.

He moaned and took the kiss deeper. Panting now, she urged him to the bed, trying with one hand to pull up her night rail while she settled back against the pillows. She parted her legs and drew him toward her, her trembling fingers fumbling with the buttons of his breeches.

He caught her hand and stilled it, then moved her

cupped palm slowly over his rigid length. "S-sweet," he gasped, the sound nearly a groan. Then, to her surprise, he pulled her fingers away and kissed them. "But not yet."

"Not yet?" she echoed, bewildered. "But…are you not—ready?"

"You are not," he said.

"But…I am!" she wailed, fretful with need and mystified at the delay. "D-do you want me to do… something else?"

He chuckled. "Nothing, my sweet sparrow. Just let me look at you."

She stared at him, wondering if they were speaking the same language. "You…are looking at me," she pointed out.

"True," he returned gravely, though his lips twitched as if at some private joke. "But I can't see nearly enough."

"Then light another candle," she said crossly and bit her lip, tears threatening. Was she doing something wrong? Suddenly she felt awkward and unsure. Had her boldness revolted him? Surely he wouldn't— "You're not going to leave?" she blurted.

His smile changed, from amusement to tenderness, and the warmth of his gaze held her motionless. "Never, my sparrow. I'll never leave you."

The words caught her like a blow to the chest. Scarcely able to breathe through the tightness, she'd not have managed a reply even had her brain been functioning well enough to formulate one. All she knew was she wanted to be joined with him, her body a gift offered joyfully, gratefully for his pleasure.

Leaning on one elbow, she reached back for him. But before she could seize his breeches flap, he reached over to grasp her ankle. Puzzled once more, she stilled, watching as he bent low over her leg. And kissed the soft skin at the instep of her foot.

She gasped, the sensation both ticklish and powerfully pleasurable. The vibrations he set off there seemed somehow to directly intensify the prickly, achy tenderness of her breasts, the pulsing fullness between her thighs. Then he lifted her foot and stroked the hot wetness of his tongue across her toes, took the littlest into his mouth and sucked it.

An immediate response rocketed through her. She seemed to lose control of her limbs, felt herself sag back against the pillows, her heartbeat loud and rapid in her ears, as if she'd been chasing Misfit while playing fetch. Seeming oblivious to her disintegrating faculties, the earl made a leisurely progress across her toes, stimulating each in turn, then inching her night rail higher to kiss her ankle, tantalize her shins with his tongue.

By now well beyond the ability of speech, but for her rasping breaths she lay silent, in thrall to his touch. With excruciating, intoxicating slowness he explored the curve of her calves, the dimple beside her kneecap. She rejoiced with incoherent gasps as he moved over her knees to the trembling smoothness of her inner thighs, his caress of that exquisitely sensitive flesh so intense it neared pain.

He halted when she flinched away, chuckled deep in his throat when she seized his neck to urge his mouth back down to her. He slowed his pace still further, letting her accustom herself to the shocking newness of his intimate touch. Some remote part of her mind watched in horrified titillation as the wanton creature who now resided in her body begged with whimpered moans and a clenching of hands for him to continue his deliciously slow progression toward a goal she could hardly yet believe.

When at last he reached there, gently urging her thighs wider so he could caress the outer petals and seek the hidden bud within, she could wait no longer. With an inarticulate cry she pushed him back, jerked free the buttons of his straining breeches. "Now," she begged, desperation giving her voice. "Please."

"Sparrow," he said on a gasp as at last she felt the weight of his bare chest against her. She clutched his sweat-slick shoulders as he fitted himself to her aching passage, and unable to wait a second longer, thrust her hips to carry him within.

So incredibly sweet was the joining, tears sprang to her eyes. But as he began to move in the ancient rhythm she thought she knew so well, the subtle friction immediately and dramatically magnified the throbbing sensations within her. Her skin grew feverish, her fingernails biting into his back as she writhed under him, trying to remain properly passive while her body demanded movement.

"Ah, yes, sweeting," he murmured against her mouth as, helpless to prevent herself, she rocked her hips to mimic his motion. The tautness within her spiraled tighter, tighter, a nearly unbearable torment, tearing a deep moan from her throat. Then suddenly, tension exploded in a brilliant shower of sensation that cascaded through her, a flashflood boiling through every nerve.

For a few moments afterward she lay stunned, barely conscious, barely breathing. Dimly she was aware of Beau rolling her with him to her side, and then she surrendered to the heavy lassitude stealing over her.

Sometime later she struggled back to consciousness,

to find she was still wrapped in the earl's warm embrace. His steady heartbeat vibrated against her chest; his breath warmed her hair. Utter contentment filled her, and once again her eyes stung with tears.

No matter how long or short the life she was destined to live, she would thank heaven for this precious night.

She looked up into his faintly smiling face and the love she'd tried to avoid and ignore caught her full in the throat, strangling her voice. How could she bear to let him walk away?

She cursed the tears that welled up, brushing them away with an impatient hand. She would not spoil the wonder of this night by regretting what could not be.

She wanted to pour out her love, tell him she'd never known such closeness nor tasted such pleasure, that she would treasure these moments the rest of her life. But nothing beyond tonight was possible, and so she swallowed the ardent vows she must not make and searched for something permissible. "How can I thank you?" she whispered at last.

With the gentleness that so captured her heart he rubbed his knuckle against her cheek. "How can I thank you?"

She struggled to lift herself on one elbow. He would leave now, as he must, but resigned though she was to the inevitability of it, still she sought some way to delay.

"Can I get you something? Do anything before you...go?"

"Some wine, if you have it. But, Sparrow—" his voice deepened "—I'm nowhere close to being ready to leave."

The teasing promise in his tone stopped her breath. Surely he couldn't mean...what she thought? Her experience argued against the possibility of any further coupling—but then, everything else tonight had been far beyond any previous experience. At the mere hint of it, nerves she'd thought too exhausted to function were beginning to stir and spark. "I'll g-get you wine," she said hurriedly.

"Wait a moment," he said, catching her hand as she reached for her wrapper. "Let me look at you."

She'd never been naked in front of a man before. But as he held her at arm's length, his ardent plea echoing in her ears, her self-consciousness faded. She nodded, dropped the wrapper, and stood fully unveiled before him.

Slowly he examined her, from her bare toes up her calves, her thighs, across her belly to taut, tight peaks of her breasts, her shoulders, her neck, her chin, cheeks, hair. "You are so lovely, Sparrow," he murmured. "Now, wine please, and hurry before you catch a chill."

Any tendency to chill evaporated as, before he released her hand, he leaned forward to capture one erect nipple and tease it with his teeth. She gasped, delight at this new sensation coursing through her, and grabbed his shoulder to steady herself.

With leisurely slowness he moved his mouth to tantalize the aching peak of her other breast. She was melting, nearly boneless when he at last stopped.

"Wine," he said, skimming his hand over her belly to touch the tight curls beneath. "We've not much time, and there's so much more—" he moved his finger to stroke within the warm folds "—to experience."

Somehow she managed to totter to the kitchen and bring back wine without spilling it all over. He greeted her with a kiss, pulled her close under the bedclothes to warm her, and fed her wine. And then, after they'd sipped, and talked, the earl proceeded to demonstrate just how ignorant this long-married wife had been.

He taught her, a voraciously greedy and willing pupil, how he could set off the same incredible explosion with his fingers, his tongue. How she could ready him again for joining with the urging of her hips, the goad of her mouth. Through the swift and shimmering hours of that short, matchless night he showed her how pleasure could be stimulated and conveyed, rapture a current flowing from him to her, from her to him, until it swept them together over the precipice in a timeless, sense-stunning cascade to completion.

Sometime in the quiet dimness near dawn Laura woke to find him still beside her. Joy that he had not crept away while she slept swelled in her, and she leaned up to kiss his cheek.

"Sparrow," he murmured, angling his head to take her kiss on his lips as he pulled her into a rib-bruising embrace.

She clung to him, knowing the time to delay had passed. "You must go now," she said when at last he released her.

"Yes. I'd best get back to Everett Hall before first light, lest I encounter some farm boy on the way to market who might carry tales. I'll be off for London an hour or so after." He paused, looking down at her. "Let me stop here for you on my way."

Quit Merriville. Part of her yearned to silence her mind's automatic clamor about the danger, respond only to the leap of gladness that urged her to go with him. But once again, fear and caution won out.

"I cannot. Please, I'm sorry, but—"

He stopped her apology with another kiss. "I know,

Sparrow. Though I leave you here alone under protest, I'll not take you with me by force. But when I return— and I will return, soon—you *will* agree to depart with me."

She said nothing, the bittersweet agony of his impending loss thickening her throat and preventing reply. While he dressed she threw on her wrapper and poured him more wine, then walked with him to the porch door.

He bent to kiss her, then lifted her into his arms and hugged her close. "Keep yourself safe, Sparrow. And dream of me until I return."

"I will," she said as he set her back on her feet. *The whole of my life,* she added silently.

Heart already aching, she watched him mount his horse, and with a final wave, ride off into the waning night.

After an exhausting journey that finally saw him installed back in London several days later, Beau sat at the desk in his study, reviewing the latest evidence in the embezzlement investigation. All the reports confirmed his suspicions. Now he must anticipate the perpetrator's mood and movements in order to construct the most foolproof trap to bring him down.

Sighing, he put the dossiers aside. Having done all he could at the moment to move the case forward, he might now turn his attention to the personal concern that had haunted him all through his long voyage south.

Though Laura seemed to feel she was safe in Merriville, every instinct had rebelled at leaving her there alone and unprotected. And he'd been bitterly disappointed that he'd not succeeded in winning her confidence. Though she'd confirmed the basic facts after he guessed them, she'd not let slip the smallest detail that would make the search for her real name—and thus the path to protecting her—easier or swifter.

That placed him at a disadvantage, but not an insurmountable one. After all, there were but a limited number of men wealthy and influential enough to necessitate a fugitive wife's going into hiding. Amassing a list of potential names and checking them would be a tedious process, but he would have it done. Armed with all the possibilities, he had every confidence he would eventually deduce the identity of the man he sought.

But how much time would that require?

He begrudged every day he would have to wait while the necessary information was assembled. Each one he spent apart from her heightened the urgency of his desire to claim her, tightened the spiral of anxiety about her safety. Grimly he vowed that he'd give the search no more than a month. Regardless of whether the investigation was complete by then or not, he would return for her.

Now to set the search in motion. He rang a bell to summon his secretary.

The slender, sandy-haired man entered, smiling in welcome. "My lord, good to see you back! I trust this means Kit is recovering?"

"Good to be back, James, and yes, Kit is doing much better. Thank you for doing your usual excellent job to keep the dispatches coming. I believe I've perused all the latest. I see our sailor songbird is still chirping."

The young man smiled grimly. "It appears he participated in bringing in several more cargoes on which the duty charged on the manifests exceeded the legal amounts owed, the excess being siphoned off into coffers other than those of the government. As you will have read, by covertly following the boasting sailor we've been able to definitely establish three other links in the chain. I assume, as usual, you intend to leave apprehension of the lower-level miscreants to other authorities?''

Beau nodded. He seldom concerned himself with apprehending petty criminals like the corrupt sailor. Instead, he felt it his special calling to track and eventually bring down their leaders. That men of birth and privilege who should consider it their duty to serve the nation should betray that trust inspired in him a loathing as deep as it was visceral.

''The evidence thus far does seem to point to Lord Wolverton as head of the operation,'' his secretary continued. ''Did your observations of him in the north support that conclusion?''

''Yes—the bastard.'' Beau sighed. ''Another page in the all-too-familiar story of a younger son outspending his means by indulging a weakness for gaming, women or vice. Though in my noble Lord Wolverton's case, it seems to be a combination of all three.'' With a grimace, he shook a finger at the secretary. ''Promise me, James, if you ever develop such proclivities, you'll come to me before doing something stupid.''

''So you can straighten out my warped thinking with a well-placed left hook?'' His secretary gave a slight smile. ''Surely you know, after what happened to my father, I'd be the last man on earth to—''

''I know, James,'' Beau interrupted. ''An attempt at levity to relieve my disgust at the pathetic circumstances.''

''I'm afraid I can't find any humor in it,'' the young man replied, bitterness in his tone. ''Not when my father's reputation was nearly destroyed by the false ac-

cusations of such a man. If not for you, he would have
been disgraced—"

"None of that now." Beau waved his secretary to
silence. "I suppose I'm indebted to the villain. Had
your father's predicament not outraged me into vowing
to uncover the identity of the real traitor, I might still
be naught but an idle dandy playing at puzzles."

"As if you were ever such!" his secretary scoffed.
"I'm just glad your intervention in my father's case
brought you to Lord Riverton's notice, and that his lordship succeeded in persuading you to continue the work.
And as always, I'm honored that you trust me to con-
tribute my small part. Speaking of which, what would
you have me do now?"

Beau hesitated. "I need to investigate another matter.
A personal and highly delicate one involving a lady,
which must of course be conducted in strictest se-
crecy."

"I hope you know you can rely on my discretion."

"That I do not doubt. However, since I'm determined
to tap my usual network in pursuit of wholly private
concern, a somewhat…irregular practice, I admit, you
may not feel comfortable being part of it. If you choose
not to become involved, I will not hold it against you."

"My lord," the secretary replied, "since it is you
who fund that network, I cannot see that there would
be any impropriety in your using it however you see fit.
And even if there were, after all you have done for my
family, I'm hardly likely to question any contrivance of
yours. Now, what should you like me to do?"

Beau smiled, gratified by the young man's loyalty.
"I need you to compile me a list of gentlemen who
have, ah, 'lost' a wife sometime in the past two years.
The woman will probably have been reported dead, al-

though it might be claimed she is tending distant relatives or off on a lengthy journey of some sort. She might even have been declared insane. The lady would be of good family and should have been about three-and-twenty at the time of her...departure.''

Beau had the dubious pleasure of knowing he'd confounded his normally unflappable secretary. After staring a moment, with commendable discretion, James managed to swallow the curiosity he obviously felt. ''Very well, my lord. How soon do you require the completed list?''

''As soon as possible. It's a matter of considerable urgency.'' Beau gazed out the window, seeing again Laura Martin's small form hunched before him, fragile arms and puny fists braced against a blow. Anxiety twisted in his chest. He must persuade her out of Merriville, and soon.

He turned back to his secretary. ''As you may have surmised, the husband in this case has violent proclivities. Try to determine if any of the prospects are rumored to be abusive. And, James...   ''

''My lord?''

''Your help in uncovering this shall more than repay any service I may ever have done your family.''

His secretary hesitated. ''The...lady is that important to you.''

''Yes.''

James Maxwell bowed. ''Then I shall begin the search immediately.''

A month later Laura Martin deposited her newly harvested herbs on the garden bench and wearily sat beside them, shivering in the tepid warmth of the fading late-afternoon sun.

Full winter would be upon them soon, with its inevitable complement of snow, sleet and drenching rain that would render the roads snow-drifted, iced over or deep in mire for indefinite periods until next spring's thaw.

That irrefutable fact made her shiver with a chill that had nothing to do with the wind blowing over her chafed hands. For with her woman's courses two weeks overdue, she had to face the frightening possibility that she might be with child.

Unfortunately, there was no way to know for certain—not until the child quickened, by which time the evidence of her indiscretion would be only too apparent to the entire county. But she'd never missed her time before, unless she was increasing. As she'd learned during her years of marriage, her cycles were most regular. Indeed, as a new bride, she'd counted the days, wanting to please her husband by offering him the possibility of the son he so desperately craved. But all too soon, she'd come to regard the advancing end of each cycle with dread, knowing the evidence that she'd not conceived would send Charlton into a fit of violent temper. At first, he'd been only verbally abusive, vilifying her as graceless failure of a woman, a disgrace to her normally prolific family he would never had deigned to marry had he known she was barren. Later her mouth would dry with fear, knowing the best she could hope for would be a slap across the face. Twice he'd beaten her so severely that she'd required the whole of the next month to recover.

Twice she'd conceived, a short-term protection from his aggression. She closed her eyes on a shudder. Even now, she could not bear to remember the terrible outcome of those pregnancies.

Once she'd watched the stable boys with a mouse they'd found in a grain bin. They'd teased it with a stick, pushing it this way and that, while the small creature, hemmed in between the probing stick and the tall straight walls of the bin, ran frantically this way and that.

She knew now what that mouse must have felt.

"Your character will be impugned and your standing in the neighborhood will suffer," she recalled the vicar warning. Simple speculation could cause that much harm. But to bear a fatherless child nine months after the earl's departure? She'd have no reputation left—and no livelihood, either.

How to preserve both? Swiftly she ruled out both accepting the vicar's offer and remaining in Merriville. She wouldn't serve Reverend Blackthorne such a turn, even if such a marriage would be legal, and to face down her neighbor's scorn would simply condemn herself and the child to slow starvation. No, if time confirmed that she was with child, she mustn't remain here.

Instinctively her hands slipped down to cradle her still-flat belly. Despite the risk, despite the fear that uncoiled thick in her veins at the mere thought of relocating, she couldn't regret that night. Nor could she regret the child who might have been conceived from it. A child to cherish and protect, tangible reminder that a love encompassing heart and body was not a fanciful imagining, but for one wondrous night, had truly been hers.

A child to protect as she'd failed to protect Jennie. That stark thought instantly refocused her thoughts.

For time was critical. If she wished to preserve her reputation—and the possibility of returning to her livelihood in Merriville—she'd have to leave before her condition became apparent. And if she wished to be assured of getting away, she'd best depart before full winter and the possibility of ice or blizzards that might strand her here for weeks.

Too agitated now to sit, she jumped up to pace the length of the porch. Inventing a plausible pretext to depart was no problem; as a healer, she could always say she'd been called away to assist some distant relative. But where to go?

A flurry of pacing merely confirmed the stark truth. When she'd made the decision to come here, she'd deliberately broken all ties to her former life, to family, friends and any acquaintances who might have come to her aid. Only one individual remained who knew her true identity, and she was the one link by which Charleton might yet trace Laura.

Her former governess, Miss Hollins, whose sister ''Aunt Mary'' had secretly conveyed back to Merriville a battered, dying runaway wife. Having initially come to Miss Hollins's home to tend a young governess, incapacitated by influenza at the local inn while journeying to her new post, Aunt Mary arrived to find at her sister's cottage both that unfortunate—and Laura. After the poor woman died, the two sisters had buried her in a grave bearing Laura's name. If Charleton retained any suspicions about the identity of the remains beneath the simple granite marker he'd been shown when he finally tracked Laura to Miss Hollins's cottage three months later, he'd still be watching that house—and Miss Hollins.

Another five minutes of pacing left her with the same worrying conclusion. She simply didn't have funds enough to support herself unassisted in some faraway community for nearly a year. If she were going to relocate for a time, she must have some assistance. Miss Hollins was the only person she could both trust with the truth and ask for help. She would have to risk contacting her again.

She hugged herself, fighting the bitterly familiar spiral of fear that clogged her veins and tightened her stomach. *I will protect us, Jennie,* she vowed.

There is one other option, a small voice argued. *You could seek out the earl.*

The thought brought back the image of his face, the echo of his voice, the dearly remembered touch of his gentle fingers. Longing rippled through her. Ah, how good it would be to make her way to London, to relax her constant vigil in the comforting warmth of his powerful presence, to cast this dilemma into his capable hands!

She smiled wryly. Given the circumstances, at least he'd know she wasn't trying to trick him into marriage.

The smile faded. But as she'd told him that night, powerful as he was, he was not above the law. If she risked going to London and Charleton discovered her, Lord Beaulieu could not prevent her husband from seizing her.

An even bleaker realization dawned, so awful the lingering desire to run to his lordship evaporated on the instant. As she was still legally Charlton's wife, any child she bore was also his. Were Charleton to find her, he could claim the child. Their child. Beau's son.

And he would do it, finding the act a fitting revenge. No, she resolved, let her flee to the ends of England, but should she be discovered, let Charleton believe the child she carried the by-blow of some farmer or curate, not worthy of being claimed as his own. Let him never discover the babe's true father.

Her resolve established, the fear retreated to a grim, ever-present shadow. She'd spread word of her intended departure to the squire and several of the neighborhood ladies. Briefly she considered sending a note to Lady Elspeth, who'd borne her much-recovered brother back home with her the previous week, and swiftly decided against it. The fewer who had definite knowledge of her plans, the better. She'd not even send a note ahead to warn Miss Hollins.

Misfit rubbed against her hand, whining for attention. Absently she leaned down to scratch his head, already aching with regret to leave behind the peace of her cottage, her garden, the kind solicitude of the squire and the families of their small neighborhood. Resolutely she put aside the grief, focusing her mind on beginning the necessary planning. She would leave within the week.

She couldn't risk even the smallest possibility that Charleton might get his hands on Beau's child.

Chapter Sixteen

A few days later Beau sat at the desk in his study, reviewing the nearly completed dossier on Lord Wolverton. Over the past three weeks the investigation had picked up speed, all the meticulous details painstakingly gathered by his operatives finally coming together to create a clear picture of the embezzler's web. Once Beau received the last overseas reports for which he still waited, he'd have sufficient evidence to present the dossier to Lord Riverton.

Normally by this point he'd be experiencing the deep satisfaction of another puzzle solved, tempered by the sadness of confirming once again human nature's frailty. But he'd had to exert all his self-control to keep his mind focused on business. For his private investigation of Laura Martin had not proceeded nearly as well.

Initially he'd expected to uncover her identity so he might return to Merriville before Ellie transported the recovering Kit from Everett Hall. But once his lungs cleared, Kit had improved more quickly than anticipated, a fact of which Beau could only be glad, and Ellie decided to move her brother the shorter distance to her country estate rather than trespass upon Squire Everett's hospitality until Kit was fit enough for the longer journey to London.

Beau could not now cloak a visit to Mrs. Martin under the guise of checking on his brother. To journey to Merriville and call on her without such a socially acceptable excuse would be so glaringly remarkable as to immediately give rise to precisely the sort of speculation and possible censure the vicar had warned about. Beau dared not approach her now until he had all the facts necessary to persuade her immediate removal. And those facts had not yet fallen into place.

Was she still safe? She'd been so ten days ago, for the message Ellie had written him when she'd arrived home at Wentworth Hall pointedly mentioned they'd left Mrs. Martin with their warmest thanks and a promise to meet again *soon*—his sister had underlined the word.

With more fervency than his manipulating sister could have dreamed, Beau wished to meet Laura Martin again *soon*. The month since he'd last seen her seemed an eternity. He would never have imagined that in the brief few weeks they'd spent together she would have so infiltrated his heart and mind that being away from her would create this raw sense of loss.

He missed the subtle loveliness of her presence, even garbed in hideous brown gowns, her low-pitched voice expressing some pithy comment or shimmering with humor as she joked with Kit. He missed the soft rose scent of her perfume, the polished mahogany sheen of the curls that escaped those ridiculous dowager caps. He craved the sight of her inquisitive eyes and angled chin as she gazed up at him with that endearing sparrow look.

Knowing he'd otherwise go mad with frustration and fury, he cut himself off from remembering any detail of their last night together, when she'd given herself to him with such innocent eagerness, proving to his amazement that a woman who'd borne a child could still be so heartbreakingly ignorant in the ways of pleasure. And yet he'd been fiercely glad that he was undoubtedly the first to unlock its secrets for her, exulting to know that special bond was theirs, theirs alone.

Though he might by supreme act of will block out the memories, he could not filter from his blood the sharp edge of need she'd created in him. In a curious way, the sense of her with him, in him was nearly as acute now, when hundreds of miles separated them, as it had been across the narrow space of her bed.

Each day that passed without bringing him the information he needed to claim her intensified both his impatience and his urgency, destroying his sleep, shortening his temper such that increasingly he found himself biting back the first, acid comment that came to his lips.

In fact, he realized with mild chagrin, given the lowered voices and apprehensive looks his household staff had treated him to for the past week, he must have been less successful in stifling such comments than he'd thought. A knock at the study door interrupted his resolve to do better.

His secretary entered, a sheaf of papers in his outstretched hands. "The reports from the West Indies and Bombay for which you'd been waiting, my lord."

"Thank you, James, and be seated, if you please." Indicating the armchair in front of his desk, Beau quickly perused the documents.

"We have in our possession the ledgers listing bills

of lading as they were filed upon the ships' landing in London?'' Beau asked after a moment.

''Yes, my lord, and as you expected, the cargo amounts on the bills of lading from the ships' port of origin are less than those in the landing ledger by several hundred pounds per commodity. They do match exactly the amounts in the ledgers actually forwarded to the customs office. But do we have any positive proof Lord Wolverton was involved?''

''Nothing that would stand in a court of law. Fortunately we don't need to prove a case, and in any event, the government prefers not to have such messy affairs dragged into the public forum.''

''But if the payoffs were made in cash, such that his involvement cannot be proven, how can you force his resignation?''

''By applying the weight of some telling, if circumstantial, evidence. We know he's been sustaining heavy gambling losses for years, got himself entangled with the cent-per-centers. Suddenly he paid off the loans, even though we've ascertained that his estates generated no more income. Threatened with transportation or the noose, I don't doubt the couriers who carried him the purloined funds will be only too happy to confirm whatever details we wish. Once Lord Riverton acquaints Wolverton with the evidence, I expect he will see the wisdom of resigning quietly.''

James frowned. ''It seems somehow unfair that the others will go to the dock while Lord Wolverton escapes prosecution.''

Beau shrugged. ''The ton knows how these things work. To be stripped of his office and his income will ruin him as effectively as imprisonment. And the corruption will stop, which is perhaps the most important point.''

''When will you present the information to Lord Riverton?''

''He's out of London at present. When he returns.''

''Will you continue to observe Lord Wolverton?''

Beau smiled grimly. ''I've half a mind to invite him to the Puzzlebreaker's Club, then propose to the membership that we unravel an embezzlement scheme such as he's been running, just for the pleasure of watching him squirm. But Lord Riverton prefers I keep my involvement in these investigations covert.'' He sighed. ''Usually the personal satisfaction of decoding the mystery is more than enough compensation. Now, have you any more information on the...other matter?''

Without doubt James knew full well why the solution of this present case had engendered in Beau so little enthusiasm. With commendable tact, he'd refrained from commenting on the shadowed eyes and grim weariness his employer had worn this past week like a cloak.

''As you requested, I've gone back and rechecked the records of all the nobility and gentry.'' His secretary gave him a wry smile. ''Who could have guessed there would be so many dead or absent wives among them the past two years? I'm still awaiting confirmation that Lady Worth did indeed depart with her father on a trip to collect data on indigenous peoples of the East Indies, and that Mrs. Dominick is truly visiting her cousin in Italy, but those two are the last. The other missing wives have turned up and the deaths of all the dearly departed have been confirmed by family members not directly related to the husband.'' He eyes Beau with concern.

"I'm sorry, my lord. Shall I begin to check among the wealthy merchant class?"

It couldn't be. He must have missed some clue, somewhere. Beau clenched his hands, tightened his jaw to prevent the raging frustration from escaping in some violent profanity. James was doing everything he could; Beau would not vent his anger on his hapless secretary.

"Oh, I did collect one memento," James said into the tense silence. "That epidemic of influenza two winters ago claimed the lives of several wives on my list. Thought I'd get out and do a bit of sleuthing on my own—"

"I've been that difficult to work with?" Beau interrupted with an attempt at a smile.

After raising a suggestive eyebrow, James continued, "Since several of the families are in London for the Season, I decided to call on them." He held up a hand to forestall Beau's protest. "In quite an unexceptional manner. Told them the government was collecting information on the influenza outbreak for a report."

"A sort of updated Doomsday Book?"

James grinned. "Something like."

Beau sighed, amused despite himself. "James, I begin to worry about you."

"At any rate, the deaths were confirmed unconditionally. Including that of the lady whose husband was previously my prime suspect—a thoroughly nasty individual whom reports suggest may have been capable of violence. However, in the interests of furthering research, the lady's father, a rather scholarly gentleman, lent me a miniature of his daughter. I thought perhaps you'd like to see it."

You're quite a scholar. No, but my father was. As the words echoed out of memory, Beau's heart skipped a beat and his mouth went dry. With a hand that suddenly trembled he reached for the small oval portrait his secretary was extracting from his waistcoat pocket.

"Apparently Lady Charleton contracted the influenza before she'd fully recovered from losing a babe in childbirth…"

The rest of his secretary's sentence faded out as Beau brought the figured gold case close enough to distinguish the features of the shyly smiling lady portrayed within. A young lady with Laura Martin's glossy auburn locks, Laura Martin's piercingly blue eyes.

For an instant he couldn't draw breath. He shut his eyes tightly, clutching the portrait in his fist, nearly dizzy as relief, euphoria and aching need rocked him in successive waves.

He opened his eyes to find James staring at him. "That…is the lady?"

"Yes. Find me everything you turn up on Lady Charleton's death, everything you can uncover about her husband. Send operatives to both families, if they're now in London—use as many men as you need. And report back to me at three o'clock with whatever you've found."

"Yes, my lord."

"And, James—"

His secretary, already at the door, halted to look back at him. "My lord?"

"Thank you."

Later that afternoon Beau returned to his study. In the intervening hours he'd conducted some research of his own. He knew little of Lord Charleton personally, the viscount being more than a decade his senior, but casual inquiries at his club elicited several intriguing tidbits.

Lord Charleton was regarded with respect but not warmth by his contemporaries. Accounted a good shot, a fair sportsman, a punctilious landlord ruthlessly precise in his duties, he drove a hard bargain in any transaction. A cold, proud man obsessed with his lineage, after being twice widowed he still had no heir, his first wife having produced only daughters and his second, the youngest child of Lord Arthur Farrington, having died two years ago of influenza after complications from a stillbirth.

In three days' time Charleton was to marry again, a Miss Cynthia Powell, daughter of ancient Devon gentry.

Soon I'll be safe, Laura had told him. And so, in a certain sense, her husband's remarriage would make her.

That his Laura Martin was the supposedly dead Lady Charleton he had no doubt—the evidence of the miniature was too compelling. And the few details he'd yet gleaned of Lady Charleton fit what he knew of Laura Martin's arrival in Merriville.

She had been gravely ill. She'd lost a babe. Whether Charleton had invented the notion of her death to derail speculation about her disappearance or whether Laura herself had somehow engineered it, Beau would soon uncover. Now that he had her name, the rest would be easy.

A thoroughly nasty individual, James had described Laura's husband. Did Charleton in fact believe her dead? Or was he still watching, waiting, as Laura believed?

Regardless of what further information would reveal, one indisputable fact had seized Beau the moment he learned her husband was about to remarry. If Charleton did not discover Laura's whereabouts until after his remarriage, he could then neither claim her nor reveal her true identity, lest he leave himself open to charges of bigamy. Though to Beau's thinking, Laura would still not be absolutely safe—Charleton would be secure from scandal only if his inconvenient former wife were truly dead.

But more than her lack of security bothered him. If Charleton's remarriage prevented the viscount from revealing the past, it also prevented Laura's escaping it. She might come to Beau as they both desired, but she'd have to remain in the shadows, unable to use her real name or assume her rightful place in society. Have to remain permanently hidden, too, from the still-grieving family that believed her dead. And most important from Beau's point of view, she'd never be able to become what he most wanted her to be—his lawful wife.

One way or another, he had to stop Lord Charleton's remarriage. One way or another, he had to convince the man to seek a divorce before remarrying.

And he had three days in which to do it.

A burning desire consumed him to order his horse this moment, to ride to Merriville with all speed. Beyond the ever-present compulsion to be with Laura again, it would be wisest to have benefit of all she knew of this tangled affair before Beau confronted her husband. But given the distance, it was impossible for him to ride there and back in only three days.

He paced the room, too restless to sit, impatient to hear whatever news James had garnered. And then, information complete or not, within the next day he must proceed. Without whatever assistance Laura Martin might have been able to offer.

Beau thought again of Laura's slight form cowering before him, her eyes distended with fear, her fisted arms raised, and the smoldering rage within fired hotter. He already knew enough of Charleton to know the man must be legally and permanently removed from Laura's life. His fists itched to deal out to the viscount a liberal measure of the sort of domestic bliss he'd offered Laura.

While he stood at the window, envisioning with grim pleasure that satisfying prospect, a knock sounded, followed by the immediate entry of James Maxwell.

The mantel clock chimed three. "Bless you, James," Beau offering a wry smile as he moved to the sideboard. "Let me pour some wine, then tell me the whole."

At just before three the following afternoon, Beau stood in the parlor of Viscount Charleton's imposing Georgian town house. As he paced the gray marble floor, awaiting his host, he surveyed the tasteful arrangement of green brocade Hepplewhite chairs and sofas, the immaculate white plaster detailing of the ceilings and overmantel that proclaimed the room the workmanship of the Adams brothers, and tried to imagine Laura here, greeting her guests in this cold, impersonal mausoleum of a room.

A few moments later Lord Charleton entered. Every nerve stiffening in automatic dislike, Beau made him the bow decorum demanded.

Charleton, a portly gentleman of middle age, barely inclined his head. Without any of the usual civilities, he demanded, "You insisted on seeing me, Lord Beaulieu? I trust the matter is of sufficient gravity. I am expected momentarily to drive my betrothed to tea."

Already simmering from the deliberate insult of not being offered so much as a chair, Beau remained silent, allowing himself a long moment to inspect the viscount, from his silvered hair to his immaculately polished top-boots. The man's face was a pasty hue that contrasted unpleasantly with the dark shadows beneath his glaring eyes. One vein pulsed at his temple, and he tapped his fingers against the smooth seam of his breeches.

As Beau allowed the silence to continue, a flush of irritation reddened the unhealthy pallor of the viscount's cheeks. *So you are easily angered,* Beau thought. *Good. Anger often makes men careless.*

"You mock me, sirrah? I shall have my servant throw you out." He turned as if to go to the bellpull.

"Not quite yet," Beau interposed, holding out a hand to block the viscount's path. Charleton stared down at it, his red color deepening.

Slowly, Beau pulled back his hand. "I understand I should congratulate you on your imminent nuptials. A happy event which will soon blot out the tragedy of your late wife's premature demise."

"You delayed my departure to tell me that? I thank you for your good wishes, but you might just as easily have sent a note. And now I bid you good day."

"I was also somewhat curious, I admit, about the circumstances of your late wife's death. Influenza following hard upon childbed, wasn't it?"

"Yes. Tragic. She was a dear young thing, my poor Emily. Now, if you will excuse me—"

"Emily Marie Laura Trent, she was, yes? Curious though, that although the child's birth took place at your country estate at Charleton's Grove, your wife was buried nearly a hundred miles away, in Mernton Manner."

The viscount waved an impatient hand. "Still distraught over the child's death, she begged to visit her old governess and I hadn't the heart to deny her. She took sick there, and by the time I arrived—'' he uttered a deep sigh ''—it was too late. My poor dear Emily was already two weeks buried.''

The speech sounded so carefully practiced, Beau had trouble hanging on to his own temper. ''Two weeks to journey a mere hundred miles to the side of your beloved and desperately ill wife? That seems a trifle… tardy.''

The viscount gave him a frosty glance. ''As it was—''

''As it was, you weren't in Charleton's Grove when your wife left your house—but in London. And once your staff notified you of her disappearance, it took you another ten days to track your 'poor dear Emily' to Mernton Manner, which is why you arrived after her tragic demise.''

The vein at Charleton's temple pulsed faster. ''I hardly see how my personal affairs are any concern of yours, Lord Beaulieu. So if you would leave my house—''

''Just one more thing, my lord, and I'll go.'' Beau braced himself to pose the crucial query. ''Lord Charleton, are you sure the woman buried at Mernton Manner is in fact your wife Emily?''

Surprise that could not be feigned swept over the viscount's features. ''What are you suggesting?''

Beau held up the miniature James had obtained. ''Is this a portrait of your late wife?''

Charleton glanced at it quickly. ''And if it is?''

''Then I must inform you, Lord Charleton, that your wife is very much alive.''

Chapter Seventeen

Charleton stared at him. "You must be out of your mind. My wife died two years ago at Mernton. Her governess, Miss Hollins, swore to me it was so."

Beau smiled thinly. So Laura had devised the ruse, with the help of her friends. "I'm sure she did. To protect the woman she knew you'd abused throughout the whole of your marriage. A woman who still lives, Charleton."

"How do you know this?"

"Because I've seen and talked with the woman in this portrait, barely a month ago. A very retiring, very private woman who lives alone and carefully avoids public notice. A woman hiding from a past—and a man."

The viscount stood absolutely still, his eyes locked on Beau's unflinching gaze, as if trying to read there the veracity of his claim. It seemed after a moment Beau convinced him, for the pale skin mottled with rage.

"So she lives, that pathetic excuse for a wife? And has hidden herself from her obligations to her lawful lord for two whole years? I'd not have thought the quivering coward capable of so successful a deceit."

Gritting his teeth, Beau held himself rigid, resisting the demand steaming through his blood to mill Charleton down here and now. While he struggled to keep himself under control, the viscount took a few agitated steps, then whirled to face Beau.

"And your interest in this matter? Ah, of course, now I see it! You must be the little slut's lover! I should have taken a thicker strap to her years—"

Unable to stomach more, Beau grabbed the viscount by the neckcloth, effectively choking off any further speech. "Say one more disparaging word about your *'dear* departed wife' and I swear it's your funeral, not your wedding, the journals will announce." He released the neckcloth and pushed the man back. "Since your previous comments have rendered unnecessary any further testaments of inconsolable grief, let us dispense with pretense. You care nothing for the former Lady Charleton, and indeed are on the point of replacing her. You could, of course, choose not to believe me and proceed. However, should events prove me to be correct, taking a new bride whilst still in possession of another legal wife might later prove rather… embarrassing."

Only then did the implications of Laura's existence seem to penetrate. The viscount turned white, then redder than before, a froth of foam developing at his mouth as his eyes bugged out and his hands and body shook with rage. For a moment Beau feared the man might succumb to an apoplexy right before him.

"A…disconcerting turn of events, I will agree," Beau interposed before the livid viscount could spew more venom. "Which is why I recommend that you take the prudent course of divorcing your current wife before claiming another."

Again, Beau seemed to have surprised Charleton. He inhaled sharply, pulling himself up to full height. "Divorce? Impossible! There's never been such a stain on my family honor!"

"A tad less of a stain than bigamy," Beau pointed out. "And I'll be happy to provide the grounds. You may accuse me of criminal consort. I shall take full responsibility before the lords, so there will be no trouble getting a bill passed. Indeed, my friends in the upper chamber will insure the process is as speedy and private as possible. Perhaps your current intended could be induced to wait until the bill is finalized, though I fear the natural speculation surrounding so unusual a case may cause an abrupt cooling in that lady's sentiments. In that instance, you have my profoundest regrets."

He made the viscount a mocking bow. "I realize this comes as a shock. I shall invite myself to a chair while you think it over, after which I am sure you will realize there is but one viable course. Once you've given me your word as a *gentleman*—" Beau nearly choked over the word "—that you will meet with your lawyers to begin drawing up a bill of divorcement, I will bid you good day."

The viscount's eyes narrowed to slits. Clenching his hands into fists, he took a step toward Beau.

Come on, Beau urged silently, nearly bursting with eagerness to get his fists around the older man's throat. But then, conscience forced him to warn off an opponent whose age and condition made him no match for Beau. "Don't tempt me, Charleton," he breathed.

Doubtless the villain preferred victims who couldn't fight back, Beau thought, disgusted, as with a flash of fear in his eyes, the viscount backed away. Charleton staggered to a sofa and dropped onto the seat, panting, then extracted a handkerchief from his waistcoat pocket and mopped his brow with trembling hands.

The actions looked somehow calculated, Beau thought. Playing for time? After giving the man a few more minutes to compose himself, Beau repeated his demand.

"A quiet divorce, my lord. You'll give me your word."

Charleton mopped his brow again. "I—I cannot reply now. Be reasonable, Beaulieu! I've just sustained a shock, a terrible shock! I cannot be so sure what the best course of action might be."

"Surely the best course cannot be to either blunder into bigamy or to watch yourself made a laughingstock when your supposedly dead wife turns up. Proceed immediately, and I will endeavor that the entire matter be kept out of the journals and conducted with as much discretion as the subject will allow. Fight me on this…and I might be forced to make public matters even more damaging to your esteem."

The mopping handkerchief stilled. His nervous prostration vanishing, Charleton whipped a hard gaze to Beau. "What are you insinuating, Beaulieu?"

"Tragic to have lost both wife and child. But the babe wasn't stillborn, as the papers reported, was she?"

"N-no, not precisely. She was young enough, poor tot. A fever, such as infants are so prone to contract. Given the…distress I was suffering at the time, you can hardly fault me for not troubling to correct the journal accounts."

"Your memory of the events does appear a trifle hazy, Charleton. Let me refresh it. The child didn't die of a fever, either—the nurse tending her reported the child was well and thriving. Until the morning two weeks after her birth when you entered your wife's chamber, shouting that you would take the worthless daughter she'd produced and have the brat fostered out. While you beat the nurse away from the cradle and dragged her out of the room, Lady Charleton struggled from bed to try to protect her child. When the maid crept back after your departure, she found the babe dead in her bed and your wife unconscious on the floor.''

For a telling instant, the viscount stared at him in silence. "I'll listen to no more scurrilous innuendo. You will leave my house this instant, or I shall have you forcibly ejected.''

Beau nodded. "I shall leave readily enough, as soon as you give me your promise to start divorce proceedings. Quick and private, or long and...untidy. But either way, a divorce. Which course do you choose?''

"I cannot answer that now, today! I—I must consult my lawyers, decide what is best. And the shock to the delicate nerves of my dear betrothed! As a *gentleman*—'' Charleton sneered ''—though I have a difficult time applying that description to a man who has assisted in hiding a wife from her lawful husband—you must allow me more time.''

"As a husband who repeatedly violated his vow to cherish and protect, you've even less right to it,'' Beau snapped back. "I'll have your word.''

"I cannot and will not give it! You may sit in my parlor until midnight, but I'll tell you nothing today.''

Beau studied the viscount's face, beating back anger, impatience and disgust to make a dispassionate assessment. His observation forced him to reluctantly conclude that he would not be able to wrest an agreement out of the man today.

So be it then.

He gave Charleton the briefest of bows. "I'll return tomorrow. I'm sure by then your counselors will have convinced you a swift and private divorce is preferable. For make no mistake, if you still refuse to cooperate, I will initiate legal proceedings against you in the matter of your daughter's death. I expect the notoriety of a trial for infanticide would be even more damaging to your betrothed's delicate nerves."

Charleton made no reply. Beau turned and walked out, his satisfaction soured by an edgy unease.

He'd gotten part of what he needed—a confirmation of Laura's identity and the initiation of the demand for a divorce. If by tomorrow the viscount still refused to take the necessary action, Beau would set his lawyers in motion.

As Beau had assured Charleton, having long ago accepted that a divorce, with all its potentially scandalous repercussions, was the only way to make Laura legally his, he truly did not care whether doing whatever it took to free her was discreet or the subject of ribald conjecture in every scandal sheet in the metropolis. His elder sister was well established, protected from harm by the influence of her husband's family even should the proceedings render Beau himself a social outcast, as well it might. Kit was young enough that the worst of the scandal would have died away before he was ready to marry. In any event, Beau thought cynically, the possession of a handsome fortune tended to erase any lingering blots on a prospective suitor's escutcheon.

It might—or might not—render him worthless for Lord Riverton's purposes—that would be for his lordship to decide. But even if taking this step ended his clandestine public service, freeing the woman he loved mattered more.

And as for Laura—how would she react to being dragged into prominence in so controversial a case? Having been dead to the world for two years, he hoped with all his heart she would conclude that the boon of being freed from Charleton's menace was worth possibly being ostracized by society afterward.

If she did not, he realized that chances were good that she might never forgive him for making this move without consulting her. But with so little time left to buy them a future, risking that was a chance he simply had to take.

His sleep troubled by images of a howling Charleton hovering over a cowering Laura, Beau awoke early and unrefreshed. Waiting only for a shave and a tankard of home-brewed, he called for James.

The first item in his secretary's morning report rocked him to his toes. Charleton, the agents Beau had detailed to watch his movements reported, had departed London at first light.

An unease speeding uncomfortably close to panic coursed through him and he set his mug down untasted. Though he'd been careful to not divulge either the name under which Laura was hiding nor her current location, he couldn't shake a deep, instinctive fear that somehow her brute of a husband might manage to trace her. His mind working frantically, he heard not another word of James's comprehensive review.

The conviction bubbled up, too strong to be ignored. Full information available or not, he was going back for Laura Martin today. And agree to it or not, she was coming away with him.

Several days later Laura sat in her small parlor finishing up tea with Squire Everett. "So you see, I shall be departing as soon as possible. The note from my husband's cousin was most urgent. His family was always kind to me, and I cannot let them down now."

"Aye, one cannot ignore the demands of family. We shall miss you exceedingly here in Merriville, though! How long do you expect to be away from us?"

Laura laid a hand on her belly. "I'm afraid I cannot say. I shall send word later."

"You needn't worry about the cottage or the hound—I'll see they are both looked after. You're sure you'll not accept the loan of my carriage for the journey? It fair distresses me to think of a gently-born lady like yourself traveling on a common mail coach."

"It's terribly kind of you to offer, but—"

"Ah, well—" he waved a hand to forestall Laura's protest "—you'll not take it, so there's an end to it. Just send word when you're ready to depart. I'll drive you to the coaching inn myself—and on that I'll not budge, so resign yourself to it! We'll at least see you safely on your way. There's my Tom, waving at me through the windows, so I'll be off."

Laura felt a wave of affection and regret for the kindly squire whose hopes she would never be able to reward. "Thank you again, Squire Everett."

She walked her guest to the door and waved goodbye. She ought, she thought with a flicker of shame, to have invited Reverend Blackthorne to this farewell tea, as well, but she hadn't been sure she could have faced either the silent appeal she knew his eyes would contain—or his questions about her plans, which were likely to be much more probing that the genial squire's.

By late afternoon she'd dispensed the last of the treatments to the patients she'd been tending and headed toward home. Tonight she'd finish packing her small trunk of books and clothing, to be ready for departure in the morning.

The early dusk of a crisp winter day silhouetted her cottage against a sky painted in streaks of violet and crimson as she rounded the corner of the country lane. After pausing a moment to appreciate the delicate beauty, she trudged wearily up the front steps.

Not until she'd entered the front door and walked to the parlor did it strike her as odd that Misfit, who usually heard her approaching footsteps well before she reached the house, had not scampered to greet her with his usual joyous chorus of barks.

She'd proceeded one step into the room before her eyes adjusted to the dimness and she stopped abruptly, shock and panic icing her in place. Standing before the empty grate, cloaked in a many-caped driving coat that magnified the malevolent darkness of his bulk, stood the man she'd hoped never again to see in this life. Her desperately unmissed husband, Lord Exeter Charleton.

"My, Emily dear, how down in the world you've come. Not even a fire in the grate or a servant girl to tend you. I can't believe you left me for this—" He waved an arm to indicate the tiny, modest room.

When she remained mute, her mind still unable to grasp the enormity of the catastrophe playing itself out in her parlor, he advanced on her. "After all this time, have you no word of welcome for your lord and master? Didn't I teach you better manners than that?" As she belatedly scooted backward, he leaned over to grab her by one arm.

She dug in her heels, resisting with all her strength, but as always, she was no match for him. He dragged her to the small window, brought one beefy hand up to seize her chin and force her face to the fading light, his fingers biting into the skin.

"Humph," he snorted. "Still no beauty. Can't see what a fancy Corinthian like Beaulieu sees in you. Though we both know what he's planted in you, don't we? Say something, wench!" He dropped her chin to seize her shoulders and gave her a shake that snapped her head back.

"I—I don't know what you're talking about," she replied, forcing the words out evenly. She'd not give him the satisfaction of hearing her stutter with the terror he knew she must feel. The terror he'd thrived on inspiring in her even as he despised her for succumbing to it.

His lip curled. "Liar," he said, and backhanded her across the mouth.

The blow sent her reeling into the side chair. She lost her balance and fell heavily, putting both hands around her stomach to protect it as she went down.

He walked over to glare at her in triumph. "Don't know what I'm talking about, eh? Don't have anything in that barren belly to protect? Shall we test that little theory?" He moved a booted foot back and poised it to strike.

"Don't!" she cried, rolling herself into a ball, more desperate to prevent whatever harm he might try to inflict on Beau's child than to protect herself from any outrage he could deal her. *Never again,* she'd promised Jennie. Never again while she still breathed would she let him harm a child of her flesh.

Laughing softly, he placed his boot back on the floor. "Sniveling coward. So you're carrying his lordship's brat. Better than you managed for me, you worthless excuse for a wife. What a sorry bargain you turned out to be!''

Before she could think to react, he suddenly kicked out. Pain exploded at her elbow. Tears squeezed under her eyes and dripped onto her cheeks as she gritted her teeth to muffle her cry. He'd proved his point—should he wish to harm any part of her, she was helpless to stop him.

He regarded her thoughtfully. ''I married a tongue-tied homely bluestocking for the bountiful crop of progeny every other female of her line had always produced—and got not a single surviving son. But cheer up, my darling, we're not done with each other yet. If you provide the heir I need, I might even be induced to keep you, despite all the trouble you've caused me. The indignity of having to contrive an excuse to delay my nuptials...at least until I could determine whether or not you are in fact going to do your duty by me at last.''

He laughed again. ''Yes, I should enjoy flaunting the brat in Lord Beaulieu's handsome young face, with him knowing it impossible to wrest the child from me. I hope the bastard looks just like him.''

Laura lay motionless, not wanting to give Charleton any excuse to kick out again. Somehow she had to get away.

He gave Laura a vicious nudge with his boot. ''So up with you, my cherished wife! I shall have to keep you safe and closely guarded—until you're delivered. If it's a boy...we shall see. If you miscarry or produce another worthless female...'' He shrugged. ''This time I shall have to ensure your childbed fever is truly fatal.''

He jerked her off the floor and set her on her feet, maintaining an iron grip on her arm. Laura flicked her eyes around frantically, searching for anything she might use as a weapon. If she could just stun Charleton long enough to break away, she could flee by a back-woods path the viscount wouldn't know, to the squire's or the vicarage—

Charleton hauled her closer, put his lips to her ear. "Don't bother plotting to slip away again, my pearl," he murmured. "I know your little tricks, and stripped this miserable excuse of a dwelling of anything you might use before you returned. If you took a poker to me, I might grow so angry I wouldn't be responsible for my actions—we both know how you love to anger me, disrespectful, disobedient wife that you've always been."

He waited, but Laura remained stubbornly silent, barely hearing him as her brain worked furiously, searching for other means of escape. If not here, perhaps after they reached his carriage, or somewhere on the journey—at a posting inn—

Charleton's sigh rattled in her ear. "So inattentive, my dear wife. And we can't have that. Especially since while we wait for you to finish breeding—" he sucked her ear into his mouth, holding her rigid against him as she tried to jerk away, letting her pull free only after he'd left the hot drooling brand of his tongue around, inside it "—you're going to be a better wife to me, aren't you, Emily, darling?" He slid one hand from her shoulder down her chest, rubbing from her stomach down to the jointure of her thighs and back up, his palm coming to rest hard and flat on her belly. "Because we both know what might happen if I'm not satisfied, don't we?"

As she had so many times through the nightmares of the past, Laura clenched her teeth against the nausea rising in her throat and tried to make her mind float away, detached from the body Charleton controlled. Willing herself to reveal neither her revulsion nor her fear.

For the flicker of an instant her thoughts flew to desperate hope that Lord Beaulieu might come to her rescue. Had he somehow encountered Charleton, let slip her location? Oh, she had begged him not to intervene!

Whether he had or not didn't matter now. She was alone, as she'd always been, and whatever the earl's feelings about them, he couldn't help her. The idea of failing to protect the child she had likely conceived during their precious night together was so horrifying all thoughts but the imperative of escape slipped away.

Somehow I'll get free, Jennie, she silently vowed as Charleton dragged her from the room. *I promise.*

Shortly after dawn the next morning Lord Beaulieu rode into Merriville. Pushing on by the light of a nearly full moon, he'd stopped for a few hours' rest only because otherwise he knew he'd likely have ridden to death the last job horse he'd hired. As soon as he'd obtained a suitable replacement this morning, he was back on the road, driven by a nameless imperative.

Though all his instincts screamed at him to ride directly to Laura's cottage, 'twas best to be more discreet. Accordingly, armed with the glib excuse of having broken his journey north to stop and again express his thanks for all the squire's assistance to him and his family, he headed for Everett Hall.

Enormous relief flooded him when the squire confirmed that everyone in the neighborhood—their exemplary Mrs. Martin included—was quite well. However, once the man imparted the disturbing news that, having been summoned to tend an ailing relation, she intended to soon depart, Beau quickly exhausted his small store of patience trading civilities before finding an excuse to break away. After casually mentioning he'd stop at her cottage to pay his respects before continuing his journey north, Beau finally managed to depart.

His smile died the moment he left the parlor. Why, after vigorously resisting every attempt on his part to relocate her, would Laura Martin suddenly want to leave Merriville?

Once beyond the gateposts of Everett Hall, he spurred his horse toward the one place he truly wished to be. The "ailing relative" he dismissed out of hand, knowing the fictitious Laura Martin had none. Had she been preparing the neighborhood with a story that would preserve her reputation when he returned to spirit her away?

That theory eased the irritation and vague hurt he'd initially felt, after the hell of worry and waiting she'd put him through this past month, upon hearing the squire's pronouncement. Still, he couldn't wait to have her confirm that comforting explanation with her own lips.

It would prove a useful story, he admitted. Today they could arrange a time and place to meet, perhaps at the first posting inn after the squire saw her safely on the next mail coach. Much as he'd prefer to stop the vehicle the second it left Merriville and carry her off forthwith.

Grinning at that indiscreet but vastly appealing prospect, he tied his horse in the barn and paced through the garden, breaking into a near run as he approached the house. Would her expressive face brighten with joy, her heart leap with gladness when they met, as he knew his would?

He let himself in the back door, calling her name so as not to startle her. And receiving no response. An impatient stroll through the silent rooms confirmed his first assessment. Laura Martin was not at home.

A niggle of foreboding underlay the vast disappointment that seeped up. He shrugged it off. She was out tending patients, no doubt. Too restless to simply sit and wait for her, he paced back to his horse. He would ride through the neighborhood and track her down.

Two hours later he returned to the silent cottage, worry a cold lump in his stomach. He'd not found Laura Martin, nor encountered anyone who'd seen her today. The friendly postboy, when queried if he'd delivered to her a fictitious thank-you letter from Beau, cheerfully confirmed that Mrs. Martin hadn't received any mail in months. So much for the possibility that an urgent missive of some other sort had prompted her intention to depart.

The maid at the posting inn tossed him, along with a saucy look of invitation, the news that no passengers had embarked on the mail coach today or yesterday. Laura had not departed town by that means, then. So where was she?

He'd even, gritting his teeth, paid a short call to deliver his thanks to the vicar, ascertaining both that the man thought Mrs. Martin still in residence and that he strongly advised Beau not to call upon her unchaperoned.

As he entered the cottage this time Beau noticed immediately ominous signs he kicked himself for not having observed on his first visit. The stone-cold hearth in the parlor, where no fire had burned the night before.

The full pot of cold tea left this morning by the squire's servant, the kitchen fire she'd kindled now reduced to a few glowing embers.

Alarm eating at him, he walked into the small room he'd entered only once before.

At the sight of the tidily made bed, a flood of rigidly suppressed memories broke free to engulf him. A vivid ballet of impressions danced through his senses—her silken hair against his chest, her arms urging his head to her breast, the soft sigh and fluid feel of her arching into him. He took a shuddering breath and forced them back. *Concentrate.*

The hearth in this room was cold, as well. Neatly folded in a chest beside the single wardrobe lay a short stack of the hideous brown gowns he so detested, a few of her uncle's medicinal journals beside them.

She'd not spent the night here, of that he was almost certain. Where, then, had she fled yesterday without a word to anyone? And if she'd not spread news of her imminent departure to prepare for leaving with him when he returned for her, why *had* she gone?

As the short winter afternoon darkened to night, Beau sat in the cold parlor, disciplining his mind to consider only the facts. It now seemed obvious that Laura Martin had indeed left Merriville, taking with her not even her medicine chest, which he'd found behind the parlor door.

Why? he asked himself over and over, his mind struggling with that question like an animal caught in a poacher's trap. Only if she felt herself threatened would she have fled the home she'd clung to with such ferocity.

What, besides her husband, could have threatened her enough to force her departure did not take him long to determine. Only a scandal more lasting than rumors of dallying with a London lord, a scandal that would destroy both her reputation and her livelihood, could have sent her running from this haven, unwilling to let anyone know definitely where or for how long she'd gone. The scandal of bearing an out-of-wedlock child.

The stark realization that in the end she had not trusted him enough to send him word about it, stabbed in his gut. Staggering at the sharpness of the pain, he wrenched himself off the sofa and stumbled out to the deserted front porch.

In the darkness, silent snowflakes had begun to fall. Chill colder than their crystalline whiteness settled in his chest. Somewhere in that winter-barren wilderness, the woman he loved had fled, probably carrying his babe. And the man she'd staged her own death to escape had a better idea how to find her than he did.

He'd simply have to work harder and faster, he concluded, thrusting the agony of his thoughts back into a tightly guarded corner. For there was no way under God's heaven a villainous bully like Exeter Charleton would outsmart that consummate puzzlebreaker Hugh Mannington Bradsleigh, Earl of Beaulieu.

A moment later Beau's whole body alerted to the sound of galloping hooves approaching out of the night. Bitter disappointment squashed a rising swell of elation as the horse neared and he recognized the rider. His secretary, James Maxwell.

"Thank God you're here, my lord," James gasped as he swung down from the spent beast. "I've just ridden over from Mernton Manner—home of Lady Charleton's old governess. Charleton was there before me. Beat the poor woman nearly to death—she's still unconscious. And I very much fear she may have revealed to him

Lady Charleton's current location. You must remove her to safety at once!''

In one awful moment it all fell into place: the chest of folded clothing left open in the bedroom, the cold hearths and untasted tea, the medicine box abandoned behind the parlor door.

Terror he'd not experienced since he was a child paralyzed Beau. Unable to move, speak, even breathe, in his mind's eye he saw again the slow roll of the carriage, over and over down the long rocky slope into the ravine below, wood splintering and smashing at each contact. Saw himself awakening, after the final deafening crash, to a silence more frightening than his mother's screams. And heard again the sound that had haunted his nightmares for twenty years—his mother's dying gasp. ''Help...me.''

A jerk at his arm dragged Beau into the present. ''What is it, my lord?'' James demanded. ''The lady is not—'' he stopped in midsentence, suddenly able even in the meager light reflected by the swirling snowflakes to read the expression on Beau's face. ''Merciful God,'' he whispered.

Pain mingled with raw fury rushed into the hollow the terror left in Beau's gut as it vanished, like a flashflood into a dry streambed. Beau gasped in a ragged breath, steadying himself, grabbing hold of the anger and welding it into iron purpose.

It was too late to agonize over decisions that might have been made differently. He needed all his wits and every bit of his experience to find Laura with all possible speed. ''May God be merciful,'' he said starkly, ''for Charleton will not be. And when I find him, neither will I.''

Chapter Eighteen

Motioning for James to follow him, Beau strode into the dark house, turning up the lamp he'd lit earlier in the parlor. "Tell me everything else you've learned."

A few moments later, after his secretary had quickly outlined his most recent information—all of it confirming what he already knew, that Laura Martin was in fact Emily Marie Laura Trent Charleton—Beau issued his instructions, dousing the lamp and preparing to leave even as he spoke.

"Return to Merriville and hire every man who's willing. I want the whole village combed for evidence of a wealthy man passing by, probably in a closed carriage. Someone has to have seen them."

James glanced from the night lit by flickering snow back to Beau's face and swallowed the protest he'd probably intended to utter. "Yes, my lord. By the way, I had a message sent from Mernton to our people in London instructing them to determine the location of every property Charleton has owned or rented. The results will be sent, as fast as riders can proceed there and back, to your sister at Wentworth Hall. As that is not too distant, I thought if…events turned out to warrant the need, you might wish to set up a sort of headquarters there.''

Beau nodded his approval. ''I'm off to enlist Squire Everett and Tom. They will know all the roads hereabouts that might support the passage of a carriage.''

Together the two men strode out the door. Before mounting his tired horse, James hesitated and looked over at Beau. ''A carriage must travel more slowly than we can proceed on horseback. He has less than a day's march on us, and can't have taken her far. We *will* find them.''

''Oh, yes, we'll find them,'' Beau confirmed grimly. ''But will we find them in time?''

A week later Beau rode up to the entryway of Wentworth Hall, his sister's country home. Legs numb from hours in the saddle, he fell more than dismounted from the exhausted mount a waiting groom led away. As he stumbled into the entry hall, mind bleary with fatigue, his sister rushed over to meet him. No doubt alerted by the outrider posted at the hall's gatehouse a half mile away to watch for him, James and his brother Kit already waited in the small parlor to which Ellie led him.

Inspecting him with a worried glance, Ellie dispensed a series of rapid-fire instructions to have food, clean clothes and warm grog brought immediately.

''Come now, Beau, you must go upstairs and rest this time, at least for a few hours. You won't be of any use to Laura when we find her if you're half dead and—'' she wrinkled her nose ''—ripe as Stilton cheese.''

''I could ride a quadrant for you,'' Kit said. ''I'm fully recovered now, and I know the roads in the county as well as you.''

''Nonsense, Kit, we can't have you bringing on another bout of pneumonia by riding out in this weather. I'll stop long enough for grog and some stew. Then I must go out again. James, what is the latest news?''

"Nothing since yesterday, though I expect another dispatch momentarily.'' He hesitated, exchanging a glance with Ellie. "Really, my lord, I must insist you accept your sister's advice and get some rest. You'll kill yourself at this pace.'' His secretary tapped Kit on the shoulder. "Let's leave your brother to Lady Elspeth's care. I'll bring any new information as soon as it arrives.''

"Even the smallest bit,'' Beau called after him.

"Of course.'' Urging Kit along by the elbow, James led him out.

Beau inspected the food on the tray the butler had just placed in front of him. The smell of beefsteak and kidney pie nauseated him, and he pushed it away, choosing instead to spoon down a mouthful of stew, so hot it burned his tongue.

Ellie watched him in silence as, under her concerned gaze, he forced himself to consume several mouthfuls and drink half the spiced ale.

"James is right. Beau, I know you blame yourself for Charleton's finding Laura again! But you mustn't. You only did for her what you've done all these years for Kit and me. Tried to protect her by setting in motion the one thing that will free us *to* protect her—a divorce.''

"If I hadn't contacted him, he'd never have known she was still alive.''

"But you couldn't have predicted he would be able to trace her so quickly. And besides, nothing you said allowed him to—''

"Please, Ellie, don't!'' Beau cut her off. He tried to

manufacture a smile to soften the harshness of his tone. "Sweet sister, thank you for your care—even if I don't appear to appreciate it. And thank you for your concern for Laura. You will look after her if...when we find her."

"Of course. I love her, too, you know. And stop driving yourself so hard. We must find her soon. You will rest—"

"Aye. In here, for an hour or so, although if you're worried about my dirtying the upholstery I can bed down in the stables."

"Stables indeed!" Ellie shook her head to dismiss so preposterous a notion. "Stay wherever you're most comfortable. But...do rest, won't you? Promise me?"

"Promise." He kissed her fingers. "Now go, and I'll try to make good on that pledge."

His smile disappeared the moment she left the room. He knew Ellie, James, Kit—all of them were right. He was pushing himself—and everyone else—too hard. But he could not rest.

Not even to Ellie could he explain the demon that drove him, destroying his ability to swallow more than a mouthful, snatching him from fitful sleep. The sick despair that charged it was his own blind, arrogant belief in his ability to manage others like puppets on a string, a belief nourished by years of watching over his family and strengthened in a dozen successful missions for Lord Riverton, that had allowed Charlton to find the woman he had believed dead. Had Beau not convinced him otherwise, Charleton would never have set off after Laura with a ruthless efficiency Beau had been too stupidly overconfident to foresee.

For whatever she suffered at Charleton's hands, Beau held himself responsible.

Ah, yes, Beau Bradsleigh, brilliant mathematician, The Puzzlebreaker. The only thing that kept him from choking on his own bile was the meager fact that it was information gleaned from Laura's governess, not from Beau, that had led Charleton to her.

It didn't help much.

During the long hours in the saddle, he repeated endlessly one simple prayer. "Dear God, spare her life. Don't let the innocent suffer for my sins."

A single shred of information nourished the hope that his prayer might be answered, a hope that kept him still sane. James Maxwell's informants indicated Charleton was even more ill than he looked, with a heart complaint that had seen him bedridden twice this last year. As desperate as the viscount was for an heir, and knowing any child Laura bore would legally be his, her husband would, Beau prayed, treat her gently on account of the child she carried.

His child.

What he intended to do about that, Beau hadn't as yet devoted time or thought to determine. A future beyond locating and freeing Laura Martin did not exist.

A clatter of bootsteps on the marble floor interrupted his recriminations, and without even knocking, James burst through the door. "We've found them."

Beau was on his feet in an instant. "Where?"

"Not too distant from Merriville. Charleton's cousin owns a hunting lodge there, and our agents report that about a week ago a middle-aged gentleman of Charleton's description arrived in a closed carriage with his wife. The husband has been out riding, but the wife is reported to be ill. She's been confined in one of the upstairs chambers."

"How far?"

"Half a day's ride. Our man has rooms waiting at the closest inn. We can go in this afternoon, or hole up for the night to confer with the agents already in place, and strike in the morning."

Beau was already ringing the bellpull to order a mount readied. "Today. I'll plan it out during the ride and confirm it with the agents when I arrive."

He rode off thirty minutes later, both Kit and James insisting on coming along. Which was a good precaution, Beau had to admit. Without the restraining presence of cooler heads, when he caught up with them he'd likely kill Charleton on sight.

The plan they devised on the road required the rescuers to station themselves undetected around the perimeter of the hunting lodge, then storm it together at a prearranged signal. Beau would make for the upper room to free Laura; the others were to immobilize any opposition—and to find and restrain Charleton, well away from Beau. As he warned James, if Beau encountered the viscount he couldn't be responsible for his actions.

For the first time in his life Beau understood how a man could do murder. But he refused to let cold-blooded hatred or the heat of rage put such a blot on his own honor, however much the swine deserved to die. Besides, he couldn't very well later beg Laura Martin to grant her hand in marriage to the man who had killed her husband. As maddeningly slow as the legal route was, he would make himself wait for legal vengeance.

The information James had been steadily accumulating to implicate Charleton in his daughter's death was far too damning for the viscount to ignore it any longer. Should Charleton resist a divorce now, and Beau set his lawyers in motion, the viscount risked the noose. Though Beau was sorely tempted to turn the man over to the magistrates in any event, if Charleton proceeded swiftly with a bill of divorcement, Beau would honor the bargain he'd offered.

The delay until Laura won her freedom would be excruciating, but at least he would know she was safe. Beau had already cordoned off his London town house, put half a regiment's worth of guards in place, ready to keep a twenty-four-hour watch. He himself intended to sleep outside her door. If God granted his prayer, never again would he allow Laura Martin to come to harm.

But first, they had to rescue her from Charleton.

After a sullen-faced woman removed her luncheon tray, Laura rose to pace the small barred chamber in which Charleton had imprisoned her for the past week, wincing on her injured ankle. She'd not seen her husband since yesterday afternoon, a fact for which she'd be grateful under any circumstances, but the need to avoid or escape him now was imperative.

The lock on the door was too solid for her to attempt. Dread a tight knot in her stomach, she limped to the window. Taking a deep breath, she raised her bruised right hand to the shutter, tried to get her swollen fingers around the latch. A flash of pain so intense she gasped made her whole hand tremble. Tears starting in her eyes, she tried again, gritting her teeth against the agony.

It was no use—she couldn't make the fingers work. Cold sweat trickled down her unwashed back, between breasts that smelled of sweat and her husband. Sagging against the wall, she took deep breaths to still the rising panic, then clenched her jaw and tried the left hand, also swollen and badly bruised, but probably not broken.

The pain was less intense, but the seldom-used fingers didn't seem able to follow her brain's command to loosen the intricate loops of wire securing the latch. Fear rose in her throat again, a choking miasma, and with a little cry of frustration she dropped her hand.

Even had she succeeded in unfastening the shutters, this room was on the second floor, too high off the ground for her to jump down without injury, and her hands were in no condition to allow her to climb down the trellis. Charleton had done his work well.

Anger built at the conclusion, and with it a furious resolve. Charleton thought he had beaten her to his will, as he had so often before. He'd lamed one foot so she could not travel far, and rendered her fingers useless to master soap, buttons, or comb, so that even should she get away from him, the filthy, wild-haired creature she'd become would frighten off anyone she chanced to encounter. But she refused to let him cripple her spirit as he had her body.

She battled for herself now. Whether from distress, Charleton's hard use, or because they'd merely been delayed, her courses had begun this morning. With the agonizing slowness that was all her battered hands could manage, she'd fashioned some bed linen to use for the present, but her secret wouldn't last long after Charleton returned. If she didn't manage somehow to escape before he discovered she was not with child, he would kill her.

She'd cowered and endured to protect the babe she believed she was carrying, but she'd cower no more. If she were to die, she'd die fighting for every breath.

That, she suddenly realized, was her one hope.

Charleton expected her to submit so as not to threaten the unborn child. Which meant she had perhaps one chance at surprise in which to use her remaining strength to break free from him.

A heavy tread of boots from the hallway penetrated her thoughts. Squelching a spurt of panic, she hobbled over and settled herself back in the chair in which she'd spent most of the past week, letting her head loll to one side as if sleeping. Perhaps Charleton would merely look in and leave her undisturbed.

But the footsteps continued through the door, up to her side. She remained silent and still, eyes closed.

Charleton shook her shoulder. "Wake up, my darling."

She stirred slowly. "T-tired," she mumbled, fluttering her eyes open groggily.

Charleton gave a snort of disgust. "You were always next to useless when breeding, sleeping away half the day. But now you must get up, my precious. We're going on a little journey."

A flash of excitement she took pains not to show sizzled through her. "J-journey?"

"Yes, we've been here a week. 'Tis time to move on. Can't have that clever lover of yours catching up to us, can we?"

Lord Beaulieu was looking for her? Incredulity and then joy swelled within her, nourishing the thin flicker of hope and strengthening her resolve. She let herself rouse, as surely Charleton would expect. "Catch us?"

Charleton "tsked" in mock-sympathy. "Sorry, my angel, but you shall not be here to welcome him if he comes. Though could he see you now I doubt he'd claim you." Charleton chuckled at his own joke, then reached over to wrench her up by her shoulder. "Come along. Beaulieu prides himself on his acumen, but he's not the only clever one. He'll not find you—unless I want him to.'' He threw a cloak around Laura and pushed her toward the door.

She stumbled along as slowly as she dared, moaning from time to time as they descended the stairs, and only increased her speed when Charleton threatened to throw her over his shoulder and carry her. All the while her mind worked feverishly.

Whether or not the earl was pursuing them, she blessed him for making Charleton suspicious enough to move her, for escaping this locked chamber had just multiplied her chances of evasion. There'd be no point trying to run off immediately as they exited the lodge; she wouldn't get far and doubtless none of the servants here would help her. But sometime during this journey, she must make an attempt.

How did the door on the carriage fasten? If it was a simple latch, she might be able, when the carriage slowed along a suitable stretch of road, to bang it open, throw herself out, and roll free. Charleton would not expect such a move, and by the time he got the driver to halt the carriage, she might be far enough away that he'd not be able to track her. Mercifully, the early snow of last week had already disappeared and her slight weight on the hard ground would leave no trace.

If she miscalculated and leaped out when the carriage was traveling too swiftly, she might break a limb—or kill herself. However, since it was unlikely she'd be able to hide her condition from Charleton once they reached their destination, she'd rather take her chances with the road.

In the meantime, as Charleton hustled her out to the carriage, she did her best to appear weak, pain-racked, and quiescent. He settled her in the corner of the vehicle opposite the door, pulling a carriage robe over her belly with teeth-gnashing solicitude. "Can't have my son taking a chill," he murmured.

After tapping on the roof to set the carriage in motion, Charleton began to tie down the windowshades, blocking her view of the countryside. Laura groaned and raised a swollen hand to her lips. "Don't!" she protested in a threadlike voice. "The movement makes me ill. I must have fresh air."

Charleton hesitated. Laura took a gasping breath, as if experiencing a wave of nausea. Frowning, Charleton threw the sash back open. "Very well," he rumbled. "Move by the window. If you cast up your accounts on my new boots, you'll be sorry."

A small flicker of satisfaction steadied her nerves. The flicker grew to a flame as she covertly examined the door latch and concluded that, despite her misshapen fingers, she should be able to bang it open with one quick blow—painful as that action would doubtless be. Now she just needed the right opportunity.

She'd hoped perhaps the motion of the carriage would make Charleton sleepy, but though he made no attempt to converse with her, neither did he nod off.

The short winter afternoon grew darker. Desperation and fear making her queasy in truth, Laura abandoned her covert watch over Charleton to lean her head against the window edge, drawing in deep breaths of cold air while she searched the passing countryside for the necessary thickness of woodland.

Then as the carriage lumbered slowly around a curve, she saw ahead a perfect stretch of road: tree-bordered to give her cover, the path ahead straight and slightly downhill so the coach would pick up speed, and narrow enough that turning the heavy vehicle would be time-consuming once Charleton got it to halt. They'd passed a cottage not far back, chimney smoking. If she succeeded in evading Charleton, there might be a barn she could hide in.

The coach began to accelerate. "Dear Lord, help me," she silently prayed. Then, pulse pounding so loudly in her ears she wondered Charleton could not hear it, she slammed her fist down on the latch, shouldered the door open, and launched herself out.

Chapter Nineteen

A starburst of pain, first in her fist, then in her shoulder shattered over her as she hit and rolled. For a moment dizzy blackness tried to claim her. She fought to stay conscious, knowing she had at best minutes to scrabble into the woods before Charleton came in pursuit.

Not pausing to see if the carriage had yet slowed, she clambered awkwardly to her feet and ran, ignoring the fire in her ankle and the agony in her hands as she struggled through a curtain of brush and trees at the road's edge to paw and drag herself up a small bluff. Once she reached level ground behind a thick screen of pine saplings she paused, sweat-soaked and gasping.

Pushing herself deep into their prickly embrace, she scrambled on her knees to the edge of the bluff where she could peer down at the roadway.

Her heart leaped as she watched the carriage bowling along toward the far curve. Had Charleton not ordered it to stop? Or had the driver been unable to halt the horses, in full gallop down the slope?

Dizzy hope bubbled through her. Keeping to the bluff's edge where she could watch the road, she fought her way along the pine thicket, intent on distancing herself as far as possible from the place where she'd leaped from the carriage. When the vehicle slowed, then rounded the far curve without halting, a rush of elation buoyed her spirits.

Grateful now for the cloak that had been a hindrance during her flight, she drew it around her against the chill that had begun to penetrate and settled herself in a thick patch of brush and pine, swiping up pine needles in painful scoops to cover her trail. Too clumsy in her condition to move quickly enough to evade Charleton when he returned to track her, she'd hide here until he gave up his search.

Gaze frozen on the far curve, she waited. Just as she'd begun to hope that perhaps Charleton had chosen to leave her by the side of the road to die, the carriage came into sight, approaching the curve at breakneck speed.

She held her breath as the vehicle began to swing into the turn, much faster than she would have thought safe. And then she realized it was not the coachman whipping the horses on, but Charleton himself on the box.

Obviously not used to driving a cumbersome conveyance at such speed, he was turning it too wide. The outside leader stumbled through the ditch at the road's edge, the carriage's right front wheel fell into it a second later, causing the vehicle to rock violently sideways. For an instant it teetered on two wheels, the screaming horses straining to right it. But though seconds later it finally settled back onto the roadbed, the momentum threw Charleton off the box and into the ditch beyond.

The driverless horses, panicked now, raced onward, passing by a moment later the bluff where she hid.

Laura kept her eyes locked on the bulky figure in the caped driving coat lying motionless beside the road.

Minutes ticked away to the thudding beat of her heart. But the man in the ditch did not move.

A savage surge of joy rushed through her. Despite all that she'd suffered at his hands, a pang of guilt followed immediately after. He must be dead, or at the least badly hurt. But though she'd spent the last year giving succor to the ill and injured, she could not bring herself to approach her fallen husband and administer aid.

Someone was sure to come across the driverless team, or the coachman Charleton must have ejected from the carriage would walk back and find him. She'd limp to the cottage she'd seen, and if the occupants didn't drive her away, thinking her a madwoman escaped, she'd tell someone there of the accident.

Having salved her conscience, she struggled to her feet and picked her way through the underbrush, her wary glance still returning frequently to check Charleton's still figure. So deep was her fear and loathing, she could not yet trust he would not somehow manage to suddenly spring up and menace her again.

Hampered by her sodden cloak, her throbbing ankle and distracted by her watch over Charleton, while edging down the steep slope near the roadway Laura missed her step. Unable to grasp the saplings beside her to recover her balance, she fell.

Like a string of fireworks, pain exploded in her ankle, the hands that flailed uselessly at the nearby branches, her shoulder and then her head as she hit the ground hard and rolled downhill. This time, the blackness following the first white-hot bursts claimed her.

Out of a floating haze of cold and pain Laura heard someone calling her. No, she thought dully, better to die here rather than have Charleton seize her once more. Until the words themselves finally penetrated, and she realized the name being called was not "Emily" but "Laura."

She tried to open her eyes, but the world beyond her eyelids seemed formed from a shifting mélange of shapes and sounds that nauseated her. She'd almost drifted gratefully back into the blackness when the fragment of an image, a face too dearly loved and impossibly beyond reach to be real, shifted into focus.

Though the light as she opened her eyes wide sent a shaft of pain through her head, she held on to consciousness. "B-Beau?" she whispered.

She must have died. This must be heaven, for Lord Beaulieu's face loomed over her, then came closer as he dropped to his knees beside her. "Laura! You're alive, thank God!"

He seized one hand. The immediate burn of agony as he clutched her wrist wrenched a strangled shriek from her, confusing her. Surely one was beyond pain in heaven?

The pressure on her wrist vanished even as she cried out. Perhaps this *was* real, she thought, a bubble of wonder swelling her chest, for Lord Beaulieu did not look like the image of a peerless knight in some heavenly vision. Mud spattered up to his chin, his face was red-eyed, bewhiskered, and nearly as grimy as hers.

"Beau?" she whispered again.

Gently he eased her off the ground, leaned her against his chest. With infinite tenderness he carefully took each swollen hand in turn, examined it, then placed a whisper-light kiss on the gouged and purpled surface. Resting both her hands lightly in the warmth of his larger ones, he laid his cheek upon them.

"Forgive me, Sparrow," he murmured hoarsely. "Forgive me."

That seemed such a nonsensical thing for him to say, she smiled. But before she could tell him so, he lifted her. The dull smoldering in her shoulder ignited to a flame that sucked the breath from her and sent her reeling backward into the darkness.

Some indeterminate time later, the gray mists in which she'd been suspended slowly cleared. She was lying in a bed, on clean white linens that smelled faintly of roses, clothed in a long, cotton-soft night rail. Her body was clean, as well, her hair in a neat braid down her side, she realized with an enormous swell of gratitude to whomever had performed that kind service.

A flutter of gray fabric snagged her attention. She turned her head to follow it, and the jolt of pain through her neck and shoulder brought her fully awake.

"She's stirring, my lord!" a woman's voice said.

By the time the acid throb quieted once more to a dull ache, the space vacated by the gray cloth filled with the image of Lord Beaulieu's face. Dark hair combed, his neckcloth pristine white under a clean-shaven chin, his eyes clearer and less shadowed. Eyes that roved over her in intent examination.

"You're...not a dream?" she murmured.

His somber gaze softened in a smile. "No." He reached over, gently lifted her hand—swathed in bandages now, she noted—and brought it to his lips.

But if this wasn't heaven—where was Charleton?

She must have cried the name aloud, for the earl frowned. "Hush, sweeting, he can't hurt you. He's dead, Laura. The coachman told us after his master demanded that he stop the carriage and turn it around, Charleton kicked him off the box, grabbed the reins and sprung the horses. He may have thrown himself off going 'round the turn, or perhaps the excitement was too much for his failing heart. In any event, he fell, his head striking a rock when he landed. He's gone, Laura. You're free.''

Free. The precious word resonated through her, a word she still could barely trust herself to believe this side of heaven. Tears came to her eyes as she smiled at Beau. ''Thank you,'' she whispered.

To her surprise, a muscle twitched as he clenched his jaw, his expression growing grim. Without replying, he laid her hand carefully back on the bed and turned to nod over his shoulder. ''I've brought someone I thought you might wish to see,'' he said as he looked back at her.

She heard a rapid click of nails, then a familiar bark. A warm, wet nose pushed against her fingers.

''Misfit,'' she murmured.

''James found him in the garden behind your cottage, kicked bloody but still breathing. We brought him with us to my sister at Wentworth Hall, which is where you are now.''

''How did you find—''

''Rest now. I'll explain everything later. There's someone else who's been waiting to see you.''

Cautiously she angled her head up just a fraction to focus on the tall, vaguely familiar figure walking toward her. Then her eyes focused on a straight line of nose, the thick thatch of sandy hair going silver. Recognition, sharp and poignant, clogged her throat.

''P-papa!'' she stuttered.

Lord Beaulieu stood aside as her father bent to kiss her forehead, his bright blue eyes glassy with tears. "My precious child," he said, his voice ragged, and gathered her in his arms.

In the afternoon of the next day, as golden sunlight filled her chamber, Lady Elspeth, Lord Beaulieu, his secretary, James Maxwell, Kit and Laura's father, Lord Farrington, stopped in for a visit. The earl allowed Mr. Maxwell, who, with her father, he credited for gathering the bulk of the clues that enabled them to track her, to narrate the story of how the rescue had taken place, Kit and Lady Elspeth inserting details along the way.

"You should have seen Beau when we reached the hunting lodge to discover Charleton had already taken Laura away," Kit broke in. "I swear, he was so angry I thought he would strangle the one groom we found still in the stables. But Charleton must have been one ruthless taskmaster. The fellow seemed only too happy to tell us in which direction the carriage had headed, even offering to ride along and point out the road."

"I'm just glad it all happened close to Wentworth Hall so that Beau could bring you to me," Lady Elspeth said. "We've discussed it, Laura, and your papa agrees that it would be best if we let it be known only that you and I came to be friends while you were nursing Kit, so that when the carriage in which you were traveling with your husband overturned, you asked to be brought here. Of course, the fact that you'd left Charleton can't be concealed, nor given his vicious behavior—" her voice took on a ferocious note "—should you be ashamed of doing so, but since it is everyone's desire that once you've recovered, you be restored to your place in society, we feel it best that the details of Charleton's death, and my brother's part in your rescue, not be revealed.''

''As soon as you feel ready to travel,'' her father said, ''I'm taking you home. Jack, Rob, Trent, Louisa, Charlotte and their families are all gathering at LeGrange to welcome you.'' His voice trembled. ''I only wish your dear mama were still alive to see it.''

Lady Elspeth patted Lord Farrington's hand. ''Your father has agreed to let you come to London with me for the Season. My husband won't return from Vienna until mid-Spring, and I shall be desperately dull without him. Having you with me there will make the time fly so much faster.''

After she'd thanked them for their help once again, asking the earl to also extend her gratitude to Squire Everett, Tom, the villagers of Merriville and all the men who had ridden quadrants across the countryside looking for them, she saw the earl give Ellie a nod.

Her hostess rose. ''Come, everyone, let's let Laura rest. I've ordered tea sent to the winter parlor.''

In a babble of voices, her visitors departed. All but Lord Beaulieu.

He hesitated by the doorway. ''Do you mind if I remain for a few moments?''

''Please, stay.'' Even in her weakened condition, her pulse leaped at the prospect of being alone with him.

To her great disappointment, however, he did not seat himself beside her. ''I must apologize once again for—''

''Oh, no you mustn't!'' she protested, rising up to reach out a hand to him, then gasping at the pain.

''You mustn't distress yourself,'' he said, rapidly approaching her side and reaching tentatively to touch her bandaged hand. ''I am so sorry for this.''

"Were it not for you, I would have suffered much worse. Charleton only moved me because he feared you were in pursuit. And if you'd not been pursuing so closely, I would likely have died of injury and exposure before someone happened down that road."

The earl hesitated, stroking her clumsy hand gently. "Did he not have good reason to treat you kindly?"

"Charleton never saw reason to do that," Laura said flatly. She looked away, avoiding his gaze.

"And there's naught else you need to tell me?"

Once, she might have replied by confirming both she and her husband had believed she carried Beau's child, that Charleton had spared her because of it. But ironically, the marriage that had trapped her had also permitted her to speak freely. She might tell the earl the truth, knowing regardless of his response, he could do nothing.

But with her husband dead, she dared not admit the possibility. And she certainly couldn't confess that she loved the earl.

For if she did, the honorable, protective Lord Beaulieu would doubtless feel bound to ask for her hand.

She would not trap him in marriage with this oldest of tricks, nor did she wish to be tied once more to a man unless she were certain his feelings for her ran as deep as hers for him.

Of that, she had no assurance at all.

The earl stood beside her, patiently awaiting her reply. Laura sensed the questions still swirling in him, and knew she was too weary to evade them. Much as she hated to send him away, given how seldom she was likely to see him in future, she said, "Nothing of importance. I—I am rather tired. Could we speak again later?"

He hesitated, and for a moment Laura thought he might refuse. "I will leave you to your rest," he said at last.

But for another long moment he remained, studying her face before bending as if to kiss her. Instead, he merely touched his lips to her hand. Feeling bereft already, she closed eyes that stung with tears.

With a bow, Beau turned and left her room. Pensively he approached the stairs, but not yet ready for company, changed his mind and headed for his chamber instead.

Had Laura ever been with child? He'd given her a perfect opportunity to admit it, yet she had said nothing. If so, why had she not sent word to him in London? If not, then why had she spread that story about needing to leave Merriville? Had she been preparing the way for his return?

Before all that had transpired this past two weeks, he would have bluntly asked her those questions, demanded that she answer. But he no longer had the right to demand anything of her.

He'd hedged on his own promise to reveal everything, as well. Some facts he would never relate to her. The terror that sliced through his gladness as he carried her unconscious to the coach, cradled her in his arms for the endless drive to Wentworth Hall. His burn of anger mingled with shame after the doctor detailed her injuries, a sprain of her right ankle, broken bones in various fingers of both hands, a concussion from her fall onto the roadway. Ellie sobbing against his chest in horror and anguish after she and her maids finished washing Laura's bruised, filthy body.

Only one other person had he ever failed as he had

Laura. His mother's death he could not rectify. But Laura's injuries he could make right.

She'd been wed when barely out of the schoolroom to a man who abused her trust and forced her into a deception that had stolen two years from her life. Not until she had resumed her rightful place in the ton, respected, comfortable, and free to select the husband of her choice, would he feel the debt he owed her repaid.

Except for the harm she'd suffered, in the curious fashion of providence, the way things had worked out was probably better than the plan he'd initially devised. Being freed from Charleton by death avoided the scandal and possible social ruin a divorce would have entailed. The carefully edited facts they had all agreed to present to the world would allow Laura to reenter the society of her birth with a minimum of gossip and speculation. In a fitting twist of irony, Charlton's as yet unaltered will even left his former wife a rich woman.

Reestablished in society, as a lovely young widow of wit and considerable wealth, she would doubtless attract every unattached gentleman in London with any pretense to intelligence. Then after a suitable interval, when she'd been courted by enough suitors to decide the kind of man she truly wanted, only then would he permit himself to press his own suit.

The selfish, needy part of him that ached for her smile, her voice, her touch, urged him to beg for her hand now, before she was exposed to the practiced courtesies of a throng of other suitors. But though in his own mind, the injury he'd inadvertently allowed her to suffer outweighed any gratitude she might owe for her rescue, she seemed to feel indebted to him. Much as he longed to claim her for his wife, he'd not propose now and have her marry him out of gratitude. She deserved the time to learn her own mind and make a choice untainted by obligation.

After that proper interval, however, he intended to do everything in his power, perhaps even try to seduce her into a repetition of the glorious night they'd spent together, to insure *he* was her choice.

But for now, he must keep his distance. And wait.

He was much more successful at the last resolve than the first. Returning to London after escorting Laura and her father home to her family, he'd called immediately upon Lord Riverton and turned over the dossier on Lord Wolverton. That minister's subsequent resignation and Beau's behind-the-scenes maneuvering to help bring the lesser criminals to prosecution occupied a number of days.

But now that Ellie had come back to London, carrying Laura along as her guest, despite good intentions to the contrary he seemed nearly every day to find some compelling reason to call on them.

Of course, with Ellie's husband Lord Wentworth still abroad on his current diplomatic mission, it was only natural he should complete for her the small commissions Wentworth would normally have performed. Natural, as well, that he grant Ellie's request to escort them to the various social engagements at which Ellie was introducing Laura.

Like the musicale at Lady Harding's tonight. Having settled the ladies in chairs nearest the musicians, he was now procuring them some refreshment.

"I say, Beaulieu, 'tis a charming lady your sister's brought to town with her," Baron Brompton, an acquaintance from his Oxford days, said as they both obtained glasses of champagne from a passing footman. "Widow with a tidy fortune, I hear."

He'd never much liked Brompton, Beau concluded as he made a noncommittal murmur.

"Glorious auburn hair, too." Wexley, a tulip who prided himself on his discriminating taste in female beauty, inserted himself in the conversation. "Upon my word, a perfect foil for that alabaster skin."

"If you approve her, Wexley, she's bound to become the next Incomparable," Brompton said with a groan. "I'd best try to work myself into her good graces before word gets around and every Pink and Tulip in the ton has a go at her. Does she like champagne, Beaulieu?"

"*I* am bringing my sister and Lady Charleton champagne," Beau informed him, finding Brompton more irritating by the minute.

"The next glass, then," Brompton said cheerfully. "Ah, the musicians are tuning up. I must find a seat."

After forcing himself to return Brompton's cordial bow, Beau hastened to bring the wine back to his ladies. For a moment he surrendered to the temptation to linger, but when Ellie invited him to take the chair next to Laura, Beau knew he must refuse.

There was no way he could sit close enough to feel the warmth of her body, breathe in the subtle rose scent of her perfume and maintain the semblance of detachment to which he'd pledged himself.

Mumbling an excuse, he walked to the far side of the room.

Of course, he knew his devious sister was doing all she could to encourage his constant attendance. But he couldn't bring himself to feel the irritation her well-intentioned meddling might have otherwise inspired in him.

It was too poignant a pleasure to gaze at Laura's beautiful face, admire the elegance of her figure clothed in a fashionable gown that emphasized her slender loveliness, enjoy the music of her voice, infinitely sweeter to his ears than the admittedly excellent fugue the well-trained performers were now playing.

Indeed, the chamber orchestra's melody scarcely registered in his senses. Freed by the concert from the need to make polite conversation or to control his constant, aching desire to be near Laura, he could simply stand and drink in the sight of her, observe the graceful line of her neck as she leaned to catch something Ellie was saying, the copper flash of her curls reflecting the massed light of the candelabra suspended above her.

Though he did retain enough self-control to refrain from engaging her in direct conversation. And he ruthlessly avoided the insanity of encountering her alone, knowing the temptation to speak with her, touch her, then would be far beyond his power to resist.

Still, his heart twisted with longing each time he saw her, his faltering resolve bargaining with the rigid sense of duty. After first vowing to hold himself aloof until the end of the Season, he'd reduced the waiting time to three months, then two.

Just two months. Surely he could last that long.

Surely in that time she wouldn't fall in love with any of the overly handsome, overdressed, overconfident Corinthians who hurried to surround her as the musicians took their break, as gentlemen had clustered around her at each social function to which he'd escorted her.

Yes, he'd survive two more months—but only, he decided, downing his glass, if he didn't have to torture himself watching other men court her. Feeling a pressing need for liberal quantities of the hard liquor available at his club, and afraid if he stayed a moment longer he would succumb to the urgent desire to wrench Baron Brompton's plump arm off the back of Laura's chair—and possibly out of its shoulder socket—Beau made himself cross to the landing. He'd summon James to escort the ladies home.

Sternly forbidding himself from gazing back for one last glimpse, he descended the stairs.

Laura looked over the shoulder of the pleasant young man offering her a glass of champagne to see Beau turn abruptly on his heel and exit the room.

He was leaving them again, she thought with a rush of dismay, as he had on each of the several occasions he had escorted them out. No doubt he'd send James or Kit or one of Ellie's friends to squire them home.

Her enjoyment of the frothy wine and frivolous conversation vanished. The first parties Ellie had taken her to upon their return to London had been amusing, even exciting. But to one who was shy by nature, and who had lived virtually without society for the past four years, the endless string of social engagements that made up the life of most ton ladies seemed to her like a steady diet of sweetmeats—overly sugared and ultimately unfulfilling.

She'd not yet determined what she meant to do. Ellie evidently hoped her friend would attract eligible suitors, one of whom might secure her a permanent place in society by inducing her to remarry.

But there was only one man for whom Laura would be willing to brave that institution again. And though she'd hoped Lord Beaulieu's devoting himself to her rescue meant he still harbored strong feelings for her, of late she'd seen no evidence whatsoever to support such a conclusion.

Perhaps he'd worked so tirelessly merely because he felt responsible for Charleton's finding her again. He'd hinted as much while she was under Ellie's care at Wentworth Hall. And now that she was safe, restored to health and society, he felt his obligation to her at an end.

Perhaps his strong preference for her company when he'd been in Merriville was simply the natural inclination of a healthy male to seek agreeable female companionship. Here in London, with ladies of much greater beauty and address available, she no longer merited his attention.

Her sagging spirits plummeted further.

None of the laughing compliments she received during the interlude—with a polite smile and a cynical ear—succeeded in reviving her interest in the evening's entertainment. With stoic calm, she waited for the party to end.

Her depressed spirits did not escape Ellie's sharp eye at breakfast the next morning.

"You look somber. Are you not feeling well?"

"No, my head is fully recovered and my hands are much better." Laura paused. "Please do not think I do not appreciate all you are doing by reintroducing me to society, but—"

"Nonsense," Ellie interrupted with a wave of her hand. "Your family was most eager to present you. They only permitted me to do it as a favor, to help take my mind off Wentworth's absence."

Laura felt a pang of envy at the obvious mutual affection her hostess was privileged to share with her husband. "You miss him very much."

"Dreadfully. And value your company immensely, as does Catherine. So let's have no more rubbish about gratitude."

"But you see, I—I just can't summon much enthusiasm for society. I never really had a place here, and in any event have occupied a different station for so long that it all seems—excuse me if this sounds offensive—rather frivolous. I know I cannot resume the work I did in Merriville, but I should like to do something useful."

Ellie gave her a knowing little smile. "When the right gentleman appears, you will know exactly what you wish to do. Unless I miss my guess, he already has. You have only to encourage him."

Laura stared at Ellie. Not bothering to pretend she did not understand her friend's inference, she instead blurted, "How can you know that?"

Ellie laughed. "Because my darling brother Beau can't seem to let a day pass without calling here. I assure you, he has not always been so assiduous in his attentions to his only sister."

"Your husband is away. He wants to assist you. And you've asked him to escort us to several parties."

"He's managed to delegate those duties before. Besides, when you enter the room, his eyes never leave you, whilst on his face there's such a look of yearning it fairly moves me to tears."

A wild hope soared and then plummeted. Shaking her head in denial, Laura said, "If he does care for me as you insist, why has he said nothing to me of his feelings?"

Ellie's teasing look faded. "Ah, Laura, you must understand Beau suffers from a nearly suffocating sense of duty. Though I can't imagine what he thinks a child of six could have done to rescue Mama after their carriage accident, I do know the tragedy still troubles him. As long as I can remember, he's been fanatical about safeguarding all those under his protection. As I imagine you realize, he holds himself responsible for the harm you suffered at Charleton's hands. In some perverse masculine way, I expect that makes him feel he has no right to ask for your love.''

''Shouldn't that be my decision?''

''When has the male species ever asked a female's opinion on something they believe involves their precious honor?'' Ellie replied with asperity. She leaned over to take Laura's hand. ''I'm nearly certain Beau loves you, but that for obscure reasons of his own, refuses to act upon it. If you do care for him, before he succeeds in mortaring that emotion behind a wall of new duties, I advise you to *make* him act.''

Uncertainty and longing tore at Laura's heart. But before she could fashion some reply, Ellie waved her to silence.

''You needn't say anything. Truly, I don't wish to interfere. But after all you've suffered, I do so want to see you happy. Both of you.'' Planting a quick kiss on Laura's cheek, she rose from the table and left Laura to her thoughts.

For a long time after Ellie's discreet departure, Laura sat at the table over her cold toast and cooling tea.

If Beau did feel something for her, it was hardly the gentleman who'd be considered unworthy.

Despite Ellie's grand plans, Laura had few illusions about her eventual place in society. Although for the moment, under the sponsorship of the well-respected

Lady Elspeth, the ton seemed willing to accept her, Laura was quite certain not everyone would welcome her entry into that privileged circle. With a rueful smile she envisioned the reaction Lady Ardith Asquith would experience upon discovering her dowdy neighbor from Merriville was now the eligible widow Lady Charleton.

Laura expected the beauteous blonde would lose little time spreading throughout the ton as many salacious details as she could recall about the woman she'd known as Laura Martin, who expended herbal treatments to farmers and peasants and lived alone in a humble cottage. The elegant courtiers who now lisped praises about her shell-like ears would likely cease their versifying once Lady Ardith had done her work.

The mistreatment that had forced her to that deception would garner enough sympathy that she'd probably not be ostracized. But many in society might consider she'd failed in her duty by abandoning her husband and disgraced her class in her subsequent choice of employment. Though her tidy fortune would guarantee that not all her courtiers abandoned her, gentlemen of high birth and discrimination would probably conclude she was unworthy to be offered their hand and name.

Gentlemen of such rank and distinction as Lord Beaulieu. Even if he did still feel something for her, as Ellie seemed to believe, Laura was reasonably certain he did not view her as a potential wife. Mercifully, Ellie could not know they had already shared the greatest intimacy possible between a man and a woman.

Though she doubted she would ever marry again, she knew for a certainty that she loved Beau Bradsleigh. Whatever her new status, Lady Charleton would be more than happy to become what the earl had clearly wished to make Laura Martin during his sojourn in Merriville. His mistress.

Did he still desire her? If so, he would hardly, given Ellie's obvious belief that he intended to offer marriage, dare instead to offer her carte blanche while she was residing under his sister's roof.

Was that the reason he was so carefully maintaining his distance?

She did not know. But there was an easy way to find out, one that meshed with the vague plans she'd already been formulating for her future.

In the two weeks she'd spent becoming reacquainted with her family, she'd realized that, despite her papa's pleading that she come back to live in the home of her birth, she had been too long her own mistress to become permanently a dependent in his household or any other's.

Charleton's money, every farthing of it earned in blood, gave her the means to live on her own.

A glimmer of excitement penetrated the fog of depression that had settled over her last night. She would begin looking for a suitable house this very day. For the first time in her life, she would be mistress of a future free from fear and ripe with intriguing possibilities.

The most intriguing of which was divining the intentions of Lord Beaulieu.

Chapter Twenty

The next morning Beau received a highly unusual summons from his sister to attend her at breakfast on a matter of pressing importance. Intrigued, and drawn as always by the bittersweet possibility of seeing Laura, he presented himself in Curzon Street at the midmorning hour she considered appropriate for breakfast.

"Darling Beau, thank you for coming on such short notice!" She leaned up to take his kiss on her forehead, then waved him to the sideboard. "Please, fill a plate. The eggs are particularly fine this morning."

"Thank you, no." Beau refrained from mentioning he'd broken his fast an unfashionable several hours earlier. "So, dear sister, what is this matter that cannot wait?"

"Laura wants to leave me!" Ellie paused dramatically as a shaft of surprise and worry lanced through him. "She says though she's grateful for the hospitality I've extended, she's still most anxious to set up her own household. I tried to argue that a lady of gentle birth simply does not live alone, but she would not be dissuaded. She did agree to have her old governess come to bear her company, and to delay her departure until after Arthur returns next month. But the darling wretch hasn't wasted a moment. She told me last night she's arranged appointments to view houses for let this very morning!''

Beau's alarm eased. Laura wouldn't be leaving London. '''Tis not so surprising. She has been managing on her own for more than two years now. And she can certainly afford it.''

Ellie frowned at him. ''If you're not going to support me, I wonder that I troubled to summon you. But there was another reason. Knowing so little of the city, Laura asked me to view the houses with her. But I'm feeling so vaporish this morning I dare not stir from the house. You must escort her for me.''

Beau inspected his sister with a raised eyebrow. Buttering her third slice of toast with an air of innocence, she looked hale enough to ride to the hounds.

Far be it for him, however, to question the veracity of a lady. Especially his sister.

He opened his lips to accept, and then hesitated.

To drive Laura in his curricle would be one thing. The side of his body tingled at the mere thought that she might be seated as close to him as the narrow vehicle demanded, but with the two of them out in plain view for any passerby to see, he felt reasonably sure he could maintain the required aloofness.

But alone with her, wandering through a deserted house? Through shuttered libraries like the squire's, where they'd spent long hours chatting, empty parlors like the snug room in her cottage where she'd invited him for tea, dustcover-shrouded bedchambers... Fire ignited in his belly and sweat broke out on his brow.

''Beau!'' Ellie recalled his attention, her lips in a pout. ''Surely you don't mean to refuse. You know the city as well as I, and certainly have a better grasp of the proper rents and such." She smiled sweetly. "I can't think of anyone better qualified to advise her. Ah, here she is now."

Wearing a carriage dress of deep cerulean blue nearly as brilliant as her luminous eyes, Laura walked in. The simple gown molded to her form, its color a perfect foil to her flawless skin and burnished auburn curls.

The unspoken connection that always linked them crackled anew, stronger than ever in the heat of his desire. He couldn't seem to take his eyes off her or to make his mouth produce syllables.

"Laura, dear, bid Beau good day," Ellie said. "I'm afraid I'm feeling too poorly to accompany you this morning, but Beau has agreed to escort you in my place."

At Ellie's words Laura halted and made him a curtsey. "Good morning, my lord." Her eyes when she looked back up were uncertain. "I—I could take a maid with me. I should hate to interrupt your busy schedule."

"Nonsense, I'm sure he can spare a few hours," Ellie replied. "And Beau is better able to advise you on the desirability of the locations, the suitability of the rent and such, even than I."

Laura's eyes fluttered back to his face. For a long moment she gazed at him, lips parted but saying nothing, as if she'd lost her train of thought.

Which was only fair. His had derailed the moment she entered the room.

"It's settled, then," Ellie said, turning to him with a mischievous look that had, during her growing-up years, always signaled trouble. "Unless you'd prefer me to send her with James?"

Send her with James? To prowl about deserted li-

braries, parlors and bedchambers unchaperoned? Not
bloody likely!

"I'd be delighted to escort you, Lady Charleton,"
Beau said, finding his voice at last. "That is, if you are
agreeable."

"Of course she is. Laura, I know you've already
breakfasted, so you may leave at once. So as to take up
as little as possible of Beau's valuable time. Brother
dear, you must make sure my darling Laura accepts
nothing less than a bargain she cannot resist. Now, off
with you."

Grinning, she blew them both a kiss.

There seemed nothing to do but depart.

"Lady Charleton," he said, and offered her his arm.

She was silent as they walked out the entry, silent
still as he helped her up into the curricle, not speaking
until he'd clambered in himself and dismissed his tiger.

"The first house is on North Audley Street," she
said.

Beau flicked the reins, acutely conscious of her beside him on the narrow seat. The rocking motion of the
carriage jostled them together as he navigated the
crowded street, his arms bumping hers as he worked the
reins, his thigh pressing into her warmth as they
rounded a curve. By the time they reached the Audley
Street address his body was in flames, his oak-solid will
reduced to splinters and his mind consumed, like a desert wanderer thirsting for water, with fighting the raging
desire to touch her.

He secured the carriage and helped her down, keeping the touch that burned into his palms as brief as
possible and praying the dwelling had a housekeeper in
residence. Until from her reticule Laura produced a key,

saying the estate agent had instructed her to let herself in, as the house was unstaffed.

His hands trembled from the force required to keep them at his sides. Desperately he searched through his mind for Latin verbs to decline, pausing halfway through the present tense of *venio* to unlock the front door.

How he was going to manage walking her unchaperoned through this deserted house?

Laura followed Beau through the door of the Audley Street dwelling, her heart thudding against her ribs.

Ellie, bless her, had presented Laura a perfect opportunity to determine whether or not the earl still harbored any desire for her. Now she just needed to summon up the courage to seize it.

He'd been so unencouraging when Ellie pressed him to drive Laura that she was on the point of declining his company when at last he offered his escort. Given his obvious reluctance, she probably should have declined it. But she'd not been able to bring herself to do so.

Just as she'd not been able to tear her eyes away from the virile face and form that dwarfed Ellie's small breakfast room, filled it with the vibrant aura of his compelling presence. She'd not been able, either, to dredge up a single shred of conversation during the drive here, so content was she to simply revel in the glorious, rare pleasure of his nearness.

On the other hand, a dispassionate review of his behavior thus far indicated that he didn't seem nearly as happy to be with her. He'd not troubled to initiate conversation, had handed her down with brusque efficiency and unlocked the door with jerky, almost angry motions. Her confidence, never high, wobbled further.

And yet. And yet she felt as strongly as ever that sense of spirits entwined, a bond that drew her to him at every meeting, brought her thoughts back to him even when they were apart. Did he feel it, too?

She'd promised herself when she embarked on her new life that she would never again be afraid or hang back in the shadows. Time to put that brave resolve to the test.

But nervousness made her palms damp, set her babbling nonsense about turnips while they viewed the kitchen, the price of ticking as they toured the parlor and dust on voile curtains as they climbed the stairs. Heart pounding at her ribs, she led the earl to the front bedchamber.

Which contained naught but a large, curtained bed.

Laura nearly giggled, giddy from nerves stretched taut—and remembered longing. *Now or never.*

"B-Beau," she said, her voice unsteady. "May I call you Beau, as I once did, even though we're now in London? It s-seems somehow too formal to refer to you as 'my lord' while we're inspecting bedchambers."

Was that a groan? No, she must be mistaken.

"As you wish," he replied, his voice tight.

"You may call me 'Laura,' of course. That's more suitable to the intimacy of the room, do you not think?"

He made no reply, halting in the doorway, fingers gripping the door frame as if he found the room too distasteful to enter.

"Come, you must see it from the inside," she urged. "Or do you not find the contents of the room pleasing?"

His knuckles were white, she noticed as, gathering her courage, she reached down to grasp his hand.

A shock seemed to ripple between them. For an instant he clutched her hand in a crushing grip, then batted it away. "You—ah, it appears... That is, the room is... fine."

He took a few stumbling steps away from her into the chamber and halted again, as if unsure where he should go. Her small store of confidence dwindled further.

Desperately she wished she had even a particle of experience at enticing a man. Why hadn't she watched more closely the behavior of the buxom upper housemaid all Charleton's staff had whispered was round-heeled?

She made herself walk away from him toward the bed in what she hoped was a slow, hip-swinging, sensual glide. Mercifully she reached it before her wobbly knees gave way.

Landing on the feather mattress with a thud more inelegant than seductive, she looked back at Beau and patted the spot beside her. "Come test it out with me."

His eyes widened and he swallowed hard. "T-test it?"

"Yes. After all, if I rent the house I shall be spending long hours in this bed. I should know if they are going to be...enjoyable. You can help me decide."

"A-about the bed?"

"Naturally. The floor appears a trifle too hard."

It's not the only thing, she thought he muttered.

"Please, Beau, I—"

"All right, I'm coming. That is, I'll help you...with the, um, bed." He lurched toward her to deposit himself on the edge as far from her as possible.

Before he could move away she scooted closer and seized his arm. The feather ticking obligingly bent to pinch them closer together.

"Oh, my, the mattress does sag...rather interestingly," she said, looking up into his face so tantalizingly close.

His eyes locked on hers, his labored breaths visible in the frosty room. Slowly he lowered his head toward her, his lips pursing deliciously.

Yes! she silently exulted, stretching up toward him, her eyelids fluttering shut.

Until two strong hands seized her shoulders.

"Laura, what in the world are you trying to do?"

Eyes snapping wide, she stared up at him. "S-seduce you," she blurted a moment later, too rattled and mortified to dredge up a convincing lie.

To her enormous relief, he didn't laugh at her, though his lips did curve into a tender smile. "My rash sweetheart, a respectable matron just embarking on her first Season back among the ton needs to be much more careful of her reputation."

His hands had gentled, but they still grasped her shoulders. She lifted her own to cover his.

"Beau, I don't care about reputations and Seasons. All I want, the only thing I want, is what you and I shared in my cottage the night before you left for London. Please, tell me you still want that, too."

He exhaled a ragged breath, but twined his fingers with hers rather than brushing them away. "Sweeting, you were a child bride, an abused wife, a desperate runaway. You've never had the chance to experience what should have been yours by birthright—the opportunity to entertain a variety of suitors and make a real choice.'' His voice lowered. ''Once you have, perhaps I can forgive myself.''

''Forgive yourself?'' she echoed, incredulous. ''For what? Befriending a lonely woman who could hardly remember what it felt to have a friend? Caring enough for her to want her freed from the man who'd terrorized and abused her? Spending more than a week searching night and day to rescue her? No, I don't wish to forgive you all that! Oh, Beau, I know you blame yourself for Charleton's finding me again, but the fault was more mine than yours.

''No, hear me out.'' She put a finger to his lips as he started to speak. ''If I had followed my heart and confessed the truth—all of it—if I'd not forced you to proceed in blind ignorance, none of that would have happened to me. It was so hard to trust again, Beau. But I do trust you now, absolutely. With my body and my love.''

He startled her by dropping to his knees before her in one fluid movement. ''I had intended to wait, not wanting to press you for fear you might come to me only out of gratitude. I still think you shouldn't give me an answer until you can be sure about your choice. But I can't hide any longer that it is my dearest wish that, once you've taken the time to truly know what you want, you'll accept my heart and hand.''

His heart and hand? ''D-do you mean you want to marry me?'' she asked incredulously.

''More than I have ever wanted anything.''

Shock, humility, and a deep sense of conviction filled her. ''Oh, Beau, I'm five-and-twenty. I've buried a child, survived illness, loss, isolation and pain. Do you really believe I don't know right now what I want?''

''Are you sure, my heart?''

"I want the man who taught me to trust again. Who gave me the most perfect night of my life, the only time I've ever felt desired and cherished. Were I to have as many suitors as the night sky has stars, my choice would always be you."

She grasped his hands and stared down at him, willing him to believe. The lazy, wicked smile that slowly lit his face ignited a heat in her belly to match the conflagration burning in her heart.

"One perfect night, then," he agreed, rising from his knees to lean her back against the dustcloth-draped pillows. With hands as feverishly hot as hers, he helped her tug off his greatcoat, his vest, his shirt, unbutton her pelisse and slide up the skirt of her gown, seeming as desperate as she for the feel of her naked skin against his. "Starting right now, my greedy darling," he whispered, "one perfect night to last us the rest of our lives."

* * * * *

My Lady's
Pleasure

Chapter One

If fornication were going to occur, it wouldn't be in her hayloft. That decided, Valeria Arnold frowned as she watched her maid, Sukey, loosen her bodice lacings to reveal more of her generous bosom, then turn the corner of the path leading to the barn, "assignation" written in every sway of her ample hips.

Now, how to enforce that resolution?

Valeria had been coming in for tea after her usual morning ride when she noticed Sukey, after a furtive backward glance, slip her sleeves off her shoulders and scurry out the kitchen door. Since the maid was now out of sight and well beyond hailing distance, if Valeria truly wished to stop her she'd have to follow the girl.

Well, if one must do something unpleasant, best to proceed quickly and be done with it.

Laying down her riding crop, Valeria lifted her chin and strode to the door. At the last moment she paused to pick up a stout walking stick from its stand beside the cupboard. In case her firmest governess's manner wasn't enough to dissuade the ardent youth awaiting Sukey, it wouldn't be amiss to come prepared.

Her courage nearly failed her when she reached the barn.

From within its stout walls emanated Sukey's high-pitched giggles, interspersed with soft shufflings and low-toned masculine murmurs. Valeria took a deep breath and wiped nervous palms against the woolen skirt of her habit.

She'd call out a warning. No sense barging in unannounced and surprising them at...whatever they were now doing, she decided, her cheeks warming at the thought. The idea of viewing a man whose unclothed body was not in the last throes of deadly illness fired that warmth to flame.

Nonsense, she told herself, raising chilled hands to cool her hot cheeks. A respectable widow shouldn't be having such thoughts. Especially—honesty compelled her to add— when in this remote corner of Yorkshire there was so little opportunity for her to act upon them.

She pulled the barn door slightly ajar. "Sukey Mae, are you in there? Cook needs you in the kitchen at once!"

At the sound of a gasp, followed by frantic rustlings, she entered.

Valeria saw Sukey first, hastily re-lacing her nearly bare bosom while her skirts, which must have snagged the edge of a nearby hay bale when she dropped them, were still hiked up to reveal a froth of white petticoat. Valeria's gaze moved to the man beside Sukey and stopped dead.

Tawny hair gleamed in the shaft of early morning sunlight, and the tall, well-muscled body that lazily rose to impressive full height was not that of the fumbling farm boy she'd expected. Golden cat eyes swept her with a glance from head to toe, their expression half annoyed, half amused, as finely chiseled lips curved into a smile.

"A ménage à trois? Who would have thought to find such delights in the wilds of Yorkshire?"

His voice whispered of Eton and Oxford, even as the fineness of the half-unbuttoned linen shirt, the width of the cravat tossed on the hay, and the expensive simplicity of the form-hugging buff breeches shouted Bond Street.

The stranger's smile broadened, and Valeria realized she must have been staring with mouth agape. Though in truth, such a man was as out of place in this remote section of England as if he'd dropped from the moon. Wherever had Sukey stumbled across this London dandy?

Valeria shut her mouth with a snap. Before she remembered her purpose, though, she had to admit a certain sympathy for the susceptible Sukey. With his smiling eyes and rakish grin, the gentleman before her could tempt a saint to dalliance.

"Sukey Mae Gibson," Valeria said, her first attempt at a stern tone coming out more like a croak. "You will return to the kitchen. We'll speak of this later."

Finishing the ties of her bodice with a jerk, Sukey gave her a sullen look. As she stepped past him, the unrepentant rogue had the audacity to wink at the girl. A foolish grin sprang to her lips before she turned back to Valeria. "But Mistress—" she whined.

"At once, Sukey," Valeria interrupted. "Before I forget that it is a Christian virtue to forgive."

What no other housewife in the county would, Valeria added mentally, with a rueful sigh at the compromises poverty compelled.

She kept her unflinching gaze locked on Sukey until the maid, with slow, reluctant steps, exited the barn. Then Valeria turned back to level the same stern look on her uninvited visitor.

"You, sirrah, will do me the favor of leaving my property by whatever means you came, and returning to wherever it is you came from."

Apparently possessing not a particle of embarrassment, the man merely inspected her once more from head to toe, his gaze curious. "Will I now?"

He spoke the words with a slight lilt, whose origin her precise mind was distracted into trying to ascertain until she realized the rogue was approaching. Before she could move, with a smooth panther's gait he had reached her and seized a curling wisp of hair, escaped from its pins during her ride, between two tanned fingers.

"You so unkindly interrupted my morning's plans. Why should I not take you instead?"

Seen up close, the golden eyes mesmerized. For an instant, she couldn't seem to move—or breathe. Then she caught the odor of brandy, the lingering scent of cigar smoke. He was more than half disguised, she realized. Rather than rising early, he'd probably not yet been to bed. Her first thought—to wonder again where in the world he had sprung from—was rapidly swamped in acute awareness of the heat and scent of him hovering over her.

"You shall not," she said sharply, dragging herself back from lassitude to slap his hand away.

"And why is that, pray? 'Tis ready for kissing you look."

Since her rapt gaze *had* focused on his lips, she'd best not debate that. "You have the appearance of a gentleman, sir, and therefore would never take an unwilling lady," she pronounced.

To her surprise, the man threw back his head and laughed. "Sure, and you're wrong on both counts! Shall I show you how much?" With the spurned hand, he reached out to tilt up her chin.

Valeria's gaze locked with his. She tightened her grip on her walking stick, though as the gentleman's height and reach far exceeded hers, should he really choose to attack her the wooden pole wouldn't prove much of a weapon. But despite his threat, she felt no fear.

"I'd prefer you didn't show me. I'd also prefer if you'd refrain from enticing my maid."

He released her chin, his glance sympathetic. "You waste your time there. The girl's as light-skirted as they

come. If not me, 'twill be another lad she raises her petticoats for, sure as dawn follows moonlight.''

Valeria stifled a sigh. "But not in my barn."

With a lithe movement the man caught up his discarded
jacket. ''I wouldn't be too sure of that.''

Nor was she, but she wasn't about to discuss with this
bosky stranger what necessity forced her to tolerate. "I trust
you can find your way out. Good day, sir.''

She turned on her heel, but the man caught her shoulder.
Startled, she looked back at him.

''Is it sure you are that you're unwilling?''

A shudder of heat radiated from his hand throughout her
body. Something buried deep within her, a longing long
denied, stirred in response.

Don't be a fool. Jerking her shoulder free, she stepped
away. "Yes," she said crisply, and strode off.

His soft chuckle followed her. Just before the barn door
closed, she heard him murmur, "Liar."

Was she unwilling? Valeria wondered as she made herself walk purposefully to the house, resisting the temptation
to glance back and watch the man leave.

Of course she wouldn't consider lying with a chance-met
stranger—certainly not one so undiscriminating that he'd
been about to tumble her maid! But neither could Valeria
deny that the stranger's sheer virility had awakened a firmly
suppressed desire for the physical bond marriage promised.
A promise that, in her case, had never been fulfilled.

The inevitable wave of pain, muted now, swept through
her. She couldn't prevent herself thinking of Hugh—tall,
broad-shouldered, black hair curling over a gold-laced uniform collar, dark eyes gleaming with health and high spirits. The man who'd been her brother's best friend, hero of
her adolescent fantasies, and briefly, her husband.

He'd want her to remember him like that—not as he'd
been last summer, wasted with fever, his flesh hanging on

a too-large frame, eyes sunken in a face yellowing with the pallor of approaching death. Shuddering, she once again banished the image. Best to bury it deep, along with any memory of her disastrous wedding night.

Impatiently she shook off a vague sense of guilt. It was only natural, having known so little of the delights of love, that she'd be tempted by a cat-eyed stranger whose lips and hands promised expert skill in the arts of seduction.

Doubtless more skill than her erstwhile suitor possessed. The idea of comparing stodgy Arthur Hardesty to that tawny-haired personification of male carnality was so ludicrous, she had to laugh out loud.

Her attraction to the stranger was equally laughable. Should she ever meet him in his true setting—a London drawing room—she would hold as little appeal for such a man as her low-born maid.

Still, if she wished to relieve the tedium of her dull existence with visions of a torrid interlude, 'twas a harmless enough diversion. Wherever the stranger had sprung from, he wasn't local. Probably he was some traveler passing through whom Sukey had somehow encountered at the posting inn when she went to town for supplies.

Aye, no need to chastise herself for wistful fancies. After all, Valeria would never see the rogue again.

Laughing softly, Teagan Michael Shane Fitzwilliams let appreciative eyes linger on the retreating figure of the lady in black. With curves as delightful, if not quite as ample, as those of the maid she'd routed, Lady Mystery was much more intriguing.

Euphoric over winnings that would keep him in clean linen and adequate victuals for the next several months, Teagan had decided to take a dawn ride to blow away the smoke and liquor fumes of a hard night's play. Had he not still been three parts castaway, he'd never have followed—

it would be a misnomer to term responding to that walking advertisement for the world's oldest profession "seduced"—the saucy maid whose bold glances and ample curves had attracted his attention at the posting inn.

Though his body still protested the abrupt termination of its favorite recreational activity, his head was more than willing to exchange a quick tumble for the possibility of a more challenging partner.

The maid had called her "mistress," so his proper lady must be in charge of the small manor whose stone walls he glimpsed beyond a curtain of trees as he walked out of the barn. A widow, in her somber black garb? Or mayhap a woman who cared little for her husband, for no wife who enjoyed bed sport would risk employing a wanton like Sukey.

Either way, he'd read attraction in her eyes—and longing. Exactly the combination that offered the potential of a mutually profitable interlude.

Though serviceable, Lady Mystery's habit had never seen the inside of a London emporium, his discriminating eye said. But the hothouse flowers of the metropolis, with their endless need for flattery, gossip and manipulation, had been growing rather tiresome of late.

Let the other men pursue the tarts Rafe Crandall had brought to occupy those of his guests who tired of hunting or card play. Teagan would seek out his host and make some discreet inquiries about Lady Mystery.

A woman for whom he'd felt an immediate attraction. His half-aroused body hardened again. It had been a long time since he'd been able to combine business with pleasure.

His exacting eye for detail pulled up another memory, and his glow of anticipation faded. As he now recalled, her black habit had been not just unfashionable, but worn.

He tried to summon up a niggle of hope. Perhaps Lady

Mystery saved her newest garments for impressing the ton during her sojourns in London. If not, it appeared his comely widow was none too plump in the pocket.

Not even the sight of Ailainn, the glossy black stallion that was his one indulgence, erased his irritation at that conclusion. Society might deem Teagan totally irresponsible—an image carefully cultivated to provoke maximum irritation in his mother's sanctimonious English relatives—but he'd learned early the pain of a starving belly and an empty purse. A man living solely by his own wits could not afford to neglect his game and pursue a woman merely for the enjoyment of it.

He should put her out of mind, he concluded as he mounted Ailainn and caught up the reins.

As the stallion trotted down the path to Rafe's hunting box, Teagan urged his mount to a gallop. The sheer beauty of the animal's powerful stride, the siren song of the wind rushing by him—scouring away the smoky debris of yesterday, making him new—carried off his vexation and revived his spirits.

Pulling up the stallion at a rise overlooking his host's dwelling, Teagan threw back his head and laughed aloud, caught up in the sheer joy of being alive on such a glorious morning.

Perhaps it was the same quixotic stubbornness that had led his mama to defy her family and follow her heart and the sweet-talking rogue who'd left her to die alone in a Dublin hovel. A man, her censorious relatives never tired of reminding him, Teagan resembled to the life.

Or that all Irishmen were fools—had his English relations not drummed that fact into him as well?

Whatever prompted him, stubborn fool of an adventurer that he was, he decided on the spot to pursue his Lady Mystery anyway, be she wealthy or not.

Chapter Two

Surveying the ruins of what had been her favorite vase, Valeria stood in the parlor trying to curb her temper. It being of little use to chastise the already weeping Sukey, she'd sent the useless girl to her room.

Valeria bent to pick up the largest remaining piece, a whimsical array of birds and flowers in blue and white pottery that had been her brother's last gift before he was killed at Talavera. Like Elliot, the vase was now shattered beyond repair. She took a deep, shuddering breath, working hard to suppress her own tears.

Remembering brought only sorrow, and heaven knew she'd grieved enough. She forced herself to concentrate instead on the practical matter of gathering up the shards.

She had to grin wryly. Her dressing-down of the hapless Sukey had succeeded all too well. Finally appearing struck by the dire future that awaited her on the streets or in a brothel, should Valeria repent of her mercy and discharge the girl, Sukey had been tearfully eager to please. But since, as she'd sobbed to her mistress after this latest mishap, she was still "powerful agitated by that smooth-talkin' London gent," the girl's distracted efforts this morning had resulted first in burning today's bread, then in scorching Valeria's best lace tablecloth and now in the destruction of one of her last physical links to her brother.

To distract herself from the anguish of that thought, Valeria deliberately conjured up the handsome stranger who, she had to admit, had left her a bit "agitated" as well. She was still kneeling, a half smile on her face, her mind tracing the image of his delicious physique and knowing eyes as one's thumb would caress the smooth surface of a gemstone, when Mercy, her nurse-turned-lady's maid, peeked in the parlor door.

"There ye be, Missy! Sorry I am to tell you, but Sir Arthur and Lady Hardesty are here. I tried to fob 'em off, but knowin' you was home, they insisted they must see you."

Valeria groaned. With Cook muttering in the kitchen over the bread, her elderly butler in high dudgeon about the ruined tablecloth and the estate books still needing attention, she had neither time nor interest in these uninvited guests courtesy now compelled her to entertain.

Uttering Portuguese profanities under her breath, she raked the broken pottery into her handkerchief. "Did you answer the door?" she asked over her shoulder.

Her old nurse bent to help. "Aye. Sorry, Miss Val, but Masters were still in the pantry, sulkin'. I'll take these to the kitchen for you."

"Blast. Then I shall doubtless have to endure Lady Hardesty commiserating on how my 'unfortunate circumstances' force us to retain a butler too old to perform his duties." With a sigh, Valeria stood and handed her nurse the handkerchief. "Please do take these. I'd prefer not to have to explain what happened, and invite another homily on why it was false charity to hire Sukey."

Valeria dusted off her hands and gave her hair a quick pat. "Send them in, then, since you must."

Her impressive bosom jutting before her like the prow

of a warship, Lady Hardesty sailed into the room. "My dear Valeria! So kind of you to receive us unannounced. And I do hope poor Masters is not ill. Your maid Mercy had to admit us."

Valeria damped down her irritation. "He's quite well, thank you. Not expecting callers this time of the morning, he was busy with other duties."

"Yes. So unfortunate it is not within your means to employ an underbutler or a footman to assist him."

"Should you like tea?" Valeria asked, determinedly ignoring the comment.

"Oh, yes. 'Twill help settle my nerves, which, I declare, are quite shattered. Only the knowledge that it was my inescapable duty to poor Hugh gave me the strength to drive out today!"

"Here, sit, Mama, and make yourself comfortable. Lady Arnold, I trust I find you well." His forehead perspiring under the burden of escorting his suddenly drooping mama to the sofa, Sir Arthur managed to sketch her a bow.

"Quite well, and you, Sir Arthur?" Valeria did not bother to inquire what dire news had prompted Lady Hardesty to drag herself from her morning room, knowing the woman would soon inform her at length, whether Valeria wished to know or not.

With a pant, Sir Arthur settled his mother's bulk on the cushions, then turned to fix a smile on Valeria. "You are looking particularly lovely today."

Since she was garbed in one of her oldest gowns, with her hair still sprouting wisps blown free by her ride and her sleeves ornamented with flour, she could manage only a noncommittal murmur in reply.

Arthur did possess a sweet smile, Valeria reflected. If it weren't for the fact that his sweetness was cobbled with an intellect dim enough to consider such absurd compliments flattering, a body already tending to the corpulence so evident in his mother—and a mother who kept him firmly under her thumb—Valeria might think more seriously about letting Sir Arthur relieve her of the burden of managing this barely profitable sheep farm.

"...awful danger!" Lady Hardesty tapped Valeria on the arm, recalling her wandering attention. "A peril to every decent woman in the neighborhood!"

"What Mama means," Sir Arthur inserted, "is that Rafe Crandall—Viscount Crandall's youngest son—has brought a party of rather...disreputable guests to his hunting box."

"A property, my dear, that borders your land!"

"For seven and one-half acres on the west," her son clarified. "Although the greater length of it, one hundred thirty-six acres, adjoins Hardesty's Castle."

Of course Sir Arthur would know to the acre where the property lines went, Valeria thought. Her suitor, she often suspected, valued her more for owning fields that marched with his own than for any beauty or charm she might possess. A lowering reflection, that.

"And the...persons that wild boy brought with him!" Lady Hardesty continued. "Why, 'tis perilous for any decent woman to walk the streets. After all your devotion to him, I knew dear Hugh would want me to warn you to stay behind locked doors until that revolting party departs."

While Sir Arthur looked at her and saw acreage, his mother perceived a woman who'd nursed her son's boyhood friend for months. And who thus might be expected to meekly do the bidding of a second husband—or mama-in-law. Not in this life, Valeria silently vowed.

"Now, Mama, 'tis not as dire as all that," her son soothed. "I daresay as long as Lady Arnold remains on her property she will be quite safe. However, as some of the guests will be shooting—and probably not in a condition of absolute sobriety—it would be wisest for her not to ride."

"There's a greater danger to riding out than bosky hunters. Arthur, did you not tell me you'd seen the man yourself yesterday at the Creel and Wicket, bold as brass?" Lady Hardesty shuddered. "Why, they say those golden cat's eyes can hypnotize an unwary woman."

Valeria's attention had wandered again, but at those words she snapped to attention. "C-cat eyes?"

"Nonsense," Sir Arthur reproved. "Ladies have always found Teagan attractive, but I've heard naught of hypnotizing."

"Who knows what Irish riffraff is capable of," Lady Hardesty sniffed.

"Only half-Irish, Mother. His mama was good English stock—the Earl of Montford's daughter, you will remember. How else could Teagan have gotten into Eton and Oxford?"

"One of the guests is a rake and the, ah, natural son of an earl's daughter?" Valeria asked, pulse leaping at the memory of golden eyes and smiling lips bent kissing close.

"No, she actually married the Irishman—her father's *groom!*" Lady Hardesty said. "To think Lady Gwyneth would show so little consideration of what is due her station!"

Irish, Valeria thought. So that explained the lilt.

"'Twas only what she deserved," Lady Hardesty continued, lips pursed in disapproval, "when the blackguard deserted her and the child, leaving her to die penniless. Why, 'tis said the boy lived on the streets until some clergyman was kind enough to restore him to her family. By which time he was already an accomplished thief."

"You exaggerate, Mama. Teagan must have been only six then, for when I met him at Eton he wasn't yet seven." Sir Arthur turned to Valeria. "We're speaking of Teagan Fitzwilliams, Lady Arnold. His reputation is very bad, I fear. But the young man I knew was not evil, merely wild."

"Wild enough to study vice early. Didn't you tell me they called him 'cheat' at school?"

"'Jester,' Mama. For the card tricks and sleights of hand he used to perform for us."

"Whatever he was as a boy, you can't deny he's turned into a gambler and a heartless rake."

"I cannot condemn him simply because he makes his living at the green baize table, Mama. What else was he to do, pray, when his mother's family virtually cut him off after Oxford? And, I must own, I think the stories of the many women he's supposedly seduced vastly exaggerated."

Lady Hardesty sniffed again. "Of course they cut him off. How could they not, after he was dismissed for seducing the wife of the dean!"

"'Twas his mentor's daughter-in-law, Mama."

"Well, the entire ton was in an uproar over the way he carried on with the wife of old Lord Uxtabridge. Now, you may say I exaggerate—" she turned to her son, who with half-open mouth did seem to be about to protest once more "—but Maria Edgeworth has sent me all the town news for years, so I believe I can speak with more authority about this matter than you!"

Having effectively squashed her son, she addressed Valeria again, clearly eager to spill yet more gossip. "After Uxtabridge, who should have known better than to buckle himself to a chit young enough to be his granddaughter, there was Lady Shelton, and—"

"Mama, you're putting Lady Arnold to the blush," Sir Arthur exclaimed, regarding Valeria with alarm, as if he expected her to swoon at any moment.

Glad her thick-headed suitor read embarrassment in the flush of excitement he must have perceived on her cheeks, Valeria was, for once, shamelessly eager to plumb every tidbit Lady Hardesty could be induced to offer. "My nerves are quite steady, though I thank you for your concern, Sir Arthur," she said placatingly. "But I believe Lady Hardesty is correct. I ought to know the whole."

"Indeed." Her ladyship flashed her son a superior look. "Gentlemen try to dismiss the villainy of their sex, but we ladies must acknowledge it if we are to protect ourselves adequately. And I would consider myself failing in my duty to dear Hugh were I not to insure that his sweet widow, whom I trust has no idea of the devilment of which men are capable, was sufficiently armed."

Valeria had the grace to feel a twinge of guilt, but not enough to stop the flow of information. "I appreciate your concern," she said demurely.

Lady Hardesty patted her hand. "You know I look on you almost as a daughter, dear Valeria. So, though it grieves me to speak ill of one whom Arthur once considered a friend, I must warn you Maria tells me this Fitzwilliams fellow never loses a hand, leaves a bottle, or spares an opportunity—excuse me for stating the matter so crudely—to debauch a complacent man's wife."

"Being a widow, I should be safe then."

Her ladyship ignored the remark, as she did any attempt to deflect the conversation from the direction in which she desired it to proceed. "I daresay no woman is safe. Indeed, I begin to feel it my duty to dear Hugh to insist you stay with us at Hardesty's Castle until Crandall's party and That Man have departed the neighborhood."

Valeria caught her breath in alarm. That would guarantee she'd never encounter the rogue again—and make her a prisoner to Sir Arthur's ponderous suit and Lady Hardesty's none-too-subtle maneuvering.

"Indeed, Lady Hardesty, you are much too kind!" Valeria said quickly. "But I could not put you to so much trouble, with your nerves in such a state. Besides, the shearing will soon be upon us. I simply couldn't leave such important preparations to mere underlings," she concluded, hoping to draw support from Lady Hardesty's well-known contempt for social inferiors.

"You have an admirable sense of duty, Lady Arnold," Sir Arthur said. "Perhaps I could step in to assist—"

"Oh, no, Sir Arthur! With the vast responsibilities of your extended acreage, I simply couldn't ask you to burden yourself with supervising mine as well."

"Dear lady, no service I could do you would ever be a burden."

Oh yes, he'd love to assume the management of each and every one of the six hundred-some acres Hugh had left her, she thought sardonically, and then caught Sir Arthur flashing his mother a significant look.

Lady Hardesty rose. "Valeria dear, I nearly forgot. I brought with me my receipt for whitening lace, which by the looks of the hangings in the entryway, your housemaid could certainly use. If you'll excuse me a moment, I shall take it to her."

Valeria rose as well, determined to forestall this blatant attempt to leave Sir Arthur alone with her. "So kind of you, but another time, perhaps." After frantically scanning her mind, she hit upon an excuse that might prompt the Hardestys' speedy exit. "You see, Sukey Mae is laid down on her bed at present. Nothing to worry about—a putrid cough only. I was about to prepare her a tisane when you arrived. Indeed—" she added a delicate cough "—my own throat is so scratchy, I believe I shall prepare myself one as well."

While Sir Arthur shot up from the sofa with the speed of a Congreve rocket, Lady Hardesty hastily deployed a handkerchief over her nose. "Lady Arnold, you should have warned us immediately that you were feeling unwell! Surely you recall the delicacy of my lungs. Come, Arthur, we mustn't linger." Her hawklike eyes looking aggrieved over the handkerchief, she headed out.

Valeria followed them. Despite her praise of careful nursing, Lady Hardesty had such a horror of illness she'd not come next or nigh her "dear Hugh" in all the months he lay dying, Valeria recalled bitterly.

Remembering that, she allowed herself to cough again, harder this time. Lady Hardesty speeded her steps.

"I'm sure I'll be right as rain in a day or so. Thank you so much for stopping by," she called after her departing guests. And then stood, immensely pleased with her ploy, listening to the echo of the front door's slam.

An Irish rogue, she thought, lips curling into a bemused smile as she wandered back into the parlor. An Irish rogue with a winning smile and an intimate gaze that could charm leprechauns out of the air, she suspected.

And foolish women out of their virtue.

A cheat and a liar, as Lady Hardesty claimed? Knowing how the worst sorts of rumors made the best gossip, she was more inclined to credit Sir Arthur's memories of an orphan barely tolerated by his mother's disapproving family.

Valeria recalled the keen intelligence of those golden eyes, the hard strength of that muscled body. But with very little effort, having been orphaned young herself, she could imagine what it must have been like for a boy of six, forced to scrabble for survival on the streets after losing his one remaining parent. A boy suddenly transported out of everything familiar, and given over to relations who, if she knew aught of aristocratic English families, never let the child forget that his father was a wastrel, his mother a fool and he an Irish beggar dependent on their charity.

Small wonder the lad had grown up a hellion.

But not, she was quite certain, a heartless womanizer.

Despite his disclaimer to the contrary, Mr. Fitzwilliams

had behaved as a gentleman. After all, she'd been alone with him, virtually defenseless, with little chance of retribution to follow should he have taken advantage of her. A true predator—with a shudder she recalled encountering several such individuals while in India with her father—would never have passed up such a golden opportunity.

No, he'd not acted the rake, and his teasing words had left her enticed rather than threatened.

Of course, having Lady Hardesty command it and Sir Arthur recommend it, she couldn't possibly remain at home. She would ride in the morning, as she always did.

And if she should encounter the fascinating Mr. Fitzwilliams?

Her heartbeat galloped and she felt shaky. Heat flushed her cheeks, then cold. In the pit of her stomach a curious spiral began, and the tips of her breasts tingled.

Yes, she lusted after the man—as apparently so many other women had before and probably would after. Still, she couldn't stop her fevered imagination from wondering what it would be like to have the rogue's lips upon her own, those long tanned fingers caressing her, that strong torso leaning over her, thrusting the most intimate part of his body into the most intimate part of hers. A powerful wave of desire and longing swept through her.

And as she struggled in rural remoteness, striving to accumulate the financial means of escape, it seemed the vague yearnings of girlhood only sharpened. She'd scarcely been married before being widowed, so the passion churning within her had never been allowed free rein. How she ached to fully experience that rapture of which bards through the centuries had sung, sensual delights which, unless Arthur Hardesty finally wore her down into accepting his suit, she might never taste.

With Arthur, a taste would likely be all she'd get.

She was back on her knees, brushing together a few bits

of the broken vase that had escaped her hasty earlier inspection—and by some mercy, Lady Hardesty's gimlet eye—when the idea struck her. Her hands froze on the shard.

Teagan Fitzwilliams, Lady Hardesty claimed, was a master of seduction. As Valeria knew from personal observation, that tall, golden, compelling gentleman appeared to be everything a woman could wish for in a lover, capable of making even an on-the-shelf widow like Valeria feel desired.

Teagan Fitzwilliams would be in the vicinity of Eastwoods for a few days only. And if, in that time, he happened to initiate her into the rituals of passion of which he was so obviously a master, no one need ever know. Should she encounter him, and he rebuff her, no one would ever learn of her humiliation. And should he take her, after a few days he would depart, sparing her the embarrassment of ever facing him again.

But in her heart, her body, the wonder of the passion with which he gifted her would burn forever.

She raised a shaking hand to her face. She must have taken leave of her senses. The idea was insane!

But once conceived, the notion refused to be dislodged. Her senses hummed with it, thrilled to it, beat with an urgent pulse that whispered, "Do it."

A sharp pain pierced her finger and she opened her fist. She'd clutched the pottery shards so tightly one had cut her.

Would that her feckless mind should receive so painful a check, she thought, inspecting her bleeding finger. If she did something so rash, so wanton, so...unladylike, she was apt to suffer much more than embarrassment. Men might indulge their passions with impunity, as her reckless body urged, but men did not bear children. Could she be irresponsible enough to risk that?

But her courses, always extremely regular, would be upon her in a day or so. Mercy had blessed that very fact three years ago, confiding on Valeria's wedding night that as no woman Mercy had ever known had conceived so near her time, Valeria would be spared the possibility of bearing a child who might never see its soldier father.

There wouldn't be a child. But there could be pleasure—pleasure such as she'd never known and likely would never have a chance to find again.

She wouldn't dare.

How could she not?

Trying to squelch the unaccustomed turmoil in her normally well-regulated mind, Valeria rose on shaky legs and went to dispose of the broken pottery bits. Noticing the blood pooling from the cut, she brought her finger to her mouth.

The suction of her lips against her throbbing digit set her body tingling again. How would it feel were it his lips against her hand…her belly, suckling her puckered, aching nipples?

Another wave of heat swept her, then a light-headedness that made her dizzy. She stumbled into the kitchen, startling Cook by leaning against the dry sink to splash water on her flaming cheeks.

She would think on this no longer. Let fate decide.

She would ride tomorrow as usual. If she happened to encounter Teagan Fitzwilliams…let happen what may.

In the late afternoon, after a thorough washing and pleasant dreams of a certain dark-haired lady in a black riding habit, Teagan went looking for his host. He ran him to ground in the back parlor, playing billiards for pound points with several other gentlemen. For a few moments Teagan simply watched, gauging the mood and degree of sobriety of the group so as to decide how best to discreetly obtain the information he sought.

Rafe, as usual, had a half-empty glass of brandy in hand. Markham and Westerley, dissipated younger sons of an earl and a marquess respectively, looked equally live to go. Only the last member of the group, a plainly dressed older gentleman, appeared completely sober.

In fact, as he was normally rather a straight-laced government man, Lord Riverton made an odd addition to Rafe's assemblage of hard-drinking, high-stakes rowdies. However, as the man had cheerfully lost a considerable sum to him last evening, Teagan was prepared to be affable.

"Gentlemen." Teagan greeted the group.

"Ah, Jester." His host turned spirit-brightened eyes toward him. "Good night you had, eh? Riverton went down by several thousand, and Markham here should have provided you enough to pay off your tailor."

Teagan gritted his teeth. Suppressing the automatic anger that still flared at his well-bred, well-heeled acquaintances' mockery, even after ten years of playing this role, he forced himself to make a light reply. "Aye, and it's a new pair of Hoby's best boots I intend on winning from him tonight."

"Here, here!" Westerley called as Rafe slapped Markham on the back.

"Before that, I've a mind to do some riding. I wondered—" Teagan began.

"Try the red-haired tart," Rafe interrupted.

As the other men hooted, Markham added, "The blond filly's got a nice tight saddle as well."

After waiting for the merriment to subside—and noticing Lord Riverton's curious glance focused on him, Teagan continued. "I appreciate your recommendations, gentlemen, but 'twas riding of a more equine nature I intended. My black needs exercise."

"Damme, why won't you sell that beauty to me?" Markham complained. "Don't know how you afford him."

"Why, by winning blunt from obliging gentlemen such as yourself," Teagan replied.

"For the black I'd pay you more than enough to keep you in booze and strumpets for a year!"

"A tempting prospect." Teagan assumed a thoughtful pose, as if considering Markham's offer. "But then, were I to turn Ailainn over to the likes of a rider like you, sure and the stallion would never forgive me."

While the other gentlemen laughed, Teagan addressed Rafe. "Can I ride in any direction, or have you left a jealous husband hereabouts who's like to shoot at me if I stray onto his land?"

Rafe grinned. "Jealous husbands are your forte—I stick to doxies. Might want to stay away from the north—Sir Arthur Hardesty's just the sort of sanctimonious prig to chastise a fellow for trespassing. Not much of a view to the west, but the woods to the east are pretty enough." His grin widened. "Especially if the widowed Lady Arnold happens to be riding."

"A widow, you say?" Westerley chimed in. "Sounds like just the thing for the Jester! Wealthy, is she?"

"Alas, no—sorry, Jester, she's nearly as indigent as you," Rafe answered. "When her soldier-husband cocked up his toes, the barony and its land went to a cousin. He grew up here at Eastwoods—his mama's property, so it wasn't entailed. If that little sheep farm brings his widow above five hundred a year, I'd be vastly surprised."

"Definitely not for the Jester, then," Westerley said. "He prefers 'em rich—and grateful."

Teagan merely raised a noncommittal eyebrow. Outwardly he followed the conversation, nodding or commenting as required, while his mind ticked off the tidbits of information. So she was "Lady Arnold." Well, until he learned her given name he'd continue to call her Lady Mystery. He didn't wish to think of her by the mark another man had left on her.

About all he'd left her, apparently. No wonder she looked so hungry. He felt an answering hunger sharpen within him.

"Pretty widow, you said, Rafe?" Markham was asking. "Maybe 'tis my duty as a gentleman to ease her loneliness."

That comment jolted him out of reverie. The idea of the corpulent Markham forcing his inebriated hands and whoremongering body onto Teagan's slender Lady Mystery spiked the rage that always smoked beneath his surface.

"Really, Markham," he drawled, "if the lady's truly as comely as Rafe says, I fear she'd prefer the sheep."

Markham glared, but with the other men seconding Teagan, didn't hazard a reply. When he stopped laughing, Rafe added, "Even were Markham as handsome as Jester, I doubt the widow'd have him. Totally devoted to poor old Hugh, she was. He'd taken some sort of ghastly wound, and she nursed him for months. Died in her arms, the story goes." Rafe thumped his chest and sighed. "So romantic."

"Stop, you'll have me in tears." Westerley tittered. "I might have to make a condolence call—if she's worth the trip, Rafe?"

"Only if you like a heart-shaped face with big brown eyes, lots of wavy dark hair and a figure…" He traced an hourglass shape with his hands.

Enough, thought Teagan. Lady Mystery was *his*. "Doubtless you'll sober up sufficiently en route that you won't run your mount into a tree," he said. "Best hurry off, though, since you'll have to sit an interminable time sipping tea in a stuffy parlor while you figure how to charm her out of her skirts. But if you'd rather do that than avail yourself of the beauteous company our kind host has so

thoughtfully provided...'' He let the sentence trail off and
shrugged. ''The redhead's a hot one, you said?''

His irritation apparently forgotten, Markham brightened.
''Aye. Come to think of it, this game is cursed flat. Think
I'll go find that little ladybird.''

''Give me your cue, then, Markham,'' Teagan said.
''Westerley, are you off, or can I count on lining my pockets with more of your gold?''

Teagan held his breath while the man stood frowning,
knowing he could not push further without arousing suspicion. ''I'm in,'' Westerley said at last. ''No female's
worth sobering up for, 'specially not one that needs persuading. Save me the blonde, eh?'' he told Markham, and
leveled his cue.

Relieved, Teagan looked up to find Riverton studying
him. His lordship had taken no part in the banter, continuing with his game as if oblivious. As he looked at Teagan
now, though, the man's lips slowly formed a grin.

Teagan had the oddest feeling Lord Riverton realized
exactly what he'd wished to accomplish in that conversation.

Nonsense, he thought, shaking off the notion. He raised
his cue, took a careful breath and sighted the ball. If Lady
Luck continued to smile, when next he went riding, his
pockets would be plumper by several hundred pounds.
Business accomplished, he'd have earned the leisure to pursue only pleasure—his, and that of one special dark-haired
lady.

Chapter Three

As her mare crested the ridge, Valeria looked down across the pasture to the stone roof of Eastwoods and tried to quell a sharp disappointment. She had nearly completed her normal route—had dawdled, even—but had caught no glimpse of a cat-eyed rogue. Either he did not ride this morning, or he'd taken care to avoid censorious widows.

The depth of her disappointment irritated her nearly as much as the pitifully nervous, flustered state in which she'd begun her ride. Specter, her gray mare, had sidestepped as Valeria mounted, and shied at every turn during the first half hour, unsettled by her equally unsettled rider. At least now Valeria had herself well in hand.

Irritation drained away, and, as she gazed at the view that signaled the end of her ride, a deep sadness welled up. There'd be no knight on a white charger to steal her from the tedium of her day and lift her to a glorious, fleeting pinnacle of delight.

No, she thought as she let the mare pick her way down the steep hill to the mowed pasture, today would settle into the same rhythm as all her yesterdays since Hugh's death, offering nothing more exciting than bills to pay, the shearing to schedule, Cook's complaints to soothe and Sukey Mae's inattention to correct.

Reaching level ground, she tautened the reins. Enough lamenting. Valeria Winters Arnold, soldier's daughter, would simply make the best of whatever life offered, which at this moment meant urging her mare to one last gallop across the meadow into the orchard.

Sensing her mistress's mood, Specter whinnied, clearly eager for the run. After spurring the horse to a gallop, Valeria narrowed her eyes, the better to savor the tempest of wind through her hair, against her face. Almost, she could imagine herself back on the vast brown plains of India, racing with Papa and Elliot on her first pony. Sharp longing pierced her for that lazy long-ago when every day brought new vistas, new experiences, and life seemed brimming with possibility. Tears, not entirely from the bite of the wind, pricked at her eyes.

Not until she was pulling up under the canopy of apple branches did she hear the pounding of hooves behind her. Surprise and dread clenching her chest in nearly equal measure, she turned in the saddle.

Racing toward her on a magnificent black stallion, golden hair incandescent in the sunlight, came Teagan Fitzwilliams.

Her hands went to ice, her mind to a blank. When he reined in beside her, laughing, she could think of absolutely nothing to say.

"Sure, and a fine morning it is for riding, ma'am. 'Tis a lovely mount you've got there."

His unusual cat-eyes seemed to catch and refract every golden sunbeam, appearing ten times more luminous now than in the shadowed barn yesterday. "Y-your stallion is finer..." she began before, captivated by the twinkle in their kaleidoscope depths, her words trailed off.

Lady Hardesty was right, she thought wonderingly. His eyes did hypnotize.

She realized she was still staring, her lips half-open. Lud, she must look like a drooling dimwit.

So much for enticing him! She felt the heat of embarrassment all the way to her toes.

Before she wrenched her glance away, though, she got a good enough look to realize that full sunlight magnified not just the attraction of his eyes, but the perfection of every feature—straight nose, high cheekbones, sensual lips, thick hair of a shade that mingled corn silk and strawberry, and cried out for a woman's fingers to comb through it. Even his tanned skin was marvelous, dusted with an endearing sprinkle of freckles.

Merciful heavens, how could plain little Valeria Arnold think such a godlike creature would ever give her a second glance?

Her fingers trembling again, she fumbled to pull the slack reins taut, ready to kick Specter to a canter and ride away before she humiliated herself totally. But when Mr. Fitzwilliams spoke again, courtesy forced her to halt.

''What reward shall we offer for so capital a run?''

Kisses was the only idea that popped into her head. As she could scarcely say that, she said nothing.

''Have you brought no treats? Whist, and with the trees so bare. Mayhap your mare can wait, but the stallion must have his now.''

Struck by all the double meanings, she jumped when he reached out—then pulled an apple from his jacket pocket.

He meant the horses. Of course he meant the horses. Another wave of heat scorched her cheeks.

She ducked her head, mortified. She couldn't do this. She simply wasn't cut out for it.

At last she dared to raise her face, compelled by a need so acute she could taste it, helpless to depart without stealing one last, longing look into the forbidden face of pleasure.

Motionless, he stared back while she simply watched him, enraptured once more by the dancing light in his eyes.

Before she could summon the will to tighten her reins

and kick her horse forward, Mr. Fitzwilliams jumped down from the saddle and stepped over to trap her gloved hand.

Her gaze flew back to his.

"Don't go, sweet lady," he whispered.

Bittersweet anxiety paralyzed her chest, robbed her of breath. She must turn away, she must, before his knowing eyes read in hers the naked hunger blazing there.

Then he smiled again. "Dismount, if you would. I've enough for us both."

It took an instant for her to realize he meant the apple. Breaking it in two, he held up a piece and waited.

She eased herself to the ground. After she took the chunk he offered, he turned to feed his half to the stallion. Specter nipped her fingers when she held on too long to the mare's portion, watching him, her heartbeat quick-stepping like infantrymen on the attack.

"T-thank you," she managed finally.

"Did you not think I'd come back?" he asked, facing her once more.

She moistened her dry lips enough to speak. "Nay."

"How could I not? There's unfinished business between us, Lady Arnold."

"What busi—oh! You know my name!"

"I made sure to find out."

Panic swept through her and she rifled a glance toward the house. "But I mustn't be seen—"

"Whoa, steady now. No one knows I came."

"Is a rogue discreet, then?"

His eyebrows lifted, the half smile fading. "Ah, I see you've been warned. It's flattered I should be, I suppose, if my very appearance in a neighborhood is enough for good folk to spread the alarm."

To her surprise, she heard bitterness under the banter.

"I'm a desperate character, a thief and a rogue. Have I the right of it?"

"'Tis what I was told," she admitted.

"And what does the lady think?"

Her next words seemed to form of their own accord, without thought or volition. "I want you to kiss me."

Aghast when she realized she'd actually spoken the thought aloud, she braced herself for his laughter.

Instead, the cynical twist left his lips and his smile turned brilliant. "Anything for my lady's pleasure."

After looping his reins around one gloved hand, he stepped to her and tilted her chin up with the other.

The bottom dropped out of her stomach and she couldn't feel her fingertips. Every nerve in her body switched off save those at her lips, which awaited in screaming impatience the slow descent of his mouth.

Her eyes fluttered shut as she felt the warmth of his breath, then the gentle brush of his lips, soft as butterfly wings, teasing. When he brushed her lips again, this time tracing them with the wet blade of his tongue, he had to grab at her waist to keep her from falling.

The stallion shifted, tugging at the reins, and Teagan backed away. "So sweet," she thought he murmured, his voice thick, his breathing rough. But she wasn't sure she was hearing properly over the roaring in her ears.

She simply couldn't let him ride off yet.

Desperate purpose stiffened her and she called out, her voice sounding odd and breathy. "Mr. Fitzwilliams! Your…your horse. There's hay. In—in the barn." With a jerky motion she indicated the trail toward the manor.

To her mingled horror and relief, he nodded. And after he assisted her to remount, when she kicked Specter to a trot, his black followed.

She'd waited for him. A grin of pure delight on his face, Teagan kept Ailainn in line behind Lady Arnold, the better to savor the sight of her trim posterior bouncing on the sidesaddle.

The black habit was more threadbare than he remembered, but that confirmation of her poverty he readily excused, for the thin material molded that much more closely over the full breasts, slender shoulders and long, graceful line of leg. Curves as enchanting, as enticing as he remembered, and more.

A day of fantasizing over what he would do with and to those curves had strengthened desire to a fine edge. Teagan wanted his Lady Mystery as he'd not wanted any woman in a very long time.

But desire was only partly responsible for the savage, purely male satisfaction that swelled his chest. In her every hesitant move, in the enormous dark eyes clouded with confusion and hunger, he read the incredible truth.

Lady Arnold had never done this before.

All the women with whom he'd trysted, back to the very first, had been in greater or lesser degree masters of the game of seduction, using with practiced skill all the feminine weapons of enticement.

Lady Arnold, though, like the half-gentled colts he'd trained in his youth, was attracted but wary, ready to bolt at the first alarm. Her indecision, her utter vulnerability spoke strongly to him on some deep level beyond reason or explanation.

It sharpened his need, honed every sense knife-blade keen—and filled him with an odd tenderness. Lady Arnold, he vowed, would never regret taking her first lover. He would give her everything for which that yearning, doe-eyed glance begged—everything and more.

He mimicked her movements, slowing their pace to let the horses cool, then dismounting to lead them into the stable yard, delay heightening anticipation.

She motioned for him to bring Ailainn to a stall in the barn where he'd first met her—was it just yesterday?—then went to swiftly unsaddle and corral her mare.

Once finished, she hesitated at the paddock rail, her back to him, as if marshaling her courage. With a sigh that shook her slender frame, she turned and walked toward him, high color in her heart-shaped face.

He kept motionless, barely breathing, for she looked as if even now she might change her mind and flee. As she neared with hesitant steps, he slowly reached out his hand, wanting to lure her closer, ease for her the moment of first contact.

Trust me, he silently urged.

Lips trembling too much for the smile she tried to form them into, she raised her hand to his. Pure energy crackled between them as their fingers touched.

She gasped, moved as if to back away. He tightened his grip, pulling her gently toward him, then raising her gloved hand to his lips and holding it there until her resistance faded. Once again, her eyelids fluttered shut.

Teagan battled a fierce desire to seize her in his arms, free right now from its chains of uncertainty the passion simmering in her body. With vivid clarity he could picture her writhing beside him, under him, and knew he could guide them both to release more intense than they'd ever before experienced.

"Shall we go into the house?" he asked.

With a flutter of lashes, her eyes opened, panic once again in their depths. "No, I cannot! My maid...the butler... No, it must be here." She pulled her hand free and pointed to the hayloft. "Th-there."

As if having suddenly reached an irrevocable decision, she strode quickly to the ladder leading up to the loft, shedding her bonnet as she walked.

He followed, grinning, ambushed once more by tenderness. His sweet Lady Mystery, hiding out not from a jealous husband but from her household staff.

He wanted better for their first loving than a rapid tumble in a haybarn—fine linen sheets, champagne, hours of the slow teasing build to ecstasy. But he sensed for right now, this was all she'd allow. More, longer, later, he silently promised as he followed her up.

When her booted foot slipped on the ladder, he caught her against him, her deliciously rounded derriere pressed against the aching fullness at his groin. For a moment neither could move. Teagan's hands were shaking almost as much as hers by the time they reached the hayloft.

She scooted across the loft to stand facing him, back against a fragrant stack of hay bales, hands fluttering nervously at her sides.

Lady Mystery had no idea what to do next.

Though he knew each second of delay must be stretching her overwrought nerves to the breaking point, he simply had to take a moment to drink in the sight of her. Thick, dark brown hair, a froth of curls escaping the pins at her nape and temples. Pale face that was all huge brown eyes over a straight little nose and trembling, plum-plump lips. High pert breasts made to fit into his hands; rounded hips made to fit against his body.

"What's your given name?"

She started. "V-Valeria."

Though she had nowhere to run now, he approached slowly. "By the blessed saints, you are beautiful, Valeria."

Her gaze never left him, yet still she jumped when he gently cupped her face in his hands.

And nearly destroyed his control by reaching up to clutch his fingers and whisper, "Please."

Only a direct hit by a lightning bolt could have stopped him then. He meant to merely brush her lips, as he had before, but when she opened her mouth at his touch, sparks of fire danced through him. He responded in kind, trapping the fullness of her lower lip and tongue against his teeth. His arms whipped around her shoulders to pull her close, while he nibbled the sweetness of her mouth, then delved deeper to explore the velvet wonders within.

He wanted to proceed slowly, but he absolutely had to

feel the weight and softness of her bare breasts in his hands. Feverishly he unbuttoned her spencer and cast it aside, then worked at loosening the fastenings of her gown.

She tried to help, her hands bumping into his in equal haste, until at last he pulled the gown free to run his fingertips across the tightened nubs of nipple and around the warm, satin globes.

He caught her gasp on his tongue and drank deeply as his hands plied her breasts, her body shuddering at each stroke. Her flailing fingers snagged his shirtfront, then, awkward, tentative, began to insinuate their way inside.

He nearly lost control when one slim finger found bare skin. Gasping in turn, he had to pull back. And he froze as, with awe in her eyes, Valeria carefully unfastened the shirt buttons and bared his chest.

She glanced up, as if seeking permission, and he gave a curt nod. Reverently, as if he were a precious object, she placed both palms against his flesh, then traced her fingers over the muscles of his arms, his shoulders and down to the nipples.

''Beautiful,'' she whispered.

His chest tightened with emotion almost as powerful as the desire thrumming in his blood—the unique sensation of being cherished.

''B-beautiful,'' he repeated, watching her.

With a hunger stronger than any he could ever remember, he craved complete union, the feeling of his body sheathed in hers, the total possession of her whimsical, greedy honesty.

Swiftly he spread a nearby saddle blanket, urged her down upon it, stripping off her chemise and skirts as he went, then shucking his own garments. Her eyes closed and her head lolled back when, with lips and teeth and tongue, he paid homage to the perfection of her breasts.

At first she stiffened when he slid his hand up the smoothness of her inner thigh, until he soothed her with more drugging kisses. Her nails bit into his shoulders when he lowered his mouth to suck hard at the taut nipples, while inch by inch his fingers crept up her thigh. And she cried out when he at last delved inside, to find her wet and ready.

But though his need was now so acute that delay was almost pain, he first wanted more. And so, crooning encouragement, he suckled harder, licked the moisture in the valley of her breasts and moved his thumb around and over her hidden pearl, deepening the pressure until she reached her peak. With triumphant tenderness he watched a burst of ecstasy light her eyes before robbing her of sense and sight.

After a few moments, when her crazed breathing steadied, he nudged her legs apart. Though he craved a taste of her, he knew with the small nugget of brain still functioning that he couldn't last much longer. Still he staved off completion a bit longer, to rally her with kisses on her pleasure-bruised mouth, until her breathing quickened and her passion-rosy nipples once again stiffened.

Only then did he position himself over her. But a maelstrom of mind-melting sensation began swirling within him as soon as he eased his needy member into her. The final shreds of control dissolved and he drove hard, unable to stop or even slow the explosion he'd staved off so long.

Even so, after the smooth glide of entry he noted unexpected tightness. His last conscious thought, before a wave of pleasure carried him into the nearest thing to heaven on earth, was the incredible realization that he was indeed Valeria's first lover. Her very first.

Drenched in sweat, her breath still coming in gasps, Valeria slowly struggled to consciousness.

She was lying in her hayloft. Naked. With a handsome man half reclining on her chest, a man who had just transported her on what had been, except for the last painful bit, the most excruciatingly intense, unforgettable adventure of her life.

A ferocious gladness filled her. Whatever happened now, she'd never regret this. Even the shameful knowledge that yesterday she'd almost dismissed her maid for the same indiscretion she'd just committed couldn't overshadow her joy.

She was smiling at the thought, heat still simmering in her veins, when the man who'd tenderly initiated her into the wonders of love play hauled her to her feet.

And stood, magnificently proud and naked, arms crossed, glaring down at her.

Eyes shocked wide open, she goggled at him.

Before she could even begin to figure out what made him suddenly so angry, he gestured toward the blanket.

A blanket, she discovered to her dismay, that was liberally stained with blood.

"Now, madam, might you do me the gracious favor of explaining just how it is you came to be a widow without having ever been a wife?"

"It must be my courses—" she began.

"Nay, don't think to fob me off. I've experience enough to know you had none, even though I've never before taken an untried lass."

Numbly she felt at the stickiness on her legs. "I'm b-bleeding?"

Some of the panicky surprise in her voice must have penetrated his rage, for his grim look lightened. "'Tis not uncommon the first time, I'm told, and 'twill likely stop soon." The momentary respite quickly ended, though. "So what were you about, woman? Surely you didn't think to catch yourself a husband!"

"Certainly not!" she exclaimed, aghast. "Even did I want one, I cannot imagine a less likely candidate for matrimony than you!"

The undisguised horror in her tone might have been

taken as an insult, but instead Teagan's face cleared. "Saints be praised, you recognize that truth! Here, then." He fished a handkerchief out of his coat pocket.

Suddenly recalling her own nakedness, she snatched the handkerchief with one hand and her discarded chemise with the other. Wrapping the latter around herself, she rummaged at the periphery of the rumpled blanket for the rest of her garments.

A touch at her shoulder made her jump. She looked over at Teagan, clothed now in his breeches. "Let me," he said, gently tugging on the chemise. "It's a fine lady's maid I make."

She allowed him to help her into the chemise, her nervousness returning now that the fire of passion had cooled. Embarrassment threatened as well, and she blessed her wisdom in choosing as a lover someone she'd need never see again.

But as he turned her around to face him, she couldn't help reaching once more to touch the satin steel of his chest, slowly stroking with the pads of her fingers each sculpted muscle.

He caught up her hand and kissed it. Then, when she reached for the gown he still held, he moved it beyond her reach. "Nay, I'm not leaving until you tell me why. Why me, today. And how any man breathing could have left so lovely a bride untouched. Unless you were wed by proxy?"

"No."

"Then why?"

He pinned her with that piercing, cat-eyed stare. Still too rattled to manufacture a lie, she blurted out the truth. "He never wanted me. Hugh was my brother's best friend. When he returned from Spain to tell me my brother had died, he asked me to marry him. I didn't figure out until later he did so only out of duty."

"When he left you on your wedding night?"

All the disappointment, humiliation and heartache of that night swelled up from memory, nearly choking her.

"Y-yes."

"But the story goes that he died in your arms. Was that a lie?"

"Nay."

"Then he must have come to—"

"Don't!" she cried, not wanting Teagan to probe into truths still too painful to be borne. And then, suddenly, she was furious with him for stripping her naked, not just to the skin, but to the soul.

"Oh yes," she spat out, "Hugh died in my arms. But not because he'd come to love his friend's poor orphaned sister. He died too delirious with fever to know in whose arms he lay. Aye, died with a woman's name on his lips— but it wasn't mine."

She closed her eyes and put shaking fingers to her temples, as if to squeeze shut the floodgates of memory.

After a few moments of silence, during which she recovered a modicum of control, Mr. Fitzwilliams said quietly, "He was a cad, then."

"Nay, you mustn't think that! He never betrayed me. The lady he loved had refused him some months before he married me, I later discovered. Hugh rejoined the army the day after our wedding and did not return until he was sent back gravely wounded."

She faced Teagan squarely. "So I was never a wife. But I longed to experience passion, to know what force it is that can drive men and women to such extremes of courage and folly. Situated as I am here, with little hope of ever moving in larger society, I thought you might be the perfect gentleman to show me. With, of course, no further obligation on either part."

He considered her. "You chose me as your tutor?"

She blushed. "I hoped you might be."

To her relief, for she half expected a revival of his anger, he made her a deep bow. "'Tis fair honored I am at your confidence in my…abilities. However, I fear I've not nearly lived up to that trust. Yet."

"Yet?" she echoed, her eyes widening. "There's… more?" Valeria couldn't imagine how those sweet sensations could possibly intensify without stopping her heart entirely.

He chuckled. "Many and wondrous are the ways to heaven, my lady."

Already the potent promise in his eyes, the smile dancing at his lips sent coils of anticipation spiraling to her now-quiescent core. She ought to finish dressing, send him on his way, and yet… "Show me."

He made a sweeping gesture. "Here? Now?"

"Neither Cook nor the butler ever venture to the barn, and I told my maid Mercy I'd ride long today. 'Tis the groom's day off and I sent Sukey Mae to town." Valeria hesitated, still shy of expressing her desires. "I've time, if…if you have."

"All the time in the universe," he whispered, and pulled her back to the blanket.

Then, at teasing length, he proceeded to reveal to her the full shattering beauty of ecstasy untarnished by pain.

Much later, as she lay in his arms, damp and sated, her mind floating in a sensual haze, the sharp bark of a dog warning of intruders jerked her alert.

"Heavens, that might be Sukey Mae returning. I must go."

She sat up, but as she reached for her chemise, he stopped her, bending to capture one nipple and worry it between his teeth.

The now-familiar warmth pooled at her center and coiled in her belly. She arched her neck, indulging herself one final moment in delightful torment. Then she gently pulled his head up to meet her lips.

She used her tongue as he'd taught her, wanting to convey not just her new knowledge but her thanks. A soul-deep thanks for this gift of pleasure he'd brought her—which mere words were hopelessly inadequate to convey.

Nonetheless, she would speak them. "Mr. Fitzwilliams."

"Teagan," he corrected. "Sure, and 'mister' is a bit too formal now."

She had to smile. It *was* ludicrous to fall back into the convention that did not allow the use of given names until after a formal, third-party introduction.

"Teagan. I must go, but first I would thank—"

"Nay." He stopped her with a finger to her lips.

"Should I not thank you?" She smiled slightly. "I'm sorry, I don't know what one—"

His hands flashed up to grip her arms so tightly she fell silent. "God forbid you should ever know," he said fiercely, and kissed her.

She'd feared it would be awkward, going about the business of dressing, tidying her hair. But once again, Teagan made it easy for her, commanding her to button up his shirt, alternating between straightforward lacing of her garments and teasing touches that let the sensual spell linger and slowly, slowly dissolve.

Ah, how swiftly she could come to crave his touch.

She dare not permit that. "When does your party expect to depart?"

"In a few days." He stopped fastening his waistcoat to study her face. "Will you ride tomorrow?"

She didn't pretend to misunderstand. "To fulfill a dream is splendid. But to try to live it again and again would be…dangerous." She swallowed hard. "It might then be very difficult to let it go at all."

He remained silent a long moment, his face unreadable, then nodded. "'Tis rare to find a lady as wise as she is beautiful."

A ridiculous hurt pierced her. What had she expected? That this handsome man, who probably had to turn away eager women wherever he went, would seek to persuade her?

Trying to reassemble the shattered bits of who she used to be, Valeria descended the ladder, then watched, already lost in bittersweet anguish, as Teagan prepared to ride away.

Before mounting the stallion, he walked over to give her one last kiss.

"Having plucked about as much as I can from the pigeons at Rafe's, I shall probably head back to London. If—if there should be some unexpected...consequence to this morning's pleasure, you will let me know?"

She gave her head a negative shake. "There won't be." She didn't wish to wound him by adding she could think of no one less qualified to assume the duties of fatherhood.

Nonetheless, he seemed to guess her thoughts. "Of course not. Whist, and what finer papa could a lad wish for than a shiftless Irish gambler?"

Before she could reply, he had hoisted himself into the saddle and swept her a bow. "Goodbye, Lady Arnold. God be with you."

"Mr. Fitzwilliams."

Wheeling the stallion, he set off across the stable yard toward the orchard. And did not look back.

A sinking feeling invaded her chest, as if her heart were a small pebble that had just been tossed into a very deep pond.

It was imperative that he ride away, she reminded herself.

A far greater danger than discovery stalked her. Were the fascinating Mr. Fitzwilliams to remain in the neighborhood, she was not at all sure she could prevent herself from attempting to seek him out. Her senses, awakened to delights of which she'd formerly had only the haziest conception, already clamored for more.

More of what the supremely skilled Mr. Fitzwilliams had

given her. What, she forced herself to acknowledge, he would in future give, with equal skill and thoroughness, to other ladies. She dare not read into their interlude, searing as it had been for her, any more than that.

Lud, though, 'twas a wonder women did not follow his carriage or throw themselves before his horse.

How ignorant she'd been when she'd blithely decided to satisfy the wonderings of her mind and the cravings of her body with one brief, blissful episode. Thinking she could then put it all behind her and go on unchanged, as men seemed to do so easily.

Only now, as her eyes followed the figure on horseback climbing the hill beyond the orchard, was the sober truth sinking in to her already-sorrowing mind and her already-needy body.

A woman couldn't give herself to a man without losing a part of her soul. And some irretrievable piece of hers was now disappearing down the ridge beyond Eastwoods in the possession of a wandering rogue she'd never see again.

Bemused as well as satisfied, Teagan guided Ailainn through the woods toward Rafe's hunting box. Faith, he still wasn't sure that he'd not just trysted with a goddess come to earth as a wood nymph.

Certainly Valeria—he let the music of her name play through his mind—had been nothing like any mortal woman he'd bedded, and he'd bedded a fair number. No, in a world where everything had its price and everyone who permitted the Jester close demanded his best performance, she had entreated only with her eyes and a whispered "please." Using no artifice to entice, intent not on punishing an errant husband or enlivening a selfish boredom, but on capturing wonder, she had, with her innocent yet powerful response, brought to passion a sweet majesty long since lost to him.

Could it be he'd encountered that rarest of all jewels—

a truly honest woman? One like his mother, who'd flouted her father's authority to follow the man she loved, faithful until the day she'd died—abandoned by that man.

The father whose irresponsible blood also flowed in Teagan's veins.

No, even if Valeria Arnold were gold, it was among dross that the Jester belonged, he reminded himself. With his pockets now well-lined with Rafe's and his friends' blunt, best to put this all-too-fascinating wood sprite out of mind and return to London immediately. After all, the winnings would last only so long. He must plan the Jester's next performance.

And extinguish this frighteningly intense desire to wheel Ailainn around and ride back to her.

Chapter Four

A week later Valeria pulled Specter to a halt before the barn. After giving the mare a final pat, she dismounted and handed the reins to the waiting groom.

Her cheeks warmed as she watched him lead the horse into the shadowed interior. She'd not been inside the structure since her tryst the week previous, an interlude so shocking, splendid and entirely beyond the scope of her normal staid existence that she now had difficulty believing it had really transpired.

Except for the constant, subtle hum of her awakened senses, the sharp and disquieting need that pulsed through her whenever, in some unguarded moment, her thoughts drifted back to that unprecedented morning. As all too often they seemed to do.

Firmly arresting the insidious longing to think on it again, she jerked her attention back to her conversation this morning with Gilbert, the farm's competent but rather taciturn foreman. Reviewing the laconic replies to her inquiries about the upcoming shearing, Valeria thought ruefully that Gilbert, having dealt with sheep all his life, seemed to commune with the beasts more readily than with two-legged beings. Given the state of her finances, however, it appeared Valeria would have a long, uninterrupted span of years in which to learn how to extract from him the information she needed.

Unless, out of boredom and despair, she finally accepted Arthur Hardesty's offer.

A shudder shook her frame. After that interlude in the hay barn, she would rather embrace the genteel poverty of Eastwinds.

She was trying, without much success, to raise her spirits out of the doldrums into which those dispiriting reflections had cast her when she spied Mercy, bonnet and apron blowing in the wind, trotting toward her.

Since the maid had suffered an injury to her ankle in India and normally avoided walking, Valeria felt an immediate frisson of alarm. "Is something wrong?" she called as the woman approached.

"I don't know," Mercy gasped, pausing to catch her breath. "There be a courier come with a message for you, sayin' he's to stay till you give him a note in return."

"A courier?" Valeria echoed in surprise. "From whom?"

"Wouldna say, Mistress. Nor would he even hand Masters the note, sayin' he was ordered to deliver it to you personal!" The elderly maid snorted in disapproval. "There's wishin' I was that your papa's batman were still about to give 'im a right proper set-down!"

"No matter," Valeria replied, falling into step beside the maid. "I expect we shall soon learn his errand."

When they reached the manor, Mercy halted. "Into the parlor with you now. I'll go round to the kitchen and fetch you up some tea whilst Masters tells Mr. Airs-and-Graces he can bring you the missive."

Within moments after Valeria had put up her whip and gloves and repaired to the parlor, Mercy entered the room with a tray of steaming tea, a young man in dark blue livery following in her wake. The maid jerked her chin at the newcomer. "Here he be, Mistress—whoever he be."

"Saunders, ma'am," the courier said, doffing his hat and offering a bow. "Sent to yer with this—" he held out a sealed letter "—by my mistress, Lady Winterdale."

Valeria scanned her memory. "The Dowager Countess of Winterdale?"

"Yes, ma'am. Begging yer pardon, Lady Arnold, if'n I disturbed yer house—" he glanced at Mercy, who gave an audible sniff "—but my mistress said as how I weren't to speak to no other but you, and was ta put this straight into yer hand. She also said I were not ta be quit o' this place till I had yer message in return."

"Very well, Saunders. I'll ring when it's ready. Mercy, would you escort him back downstairs, please."

After nodding a dismissal, Valeria deposited the vellum packet on the table beside her chair and poured herself a cup of tea, wondering what was so urgent that her husband's grandmother, a woman she had never met, thought it necessary to send the news by courier.

Word of some special bequest?

A thrill shivered through her before she laughed, dismissing so fanciful—if appealing—a notion. For one, Lady Winterdale was obviously very much alive, and besides, if someone had bequeathed her late husband anything of value, notice of it would surely come through a lawyer.

Seating herself, she broke the seal and began to read.

My dear Valeria,

It was a great sadness to me that my indifferent health precluded my attending your wedding to my grandson at Portsmouth, and an even greater one that illness prevented my journeying to Eastwoods to see Hugh before his tragic demise.

I have heard much of your devoted care to him during his long decline. Now I beg you will show compassion for the grief of an old lady and come to London, that you might relate to me every detail of Hugh's last few months.

I've instructed my courier to wait upon your reply, that I might know when I can look forward to your arrival. Until then, I remain, yours...

After the usual expression of compliments, the note ended with the dowager's signature in an impressive looping scrawl.

Valeria sat back in her chair, irritation and amusement mingling with her surprise. Summon her to London, did the countess, and with such arrogant assumption of Valeria's instant obedience that she'd had her messenger wait upon Valeria's reply!

Granddaughter-in-law or no, she was not a lackey to spring to the countess's bidding. Though she had to admit the idea of visiting the grand metropolis of London, a city she'd never seen, was vastly appealing.

London, center of business and trade, of government, of Society. London, where the members of the ton—that privileged world to which she belonged by birth but to whom she had never been presented—would gather for the Season.

London, where one charming and unforgettable Irish rogue was doubtless now residing.

A rush of excitement tingled her nerves. Don't be a looby, she chastised herself. Even if she did not resent the command thinly veiled beneath the politeness of the dowager's invitation, the cost of such a journey made it out of the question. Much as she sympathized with the old lady's evident need to cling to every memory of her beloved relative—a need with which Valeria was all too familiar.

Mindful of the waiting courier, she quickly composed a

reply, which, while honoring the countess's grief, was nonetheless firm in refusal. After sanding and sealing her note, she regarded it with a sigh.

London. Like so many other exotic lands and adventures she longed to experience, distance and poverty rendered this one just out of reach.

But one adventure she had claimed. A fierce gladness filled her that she had triumphed over modesty, upbringing and abject terror to seize the opportunity life had granted her. Especially since with the beginning of her courses, she now knew that stolen interlude had not left her a permanent and scandalous memento of her recklessness.

She suppressed a grin when Masters appeared practically the instant she rang the bell pull. No doubt her servants were as agog to learn the courier's message as they were insulted by his method of delivering it.

"Would you tell Saunders I have his message ready?"

"At once, my lady." However, Masters hesitated. "I trust nothing of an...alarming nature has occurred, ma'am?"

"No, Masters. My husband's grandmother merely wished to convey her sympathy on my recent loss."

The momentary crease of his brow told her Masters found that excuse for a courier-delivered message unconvincing, but he forbore further questioning. "I'm relieved to hear that," he said, and bowed himself out.

As she awaited the courier, Valeria mentally reviewed the list of small, dull, but necessary chores that would occupy the rest of her day. Another sigh escaped. Valeria Arnold, good soldier's daughter, would do what she must without further repining. Still, how exciting it would be to be reviewing instead the plans for departing to London!

A sharp knock at the door pulled her from her lapse into melancholia. "You may give your mistress this, with my compliments," she said, holding out the letter.

Saunders took it and bowed. "If'n I may be so bold, Lady Arnold, when can I tell my mistress ye'll be comin'?"

Taken aback, Valeria hesitated. It seemed odd indeed that the countess would have made her servant aware of her invitation. "I shall not be going to London," she replied.

"Then, begging your pardon, ma'am, my mistress said I was to give yer this—" the courier reached into his vest to extract another folded square of vellum "—n' this." From his trouser pocket he produced a fat leather purse.

Valeria heard the distinctive clink of coins as he transferred the articles to her outstretched hand. Her heartbeat leaped as her palm dipped under their weight.

For a moment she simply stared at him. "I—I shall require another moment, please," she said. After he bowed himself out, she hurried over to lay the money bag reverently on the desk, then ripped open the countess's second note and rapidly scanned the contents.

With numb fingers Valeria set the missive aside, loosened the pouch's drawstring and poured the coins onto the desk. Ten, twenty—there must be fifty golden guineas! No wonder the courier had been instructed to confide his message to none but the recipient.

Her mind still a swirl of disbelief, on knees gone suddenly weak she sank into her chair and, slowly this time, reread the countess's note.

My dear Valeria, I feared when my grandson went off soldiering, he would neglect his estates such that, with the barony's assets passing to Hugh's cousin upon his premature demise, he left you little beyond that wretched farm. Hardly a fitting repayment for your devoted care!

Lest a lack of funding prevent your accepting my invitation, my servant has been ordered to advance this

sum and arrange your food and lodging for the journey. I shall live in happy expectation of meeting you
shortly.

A rising excitement swamped any lingering vestiges of
irritation over the countess's high-handedness.

Gilbert could handle the shearing without Valeria, and
the small tasks awaiting her attention could just as easily
be accomplished a month or two from now. Could she but
persuade herself to accept the countess's largesse, she had
no compelling reason to refuse the invitation.

Ah, to escape this dull backwater—and in London! Pre-
mier city of England, seat of government, finance and Society…residence of Teagan Fitzwilliams.

'Twas ridiculous how her breath fluttered at the very
thought. Even should she go, London was a huge city. A
half-Irish gambler of dubious reputation would hardly frequent the same circles as the Countess of Winterdale.

However, were Valeria to go, she should be able to steal
a few hours in which to explore the fascinating metropolis
Elliot had described to her so enthusiastically. The soaring
heights of Westminster Cathedral and the perfection of Sir
Christopher Wren's masterpiece, St. Paul's. St. James's
Palace, surrounded by its vast park, and the grim silhouette
of the Tower brooding over the Thames. The pleasure gardens of Vauxhall, illumined at night by thousands of lights;
the docks by day crowded with ships unloading cargos from
exotic lands she so longed to visit.

Awe at actually being able to view such glorious vistas
scoured away the remnants of her resistance. Swiftly she
withdrew more paper and sharpened her pen.

But as she rapidly composed her acceptance, a guilty
excitement that had nothing to do with cathedrals, cargoes
or commerce thrummed through her.

* * *

Three weeks later, Valeria sat beside Mercy in the comfortable carriage Saunders had arranged, anxious for her first sight of the countess's town house. Though in India she'd viewed sprawling cities and the opulent splendor of a nawab's palace, she still found the vastness of London impressive, and the classically designed and detailed dwellings of Westminster and Mayfair most beautiful.

Lady Winterdale's residence, she discovered as the carriage halted at last, was a three-story brick residence set on the lush green expanse of Grosvenor Square.

"'Tis lovely, is it not, Mercy?"

"As long as the roof don't leak nor the chimney smoke, I shall like it well enough," the maid replied prosaically.

"I expect you can count on that!" But as Valeria ascended the stone stairs, sudden nervousness afflicted her, and she smoothed her wrinkled pelisse with anxious fingers. The owner of such magnificence was certain to be pained by her outmoded, rather worn apparel.

The gesture didn't escape Mercy's sharp eye. "No use fretting yourself, Miss Val. Lady Winterdale knows how you're circumstanced, and if she don't, she ought to!"

True enough, Valeria reassured herself as she entered the vast marble foyer. It really did not matter whether or not the old lady approved of her. Valeria was here only to recount the episodes Hugh's grandmother had requested, and after that would be on her way back to Yorkshire.

The butler, a forbidding personage with a stiffly starched collar and expression to match, directed Mercy to meet the housekeeper, and bade Valeria follow him to a guest bedchamber.

"Lady Winterdale will receive you after you've refreshed yourself from the journey," the butler said. "Molly can assist with whatever you require."

An apple-cheeked young servant awaited her within a spacious chamber furnished in Chippendale mahogany and rose satin. After the butler departed, the girl confided that the countess had assigned her to be Valeria's personal maid for the duration of her visit.

Eagerness to remove the grime of the road and curiosity to meet her benefactress spurred Valeria to make quick work of repairing her appearance. After insuring every braided hair was in place and her dowdy gown as presentable as a few moments' ministrations could make it, she rang the bell pull.

The butler led her to a much larger bedchamber whose tall Palladian windows overlooked the gardens behind the town house. The figure reclining on the ivory brocaded sofa in the room's center looked up as she entered.

"Lady Arnold of Eastwinds," the servant intoned.

"Countess, thank you for your kindness in bringing me to London," Valeria said with a curtsy.

"Come closer, gel, and let me have a look at you," the countess said. "Jennings, bring us sherry."

The butler hesitated and cleared his throat. "Your physician recommends only tea, my lady."

The countess grimaced. "Impudent sawbones! If I can't have a glass of sherry to celebrate the arrival of my grandson's wife, I might as well cock up my toes now."

Valeria thought she heard a sigh escape the butler before he turned to her. "Tea for you, Lady Arnold?"

"If you please."

"Old retainers," the countess muttered after the butler left. "Never know their place. Now come, give me your hand. I shan't bite, you know."

Valeria approached as bidden and held out her hand. As the dowager took her fingers in a surprisingly robust grip, each woman silently appraised the other, Valeria searching for signs of the man she'd loved.

With her slightly hawked nose, broad brow and well-shaped lips, the countess must have been striking rather than handsome as a girl. Though the face and figure gave little testimony to the closeness of blood between this woman and Valeria's late husband, the sharp, piercing black eyes that watched her every step were so reminiscent of Hugh's that Valeria felt an automatic pang.

Just so had Hugh scrutinized her, when he'd first accompanied Elliot to her father's billet. An impetuous fifteen-year-old delighted by her beloved brother's visit and overwhelmed by his handsome friend, she'd pelted the two with pebbles as they rode up the lane, desperate to attract their notice. Caught in bittersweet longing for those long-ago days, she said, "Hugh had your eyes."

The countess's expression softened. "Aye. You loved him well, did you not?"

"Yes." *But he didn't love me.* Surprised by the acuteness of her lingering pain over that bitter fact, Valeria could think of nothing further to say.

"Sit." The countess indicated a wing chair next to her. "Aside from the several letters I believe he dictated to you, I know nothing of how Hugh fared after he was wounded. So, tell me everything."

"Of course." Pausing only long enough to sip gratefully at the hot tea the butler brought, Valeria described to his grandmother the shock of viewing Hugh's bloodied body, rigid with pain and incoherent with fever as he was unloaded from the transport ship. Then the desperate first weeks when he hovered between living and dying, the slight improvement that allowed him to be conveyed back to the small farm at Eastwinds where he'd grown up...and the final, slow decline.

"You were with him at the end?" the countess demanded.

"Yes, my lady."

"Did he have any last words?"

Lydia...Lydia?

The echo of Hugh's hoarse whisper invaded her ears, unleashing a cache of infinitely painful memories.

"H-he was not speaking very clearly toward the end," Valeria evaded. She didn't want to recall the anguish she'd felt at discovering her husband had never stopped loving the girl who'd refused his suit—anguish mixed with anger at his approaching death, and despair that she was helpless to prevent it. Or the stubborn, hopeless love that had prompted her to comfort despite the blow his words had dealt her.

"I'm here, my dearest," she'd whispered back.

"Kiss me, Lydia," he'd gasped. "One…last time."

And so she'd pressed her trembling lips to his hot, cracked ones, cradling his emaciated body close while her tears fell and evaporated off his fevered skin, her heart splintered by the knowledge that she could ease his final suffering only by pretending to be someone else.

Once more tears gathered. She swiped at them, angry with the countess for exhuming the ugly, hurtful truth.

She looked up to find the old woman staring at her. "He thought of her, didn't he? His precious Lydia."

For a moment Valeria could not breathe. Then, the habit of replying truthfully too ingrained for her to quickly dredge up a lie, she sputtered, "He…I…how dare you ask?"

"Don't trifle with me, gel! I'll have an answer. Or did you think to come to London and wheedle me with lies, mayhap claim some of the bounty that would have been Hugh's, had he lived?"

Valeria felt her face whiten, then suffuse with color. Slowly she rose to her feet.

"I have provided as full an account of Hugh's demise as I can. That being done, you can have no further use of me. Thank you for the tea, Lady Winterdale. You needn't summon your butler—I can find my way out."

Too furious even to consider how she was to manage the expense of the return journey, Valeria curtsyed and whirled around, intent upon summoning Mercy and quitting the house as quickly as possible. Only to find her wrist caught in the grip of one thin, clawlike hand.

"Here now, where do you think you're going, you silly chit?" the dowager said, tugging on the arm she'd captured. "Sit back down! I may be old and invalidish, but my sources among Society are excellent. You have no friends or relations here. A lady don't stay alone at a hotel, though if that wretched pig farm leaves you with more than a feather to fly with, I shall own myself astonished."

"Sheep. We raise sheep," Valeria replied through clenched teeth. "And Eastwinds is doing quite well. If you will kindly release my wrist, I wish to leave."

"Well, *I* don't wish it," the Dowager returned. "'Tis one of the few privileges of age, missy, to conduct oneself badly and get away with it. But I intend to explain myself, so climb down from the boughs and hear me out." When Valeria remained stiffly upright, the countess gave her wrist another shake. "Sit, I say!"

After briefly entertaining—and discarding—the notion of arm-wrestling her husband's elderly relation, reluctantly Valeria sat.

Waiting a moment, as if to make sure Valeria would not spring up and quit the room if she released her, the old woman let go of her wrist.

"Since you require it, I shall remain," Valeria said. "However, I shall not answer any further questions, nor do I possess any interest whatsoever in any bequest you might have intended for Hugh."

"If you haven't any interest in additional funds, you're a nodcock, girl, and not the intelligent lady I believe you to be! Not but that I don't think the better of you for being offended by my plain speaking. No sly-smiling, weasel-faced flattery from you, which just confirms the good I've heard of your character.'' The countess nodded approvingly.

Rendered off balance by the sudden shift from attack to praise, Valeria sat silently, a sliver of amusement piercing the defensive shield of her ire.

Before she could formulate a suitable reply, the countess continued. ''First, let me assure you I consider it the best of good fortune that the bird-witted Lydia Fontescue refused Hugh's suit! Oh, she claimed to love him—'' the countess paused to give a disdainful sniff ''—until she learned he meant to go fight with Wellington. Not for Miss Lydia to chance being left on the shelf, should her fiancé die in some heathenish land!''

The discomfort Valeria might otherwise have suffered at being forced to endure a discussion of the woman her husband had loved was blunted both by surprise at the countess's outspokenness and a grudging sympathy with the illwill the woman obviously still harbored toward the lady who had rejected her grandson.

Allowing Valeria no chance to insert a comment, Lady Winterdale continued. ''Lydia snagged herself the viscount she wanted. Already running to fat, Aylesbury is, with barely a thought in his head beyond the cut of his coat. And he ruined her figure, getting her with three puling imitations of his spavin-shanked self.'' The old woman shook her head in disgust. ''Still, Lydia wasn't the only lackwit, if by the time of his death Hugh hadn't come to appreciate the lady he did wed.''

''Please, Lady Winterdale, I don't want—''

''There now, girl,'' the countess said, patting her hand. ''You mustn't think too badly of him. You were married so briefly, and then him coming back more dead than alive… But he was ever a smart lad, and had the good Lord granted him more time, I'm sure he would have overcome that silly infatuation and learned to value you as he ought.''

His grandmother believed Hugh might have come to love her? Once again tears stung Valeria's eyes. How many long, lonely months had she hoped and prayed for that eventuality, until the final crushing disappointment?

Before she could master herself enough to reply, the countess sighed. ''Enough about the past, then. We must decide what's to be done with your future.''

''M-my future?'' Valeria stuttered, once again disconcerted by the dowager's abrupt shift.

''Of course, yours. My sources tell me that your papa, apparently as lackadaisical about what was owed you as my grandson, never gave you a Season. How are you to reestablish yourself in Society if you're not even out?''

''It is rather difficult to arrange a Season from Bombay, and then Papa was ordered straight from India to the Peninsula,'' Valeria retorted hotly.

''Ought to have sent you back home, even though your only relations are cousins several times removed. Still, your mama's people never stir from that medieval pile in Westmoreland and your papa's kin in Devon are just as bad. But we've matters of more import than abusing your relations, gel,'' the dowager continued, cutting off Valeria's protest. ''So you may cease looking daggers at me. Something must be done now. You've had sufficient time to mourn Hugh. You're still young, of excellent birth, and sufficiently attractive that your chances of remarriage are quite good. I mean to present you, missy.''

''Present me?'' Valeria echoed, both bemused and annoyed by this further evidence of the countess's high-handedness. ''My lady, I cannot conceive how—''

''True, you're a bit old,'' the lady continued, dismissing Valeria's interruption with an imperious wave, ''and though that lamentable farm will provide little enough dowry, once we've gotten you suitably attired, I have every expectation of bringing some respectable candidates up to snuff. My health don't allow me to go out, so I've arranged for my niece, Lady Farrington, to squire you about. Alicia will arrive tomorrow and escort you to the mantua-makers the instant her trunks are unpacked.'' The countess surveyed Valeria with a grimace. ''You're not to stir from the house until your new wardrobe is delivered.''

''Do I have no say in this whatever?'' Valeria demanded when the countess at last paused for breath.

''You may thank me,'' she replied, the hint of a smile belying the tartness of her tone.

Valeria shook her head, trying to gather her disordered thoughts. Had she possessed sufficient funds, she probably would have chosen to come to London and enter Society after her year of mourning ended. Still, generous as the countess's plans were, she wasn't at all sure she should— or wished to—place herself under such obligation to her husband's imperious relative.

'''Tis all so unexpected. I must reflect—''

''What is there to reflect upon? You'd be a looby to refuse such an offer, and you know it. Now...'' the countess turned her compelling, black-eyed gaze upon Valeria, and once again the old woman's resemblance to her grandson reverberated painfully through her ''...there's naught to do but be sensible, thank me prettily and begin considering which new fashion will best become you.''

''But I'm not so sure I wish to remarry,'' Valeria countered stubbornly. ''Even were I fixed upon it, there's no guarantee, despite your generous support, that I would in fact attract an offer that would be acceptable to us both. I should not wish you to invest funds in an endeavor so uncertain of success.''

''Perhaps you'd not find a suitor to your liking,'' the countess conceded. ''But you must admit, Miss Contrary, that you've a much better chance of finding a suitable candidate here and now than at any other time or place. I'm not set on marrying you off, child. Should you end the season unwed, I'll consider my duty to Hugh done, and that's an end to it.''

Silently Valeria reconsidered the countess's proposal. As the old woman said, should she ever wish to remarry—or more importantly, to have children of her own—she would be foolish to turn down this singular opportunity. And in addition to that possibility were the attractions offered by the city itself.

Ah, to have months to explore it, rather than a few days. And after years of struggle, heartache and poverty, the prospect of simply enjoying the frivolity of Society life, garbed in a wardrobe of fashionable new gowns, was wonderfully appealing.

Reluctantly, Valeria tried to close her eyes to this attractive vista. 'Twas one thing for her to allow the countess to pay her way to London, that she might render the old woman some service, quite another to accept from this near stranger the staggering sum Valeria suspected a Season would cost. "I must again thank you for the offer, but I cannot feel I could accept such great largesse. Despite my marriage to Hugh, I have no claim upon you.''

"Pft!'' The countess made an impatient sound. "'Tis all well and good to be independent, gel, but don't whistle away a golden opportunity out of misplaced pride.''

A pride she'd undoubtedly be forced to swallow over and over, were she to remain here, subject to the whims of this imperious and unpredictable woman. Perhaps her modest sheep farm—with Arthur Hardesty as a last resort—was not so unappealing an alternative.

Her hawklike gaze on Valeria's face, the countess must have seen the conflicting emotions mirrored there, for after a long moment she sighed. The fierceness seemed to drain from her and she sagged back against the sofa cushions. For the first time Valeria caught a glimpse of how truly ill the old woman was.

"My husband, children, grandchildren have all left me," she said quietly, her voice now subdued and weary. "Except for the foolish Alicia, who cowers every time I speak to her, I've no near relations still living. I like your spunk, my dear, your independence—and your devotion to Hugh. The doctors tell me I haven't long left. It would...comfort me to have you with me until the end."

The countess turned to look directly at her, and Valeria could read in her eyes how much it cost the proud autocrat to have to admit her weakness. "Would you not humor a sick old woman, and remain in London?"

Though her lips had been poised to utter a refusal, that sudden change from dictatorial to vulnerable touched something deep within Valeria. She, too, knew what it was to lose all those dear to her, to dine at a solitary table, sit before a solitary fire with only loneliness and memories for company. Neither wealth nor title could save the countess from the same fate.

Valeria could.

"I...I hardly know what to say."

Once again the dowager reached out to take her hand, her grip this time trembling, uncertain. "Say yes. You'll not need to suffer my company long, if the sawbones are correct. Can you really be so contemptuous of pleasure that you could not enjoy yourself in London for a few months? You need not remarry if you do not wish it. Stay, and let me repay the debt I owe you for nursing Hugh in spite of...everything."

"I loved Hugh," Valeria said. "No repayment is necessary."

"Then stay out of kindness for the grandmother who loved him, too. Please."

Crafty old beldame, Valeria thought, more than half convinced she was being cleverly manipulated. To refuse largesse was one matter, but how could one turn down a dying grandmother-in-law's last request?

"Very well, Lady Winterdale. I will stay."

The countess nodded. "Good. And you may call me 'Grandmamma,' as Hugh did. Now, if you will leave me, my dear, I fear I must rest."

Shaking her head at how brilliantly the countess had outmaneuvered her, Valeria curtsyed and walked away. But as she paused to open the door, she looked back to see the woman already asleep, something that looked suspiciously like tears seeping from under her eyelids.

Valeria paused, her cynical suspicions softening. Perhaps the old woman genuinely wanted her company—or at least a more worthy opponent with whom to clash swords than the apparently timorous Alicia.

As Valeria silently tiptoed out, a surge of excitement buoyed her spirits. She'd send her London maid out for a guidebook this very afternoon. Since it appeared she'd be treated to a several-month sojourn in the city, Valeria intended to profit from it—and not restrict her explorations solely to the handful of residential squares and business streets frequented by the ton.

No, she meant to discover all of London, even those less fashionable districts where she might chance encountering one handsome, charming half-Irish gambler.

Chapter Five

Though the early spring sunshine a month later did little to drive the chill from his chamber, the golden beam caressing his face was intense enough to roust Teagan from slumber. Rubbing a hand over the rough stubble at his chin, he squinted and sat up, a precipitous action that sent sharp pain lancing through his head. Groaning, he squeezed his eyes shut and leaned back against the pillow.

The cotton dryness of his swollen tongue and the bitter taste in his mouth must be relicts of the cheap brandy at the gambling hell Rafe Crandall had taken them to last night. The results of his evening's play were scarcely sweeter than the brandy residue.

Slowly this time, he eased himself to a sitting position and fumbled for the water pitcher on the bedside table. After cautiously opening his eyes just wide enough to pour a glassful, he shut them again and gulped it down.

Mhuire, but he was tired of drinking and dicing, the smoke and stink of stuffy, crowded rooms, the feverish eyes of brandy-soaked men caught in gaming's thrall, the endless charade of playing the reckless, jovial rogue. Laughing at coarse jokes he'd heard too many times, forced by necessity never to be able to turn down a wager over cards or a billiard cue, spending his nights in the company of men whose endless pursuit of superficial pleasures he cordially—but silently—despised.

He took another long draught of water and reached for the breeches he'd flung on the bedside chair near dawn this morning. After inspecting those pockets and the slim money pouch he extracted from the waistcoat dangling off the chair back, he reclined against the pillows once more.

Despite the brandy, his memory was only too correct. Though Teagan had not lost the entire stake he'd brought with him into the hell last night, his precious cache of coin had been severely reduced.

Sighing, he rose and walked to the washbasin. His landlady, Mrs. Smith, bless her, had the pitcher filled and a clean towel set out. For a moment he lost himself in the simple pleasure of scrubbing away the night's grit and smoke, reveling in the feeling of freshness despite the clanging set off in his head by the motion of bending over.

He would come about again, he told himself as he toweled his face dry and contemplated the effort necessary to shave. As a man whose whole income derived from gaming, he'd developed a strategy that for the last ten years had kept him, if not in luxury, at least one step ahead of the magistrate. Avoiding contests whose outcome depended solely on chance, he concentrated his efforts on games in which skill—a skill he'd worked hard to perfect—normally balanced out the capriciousness of pure luck.

Normally. But every so often, as if mocking his attempts to circumvent her, Lady Luck seemed to send him a succession of hands so bare of promise that even his experience and expertise couldn't manage to turn them to advantage. He'd just suffered a month of such hands, and the tidy bankroll of winnings he'd brought back with him from Rafe's house party had dwindled dangerously low.

A knock on the door interrupted his glum reflections.

"Thought I heard ye stirrin', sir!" His landlady entered with a bundle under her arm and a steaming tray. "And by the time it were when ye brought yerself home this morning, I expect ye could use a bit o' this."

The sharp tang of fresh coffee eased the queasy swirl left in the brandy's wake, and the aroma of fresh-baked meat pie made him realize that, having had no dinner the previous night, he was famished.

"Mrs. Smith, 'tis a blessing you are!" His mouth already watering, Teagan reached for his money pouch.

"Nay, put away yer coins," she said as she set down the tray. "I've just made the meat pies, and the coffee be fresh. Have 'em while they're hot."

Teagan took the mug and gulped a reviving draught of the coffee, then set about the meat pie. "Ah, sweet lady," he said after the first savory bite, "you're an *aingeal* flown straight down from heaven!"

Mrs. Smith chuckled. "An' ye're a lad with too honeyed a tongue! But a good tenant ye are for all that, always payin' me reg'lar, never pinching the maid nor bringin' in raff 'n scraff to brawl 'n gamble. I'd rather have yer plain "Mr." than half a dozen lordlings with fancy titles runnin' up their bills 'n sendin' their man bangin' on me door, hollarin' fer me to fetch 'em this 'r that."

"Why, Mrs. Smith, I shall have to change my new coat for an altar boy's robe, such a saint ye make me out to be," Teagan replied as he reached for another meat pie.

"Not a saint, I'll reckon," Mrs. Smith replied as she crossed the room, "but a true gentleman, fer all that ye carry on about bein' naught but a rogue." She deposited a bundle of folded linen on the bureau. "Maisy said to tell ye them new shirts iron up real nice. An' 'twas kind o' ye to give her an extra copper, her mum being sick 'n all."

"She does her work well," Teagan said, thinking of the young girl—she couldn't be much older than eight—with her thin shoulders and slender hands, sweat beading her face as she hefted the heavy iron and guided it across the endless stacks of linen shirts.

How could he not despise his aristocratic cronies who carelessly threw away hundreds of pounds on a single round of cards, when so many honest folk made do on so little?

"Ah, did ye not see the parcel what was delivered to ye yesterday? I set it here on the bureau. The boy what brung it said 'twas already paid for."

Teagan looked in the direction of Mrs. Smith's pointing finger to a small paper-wrapped package. After Oxford, he'd turned his back on the books he loved, but upon returning from Rafe's hunting box, winnings heavy in his pocket, he'd vowed to purchase a few of his favorites. Despite his dwindling resources, when he'd seen the small used volume of Herodotus in the shop window of the penny press, he'd not been able to resist it.

His spirits inched up a notch. Before he forced himself from his rooms this evening for another round of gaming, he would allow himself the pleasure of an hour in the intelligent company of that long-dead historian.

Mrs. Smith walked to the door, then hesitated. "There were a man come from that Hoby's yesterday, and one from that Mr. Weston as well. But I tol' 'em all the young gentlemen buy on tick, 'n ye'd always paid me sooner 'r late, and would pay 'em too, so's not to come round here bothering ye no more. That should hold 'em off a week."

Teagan looked over in surprise. "Thank you, Mrs. Smith. That was very kind."

Mrs. Smith shrugged. "The merchants' lads been comin' round here reg'lar since I bought this place caterin' to the Quality, fer it seems most o' the gentlemen never have a feather ta fly with. Spend it all on cards 'n spirits 'n women, with naught left to pay the duns." Mrs. Smith gave a sniff of disdain. "But I ain't forgot the favors ye've done me, and ifn I kin keep the collectors from botherfyin' ye till ye come about, I'm right happy to do it."

Surprised and touched by his landlady's intervention on his behalf, Teagan hardly knew what to say. "Ah, Mrs. Smith, I misspoke the truth earlier. 'Tis the very Queen of Heaven ye be, and a beauty besides!"

Laughing, Mrs. Smith waved a hand at him from the doorway. "More's the fool me, were I ta listen to yer pretty words! But go on, now, finish yer pies. There's ale in the kitchen—ring when ye're ready for it."

After she'd bobbed a curtsy and departed, Teagan chewed the rest of his meat pie and eyed the neatly wrapped package. After a few moment's struggle, he gave up, too eager to wait until after he'd finished shaving.

Quickly he unwrapped and drew out the volume. Though the cover's nicked and dented surface spoke of hard use and lack of care, nonetheless Teagan ran his fingers over it reverently. He opened the flyleaf, to find an inscription in fading black ink: "T. Williams, Oxford, 1808."

Oxford. In his head he heard Magdalene's bells tolling, surprising him with the lateness of the hour as he sat at the desk in his narrow room, immersed in the *Dialogues* of Plato. Close his eyes, and he could see the soft gold of the weathered stone of the university's halls and chapel glow in the early morning light as he strode to his professor's house.

A deep, barely conscious anger stirred, and he shut the cover with a snap. If the possession of a few ragged volumes, doubtless sold off at the first possible moment by university men more enamored of drink than scholarship, was going to sink him into a green melancholia over being torn from the one place he'd ever felt he belonged, he'd best resell the lot of them forthwith. That page of his life had been ripped out and trampled underfoot long ago.

After placing the book on the bureau, he strode to the washbasin and pulled out his shaving gear, trying to shake a lingering weariness. A ride would buoy his spirits, but Ailainn had thrown a shoe and was still at the smith's.

Teagan would make himself presentable, then go for a walk. Mayhap even spend a few precious pence to take a boat down to Hampton Court, that he might clear his mind and revive his spirits with a stroll through the gardens. And steel himself for another round of play tonight.

Perhaps he should look for another house party. The company would be more respectable and the players less fanatic than those who frequented the hells that, as he lacked entrée to the exclusive clubs of White's or Brook's, were his chief London haunts. He would be well fed for the duration, another plus, and there would be fields and woods through which he might race Ailainn, a pleasant change from the restrictive bridal paths of Hyde Park.

There might even be another lovely sprite of a neighbor.

At the thought, he slipped easily back into memories he'd reviewed all too often these past two months. What a marvel she'd been, his Lady Mystery, all wide-eyed wonder and desperate yearning, passionately curious, and yet wise enough to walk away when the time came. No, he concluded, his lips curving into a smile as he tucked the magical recollections back in their special place within his mind. There could be no other like his Lady Mystery.

But for the cost of a boat ride, there could be a temporary respite from the noise and clutter of London. For one afternoon he'd indulge himself in clean-scented air, blessed solitude…and sweet memory.

Several hours later, refreshed by his time away, Teagan strode into the Meridian, a modest gentleman's club off St. James's that had never quite achieved the cachet that allowed its former neighbor, White's Chocolate House, to transform itself into one of London's most exclusive establishments. The Meridian counted among its patrons a mix of clerks, neighborhood merchants and men of aristocratic birth whose connections were not sufficiently grand to gain them admission to the more select clubs.

Teagan noted Rafe Crandall already present, his small group nursing tankards of home-brewed.

Rafe raised a mug to him. "Ah, Jester, well met. Barkeep, a round for my friend."

As Teagan claimed a seat at an adjacent table, a young man rose from the back of the room and approached him.

"May I?" he asked, indicating the chair beside Teagan.

"Of course. A good day to you, Holden."

The young man smiled. "Much better than yesterday, thanks to you. Since you wouldn't hear me out last night, I had to find you today and—"

"Nor do I mean to listen now." Teagan cut him off, smiling. "'Tis the duty of one Oxford man to another to deflect the Captain Sharps out to fleece newcomers."

"Is it?" Insley glanced at Lord Crandall and his party. "Based on my experience, I would have concluded most Oxford men believe quite the opposite."

Teagan took a sip of the frothy ale just delivered by the barmaid. "You mustn't judge us all by the...dubious behavior exhibited by some."

"Why, Teagan," Rafe called over to them, apparently noticing the addition to their numbers. "'Tis the young bantling you've been bear-leading. Insley, ain't it?"

The young man inclined his head. "Lord Crandall."

"An odd role for you to play, Jester—rescuing innocents, rather than leading them astray," Rafe observed. "Or did his mama pay you to keep him out of harm's way?"

"Ah, Rafe, give the lad time. Even such a reprobate as you must have been green once," Teagan replied.

"Still don't think you should have won the infant's vowels back from that sharpster." Rafe shook his head. "Dropping one's quarterly allowance at a gaming hell is practically a gentleman's...rite of passage. Why, an Oxford education's not complete until one has learned mathematics at the hands of the cent-per-centers."

"For those who don't mind dishonoring their family name," Insley muttered.

Crandall sent the young man a sardonic glance and drained his glass. "We're off to see what play there's to be had at White's. Care to join us? Ah, of course, how silly of me," he said, clapping his hand to his head in an exaggerated gesture of comprehension. "Not likely to allow you into White's, are they, Jester?"

"Might be interesting to bring him as a guest, Rafe," another of Crandall's friends said. "If his cousin the earl happened to be present, he'd likely go into apoplexy."

Keeping tight rein on his temper, Teagan said lightly, "Faith, and why should I wish to enter such portals? Nothing but a bunch of bloody Tories within, who'd as soon try to string up my Irish arse for sedition as look at me."

"Shoot you for dallying with their wives, more like," Rafe returned. "We're to try that new hell near Marlybone after dinner—Devil's Den, they call it. Play's said to be deep and the lasses comely. Join us, both of you—if Insley's mama will allow him out of the house tonight."

Ignoring the jibe, the young man replied, "I expect to play a few rounds later. My sister's come-out ball is tonight, and I must put in an appearance." Turning to Teagan, he added, "Mr. Fitzwilliams, I'd be honored if you'd accompany me there."

Rafe was moving with his friends to the door, but at that, he halted. "Teagan? At a ton ball?" He leaned his head back and laughed. "You young cawker, don't you know Teagan ain't received? Not even by his own mama's family!"

"'Tis Lady Insley who'll be having apoplexy if you bring Teagan along!" one of Rafe's group added.

"Might have to toddle over and witness this spectacle myself," Rafe mused. "'Twould be quite entertaining—seeing the Jester get bounced out on his ear."

"Entertaining for certain," Teagan replied. "But not half so satisfying as a good dinner at White's."

Rafe appeared to ponder the alternatives. "Aye, Jester, you're right. As usual. But then, were you not usually right, in wagers and play, you'd have been clapped into prison for debt long ago, eh?" With a careless nod, Lord Crandall walked out, trailed by his sycophants.

"Ignorant ass," Insley said, watching them depart.

Teagan shrugged. "A bit worse than most, I agree. Though I've won a tidy fortune off him these last ten years, so I must not abuse his character too roundly."

"Would that you'd won enough to see *him* clapped in prison, and so spared us his company," the young man replied with some heat. "But no matter. I was quite sincere in my offer, by the way. Won't you take dinner with me at Crillon's and then go on to Marianne's ball?"

Teagan looked over in surprise. "That's kind of you, but however inelegantly he expressed it, Rafe was correct. My...presence is considered undesirable in proper ton circles, particularly if there are innocent maidens about."

"I can't understand why. From what I can discover, you've never debauched a maiden in your life, and have scarcely dallied with married ones the last few years."

"My behavior after being sent down from Oxford was a bit...less circumspect," Teagan replied wryly. "And once won, a bad reputation is easier kept than lost."

"Perhaps. But given the magnitude of the service you've done me, a service of which both my parents are aware, I'm sure *my* family would be pleased to receive you."

"'Twas a mere trifle."

"You may call it such, but I cannot. The horror that overcame me when I realized the extent of the vowels I'd signed, and knew that in order to make good on them I'd have to confess the whole ghastly business to papa..." Insley gave a reminiscent shudder. "Never again shall I be tempted to play beyond my means or skill. I *am* under obligation to you, whether you choose to recognize it or not, and I *should* be honored to acknowledge you, even at so public an event as my sister's ball."

The young man's declaration left Teagan at a loss, none of the usual light comments he kept at hand to deflect criticism or jibes being applicable. "L-let me accept the dinner invitation with pleasure, and leave it at that."

Insley offered a hand. "That will do...for a start."

Lady Farrington peered out the carriage window at the long line of vehicles waiting to discharge their passengers before the torchlit entry of the square's central town house and sighed. "I do wish you would have let dear Sir William escort us to Lady Insley's ball, Valeria. At least we would have had the benefit of that gentleman's uplifting conversation while we waited."

With what she considered true nobility, Valeria refrained from pointing out to her chaperone that had they departed at the hour first agreed upon, they would have arrived before this crush. "That may be true, Cousin Alicia," she replied instead, "but Sir William has already escorted us to three activities in the last two weeks. Though he is a good friend to Grandmamma, I should not wish to take advantage of his kindness."

Nor appear to be encouraging him to dangle after her, Valeria added silently to herself.

"To be sure, but 'twould be a very good thing if you could fix his interest. A truly noble gentleman, you must allow, learned and well spoken, as well as quite kind and distinguished. And at least ten thousand a year. Of course, I should not wish to imply that his income matters overmuch, but one cannot deny the possession of a handsome fortune must enhance his other fine qualities.''

''I will allow that Sir William is everything good and amiable. You have been exceedingly generous, introducing me to your friends, and bringing me along to so many delightful entertainments. But please remember, Cousin, I am in London only to keep Grandmamma company for a time.''

''Nonsense,'' Lady Farrington declared. ''I know 'tis only been a year since Hugh… But you're not getting any younger, my dear, and to whistle down the wind a gentleman like Sir William without at least making a push to—''

''Only look, I believe we're close enough to the entrance to step down. Do go first, ma'am, so Jeffers may hold the umbrella for you.''

With any luck, that would end the discussion of her erstwhile suitor for the evening, Valeria hoped, since the gentleman himself would doubtless soon join them. Surely even a lady as single-mindedly fixed on forwarding matrimony as Lady Farrington wouldn't attempt to advance a gentleman's suit with the man himself within earshot.

Valeria climbed down after Lady Farrington, wondering with some aspersion why that lady, if she were so enraptured of the wedded estate, did not expend her efforts on finding herself a husband and leave Valeria alone.

Her first month in London had been like dining on a diet of Gunter's sweet ices. But by now the time-consuming ritual of shopping for gowns, gloves, reticules, pelisses, shawls, stockings, bonnets, undergarments—it seemed every day Lady Farrington discovered another ''deficiency'' in Valeria's wardrobe that must be rectified by an immediate expedition to Bond Street—had grown tiresome. The exciting novelty of attending the apparently endless

round of at-homes, breakfasts, routs, card parties and balls
that made up the rest of Lady Farrington's existence, had
also paled.

Her chaperone's delight in introducing her new protégée
about was so obvious, however, that thus far Valeria had
refrained from begging off any of the invitations that Lady
Farrington eagerly accepted on their behalf. But her patience was wearing thin. She had about had her fill of overcrowded rooms, overdressed aristocrats and conversation
concerned solely with the latest fashions and the most scandalous on-dits.

They reached the entry at last and handed their evening
cloaks over to the butler. "Did I not tell you?" Lady Farrington said with a smile of pure delight. "Look there, at
the edge of the ballroom. Sir William awaits."

She sounded so enthused Valeria felt a little guilty for
having so little enthusiasm herself. Perhaps, she thought as
they awaited their turn in the reception line, if she'd been
able to see more of the city she'd feel less frustrated, but
it seemed that every time she tried to steal a moment to go
exploring, Lady Farrington or her grandmamma had some
objection.

That, Valeria decided firmly, would have to change. She
would simply have to make it clear to them both that she
must have more time to herself. More opportunities to venture beyond those areas in which the Upper Ten Thousand
lived, shopped and socialized.

For, if she were very honest, the fact that in the two
months of her residence she'd been nowhere that promised
even the chance she might see or hear something of Teagan
Fitzwilliams certainly added to the vague disappointment
she'd been feeling of late.

Not that she wished to actually meet him. Indeed, her
cheeks heated at the very thought. How could she look in
his face and not remember in scorching detail his lips on

hers, his mouth moving over sensitive areas of her body that a lady dare not even name? Or offer her hand without recalling the touch of those sure, knowing fingers?

But...to catch a glimpse of his handsome face in a crowd, to overhear the music of that lilting voice...to have tangible proof that the lover who had given her so incredible an interlude was flesh and not a chimera born of her lonely imagination...ah, that would be bittersweet joy.

By the time they'd finished greeting their hostess and her blushing daughter, Sir William had reached them.

"Ladies, how lovely you look this evening," he said with a bow. "Let me escort you upstairs."

He truly was an amiable gentleman, Valeria thought as she put her hand on his arm. Tall, with a lean, serious face, his dark hair touched with gray, Sir William Parham was a distant connection of Hugh's who had lost his wife two years previous. With three small daughters and no heir, he was known to be looking out for a second wife.

Valeria was more than a bit suspicious that Lady Winterdale had urged Sir William to consider Valeria for that role. Though she'd grown fond of the old woman and come to appreciate the concern behind the imperious facade, theirs still was a rather tempestuous relationship. Valeria, long mistress of her own establishment, did not take kindly to Lady Winterdale's managing ways.

In the matter of Sir William, she had to admit, apparently the old tartar was crafty enough not to try to force her choice on Valeria. Or perhaps she'd realized after their first few encounters that any attempt to bully her granddaughter-in-law, who could be just as obstinate and unyielding as Lady Winterdale herself, would most likely result in Valeria's doing the exact opposite.

Would she be attracted to Sir William, were it not for Lady Winterdale's interference? Valeria studied him covertly as, skillfully dividing his attention between the ladies on either arm, he turned to amuse Lady Farrington with a fulsome compliment. His manners were excellent, his conversation intelligent and his interests far-ranging. His attentions to Valeria were particular enough that she had no doubt of his intentions, yet not so familiar as to make her uncomfortable.

As Lady Farrington claimed, Sir William would make some fortunate lady an excellent husband. Valeria just wasn't sure an excellent husband was what she truly wanted.

Would her pulse race if he took her in his arms? Would his kiss make her blood quicken and her bones seem to dissolve…as a certain other gentleman's had done?

Would she look on him in a more favorable light if a charming rogue had not opened her eyes to pleasures far beyond what she'd imagined possible?

Having once tasted such pleasure, Valeria would never again consider binding herself to a man without it. Unfortunately, with an honorable gentleman who was considering making one a proposal of marriage, one could not discuss— or sample—the degree of pleasure obtainable without ending up with a betrothal ring on one's finger.

Valeria had not settled in her mind how she might solve that conundrum when they reached the ballroom. After escorting Lady Farrington to a comfortable chair beside her friends, Sir William bore Valeria off to join the dancing.

Just inside the entry of the Insley town house, Teagan paused to take a deep breath. Rafe had been right; allowing Insley to talk him into stopping by the ball was a mistake. He might well be ejected forthwith, and at the very least, would probably embarrass his earnest young friend or the lad's mother.

But before Teagan could tap Insley's sleeve to tell him he'd changed his mind, his eye was caught by one of the dancers at the edge of the ballroom above. A slender, graceful sprite of a lady, delicate as a butterfly in a gown of pale gold as she dipped and swayed through the movements of the dance on the arm of her dark-clad escort.

It couldn't be…and yet the shiver of awareness over his skin, the pull of connection that nearly impelled him to leave Insley's side and go to her, all clamored that it was indeed his Lady Mystery, somehow transported from the depths of Yorkshire to this London ballroom.

Trying to keep an eye on her, Teagan let Insley lead him forward, knowing it was now too late to retreat. Nor, despite the difficulties of finessing his way into Lady Insley's soiree, did he wish to leave.

He had no business intruding into the life of a respectable widow—and yet both the simmering desire the mere sight of her ignited in him and a deeper longing for something pure, honest and untainted by vanity drew him irresistibly.

That, and a natural curiosity to discover how a purse-pinched widow had ended up at this ton party in a stylish new gown.

He'd seek her out for a few moments—surely he could do that without irretrievably besmirching her reputation. Somehow he had to charm his hostess into permitting him to stay at the ball long enough to speak with Lady Arnold.

Chapter Six

After the dance ended, as Lady Arnold rose from the final curtsy, she happened to look down—straight at Teagan. Her eyes widening, the lady froze.

Teagan felt his lips curving into a smile so automatic and instinctive he was helpless to prevent it. Their gazes held, time halting in the power of that glance.

Then her eyes warmed with delight, and an answering smile lit her face—a smile that quickly faded as she must have realized the impossibility of publicly acknowledging him. But not before the heat of it rocked him to the core.

A tug at his sleeve brought his attention back to Insley. "There's Mama. Let me present you."

Teagan sucked in a deep breath. *Now for the difficult part.* Squaring his shoulders, he summoned up a smile and followed Insley, who came behind his mama to tap her arm.

"Holden, there you are at last!" she exclaimed, looking over her shoulder. "I should read you quite a scold, coming so tardy to your own sister's ball. But I'm sure Marianne will be glad to have you, late though it be."

"I've brought a friend, Mama." Insley stepped aside and beckoned Teagan forward.

Teagan made his hostess a deep bow. "A charming party, ma'am."

Lady Insley's smile died and she looked over at her son in unconcealed dismay. The fair skin of Insley's face reddened, but with a quick movement of his head he indicated that Teagan should stand his ground. "You'll remember Mr. Fitzwilliams, Mama. And remember also how indebted we are to him."

"Y-yes," she said, moistening her lips. "Indeed, but…I scarcely think Marianne's ball is the proper place—"

"To acknowledge a gentleman who has performed us a singular service? Then what would be proper, ma'am?"

Avoiding Teagan's eye, Lady Insley leaned toward her son, her voice lowered. "Holden, you cannot expect me…"

By now, a group of onlookers had stopped chatting and were watching with avid interest. Teagan hoped the humiliation twisting in his gut wasn't coloring his face. "Perhaps I'd best leave, Insley," he said quietly.

"If my friend is not welcome, Mama, then I will not stay, either."

"Holden!" Insley's mother reached an imploring hand toward her son. Stone-faced, he ignored it, waiting.

Before the small crisis could escalate further, another gentleman stepped from behind Teagan.

"Insley, Fitzwilliams," Lord Riverton said, offering his hand to each in turn. "Good evening. Lady Insley, your lord husband has just been telling me of the kindness young Fitzwilliams recently rendered the family."

His hostess goggled at him. "H-he has?"

"Indeed," Riverton replied. "I must say, I've known Mr. Fitzwilliams since Oxford, and always thought him a capital fellow. This latest incident just confirms that. But Lady Insley, we must not keep these gentlemen from the floor when young ladies are in need of partners. Let me procure you some refreshment." He offered his arm.

Lady Insley stood a moment, obviously torn between acceding to the direction of her son and this distinguished guest, and avoiding the probable outrage of the watchful mamas present should she allow this rogue of the first order to mingle among their innocent daughters.

Evidently lacking the mettle to withstand two determined gentlemen, with a sigh she capitulated. "M-Mr. Fitzwilliams," she murmured, giving him the barest nod of recognition. "I...I believe I should like a glass of punch," she said to Riverton, and latched on to his arm as if desperate to flee the scene of imminent disaster.

Though Teagan had indeed encountered the cabinet minister at Oxford and occasionally at subsequent social engagements, he couldn't imagine why Riverton should have come to his rescue. Whatever the reason, he was exceedingly grateful. He gave the older gentleman a quick nod, which Riverton acknowledged with a wink before leading his hostess away.

"I didn't know you and Riverton were friends," Insley said.

"Neither did I," Teagan replied ruefully. But his mystification over Riverton's unexpected assistance was quickly submerged in a rising excitement. Now all he needed was an introduction, and he could speak again with his Lady Mystery.

"Insley, did you notice the slender dark lady in the golden gown dancing the cotillion when we entered?"

"You must mean Lady Arnold. Lovely, isn't she?"

"Exceptional. Would you introduce me?"

"If you've the courage to brave her chaperone."

"Follow me," Teagan said, and led him to the stairs.

After a quick search, nerves dancing in anticipation, Teagan urged Insley across the crowded ballroom toward the far corner, where he spied Lady Arnold in conversation with an older lady and a tall gentleman.

He knew the instant she perceived their approach. The rigidly restrained anger that always smoldered in his gut flared briefly as he halted, silently damning his lurid reputation, for this time no welcoming warmth preceded the alarm that widened her eyes and drained the color from her cheeks. Something sharp and hurtful stabbed at his chest.

Well, 'twas only one way to reassure her. Teagan propelled Insley forward again.

Lady Arnold was even lovelier close up than she'd appeared at a distance. The soft canary-yellow of her gown set off her pale skin and the burnished richness of her dark hair, arranged atop her head in a charming confection of curls. The garment itself was a masterpiece of titillation, the tiny puff sleeves emphasizing her slender arms and elegant shoulders, the low décolletage instantly drawing his eye to the taunting swell of her breasts.

Silky bare skin, soft heavy mounds he had nuzzled and licked and kissed. Simmering desire intensified to a hunger that hammered him, sharp and urgent. For an instant he was captured by the absurd fantasy of carrying her off here and now, perhaps outside to the night-shadowed gardens or to some conveniently vacant adjacent chamber.

Distracted by the unprecedented ferocity of his need, eyes fixed on her downcast face like a mariner navigating to a lighthouse's beacon, Teagan at last reached her. Wanting to allay her alarm as swiftly as possible, he nodded for Insley to speak.

"Sir William, ladies, how nice to see you," Insley said on cue. "Lady Farrington, I've brought someone I believe your lovely protégée has not yet met. Please allow me to present my good friend, Mr. Fitzwilliams."

Ironic amusement curled Teagan's lip as Lady Farrington, consternation on her face, threw a panicked glance at the frowning Sir William. She obviously considered Teagan not at all the sort of gentleman she should allow her charge to meet, but since he was being presented by her hostess's son, she could find no polite grounds to refuse. After clearing her throat several times, she stuttered, "Y-yes, of course, Lord Insley."

The subtle insult of that long hesitation stung no less for being expected. But all Teagan's irritation faded as he looked back at Lady Arnold. After inhaling sharply, as if she'd been holding her breath, she smiled at him.

'Twas like basking in the first warm sunshine of spring after a long, frigid winter. His spirits lightening, Teagan bowed. "Lady Arnold. 'Tis utterly charmed I am to meet so captivating an addition to our London society."

"Mr. Fitzwilliams," she murmured, dropping a curtsy.

He yearned for that smile, the music of her voice, the warmth of her small hand resting on his arm. He simply had to capture her for a dance or a stroll before her conscientious chaperone found a way to dispatch him.

"This is your first visit to London, I understand," he asked, breaking the strained silence. "Won't you take a turn about the room with me, Lady Arnold? I should love to hear your impressions of our vast city."

Her smile faltered a bit. "I...I'm not sure—"

"Please," he added softly, holding out his arm.

After a short pause, during which his eyes implored hers in wordless entreaty, she took it.

The spark of contact sizzled through them. Teagan exulted as her breath hitched in a gasp, her hand clenched involuntarily upon his sleeve. Ah yes, that interlude in the hayloft had been no aberration. The passion running molten in his veins still scorched her, too.

While Sir William sputtered a protest, Teagan said to Lady Farrington, "Do not fear, madam. I shall restore her to you shortly," and urged Lady Arnold into motion.

For a few moments they walked in silence while, holding his inexplicably fierce desire in check, Teagan contented himself with devouring her with his eyes. After they'd distanced themselves from her party, Lady Arnold glanced up, and blushed once more.

"Really, Mr. Fitzwilliams, you must not look at me like that," she murmured.

Once again, her utter lack of flirtatiousness enchanted him. "And how is that, pray?"

"As if you wished to..." Apparently deciding it was best not to complete the thought, she continued with a touch of exasperation. "You know very well how you're looking at me."

"How else should I look at a beautiful lady?"

"Oh, do stop trying to put me to the blush. You'll make me cross, and then it will be very difficult to express the gratitude I owe you for not...giving way that we'd already met."

His amusement faded. "Ah, my singular reputation. Did you really fear I would embarrass you so?"

"Oh, no!"

Surprised—and gratified—by her immediate denial, Teagan nodded at her. "Thank you for that."

"It's just I had no idea what you *would* say, and feared I might not be able to fall in line quickly enough to avoid upsetting Lady Farrington's delicate sensibilities. Or arousing Sir William's suspicions."

Glancing back to the corner, Teagan found Parham watching them, lips set in a thin line, and instinctively he gripped her hand a bit tighter. *You'll not claim my Lady Mystery, you bastard,* he thought.

"Why, should anyone hint that there seemed to be some prior acquaintance, you need only say that we saw each other from a distance while riding in Yorkshire, but were never properly introduced."

She uttered a smothered choke of laughter he found totally charming. "You are the most complete hand!"

"You malign me, dear lady! Is that not perfect truth? The trick, of course, is in knowing how much to tell. Didn't you learn that in childhood? Or were you too much a paragon to need the knack?"

She laughed in earnest then. "Hardly a paragon! But much as a glib tongue might have proved useful, I'm afraid I haven't one. I found early on that Papa could always tell if I tried to 'adjust' the truth. The punishment was generally lighter if I simply owned up to my fault rather than— vainly, it generally turned out—tried to talk my way out of it. Now you, I'd wager—" she smiled at him "—can probably spin a tale with the best of them."

"Ah, yes," he replied, more than a hint of irony in his tone, "as everyone in this room is doubtless dying to warn you, I'm a pure master of the ability to deceive."

She glanced quickly around, as if suddenly conscious they were attracting no small amount of attention. "Ah. I take it your presence is not generally…appreciated at such gatherings as this?"

"No," he said shortly, regretting that truth for perhaps the first time since his Oxford disgrace. "However, Lady Farrington's credit is such that I believe your reputation can stand a single turn about the room in my company without suffering irremediable harm."

She shook her head in mild reproof. "Once again you would have me believe you are no gentleman, but you shall not succeed. Arranging a proper introduction tonight, as if we truly were meeting for the first time, as well as your…previous behavior, all give the lie to that claim. And I hope I'm not so pudding-hearted as to be afraid of a little gossip. Though the ability to dissemble well might be a useful skill. Perhaps one that, ancient though I've become, I should still attempt to master."

'Twas nonsensical that her defense of his character should move him, but it did. "Don't change, I beg you," he said more fervently than he'd intended. He tried to soften his vehemence with a smile. "Your honesty and innocence are all too rare."

Once again, his compelling gaze captured hers. After a moment, with a shaky laugh, she looked away. "What an odd notion you have of me indeed. I admit to honesty, but I'm hardly a saint, and no one growing up amongst the army in the wilds of India could be thought an innocent."

Lighten the tone, he chastised himself. Where had all his easy, practiced wiles fled? He must amuse her, lure her to linger on his arm. Make the most of what he knew, now fully conscious of Sir William glowering at them, might well be Teagan's only opportunity to speak with her.

"But I haven't asked you what I set out to discover. So, Lady Arnold, what brought you to London?"

She gave him a look that was almost—apologetic. "At the time we…met, I had no notion of coming here. Lady Winterdale, my late husband's grandmother, unexpectedly summoned me to visit her. She offered to frank my way, and I wished to see the city my brother had described to me with much enthusiasm, so here I am—under her niece Lady Farrington's chaperonage, as Grandmamma does not go out."

"And how are you finding our fine metropolis? Rather tame, I suppose, after the wilds of India."

"Well, Society is a bit…constricting, but the city itself is splendid! At least, what little of it I've managed to visit. I purchased a guide, but some of the sights my brother recommended I've not been able to get to. A lady cannot go about on her own, I've been told, but my old nurse has a bad ankle, and the maid Grandmamma assigned me does not care for walking." Lady Arnold sighed, a look of vexation crossing her face. "I'm afraid my chaperone considers nothing beyond the borders of Mayfair and the shops of Bond Street worth seeing."

"And what unfashionable locales do you wish to visit?"

She gave him a probing glance, as if wary of mockery.

Truly curious now, he prodded, "Come, you may confide in me. 'Tis the soul of discretion I am. Honestly."

To his delight, she smiled. "Very well, if we are being *honest*. But you must promise not to laugh."

"Cross my heart."

"I should like to see the West India docks and the Inns of Court. St. Paul's, but not on Sunday, so I might explore the building, even if 'tis not in a fashionable neighborhood any longer. Oh, the Tower, and Astley's, and old London Bridge." She sent him a challenging look. "There, I've just proved how truly unfashionable I am."

"'Tis the real London you wish to see, then."

Her wariness dissolved in a smile. "You *do* understand!"

"Sure, and I can—" he began. But they'd reached the end of their circuit, and before he could finish his sentence, Lady Arnold's arm was seized by her distressed chaperone, who looked as if she might at any moment succumb to an attack of the vapors, while the disapproving Sir William stepped forward to block Teagan's path, his tall form between Lady Arnold and Teagan's tainting presence.

A ridiculous sense of despair pierced him, as if light and hope were slipping through his fingers. Though he shrugged off the absurd notion, he could not prevent himself calling after her, despite knowing his invitation was certain to be spurned.

"I'm well acquainted with all parts of the city, Lady Arnold." Ignoring Sir William's muttered objection, he continued doggedly. "I would be happy to escort you to any of the sights you mention—"

"So kind of you, Mr. Fitzwilliams," Lady Farrington interrupted, "but I'm afraid Lady Arnold—"

"Is much too occupied," Sir William finished. "Besides, I'm available to take her wherever she wishes."

"Providing I have the time, of course?" Lady Arnold interposed sweetly. "Sir William, have you an interest in viewing the West India docks?"

"The docks?" he repeated with a grimace of distaste. "Certainly not! I cannot conceive what Mr. Fitzwilliams has been telling you about them, but I assure you the docks are no fit place for a gently bred lady."

"My brother Elliot disagreed, for he highly recommended them to me. And so," she said, with a glance toward Sir William and Lady Farrington, as if daring them to dispute her, "I should be delighted to accept your escort, Mr. Fitzwilliams."

"Valeria!" Lady Farrington all but shrieked. Lowering her voice, she continued in an earnest undertone, "My dear, I really don't believe that would be…prudent."

"Certainly not," Sir William echoed.

"Indeed?" The ice in her tone finally penetrated the abstraction of her two protectors, who fell silent. "Then would one of you please explain to me what possible impropriety there could be in my going out in broad daylight, my maid in attendance, with a gentleman who has just been presented to me by the son of my hostess?"

The clever girl had just outflanked them, Teagan realized with dawning admiration. To justify a refusal, Lady Farrington would have to either malign Teagan's character to his face—in itself a grievous breach of good ton—or even worse, assert that their hostess was not discriminating in her choice of guests.

"Well, I…that is…" the lady faltered.

"We shall speak of this later," Sir William interposed, throwing Teagan a dagger glance.

A mischievous look in her eye, Lady Arnold reached past Lady Farrington to offer him her hand. "Shall we say tomorrow morning, Mr. Fitzwilliams? I'm staying with Lady Winterdale, on Grosvenor Square. You know the house?"

"Y-yes, my lady," Teagan stuttered, hardly able to believe that Lady Arnold apparently intended to accept his rash offer.

"Then I shall see you tomorrow."

Teagan recovered his poise. "I shall be counting the moments."

That earned him a lift of her eyebrows and the hint of a skeptical grin. "Shall you, now?" she drawled in a teasing echo of his own lilting speech. And with a nod, she at last allowed her two watchdogs to bear her away.

"I shall indeed," he murmured to her receding back, only half surprised to discover he really meant it.

Oblivious to the whispers buzzing around him, Teagan remained motionless, watching her slender figure disappear amid the crowd of guests. Did she truly understand what she had done? To contradict her guardian for interfering in the conversation of a grown woman was one thing—but to actually accept his escort?

Still marveling, he went in search of Insley. After locating his friend and paying his compliments to Lady Insley, who looked vastly relieved to have Teagan depart before spawning some social disaster beneath her roof, Teagan escaped into the cool night. He parted at the street corner from Insley, after turning aside the young man's offer to share a hackney with a promise to meet him later at the gambling club and walked off into the darkness.

He wanted time, before he resumed his gamester role at the club tonight, to recall and savor the short exchange with Lady Arnold. To muse over the strength of the attraction that drew her to him, this slight, slender woman a disinterested ton observer would account much less memorable than most of the sophisticated, stylish beauties in the ballroom he had just left.

The potent physical connection between them he readily understood, but he wanted to pinpoint just what it was about Lady Arnold's character that so captivated him. Her independence, certainly—her insistence on choosing her own way. That honest, questing intelligence. Like the classical literature that had been his joy before the disastrous end of his Oxford career, she seemed both unusual and yet hauntingly familiar; set apart from her place and time; seemingly indifferent to the dictates of fashion. Timeless.

Then he threw back his head and laughed at his own whimsy. To be sure, he'd met Lady Arnold under extraordinary circumstances, magnified to even more epic proportions by his bemused remembrances and the depression engendered by his current run of ill-luck. Should he come to know her better, doubtless he would find she was little different than most well-born ladies—or gentlemen—he'd known: self-absorbed, rather shallow, interested in Teagan only so long as he could divert, amuse or distract her.

Something in his gut protested that cynical assessment, but he pushed it away. He'd fallen once, with his whole heart, for a woman who'd seemed to value his talents and opinions—and look where that had gotten him!

No, he would indulge this fancy only to the point of pursuing Lady Arnold until he'd plumbed to its source whatever intangible it was that attracted him. Which meant cutting short his gaming tonight so he might rise in time to present himself at Lady Winterdale's town house at the proper hour tomorrow.

A rueful grin creased his face as he changed direction and headed to the club. If Lady Winterdale's reputation as a stiff-necked, tyrannical stickler were accurate, the woman would have apoplexy at the very notion of her widowed granddaughter-in-law traipsing about London in the company of one of the ton's most notorious rakes.

Still, boldness had carried him this far, and should Lady

Winterdale's butler shut the door in his face, he'd weathered snubs before. He would call on Lady Arnold tomorrow, as promised.

Even though by morning, either the lady herself or her relation would probably have talked her out of the folly of pursuing a closer acquaintance with the totally ineligible Teagan Fitzwilliams.

Chapter Seven

Over the sound of Lady Farrington's sobs, Valeria heard the countess's tart voice emanating from the darkened hallway outside the sitting room. "How can a body be expected to sleep in the midst of this caterwauling?"

Already almost at the point of wishing to shake her prostrate chaperone, Valeria tried to keep the exasperation from her voice. "Cousin Alicia, you must calm yourself! You've awakened Grandmamma!"

That produced a momentary respite from the sobbing. "It's all the fault of that Awful Man!" Lady Farrington said tremulously. "My poor nerves cannot support any more. You must prevent Aunt Winterdale from—oh!"

Occupied in chafing Lady Farrington's chilled fingers, Valeria looked up to see the countess glaring at them, then back to discover that her chaperone had fainted dead away.

"What's happened now to put that silly fool into such a taking?" the dowager demanded as she entered the room.

Caught between dismay at the lady collapsed on the couch, concern for Hugh's grandmother and irritation at the farce the evening had turned into, Valeria said, "Grandmamma! It's much too late for you to—"

"Stuff and nonsense," the old lady interrupted. "I sleep

away half the day, anyway. Call Alicia's maid to deal with her and tell me what's going on.''

Valeria paused, reluctant to abandon her unconscious chaperone. ''Should I not look for her vinaigrette?''

Lady Winterdale made a contemptuous noise as she jerked on the bell pull. ''Let her be. Alicia swoons over something twice a month. Darcy will see to her.''

Valeria bit her lip. Not only had Lady Farrington inflamed an episode that the ton might have otherwise considered only mildly gossip-worthy, she had roused the countess, who despite her feisty words had suffered such a spell of weakness two days ago that her doctors had confined her to bed for a week. ''Please, ma'am, return to your chamber, and I will come report to you as soon as we get Cousin Alicia settled into bed.''

''Where, you're about to tell me, I belong also?'' the countess retorted. ''Very well, I shall retire. But only if you promise to bring some sherry when you come in.''

The old woman's face assumed a mulish expression that Valeria knew, from a month's experience, might very well result in her refusing to budge if Valeria did not submit. ''As you wish, Grandmamma,'' she replied with some asperity, ''but only because I'm being blackmailed.''

Leaning heavily on her cane, the dowager moved toward the door. Valeria knew better than to offer her assistance. ''Least I can still do *that*,'' Lady Winterdale muttered.

And so, after helping Lady Farrington's dresser to revive her mistress and assist her to her own chamber, Valeria snatched the sherry decanter from the sideboard and headed for the dowager's room, two glasses in hand. After the events of this evening, Valeria felt the need for fortification as well.

She found Lady Winterdale settled on her favorite sofa by the fire. At her entrance, the lady pointed an imperious finger at the wing chair beside it. "Sit now, and pour me a glass. Then explain what's going on."

Valeria took the chair indicated and tarried as long as she could in pouring the smallest amount of sherry she dared into each glass, pondering what to reply.

'Twas probably best to relate the whole. For one, given Lady Winterdale's extensive contacts among the ton, she would most certainly receive a full account from her cronies tomorrow. And as Valeria had confessed to Teagan, she wasn't very good at evasion.

She handed Lady Winterdale her sherry. "At the ball tonight, I made what Lady Farrington believes to be a very unfortunate connection."

"'Unfortunate' enough to have Alicia enacting Cheltingham tragedies in my upstairs parlor, obviously! Don't speak in riddles, child. What 'connection'?"

"I was introduced to Mr. Teagan Fitzwilliams, a gentleman who is not, as Cousin Alicia expounded to me at length on the way home, a fit person for me to know."

"The Fascinating Fitz?" The countess gave a bark of laughter. "I should think not! What maggot did Lady Insley take into her head, inviting him to her ball?"

"As to that, ma'am, I cannot say. However, Mr. Fitzwilliams was presented to me by Lady Insley's son, and seemed to be perfectly charming."

The countess snorted. "Of course he's charming. How else could he coax women who should know better out of their skirts? He's a rogue of the first order, missy! Which, of course, is why he ain't received. Lord, that I'd been there to witness what a dust-up he must have caused." For a moment the countess seemed to contemplate the vision with amusement, before fixing her gaze back on Valeria. "Did that widget Alicia swoon right there at the ball?"

"No, ma'am, fortunately not. However—" Valeria could not prevent the aggravation that entered her tone "—afterward, she was so overcome with…emotion that she nearly collapsed in the refreshment room. Sir William and I had to practically carry her to a chair, which I fear attracted no small amount of attention. I suggested she retire to the lady's withdrawing room to compose herself, but she insisted we leave the ball at once. If Mr. Fitzwilliams does have a scandalous reputation—"

"And he does."

"Then I fear that by making such a to-do over the matter, Cousin Alicia drew more notice to my meeting him than would ever have occurred had we simply remained."

With a grimace of distaste, Lady Winterdale nodded. "Blast Alicia! She was ever a nodcock."

The old woman settled back to sip her sherry. Just as Valeria was hoping she'd satisfied Hugh's grandmother with that brief summation, the countess spoke up again.

"What happened after you were introduced? Surely the rogue hadn't the effrontery to ask you to dance!"

"N-no, we took a turn about the room. His conversation was quite unexceptional. Having learned it was my first visit, he merely inquired how I liked London."

"'A turn about the room.' And did he take a turn with any other of the ladies present?"

Valeria took a small sip from her glass. "I cannot say. Immediately after we bid him goodbye, Cousin Alicia had her…episode and I was preoccupied."

"So one of London's handsomest rogues insinuates his way into a ball, finagles an introduction and strolls about— only with you?"

"As I said, Grandmamma, I do not know. He may have talked and danced with a number of ladies."

"Not if I know Lady Insley. No matter that that pup of hers was escorting him about, she'd have managed to show Teagan Fitzwilliams the door as quickly as possible, or risk outraging every marriage-minded mama present with an innocent daughter's good name to protect."

The countess fell silent and fixed a considering look on Valeria, who willed her face not to flush.

"No, gel, something ain't right here," Lady Winterdale said after a moment. "Teagan Fitzwilliams is known for squiring only the flashiest of Diamonds. Not that you're an antidote, but I can't see him being so struck by your looks that he'd use the few moments' entrée Insley provided to beg an introduction to you, not when I know for a fact there were half a dozen Incomparables present. Unless he was *renewing* an acquaintance. Do you know him, child?"

Valeria felt a sinking in the pit of her stomach. *Don't be ridiculous,* she told herself angrily. She was a woman grown, after all, and accountable to no one.

Then she recalled Teagan's words, and snatched at them. "We were not precisely acquainted, ma'am. He attended a house party in the neighborhood of Eastwinds earlier this year, and I saw him while out riding. But we were never formally introduced."

The countess studied Valeria's face, no doubt observing the heat she felt creeping into her cheeks. "Well, you're a widow, and what you've done is your own affair. No, I don't wish to know! But foolishness that may pass unnoticed in the country won't do in London, where everyone knows everyone else's business. Acquainted or not, if he has the audacity to show his face here, you must refuse to receive him."

Valeria felt her cheeks warm in earnest now. "I'm afraid I cannot do that, Grandmamma."

"And why not?"

"After I'd told Mr. Fitzwilliams that there was much of London I'd not yet been able to see, he kindly offered to escort me about the city, and I accepted his offer. He is calling for me tomorrow morning."

A long, ominous silence followed, during which Valeria prepared herself for an outburst once the countess absorbed the full meaning of her words.

"Are you daft, child? Do you wish to ruin your reputation practically before you've established it?"

"Really, Grandmamma! As you've noted, I'm a widow, not some innocent virgin. Mr. Fitzwilliams could have embarrassed me tonight by revealing a prior acquaintance. Instead, he very properly sought an introduction. And if he were the villain everyone seems to delight in painting him, when I previously encountered him, riding alone and unprotected, he might easily have taken advantage of me. Instead, he acted the perfect gentleman."

"I can imagine," the countess said dryly. "Come now, puss, I'm not so old that I can't remember the sort of...fascination a man like Teagan Fitzwilliams can exert over a woman. But there's more at stake here than the excitement of a few afternoons spent with a dashing rakehell. You must consider your future. How can you hope to fix the interest of a man like Sir William if you're wasting your time trifling with a gazetted ne'er-do-well?"

With difficulty, Valeria held on to her temper. "First, though I readily admit Sir William is a superior gentleman, I am by no means assured that he wishes to fix his interest on me, nor am I sure I would encourage him if he were. I've heard nothing that persuades me I should cut the acquaintance of a man who was introduced to me in perfectly acceptable circumstances, who has always conducted himself in my presence with utmost courtesy, and about whom the only ill that has ever been voiced is a vague innuendo based on no evidence whatsoever."

"Vague innuendo, is it? Then let me offer you some facts. Truth, missy, not rumors! While at Oxford, he seduced the wife of his Oxford mentor's son, and nearly convinced the besotted woman to run off with him."

"So I understand. But he must have been very young then—sixteen or seventeen? And the lady much older? Having once or twice observed similar cases among the army in India, I suspect it was much more likely that a bored matron seduced a handsome young man. And only the young man paid the consequences."

The countess lifted an eyebrow. "Perhaps. But any possible sympathy one might have had over that unfortunate episode was quite ruined by the blatant way he conducted his subsequent affair with Lady Uxtabridge. Strolling into Covent Garden with that woman on his arm, both of them somewhat in…disarray, and then kissing her on the lips as he seated her next to her husband in Uxtabridge's own box!" Lady Winterdale shook her head. "Shocking bad ton."

"Foolish, certainly. Of course, Lord Cranston and Lady Fellowes are much more discreet," Valeria replied, naming a young aristocrat and the married lady he'd driven out in Hyde Park the last three afternoons running. "And Sir Alewynd and Lady Lydia are merely convivial friends," she added, indicating a couple, both married to other partners, whose touching and nuzzling, followed by their mutual disappearance for a good hour or more, had caused no end of scandalized speculation at a ball the week previous.

Lady Winterdale frowned, obviously displeased to have had her arguments rebutted so neatly. "Fitzwilliams is of dubious parentage, and a gamester besides."

"He can hardly be held accountable for his parentage. And I have it on the authority of my neighbor, a collegemate of his, that turning to gambling was more necessity than choice. What other occupation is open to a landless gentleman whose family disavows him? The army requires the funds to purchase a commission, and of course, the church was not a possibility."

"A gentleman would have found another way," Lady Winterdale insisted.

Valeria raised an eyebrow. "Perhaps. But I suspect that Mr. Fitzwilliams is really guilty of no more than being half-Irish, having an unfortunate affair with one woman and a too-obvious one with another. Unless you can inform me of some other venality he's supposed to have committed. Seducing and abandoning an innocent maiden? Murder? Theft or embezzlement? Cheating at cards?"

"Not that I've heard," the countess admitted.

"Well, then. Papa told me the army taught him to value a man's actions over his parentage and prior record. I, for one, do not intend to condemn a man based on his having once committed mistakes for which the grandson of an earl not possessed of an Irish father would have long since been forgiven."

"Very well, I'll allow Mr. Fitzwilliams may have been ill-used. But life ain't fair, missy, as you should well know. 'Tis a rogue's reputation he bears, whether deserved or not. 'Tis also the way of the world that if one plays with pitch, one gets blackened fingers. For all your noble talk of treating a man by his actions, are you prepared to risk sullying your own reputation? Ruining your chances of a decent marriage?"

"Other than your kind sponsorship, Grandmamma, I cannot see that I possess anything that would entice Sir William, or any other ton gentleman, to offer for me. To be sure, you've tricked me out in fashionable garments and had Cousin Alicia introduce me around, but the fact remains that I'm a widow of no particular beauty, somewhat stricken in years, with naught but a barely profitable sheep farm."

"Don't be buffleheaded, child. Surely you know I didn't bring you all the way to London just for a Season. I mean to leave you my fortune."

Her lips already parted to continue arguing, that announcement caught Valeria entirely unawares. She paused in mid-breath, stunned. "Y-you are going to—!"

The dowager waved a hand. "Now you've made me bolt from the gate. I hadn't meant to confirm it to you yet—don't want it puffed about, lest all the rakehells and fortune hunters in London descend on you like a flock of vultures." She gave Valeria an exasperated look. "All the *other* rakehells and fortune hunters."

"Dear ma'am, I hardly know what to say," Valeria replied, still astounded. "Surely you have blood kin—"

"Don't you be telling me who I can leave my money to and who I can't! Alicia's got her own fortune, which is a mercy, since she's too great a widget to attract a gentleman of sense, and my great-nieces and -nephews are naught but a passel of idle, ignorant fools. Which I'm delighted to say that you, girl, are not."

Valeria had to smile. "A high compliment indeed."

Lady Winterdale chuckled. "Mind your manners, child. Ah, 'tis been a delight having you here, a debater worthy of my wit, someone who doesn't toady or shrink away every time I look daggers at them. But after the...last few days, I can't pretend I have forever. I'd like to see you settled. And if not in wedlock, I'd like to die knowing you'll be happy." Looking away, the countess added in a gruff voice, "Happy as you've made me these last weeks."

A lump in her throat, Valeria reached over to grasp the dowager's thin, veined hand. "Thank you, Grandmamma. I've been happy here with you."

"Then you'd best stop acting the fool," the countess replied, the tart tone back in her voice, as if regretting her momentary softening. "Which means that when he calls, you mustn't receive Teagan Fitzwilliams."

She held up a hand to forestall Valeria's protest. "Don't waste your breath assuring me you're immune to his charm.

I've known the boy since they sent him down from Oxford, and even at my age, I can't image a woman receiving the full attention of those mesmerizing eyes and keeping her senses—or her chemise—in place! Damnation, child, I didn't bring you to London after having your heart broken by a good man to watch you get your heart broken again by a bad one.''

"I have no intention of risking my heart."

"No, and I'm sure you don't, but even women of sense tend to turn idiotish when a devil as handsome as Fitzwilliams comes calling. But enough of this. I don't mean to deny him the house. You'd only sneak out to meet him then, just to spite me."

"I hope I'm not so small-minded," Valeria said primly.

"You're an unbroken filly too apt to take the bit in her teeth," the countess replied, and gave a crack of laughter. "Ah, but you remind me of myself at your age! All I ask is that you consider carefully. Sir William's a fine man. He'll give you companionship, comfort, children to occupy that restless spirit, and a permanent place in Society. Don't throw all that away for a man who'll dazzle you for a week or a month and then leave you alone with your regrets the rest of your life. You will think on it?''

Once again touched by the countess's concern, Valeria replied quietly, "Yes, Grandmamma. I'll think on it."

"Good. Leave me now, child. I'm fatigued."

A frisson of fear shook Valeria. "Are you all right, ma'am? Should I summon your physician?"

"Lord, no! There's nothing that incompetent will do but leech me, and I've had enough of bleeding. I'm not ready to stick my spoon in the wall yet. Go to bed, child. And try not to be a fool."

Valeria kissed the old woman's hand. "I'll try, Grandmamma. Good night."

Valeria slipped from the room and walked across the hall

to her own chamber. What a contradiction the countess was—gruff for the most part, which only made her very occasional softening the sweeter. Valeria realized that over the last month, the manipulative, combative old lady had managed to steal into her heart. Suddenly the fact that she would soon lose the countess's companionship and counsel filled her with sadness and a deep regret that she had not come to know Hugh's grandmother sooner.

So what did she mean to do about Teagan Fitzwilliams? The countess was wise in advising caution. It would be all too easy to be "dazzled" by the man.

However, Valeria did very much want to explore London. She had to admit that she'd feel safer, once beyond the confines of Mayfair, if she were to have a gentleman to escort her, and Sir William had already indicated his disdain for her chosen destinations. As she'd told the countess, she did not mean to eschew the escort of Teagan Fitzwilliams merely because he'd acquired what was, in her opinion, an undeservedly scandalous reputation.

Surely she was sensible enough to spend a few mornings in his company without losing her wits entirely—and tumbling back into his bed.

Attractive as that prospect might be.

A shaft of desire stabbed her at the very notion.

No, an affair with Mr. Fitzwilliams wouldn't be wise. Though she wasn't sure she wished to remarry, she also wasn't sure she did not. As the countess warned, squandering her reputation in a flagrant affair with a well-known rogue would effectively eliminate that choice.

A fraternal relationship in which she merely explored the city with him, in daylight hours with her maid to chaperone, should not. Any prospective suitor who trusted her so little that he doubted her word about the nature of her relationship with Mr. Fitzwilliams would obviously not be worthy of becoming her husband, anyway.

Husband of the *rich* Lady Arnold. A rich woman who, unlike a widow struggling to survive, would be free to marry—or not marry—as she chose.

Elation filled her as the full implications of that seeped into her mind, and she laughed out loud. She would be truly free—free from worry over want, free from the necessity to marry for security, free to pursue her own interests and desires.

That decided it. She would meet Mr. Fitzwilliams in the morning and, if he were amenable to the limits she set on their relationship, tour London with him.

As Valeria settled back into bed, she tried to damp down the glow of anticipation. 'Twas only a visit of the city. She mustn't make the mistake of seeing in Teagan Fitzwilliams either a potential suitor—or a friend.

And be he ever so dazzling, surely after what had happened before, she was too intelligent to risk handing her heart over to a man who could have no interest whatsoever in it.

At the Devil's Den a few hours later, Teagan laid down the last card of his winning hand, and to the groans of the other gentleman, drew over a stack of guineas. While scooping them up to place in his purse, he called to a passing waiter to have the butler bring his coat and cane.

"What's this, Jester? Leaving us already?" Rafe Crandall peered at Teagan through the haze of smoke.

"Merely taking pity on you, my lord," Teagan replied. "I've won enough for one evening. 'Tis time to let you other gentlemen have a go."

"I do believe our Jester's reforming his ways," Rafe announced to the group, which included Teagan's friend Lord Insley, as well as Crandall's usual cronies, Markham and Westerley. "First he visits a debutante's ball—though how he managed that feat without being tossed out on his rear I still cannot fathom—and now he means to retire to his bed before dawn! Damme, Teagan, what's about? Not trying to turn respectable on us, are you?''

''Wouldn't do him no good,'' Markham observed. ''His family won't touch him. His cousin, the earl, would rather spit on 'im than look at 'im. Told me so himself at White's t'other day.''

Teagan gritted his teeth at the casual insult and forced his usual bantering tone. ''Whist, and should I ever be in danger of earning the earl's approbation, I should have to quit England forthwith.''

''Aye, he's a dull dog, your cousin,'' Rafe agreed over the ensuing laughter. ''Probably despises you because he knows the ladies prefer your energetic and talented performance to his money and title.'' Then Rafe straightened, spilling some of the brandy in his glass. '''Od's blood, that can't be it, can it? Jester, you're not sniffing up the skirts of an honest woman, are you now?''

Careful, Teagan warned himself. Despite his constant state of inebriation, Rafe Crandall was no fool. ''Faith, and what would I want with the likes of an honest lass?''

''True, true.'' Westerley wagged the wine bottle he held. '''E's got no money to get leg-shackled. 'N anyways, no ton mama worth 'er salt would let 'em next 'r nigh some innocent virgin. Rich merchant neither. If he'd a mind to marry, Jester'd have to find 'imself a widow.''

''A rich one,'' Markham said, flicking a cigar ash off his florid brocade waistcoat. ''Dressin' well's expensive.''

''And one poorly chaperoned,'' Rafe observed. ''Very well, I concede.'' He threw up his hands in a gesture of surrender. ''Any female with money enough to tempt the Jester would have to be long in the tooth and ugly besides, not to have already been snatched up by some other fortune hunter.''

"And Jester's too discriminating to settle for an ugly woman, be she ever so rich, eh?" Westerley asked.

"Now wait a moment." Rafe frowned and closed his eyes, as if making a diligent effort to concentrate. "Isn't the beauteous Lady Arnold, my lovely neighbor from the far north, presently visiting poor old Hugh's grandmamma in London? I believe I remember m' mother nattering on about it when last I visited the family manse. And don't I recall the Jester taking a ride in her woods?"

Teagan hesitated, knowing he must choose his words with caution. After so carefully guarding the secret of their first meeting, he certainly didn't wish to say something that might inspire Rafe Crandall and his drunken cohorts to bandy Lady Arnold's name about.

Insley shot Teagan a quick glance. "Gentlemen, if you are to retain any pretensions to the name, you really must cease discussing respectable ladies in such terms."

"I believe our plain talk offends young Insley," Rafe sneered.

"Perhaps we should send for his mama to escort him home," Westerley sniggered.

Teagan gave an elaborate yawn. "If you gentlemen persist in discussing so dismal a topic as marriage, I shall certainly leave." After making them an elaborate bow, he walked with unhurried steps from the room.

Insley followed him. Once outside the club, Insley stopped Teagan with a hand to his elbow.

"No word of what happened at the ball will be spoken by me. But I expect your presence there—and the story of the lady whose introduction you sought—will be one of tomorrow's on-dits. What," Insley said hesitantly, "do you mean to do about Lady Arnold, if I may ask?"

In his mind's eye Teagan saw the image of a polished mahogany door shutting in his face. "Probably nothing."

Insley offered Teagan a hand. "'Tis your own business, to be sure. Good night, then."

After shaking the young man's hand, Teagan turned to walk pensively into the lightening dawn. Insley was correct; Teagan's impulsive claiming of Lady Arnold's acquaintance earlier in the evening would certainly become fodder for the gossip mills. When Rafe Crandall heard of it, as inevitably he would, the suspicions he might voice would fly through the ton. The ensuring speculation was certain to be far more damaging to Lady Arnold's reputation than Teagan had ever envisioned when he'd permitted himself that innocent stroll across a ballroom with her.

A sinking sense of dread dulled the rush of anticipation that had buoyed him since leaving the Insley ball. He'd erred, allowing a selfish desire for her company to lead him to defy the social ostracism he usually accepted without question, thereby calling down on her head the avid notice of the ton.

The idea of Lady Arnold's name being involved in scurrilous innuendo sickened him. And if it became known that he was squiring her about the city, the rumors would only grow worse.

His Lady Mystery deserved better than that of him.

Perhaps he would do her a greater service by not keeping their appointment, after all.

Chapter Eight

Before nine the following morning, Valeria's maid did up
the last tiny button on her favorite of the new morning
gowns, a deep peach sarcenet. After instructing Molly to
take her pelisse downstairs so she might be ready to set out
as soon as she'd offered Mr. Fitzwilliams refreshments, she
picked up the guidebook and crossed to the wing chair near
her window overlooking the garden, where crocuses and
daffodils were just now awakening from their winter sleep.

Excitement bubbling in her stomach, she opened the
guidebook and tried to concentrate on choosing the sites
for their first expedition.

Bullock's Egyptian Hall at Piccadilly, the guidebook
said, offered an excellent collection of objects gathered
from Africa and the far Americas, including an extensive
exhibit of animals and insects. She wrinkled her nose at the
idea of tropical insects, having encountered more than she
ever wished to see again while living in India.

But viewing the relics from the land of the Pharaohs
would be interesting, or perhaps they could stop by Astley's
Royal Amphitheatre, whose equestrian displays her brother,
Elliot, an avid horseman, had pronounced "spectacular."

Mr. Fitzwilliams, himself a fine rider, would probably enjoy the show.

Valeria pried her mind from contemplating the admirable figure Mr. Fitzwilliams presented while mounted on his fiery black and tried to direct her attention back to the guidebook. For the first time she wished her window overlooked the front entrance instead of the back garden.

Idiot, she chastised herself. Time would pass even more slowly were she to sit watching the street. And she certainly didn't wish for Mr. Fitzwilliams to ride up and find her with her nose pressed to the glass, as if she had nothing more urgent to do than wait for his arrival.

Though that was the truth. *Read,* she told herself again, and picked up the guidebook.

But after another half an hour, during which she lost her place a dozen times within the same paragraph, she shut the book in disgust. A glance at the mantel clock revealed the hour not yet struck ten.

With a sigh, Valeria put aside the volume and stood up. She'd walk in the garden, she decided. Jennings could summon her from there easily enough, and she could more profitably occupy herself comparing the plants now peeping out of the ground with the slower progress being made by those in her garden farther north.

Suitably attired with shawl and mittens, she set off across the rose walk. But even after she'd made a slow inspection of each of the three garden rooms, there was no news of a visitor.

Valeria sat down on a bench and lifted her face to the soft, early spring sun. Surely the hour was late enough. They *had* specified this morning, had they not?

Perhaps something had come up to delay him. But if so, why had he not sent her a note of explanation?

She took another circuit of the garden, more quickly this time. But by the end of that transit, she could no longer

avoid acknowledging the bitter truth: after she had given
him that oh-so-public invitation in the ballroom, Teagan
Fitzwilliams was not going to call.

She should be insulted. Instead, her chest tightened with
an inexplicable sense of loss.

'Twas foolish in the extreme to be so disappointed. It
just pointed up the uncomfortable fact that she, at least, had
been far too eager to see him again.

An eagerness he plainly didn't share.

Perhaps he'd just been toying with a woman who was
obviously anxious for his company. That lowering thought
revitalized her flagging spirits as nothing else had, and anger flickered.

She was being just the sort of fool her grandmother had
deplored, investing with far too much importance an excursion for which her intended escort couldn't even be
bothered to make an appearance. Perhaps he'd chosen to
speak to her on a lark, to see how much he could induce
the little country bumpkin to blush, and never had any intention of calling.

Her ire truly roused now, she raised her chin. Teagan
Fitzwilliams might not find a jaunt about London interesting enough to tempt him from other pursuits, but Valeria
Arnold was not to be put off so easily. She wished to visit
the city, and visit it she would.

She would send Molly out for a suitable map, she decided, and ask the maid which of the footmen she considered stout enough, and agreeable enough, to act as their
escort. Then she'd figure how to wheedle Lady Winterdale
into excusing the servant from his duties long enough to
accompany them.

She sprang up, ready to march back to house and summon Molly, when a footman hurried down the path to her.
''Beggin' your pardon, ma'am,'' he called. ''You've a
caller awaitin' in the parlor.''

Her wrath cooled as if doused with ice water, leaving her with a mix of surprise, delight and trepidation.

"W-who is it?"

"A gentleman, ma'am. Jennings didn't give his name."

Don't be a looby, she told herself as she followed the footman. *It might not even be Mr. Fitzwilliams.*

But her pulses, already fluttering, leaped as she walked into the parlor. By the window, golden hair glinting in the noonday light, stood Teagan Fitzwilliams.

He turned when the butler announced her, a slight smile on his face, his eyes that mesmerizing kaleidoscope of gold and amber.

"Lady Arnold," he said, and made her a deep bow.

Oh, Grandmamma was right. Teagan Fitzwilliams was all too dazzling.

Valeria sucked in a breath and ordered herself to produce coherent speech. "Good morning, Mr. Fitzwilliams. Jennings, would you bring us tea?"

After the slightest flicker of a glance toward her guest, the butler bowed. "As you wish, my lady."

Valeria made herself walk calmly toward him, wishing the butterflies in her stomach felt less like sparrows flapping bony little wings against her ribs.

She should be cool and distantly polite. After all, he was late. Very late. He owed her an explanation, and it had better be a good one.

"Won't you sit down, Mr. Fitzwilliams?"

He stepped toward her, raised a hand as if to take hers, then closed it into a fist and drew it back. "N-no, I shouldn't. I should just stand and deliver the apology I owe you for being so frightfully tardy. Actually, I had convinced myself that I ought not to come at all."

Despite her rallying speech in the garden not a quarter hour previous, Valeria felt a ridiculous sense of hurt squeeze her chest, displacing the thumping sparrows.

"If you have changed your mind and do not wish to accompany me, of course I—"

"No! No, you mustn't think that. I should love to escort you!" He gave her his full smile then, that curve of dimpled cheek and slight narrowing of eyes that somehow only made their outrageous sparkle brighter. "But," he continued, the smile dimming, "after much reflection, I concluded it would be...wiser if I did not. Indeed," he added with a lift of his brow, "I'm fair astonished you even received me. I'd rather expected to have Lady Winterdale's butler bar your front door against my encroaching person."

Valeria knew he meant the remark to be amusing. But suddenly she was pierced by the image of a golden-haired orphan, then a man, standing on the front steps of a succession of houses while a lifetime of doors slammed in his face.

She pushed the disturbing vision aside. "And why is that? I've not been long in the city, but I thought it was customary for a gentleman to call on a lady to whom he'd been properly introduced the previous—"

His wry chuckle startled her into silence. "Whist, and you did roll them up, horse, foot and guns! A clever stratagem, my lady, but a sophist's trick, as we both know. As I'm sure your guardian has explained to you at length, mine is not an acquaintance you ought to pursue."

Valeria lifted her chin. "I'm not a green girl, to be told who I should see and who I shouldn't."

"'Tis not a bad thing to attend to those who have your best interests at heart. Which is why, in the end, I decided to come this morning. That, and the belief that your kind defense of me deserved better than the rudeness of my not keeping our appointment at all."

His face had grown serious, and Valeria felt the spirits sent soaring when she beheld him standing by the parlor window once again sink.

"So...you're *not* going to escort me."

He looked away, as if the hurt she hadn't been able to keep out of her voice was reflected also on her face.

"It was inexcusably selfish of me to seek you out last night. You *are* new to the city, so you may not know, but I assure you every spiteful cat and idle dandy in the ton is speculating over their morning chocolate today about why the notorious Teagan Fitzwilliams sought an introduction to a shy country widow. And given his temperament, when my Yorkshire host, your neighbor Lord Crandall, hears of it, he will certainly draw conclusions detrimental to your reputation that, I'm afraid, he will be only too happy to broadcast to the largest possible audience."

Teagan paused, his face grim as if envisioning the uproar. "Fortunately," he continued, "the ton, though malicious, has a short memory. If we have nothing further to do with each other, some new scandal will soon occur to displace the rumors. So regrettably, I must withdraw my offer. After the...kindness we have shared, I cannot permit an association with me to tarnish your sterling character."

Valeria stared into his eyes, but could detect neither irony nor falsehood. Though Mr. Fitzwilliams wished for her company, he would eschew it...to protect *her* reputation.

A tiny knot of gratification and wonder grew in her incredulous chest. And the ton believed him no gentleman!

Valeria couldn't help the smile that sprang to her lips. "As it happens, after hearing the account of our 'introduction,' Grandmamma drew the same conclusions."

Mr. Fitzwilliams had turned toward the window, but at that he whirled to face her. Surely that wasn't...a blush beginning to color his cheeks?

"She believes that I...that we—?"

Valeria nodded, still smiling.

He blew out a gusty breath and ran a hand through his hair. "I wonder she didn't have me shot on sight."

"She did warn me that the 'foolishness' a widow might indulge herself with in the country would not be possible in London, where members of the ton seem to do nothing but spy on and gossip about all the other members of the ton."

"She's a wise lady, your grandmamma."

"Yes. I agreed that such…reckless conduct would be out of place here. But I also informed her that I refused to allow the prejudiced opinions of the fashionable world to dictate my actions. As I myself find nothing to reproach in your behavior toward me, and since you know all of London well—by the way, you do, don't you?"

"Y-yes, but—"

"Then, if you are still agreeable, I see no reason not to have you escort me as we discussed. We shall explore in the mornings, as I'm obligated to make calls with Lady Farrington most afternoons, and my maid will accompany us to preserve the dictates of propriety. Though I must say, I consider her presence a nonsensical requirement, and hope she will not expire from boredom. Now, I've been going over my guidebook all morning. I fear it's too late to set out today, but perhaps tomorrow—"

"You cannot be serious! My little innocent, though you may persist in your fantasy that I'm a gentleman, I assure you that the ton speaks of me in very different terms. Broad daylight and accompanying maids won't matter a ha'pence. 'Tis a fragile thing, a reputation—a woman's even more so than a man's. You may think that by associating with me you are only being fair and impartial, but the world will not see it so. They will say I intended to seduce you, lead you to ruin. And ruined you will be."

When Valeria uttered a dismissive laugh, he continued. "'Tis no joking matter. Surely your grandmother is presenting you in hopes of finding you another husband. Rumors that you are conducting an affair with me would destroy any chance of attracting a respectable suitor, and close the doors of the best of polite society to you.''

He rounded on her, the intensity of his gaze holding hers. ''You cannot conceive what 'tis like to be cast into permanent exile from decent company, to have your name always linked to slander or spoken with sly innuendo. You would rue the loss of your good reputation till your dying day. Which is about as long as you would hate the man who caused you to lose it.'' His impassioned tone softened. ''Please, Lady Arnold, let us be able to part as friends.''

The conviction in his voice shook her to the marrow. Before she could prevent herself, she asked, ''Rue the loss of my good name, as you have rued the loss of yours?''

For an instant he froze. Then, almost as if he were physically donning a mask, she watched him wipe the earnest expression from his face, shake his head and summon up a smile. ''Me? Whist, and when had an Irish beggar's brat any good name to lose? Nay, dear lady, 'tis your own fair self that concerns me.''

''Yes, being a beggar's brat and a seducing rogue, you always worry about the reputation of fair ladies.''

The smile slipped a little. ''Nay, I haven't always.''

Despite the teasing expression still on his face, for an instant Valeria saw such bleakness in the depths of his eyes that she had the absurd desire to gather him into her arms. Mercifully, before she rashly did something that would have embarrassed them both, the look vanished.

Rattled by the intensity of that compulsion to embrace him, she could think of nothing to say.

Then a wave of awareness swept through her, some wordless sense of connection that drew her irresistibly to Teagan Fitzwilliams with an attraction that went well beyond the physical. She had known, as he had, an orphan's fate, the terror of losing all that was beloved and familiar. Known the anguish of being rejected by one she thought would love her, and left to make her way alone in an indifferent world.

They stood motionless, bound in place by the strength of what was flowing between them. A bond she *knew* was mutual just as clearly as she knew he would never acknowledge or act upon it. In order to protect her.

With the only soul she now cared about having only weeks left to live, Valeria didn't want to give up this profound, inexplicable link. Somehow she must convince him that parting ways wasn't necessary.

Jennings's knock at the door startled them both.

"You must at least take tea before you leave," Valeria said, gesturing to the settee before busying herself with the tray the butler left before them.

Her caller hesitated, obviously debating the rudeness of refusing against the prudence of an immediate departure.

"Sugar, Mr. Fitzwilliams?" She dropped her gaze to his cup so he could not catch her eye to make his excuses.

She heard him sigh, followed by the soft slide of superfine against brocade upholstery. "If you please."

Silence fell while Valeria worked to prepare their tea and her arguments. "Though I appreciate your experienced view of London society, Mr. Fitzwilliams," she said a moment later, handing him his cup, "there is another factor of which you are not aware. Although it is not yet generally known, Lady Winterdale intends to settle her fortune on me."

She risked glancing at him. The surprise on his face appeared genuine.

"That is excellent news. My congratulations."

"Now, I will allow that if country-nobody Lady Arnold dallied with a rogue, Society might well delight in shredding her reputation. However, much will be excused the heiress of the rich Lady Winterdale. I doubt I would be left completely friendless.''

He nodded. ''Aye, the glitter of gold makes an excellent cleanser. But unless you remain completely above reproach, some of the more discriminating would still cut your acquaintance. 'Tis a risk you need not take.''

''Perhaps not. But, as we've both noted, I'm not a ton lady, nor, given what I've seen of them thus far, am I sure I wish to be. Oh, I've enjoyed Grandmamma's hospitality, but I suppose I've been a soldier's daughter too long. Having lived among men who in the course of their duties put their lives at risk daily, I rather doubt I'd ever feel at home in a society whose time is spent mostly in the frivolous pursuit of pleasure.'' She smiled wistfully. ''I'm not sure where I belong.

''But,'' she continued before he could comment, ''the imminent possession of a fortune frees me from having to worry about Society's good opinion. I need not remarry unless I choose to. And I certainly would not marry a man who would believe Society's evaluation of me rather than make his own assessment of my character.''

''Such a man would certainly not be worthy of you.''

She smiled. ''Precisely. So you see, if you still refuse to honor your promise of escorting me, I am forced to conclude that your concern for my reputation is merely a pretext to avoid my company.'' She took a deep breath, steeling herself to ask, ''Will you make me conclude that?''

Mr. Fitzwilliams stared at his teacup, thumb rubbing the thin china stem, as if engaged in some inner struggle. ''I should affirm it. In truth…Lord forgive me, but I cannot. Neither, though, can I countenance harming you.''

Euphoria filled Valeria, sent a smile bubbling to her lips. ''You won't. You are merely a knowledgeable friend acquainting me with the attractions offered by your city.''

''The ton will never believe that.''

She shrugged. "The ton can believe what it likes."

For a moment he said nothing. Then, with a deep sigh, he looked up at her. "So be it then."

"Naturally, there will be no repetition of the...foolishness my aunt deplored."

His changeable eyes grew alert, their sparkle intensifying. Slowly he scanned her from her forehead down her face, her neck, to linger at her breasts before returning to focus on her lips. Heat scoured Valeria in the wake of that glance.

"Whist, will there not?" he murmured. "Is it sure you are?"

Watching the dimple that creased his cheeks and the roguish gleam in his eyes, she was not sure at all. "Certainly," she lied. "You will conduct yourself as the perfect gentleman I have pronounced you to be. So, do we have a bargain, Mr. Fitzwilliams?"

He raised his teacup to her in salute before placing it back on the table. "A bargain it is, Lady Arnold."

Her pulses leaped in joyous expectation. With a calm Valeria was far from feeling, she carefully deposited her own teacup and rose to hold out her hand. "Until tomorrow then, Mr. Fitzwilliams."

He came over and kissed it. "Until tomorrow."

Scarcely breathing, Valeria watched him walk out, her fingers burning where he had held them, her hand tingling where he had kissed. Legs turning shaky, she collapsed back into her chair.

Oh, my, this was definitely not wise. And she was going to do it anyway.

As he walked back to his lodgings, Teagan found himself breaking into a whistle.

He shouldn't be feeling this surge of energy, as if every sense had been heightened. He should be castigating himself for not having talked Lady Arnold out of the foolishness of seeing him again.

But oh, with a ferocity so deep-seated it almost frightened him, he wanted to see her. And so he'd given in, let the lady have her way.

How unique she was with her mix of innocence and worldly wisdom, her lack of concern for presenting a fashionable facade. She possessed a perception that was almost painfully acute and a straightforward manner entirely bereft of guile. Her wit delighted him, her honesty charmed him, and despite his acquiescence in the matter of seducing her again, her mere presence enflamed him more than the practiced wiles of the most voluptuous society matron.

'Twas a conflagration he'd hold at a low burn, though. He'd given her his word.

Unless, of course, *she* chose to break the agreement. His mouth dried and his body hardened at the prospect.

Even the weariness with which he faced another night's ritual of gaming faded in the face of his anticipation. For the first time in recent memory, Teagan could not wait for it to be tomorrow.

Her mind wandering, but with a polite smile on her face, Valeria served tea to the guests who stopped by Lady Farrington's afternoon at-home. She was performing the hostess's duties alone, however, her chaperone having taken to her bed again upon being informed that Valeria had not only received Teagan Fitzwilliams this morning, but was insisting she meant to go driving with him tomorrow.

Valeria sighed. She was sorry to distress Lady Farrington, who had shown her every kindness, and she hoped that her behavior would not cause undue embarrassment. But she would not allow her chaperone's opinions to overturn her own.

Given the contretemps at the Insley ball, their at-home

was attracting a larger number of guests than usual. Despite Valeria's lack of fortune, Lady Winterdale's sponsorship had been sufficient to attract to her the interest of half a dozen courtiers, though Sir William Parham had been the most assiduous. Many of Valeria's dance partners from the previous evening as well as a number of acquaintances, their avid curiosity barely concealed under an exchange of polite conventionalities, crowded into her drawing room.

By the time she had fended off for the tenth time the same probing questions about her meeting with Teagan Fitzwilliams, some of them phrased in terms so insulting to that gentleman that she was hard put to reply civilly, she was ready to trade so-called "polite society" for a clan of Aborigines that very afternoon.

She wasn't sure whether to be pleased or annoyed when Sir William lingered after the other guests departed to beg her company for a stroll about the gardens. Knowing she might not be able to respond courteously to the warning she feared he meant to deliver, she hesitated a long moment before finally taking the arm he offered.

"Thank you for allowing me to remain," he said once they'd reached the rose walk. "I wanted to apologize, which I wasn't able to do last night before Lady Farrington or this afternoon in a drawing room full of guests."

"Apologize?" Valeria repeated, defenses on alert.

"Yes. I hadn't meant to belittle the attractions you wished to see in London, nor disparage your brother's advice. Although the West India docks are an...unusual site to capture a lady's interest."

She found herself bristling. "I'm an unusual lady."

He smiled. "You are indeed."

Instantly suspicious, Valeria looked up at him. But in his hazel eyes, quite fine if not as uncommonly brilliant as Mr. Fitzwilliams's, she read not censure, but sincere appreciation. She allowed herself to relax a bit.

"I found myself wondering if Mr. Fitzwilliams kept your appointment."

Valeria stiffened once again. "Excuse me, but I do not think that is your concern."

"It is presumptuous of me to inquire. After all, you're an independent lady who's been mistress of her own establishment for years, quite capable of deciding on your own whose company you will keep. However, I—"

"Please, Sir William, you may spare yourself warning me that Teagan Fitzwilliams is a rascal whose escort will lead to my utter ruin. My chaperone has already fully covered that topic. Therefore, you—"

Sir William began to chuckle. Thrown off stride, Valeria fell silent.

"Yes," he said, controlling his mirth, "having witnessed Lady Farrington's reaction last night, I'm sure she has harangued you—at much greater length than you wished to hear! Actually, my intention was quite the opposite. If you are in fact determined to go through with your plan, I wanted to reassure you that I do not believe Teagan Fitzwilliams will cause you any harm."

This was so completely opposite what she'd expected to hear from him that Valeria was left momentarily speechless.

"It's good of you to reassure me," she managed.

"My younger brother was at Eton with him and quite admired him, actually. He kept the lads amused, winning their pennies with his card tricks and sleights of hand. Which I suppose was fortunate, since Rob says his family frequently neglected to bring him home during term breaks, so he must have needed those funds." Sir William sighed. "However, to be honest, I have to admit I cannot be happy about your spending time with him. His rogue's reputation among the ladies is well earned."

"I see. And naturally he is the only single gentleman among the ton who has ever dallied with a willing matron."

Sir William flushed at her blunt words. "He is not, of course, and you are correct in inferring that he has perhaps been unfairly maligned for behavior forgiven in others. That was not precisely what I meant."

Sir William paused and put his hand over the gloved one she had rested on his arm. "Y-you cannot be insensible of my regard for you."

Valeria was glad he'd given her an opening to speak frankly. "Sir William, I know Grandmamma must have spoken to you on my behalf, and I wish to assure you in the strongest terms that despite your fondness for Lady Winterdale, you must not feel compelled to—"

"No, it's not like that. Well, I admit, at first I called on you mainly because of my sympathy for the…circumstances she'd described."

Mortifying fear shot through Valeria. "Indeed? And just what did she tell you that inspired such compassion?"

"You will say she should not have spoken to me of your deepest feelings, and perhaps you are correct. But she knew I, of all men, would understand. I, too, lost a spouse whom I loved almost beyond reason, and…" He stopped and swallowed hard. "I…I know how difficult it is to go on. Lady Winterdale was concerned for your future, and I knew it was time that I, too, move on with my life. She hoped perhaps we might…help each other."

Remorse filled Valeria. Until this moment she had thought of Sir William only in terms of being Lady Winterdale's willing pawn, considering neither that gentleman's reasons for calling on her—nor his feelings. "I am sorry for your loss," she said, patting his hand.

He captured her fingers and held them. "Thank you. Although initially I called at Lady Winterdale's behest, I now enjoy your company for its own merits. Indeed, I had hoped we might soon reach an…understanding. Which is why I cannot help being dismayed by your introduction to Mr. Fitzwilliams. After all, he's not called 'Fascinating Fitz' for naught. Ladies seem to find the handsome rogue nearly irresistible.'' He smiled wryly. ''In comparison, I'm a rather dull dog.''

His modesty touched her. ''I think you're a very fine gentleman.''

He laughed with self-deprecating humor. '''Fine,' I believe, is an adjective a lady uses when she can't think of something more dashing. Dull or not, I'm hoping there will still be a chance for me…for us—'' He broke off, flushing. ''Forgive me. I'm putting this badly.''

Valeria looked at his averted face. No, he hadn't the mesmerizing handsomeness of Teagan Fitzwilliams. But there was strength in those broad shoulders, kindness and a deep sense of honor in his character that led him to commend even a gentleman he obviously saw as a rival. And courage to speak of his feelings when she had given him no real reason to believe they would not be summarily rejected. A most admirable gentleman, in sum.

Sir William's a fine man. The countess's words echoed in her head. *Don't throw a chance to fix his interest….*

''Let me return the courtesy of speaking frankly, Sir William. I'm not sure *I* am ready to remarry. But should I become so, I recognize that Teagan Fitzwilliams is not a likely candidate for husband. I admire you all the more for your honesty today, I value our friendship…and certainly do not dismiss the possibility that it could become more.''

Sir William kissed her hand. ''That, dear lady, is all I ask. Except perhaps that you will also allow me a chance to squire you about the city. Unfortunately, I must leave this afternoon to resolve a pressing problem at my estate.'' He sighed. ''I cannot regret enough the necessity to depart at this particular moment! But when I return, if you will permit me, I promise to escort you wherever you wish—no matter how 'unusual' the place.''

Consider carefully...and try not to be a fool, the countess had counseled. ''I should like that.''

Sir William smiled, the pleasure lighting his eyes more fervent than Valeria would have wished. ''Excellent. I'm afraid I must depart now to prepare for my journey. Shall I bring you back to the house?''

''Thank you, no. I'd prefer to remain a bit longer in the garden.''

Sir William glanced quickly around, then leaned toward her. At about the instant Valeria realized he meant to kiss her, he halted. Cheeks flushing slightly, he raised her hand and brushed his lips over her knuckles instead.

''I shall leave you now. Your most obedient servant, Lady Arnold.''

Valeria bid him goodbye, not sure whether she was relieved or disappointed he'd changed his mind.

And knowing she was even more foolhardy to wonder how his kiss might have compared to the expert caresses of Teagan Fitzwilliams.

Chapter Nine

Two weeks later, Valeria went in to breakfast with Lady Winterdale. Having never fully recovered from the spell of weakness that had sent her to her bed, the countess tired after walking more than a few steps. Since she absolutely refused to be carried up and down the stairs, she now received her friends and took her meals in the sitting room adjacent to her chamber.

Watching with a worried eye as the countess picked at her toast, Valeria filled her plate from the assortment of dishes Cook had sent up to tempt her mistress's flagging appetite. It pained her to see Grandmamma growing steadily weaker, but having received one of the worst scolds of her life yesterday for attempting to cajole Lady Winterdale into eating, Valeria knew it was useless to speak about it.

Nor could she help feeling a ready sympathy. Choosing—or not choosing—to eat was one of the few things over which the once indomitable countess still had control.

"Abandoning me again this morning, eh, missy?" Lady Winterdale said over her teacup. "Always gallivanting about, with never a minute to spare for an old lady."

"Pooh, Grandmamma, that horse won't run. You know

very well if I did stay, you'd dispatch me on an errand as soon as your friends arrived for a good gossip.''

''Wouldn't bother me to have you lurking about.''

''No, but you know it inhibits the others. *They* have too much delicacy to shred the character of their adversaries and meddle in the lives of all their relations with a witness present.''

The countess chuckled. ''Impertinent chit! You've been out five mornings already with that Fitzwilliams rogue. Can't image what else of interest you'd have left to see in London. Alicia told me that there's been no gossip about your excursions, so you're still receiving invitations aplenty.''

Valeria smiled ruefully. ''No gossip yet, although I expect there will be sooner or later. I suppose thus far either no one in the ton has been up early enough to see us, or none venture into such unfashionable locales.''

''Alicia's gone to some trouble to introduce you. I don't want you neglecting your social duties with her.''

''I won't, Grandmamma. We are to go to King's Theatre tonight with Sir William, who's just arrived back in town.''

''And none too soon,'' Lady Winterdale muttered. ''Well, and what do you think Sir William will say to all this racketing about you've been doing in his absence?''

Valeria didn't pretend to misunderstand. ''Actually, he stopped by before he left London to reassure me that Mr. Fitzwilliams would make a very safe escort.''

The countess raised an eyebrow. ''Did he? The boy's downier than I gave him credit for. Where do you go today?''

''Spring Gardens. Knowing my interest in foreign travel, Mr. Fitzwilliams recommended Mr. Wigley's Royal Promenade Rooms, which house a splendid panorama of St. Petersburg and thirty other cities. And there's also Monsieur Maillardet's exhibition of moving mechanical figures, which include a lady playing the harp and a bird that moves and sings. I can't imagine how they work, but perhaps Mr. Fitzwilliams can explain them.''

"What would a rake know about mechanics?''

"He's amazingly knowledgeable, Grandmamma. When we went to see the marble statues Lord Elgin brought back from the Parthenon, Mr. Fitzwilliams related the myths of all the gods portrayed, along with a general history of the entire Peloponnesian Wars.''

The countess snorted. "Sounds dry as dust.''

"On the contrary, I found it fascinating!''

Lady Winterdale groaned and raised her eyes to the ceiling, as if imploring the deity. "First she insists on seeing a certified rogue, now she's talking like a demned *bluestocking!*'' The countess looked over to shake a finger at Valeria. "Child, you are past praying for.''

Valeria gave her an apologetic smile. "I'm afraid I shall never be fashionable.''

"You'll return after viewing these mechanical toys?''

"N-not today.'' Feeling a bit guilty, Valeria explained, "You see, the weather has been inclement for the last week, but today promises to be fair and warm. I've decided to take a water taxi to the Tower—''

"Where the erudite Mr. Fitzwilliams will no doubt regale you with the entire history of the kings and queens of England.''

"—and if the weather holds, go on after nuncheon to view the West India docks. A locale, I know, that is even more unfashionable, but which I am most anxious to see!''

Valeria knew her eyes must be shining with an excitement she had difficulty subduing, even in her Grandmamma's presence. She looked forward this morning to not just a few hours, but an entire day of unsullied pleasure in the company of the most interesting, congenial companion she'd known since she lost her brother.

Like Elliot, Mr. Fitzwilliams seemed to take an avid interest in almost everything, and like Elliot, he never seemed to mind the questions she peppered him with. They'd had the most stimulating discussions about English law while visiting the Inns of Court, about the intricacies of investment and finance during their tour through the City.

She'd been surprised by the keenness of his mind and his obvious breadth of knowledge. And he'd adopted toward her an easy, avuncular manner that reminded her so much of her brother that within an hour of their first excursion she felt they were the best of friends.

Except for the acute awareness that simmered always just below consciousness. And occasionally bubbled to the surface in pulse-quickening moments, like when he took her arm to help her in or out of the carriage. Or once, when she slipped on a rain-slick cobblestone coming out of the shed in which Lord Elgin lodged his marbles, and Teagan caught her shoulders to keep her from falling.

Each time, they'd stood immobile, gazes locked, held as if by some inescapable force. Each time Valeria had felt a powerful urge to lift her lips to his, so tantalizingly close, to tangle her fingers in the thick golden silk of his hair.

Each time he had moved away first.

She would have thought such episodes would have spoiled their camaraderie, made her feel shy and awkward. Instead, they seemed to enhance and deepen the bond between them. When near him, Valeria felt a shivery expectation, such as long ago in India when Papa's relations had sent her a package not to be unwrapped until the holidays. Each day of waiting, speculating over the delights soon to be revealed, had enhanced the anticipation.

Though, as he'd promised, Mr. Fitzwilliams had never gone beyond the line of friendship. True, at every outing he made some teasing comment about her lips or eyes, his tone more than the words themselves conveying that he'd not forgotten the long-ago interlude in her hayloft. Twice he had followed the remark with the suggestion that she abandon convention and come back with him to his rooms.

But the offer was always delivered in such an outrageously flirtatious manner that Valeria could never be sure just how serious he was. Fortunately for the sake of her reputation, he had never persisted in trying to persuade her to cross the bounds she had set. But still...

She came back to herself with a start, to find Lady Winterdale's eyes fixed on her. Realizing she must have been gazing into the distance, a dreamy expression on her face, Valeria felt her cheeks heat.

"Excuse me, ma'am! I've been woolgathering."

"Child, I'm afraid for you," the countess said.

Valeria knew the old woman was concerned with much more than her lack of fashionable aspirations.

She took Lady Winterdale's hand and squeezed it. "I'm being careful, Grandmamma. I promise."

Lady Winterdale shook her head and sighed. "Ah, but can you be careful enough?"

A knock at the door, followed by Molly's entrance, saved her from the necessity of a reply. "Mr. Fitzwilliams is here for us, my lady."

"Thank you, Molly. Fetch the picnic basket Cook made up, and tell Mr. Fitzwilliams I'll be down in a moment."

Avoiding her grandmamma's gaze, Valeria leaned to kiss the old woman goodbye. "I'll stop by later and tell you all about my adventures."

Lady Winterdale nodded. "See that you do."

Valeria exited the room, hard-pressed to keep herself from skipping. She knew she was smiling, but such a joyous expectancy filled her, she felt like gathering the whole world in an exuberant embrace. The sense of setting out on a grand adventure buoyed her, as it had when she'd stepped onboard the vessel that had carried her family to India.

She knew Lady Winterdale worried about her barely concealable enthusiasm for her excursions with Teagan Fitzwilliams. Mercy, too, was suspicious enough that she'd nearly insisted, despite her bad ankle, on replacing Molly as Valeria's chaperone on the last two outings. Not wishing her nurse's glowering presence to dampen the delight of her limited time with Teagan, Valeria had with difficulty persuaded her to remain at home, though not before Mercy delivered a sharp warning against becoming too fond of so handsome and ineligible a gentleman.

In the back of her mind, Valeria knew her rapidly growing attachment to his company ought to worry her, too. Each day they explored, the list of sites still to visit dwindled, and soon their pretext for being together would vanish.

What she would do then, she had no idea. But with the conviction of one who had spent more than enough of her life in loneliness and grief, Valeria resolved for the present to put aside doubt, fear, or caution. She would focus instead on enjoying to the fullest the about-to-be-unwrapped gift of today.

Having dispatched Molly, as well as James, the footman Lady Farrington had insisted on adding to Valeria's party, to buy meat pies from a nearby vendor, Mr. Fitzwilliams spread their picnic cloth on Tower green.

"There, milady Valeria. Your throne, established in the driest bit of greensward I could discover, awaits."

"Thank you, gallant sir!" Valeria seated herself and, after arranging her skirts, patted the place beside her. "Sit, and I'll unpack the bounty Cook provided. We probably have no need of additional meat pies."

"Ah, but Valeria-love, how else was I to have a few minutes alone with you? Since you are so disobliging as to always refuse to steal back to my rooms with me."

"Oh, Teagan, do stop," she replied, chuckling. "You've already practiced your wiles on Molly. I believe she's more than half in love with you, which is making poor James quite jealous."

Teagan, with the quick wit she'd soon noticed in him, had skillfully taken advantage of Lady Farrington's addition to their group, realizing that, with the footman to escort Valeria's maid, he could safely dispatch the two on small errands.

'Twas a kindness to both couples, he told Valeria, the twinkle in his eyes belying the seriousness of his tone, for it prevented Molly from becoming bored by giving her a handsome young footman to flirt with, and allowed Teagan and Valeria to converse with much more freedom and privacy than might have otherwise been possible.

He'd also induced her to dispense with cumbersome titles. As Teagan pointed out, 'twas a bit ridiculous for two who had shared such intimacies to address each other as "Lady Arnold" and "Mr. Fitzwilliams" during private chat.

"You have a talent with people," Valeria observed, watching her maid and the attentive footman walk away.

Engaged in pulling the cork from their wine, Teagan made a short bow over the bottle. "Sure, and a rogue must needs charm the ladies."

"True, 'twould be hard otherwise to maintain one's reputation. But you talk just as easily with James, and can always find something to interest him, no matter how unlikely the locale. You persuaded the Tower guard to give us an extended tour after I'd just overheard him telling another group of visitors the rooms were closed."

"'Tis my Irish tongue. Faith, but it can be very persuasive."

"Can it, now?" But as she echoed his teasing tone, the memory of what that tongue had persuaded her to do invaded her mind in a hot rush of sensation. Ordinary hunger forgotten, suddenly she was starving for the taste of him, the banquet of responses he could evoke with his knowing hands and lips. Her eyes lifted to his mouth, her fingers itching to reach out and pull him the small distance that separated her greedy tongue from his.

He must have sensed her need, for his smile faded and his hands clenched on the wine bottle. His golden eyes blazed with an answering heat. "Valeria," he whispered.

"We got six meat pies. Think ye that'll be enough?"

Molly's cheerful voice jerked Valeria back to the reality of where she was, sitting on a blanket on Tower green, brightly garbed guards within sight, curious visitors wandering the grounds all about her.

"M-more than enough, thank you," she answered in a voice that wobbled only slightly, thinking how wise she'd been to provide herself with a multitude of chaperones.

Molly insisted on unpacking and dividing up the provisions, she and James then removing a short distance away to devour their meal.

"So, what did you find most remarkable this morning?" Teagan asked, handing Valeria a wineglass.

"I thought the mechanical figures most ingenious, particularly the man dancing on a circus tightrope. But I am somewhat sorry we visited the menagerie."

"Why is that? Do you not like animals?"

"On the contrary, I like them very much. I felt so sorry for the beasts, though—and pity is not an emotion I'd ever envisioned feeling for a tiger! We encountered ferocious ones in India, where they sometimes carry off livestock and even threaten the inhabitants. But those poor creatures! Stolen from their homeland, trapped in an alien place, pacing their narrow cages with no hope of breaking free..."

"Aye. 'Tis no wonder they roar with the pain of it."

The odd tone of his voice caused Valeria to look up, into

the sparkling depths of Teagan's golden eyes. *Like you,* she thought, and knew he was thinking the same.

"Is there no way out?" she asked softly.

He remained silent, staring off into the distance. Valeria began to fear she'd breached the trust between them, articulating an insight to which she ought not have given voice, when Teagan spoke.

"Sometimes I dream of using Ailainn to begin a stud farm, such as I used to run in the summers for my grandfather. A simple place in the country I can purchase when the dibs are in tune, and manage like a proper gentleman farmer. But the dibs are never in tune long enough." His wry smile took on a bitter edge. "I suppose I could try to entice a rich woman into marrying me. But I pray heaven I'll never be that desperate or that deep in my cups. What a treat for the lady, to take to husband a man who'll sooner or later abandon her, as dear Papa did us."

Before she could think what to reply, Teagan put down his glass. "Let Molly help you pack up. There's much to see at the docks, and we must view it all before four of the clock. After that, the guildmaster locks the great gates and not even the king himself could gain entry."

He sprang up and walked away, leaving her still at a loss for words to ease the ache she heard in his voice.

By the time he returned with the hackney, the light-hearted sparkle was back in his eye, and conversation grew general. And once they arrived at their destination, Valeria forgot the incident in her wonder over the long avenue of brick warehouses set on stout stone foundations, the crowd of ships straining at anchor in the swift-flowing river, awaiting their turn to disembark their cargoes.

Before her awed eyes she saw flags from a dozen nations, men in sailor's garb, in factor's suits, in flowing Eastern robes. A forest of stout posts lined the quays, bearing huge hoists and winches by which means the sailors were levering a diversity of cargoes out of the holds of their ships.

Eager for a closer look, Valeria begged Teagan to take her to the quay of the easternmost warehouse. Molly and James declined the treat, preferring to wait with the hackney.

"It's said ten thousand tons of shipping is unloaded on these docks in a year," Teagan told her.

"How do you learn such things?"

"I've often had occasion to play cards with merchants and factors. Most men like to speak of their work, if you give them the opportunity."

Valeria edged closer to the water. "See the ropes strain! What is it they're hauling up now?"

"Why, 'tis a fine Queen Anne chair and a beautiful balustrade. Or it will be, when the carvers finish it."

"Ah, 'tis a block of mahogany! Where would that come from, do you think?"

"The forests of Asia, probably, though I believe some grow in the Americas as well."

Valeria stood on tiptoe and leaned forward to get a better look at the rich, red-hued wood glistening in the afternoon sun. "How beautiful it—oh!"

Her words ended with a small shriek as one of the hoist ropes snapped and the huge block teetered, then tumbled out of the cargo net toward the dock below.

Before she could think to move, Teagan seized her and half carried, half dragged her away. As the mahogany crashed onto the quay where she'd been standing a few seconds earlier, he pulled her into the safety of a small alley bordering the warehouse.

The foreman directing the winch-handlers ran after them. "Cor, ma'am, is you all right?"

Teagan set her down and steadied her against him. "Unhurt, sir. A bit frightened, perhaps."

"Lord be praised," the man declared, and trotted back to the quay to deliver to the workmen a loud and, to Valeria's ears, completely incomprehensible harangue whose angry tone alone she could understand.

"You are unhurt?" he asked, still cradling her against his chest, his panting breaths warm against her face.

"Perfectly fine," she answered. "It all happened too quickly for me to be afraid."

"Well, I'm glad you weren't," he muttered. "I was terrified." As if to emphasize those words, he hugged her.

Surprise soon gave way to sweetest pleasure. She loved the strength of his arms cradling her to his chest, the faint scratchiness of his chin pressed to her temple. The feel of his body against hers from chest through torso, her legs brushing his, sent sparks through every nerve.

Her mind instantly recalled that other time she'd felt him full-length against her, the sultry pressure of his body touching hers intimately, while his tongue, slow and languid, spiraled her to unimagined bliss.

Fire ignited within her, kindling her bones, melting conscious will and molding it to new purpose. She felt the tremors of an answering explosion vibrate through his body.

Valeria pulled her chin from the spot he had tucked it, in the hollow of his shoulder. Slowly, as if reluctant to lose even one small area of contact, he allowed her to back off. His breathing ragged, he looked down at her.

"Please, Teagan," she whispered, and raised her lips.

This time he did not move away. Making a sound deep in his throat, he brushed his mouth against hers gently, his touch soft and almost unbearably sweet. Clutching his shoulders, Valeria traced the tip of her tongue over the lips she'd wanted so long and so badly to taste.

As if a wall of restraint had been breached, with a growl he hauled her closer, crushing her breasts against his chest.

His tongue parted her lips, delved deep into her mouth, teasing, stroking, fanning the flames within to a conflagration that burned away any thought of where they were or why she had waited so long to come into his arms.

She wasn't sure whether she'd been kissing him an eternity or an instant—whichever was not long enough—when he broke away, gasping, and pushed her unsteadily aside.

Had he not fended her off, Valeria would certainly have claimed his mouth again. She stared up at him in confusion as the fog of need began to clear.

"Ah, sweeting," he murmured, raising one shaky finger to touch her kiss-reddened lips. "We cannot."

Running footsteps approached.

"My lady!" Molly's panicked voice called across the sudden stillness. "There be a courier come from the house. 'Tis Lady Winterdale! We must return at once!"

Chapter Ten

Apprehension making it difficult to breathe, Valeria scrambled from the hackney. Jennings opened the front door before she could touch the handle, and to her surprise, Lady Farrington hurried out from the parlor, a damp handkerchief in her hand.

"Valeria, at last! She's been asking for you, and I so feared you might not return in t-time!"

Dread slammed into her chest. A queasy mix of fear, anguish and angry protest, too reminiscent of another time, another sickbed, churned in her gut. "I'll go up at once."

She fumbled with the fastening of her pelisse, felt rather than saw Teagan brush her fingers away and undo the ties, then hand it to the butler. "Go," he said quietly.

She gave him a quick nod and ran for the stairs.

Teagan watched her ascend, an echoing sadness in his heart. Though to hear her speak of her dealings with the countess, it appeared the two argued more than they agreed, Teagan knew she cared deeply for the old woman. The news brought by the courier who'd summoned them back had been alarming, and the face of Valeria's chaperone even grimmer.

Lady Farrington stood near the base of the stairway, looking up. "If she'd been at home where she belonged, Aunt Winterdale wouldn't have become so distressed."

At first Teagan didn't realize her remark was intended for him.

"I'm sure she never meant to distress her grandmother, or you, my lady," he belatedly replied.

"Well, she's home now." Lady Farrington did not turn to address him directly. "And she will have no further need of your services, Mr. Fitzwilliams." Still showing him her back, Valeria's chaperone walked to the stairs.

Before Lady Farrington had taken two steps, Jennings had the massive entry door open. "Good day, sir," he said, pointedly standing aside to allow Teagan to exit.

He was being ejected. Though the butler made no move toward him, Teagan suddenly noticed a brace of footmen standing by silently, as if to assist in his departure should he prove uncooperative.

Chagrin heated his face. With the butler's disapproving eyes burning into him, Teagan stepped mechanically toward the door. A panicky awareness washed over him when he crossed the threshold and the portal slammed closed behind him.

Not until this moment had he realized how much his access to Valeria depended upon the goodwill of an old woman who might very well be dying.

As he stood motionless on the front porch, a carriage careened down the street and slowed before the town house with a screech of brakes. Before the vehicle even stopped moving, Sir William Parham leaped out and came up the steps at a trot, giving Teagan a quick nod as he passed.

As it had for Valeria, the door opened for him before he could reach it. In the entryway beyond, Teagan saw Lady Farrington hurry down the stairs to seize the newcomer's hand. "My dear Sir William, thank you for coming! I very much fear Valeria will n-need you—"

The mahogany portal closed behind Sir William, cutting off the rest of Lady Farrington's sentence. Numbly Teagan descended the rest of the stairs.

Valeria will need you.

He clenched his teeth and slammed one fist against his thigh, fighting an upsurge of humiliation, anger, fear—and a pathetic burst of jealousy.

She's my Lady Mystery, you bastard, he silently raged at Sir William, who even now was being led into her presence, probably gathering her into his arms, comforting her against his chest.

For one ridiculous moment, Teagan wished he were a rich, well-respected gentleman worthy of courting a gently bred lady, able to offer her a home and children, able to vow to keep her in love and comfort the rest of her days.

But then, he thought as he trudged blindly back toward his lodgings, Lady Mystery had never truly been his. She was no more than a sweet illusion, a fleeting shaft of sunlight and warmth that had briefly brightened the gray sameness of his days. A searing memory of a morning in a hayloft he could now scarcely believe had been real.

Valeria hurried to the large canopied bed where the countess lay propped up against the pillows, taking shallow panting breaths.

"Late, girl," Lady Winterdale scolded as she fixed her still-fierce gaze on Valeria. "Nearly too late."

"Nonsense, Grandmamma," Valeria whispered, grasping the thin chilled hands between her warm ones. "I'm sure you'll improve. You're too ornery for St. Peter to want you yet."

A ghost of a chuckle exited thin lips already turning

waxy. "Can't cheat death forever. Do something...for me?"

"Of course," she answered, blinking back tears.

"Leaving you money. Winterdale Park, too. Go there afterward. Consider carefully...what you want to do. Promise me?"

"I promise."

"Good." The countess squeezed Valeria's hand, the faintest bit of pressure. "Remember...not to be a fool."

"I shall try. I love you, Grandmamma."

The countess smiled faintly. "My darling girl."

Then Lady Winterdale closed her eyes and softly exhaled her last breath.

And Valeria put her face in her hands and wept.

With the grim efficiency of one who had organized the ritual three times before, Valeria consulted with the vicar and sent notes to Lady Winterdale's cronies about her grandmamma's funeral service. She sat beside Cousin Alicia's bed, putting cold compresses on that afflicted lady's temples and bathing her forehead with lavender water while she wailed with a grief Valeria expressed, after her first bout of tears, only in stoic silence. She supervised the draping of the mirrors and doorframes in black, the ordering of mourning apparel for herself, Lady Farrington and the servants, and steeled herself to meet the flood of visitors who called to express their regrets.

She received Lady Winterdale's lawyer and man of business, hearing with perfect indifference the news that she now possessed cash and property that would make her wealthy beyond imagining.

An indifference that remained unbroken until the afternoon she and Molly went shopping for black lace crepe, ribbons and feathers to adorn their mourning bonnets.

At the first establishment they entered, the customer being waited upon, Lady Evelyn—an earl's wife with an expensive younger son to maintain—stopped in mid-sentence and insisted that Lady Arnold be served first. With profuse expressions of sympathy, she latched on to Valeria's arm and begged to be allowed to assist her.

Uncertain how to get rid of Lady Evelyn without appearing rude, Valeria allowed her to accompany them to the next shop. While they walked that short distance, two strolling gentlemen joined them, one a widower with five children and the other a fashionable dandy with a strong preference for the green baize tables of Pall Mall, the two gentlemen disputing with the earl's wife as to who should take Valeria's arm.

Had she not needed the black crepe and ribbons that very day, Valeria would have abandoned the shopping excursion and called for her carriage forthwith. By the time she'd purchased the few items she considered truly essential, a small crowd had gathered, the babbling group tripping over each other to try to carry her parcels, advise on the best shop to patronize, and persuade her to allow them to take her to Gunter's for some refreshment.

After finally extracting her arm from Lady Evelyn's grip, persistently refusing all invitations and having Molly yank the packages back from the hands of her too-willing assistants, she and the maid at last escaped back into their waiting carriage.

If this, she thought as they regained the blessed quiet of Grosvenor Square, was a sample of what she could expect in her new life as the rich Lady Arnold, Valeria wanted no part of it. As soon as Lady Winterdale's services were concluded, Valeria intended to honor her benefactress's wishes and leave London for Winterdale Park.

Protected in a cocoon of numbness, Valeria attended the funeral several afternoons later. Even the necessity of assisting Lady Farrington, who collapsed at the churchyard and had to be carried back to her carriage, did not penetrate that soothing fog.

With her cousin tucked up in bed and her own maid dismissed, Valeria sat alone by the flickering light of a single brace of candles in her grandmother's sitting room.

Her sitting room now.

Her tightly knit calm was unraveling in a tangle of emotions, all of which she'd experienced before. She hadn't had enough time. Though she'd come to love the crusty old lady who'd adopted her, she hadn't expressed those feelings often enough. And though she'd deluded herself into believing she was prepared for her grandmother's death, she now found she had no adequate defense against the stark loneliness that clawed at her.

In one respect this loss was better than the last, she told herself, attempting to rally her depressed spirits. She knew the countess had grown to care for her, and however poorly she'd expressed it, Valeria knew the countess had realized she was loved in return.

Valeria wandered to the bed and trailed her hand across the pristine linen, hardly able to believe her grandmother's frail frame but valiant spirit would no longer occupy it. Could it have been only a week ago that she'd rushed here to clasp those thin gnarled fingers?

From the one person she truly wished to see, the one whom she felt would appreciate her grief and whose mere presence would ease her sorrow, she'd heard nothing.

Perhaps, having been exiled from his family so young, Teagan Fitzwilliams had no experience of proper mourning protocol, and thus had not thought to call or write.

Still, she'd hoped she might catch a glimpse of him, mayhap receive an encouraging glance, during the service to which Sir William escorted her in compassionate silence.

But there'd been no sign of Teagan's handsome face or distinctive gold hair among the large crowd of mourners.

Now, alone in this empty, echoing room, she had to conclude that Teagan Fitzwilliams, probably surmising correctly that her grandmother's death would leave her too busy for sightseeing excursions, had dismissed her to go on with his life.

Would he care that she'd determined to leave London? If he knew, would he have called to bid her good-bye?

Would he have pressed her to stay?

Suddenly she couldn't bear the thought of quitting the city without making some final contact with him. She would pen him a farewell note, she decided—and realized with chagrin that she didn't even know his address.

No matter, she thought. She'd send James with the message. The servant's grapevine knew everything, and surely he would be able to track down Mr. Fitzwilliams.

Swiping away a tear, she went to find pen and paper.

As Teagan left his lodgings to walk through the drizzling gloom of the London night toward Jermyn Street, his thoughts, as they had so often this past week, returned to Valeria.

Within a day of Lady Winterdale's death, rumors began to circulate that her granddaughter-in-law, the quiet little widow Lady Arnold, had been named her sole heiress, making her very, very rich and catapulting her in the eyes of the ton from country nobody to socially prominent in the breath it took the speaker to describe her bequest.

Valeria wouldn't care about that, he knew. She'd lost a friend, not a benefactress, and though she'd been bereaved before, having already experienced what she must face again wouldn't make enduring the grief and sudden shock of loneliness any easier. Teagan had ached to be with her and offer whatever help and comfort he could.

Realizing with angry resignation that he would almost certainly have been refused entry had he tried to attend the funeral services this afternoon, he'd merely stood under the portico of the building facing St. George's, Hanover Square, and watched as Valeria was hustled from her carriage into the church and then back out again.

He'd sent her a note the day of Lady Winterdale's passing, but had received no reply. Suspecting her chaperone had not allowed it to be delivered, he'd called and been turned away three times by a stone-faced Jennings. Finally he'd come by way of the mews to the servant's entrance and asked for Molly. James had intercepted him instead, taking him into the shadows of the garden and begging him not to put Molly's employment at risk by asking her to smuggle a message to her mistress.

Lady Farrington's doing, he knew. Valeria's personal dragon of a protector would do whatever was necessary to ensure the unworthy Teagan Fitzwilliams never succeeded in intruding his polluting presence upon her cousin again.

Every man of birth and address in London now hanging out for a wife, as well as a miscellany of fortune hunters and ne'er-do-wells, would be flocking to her, the already-blessed Sir William at their head. The kindest, most intelligent and wittiest ones might even be worthy of her.

Teagan might as well face the fact that his sunlit, laughter-dappled interludes with the now rich and socially prominent Lady Arnold were over for good.

He turned the corner and looked up wearily at the light blazing from the windows of the gaming hell where tonight's play would take place. There could be no more fitting metaphor of his world of separation from Valeria, he thought with bitter amusement, than the large, beautifully appointed marble mansion she now owned and this smoke-and-tobacco stained, brandy-redolent establishment he was now bracing himself to enter.

He had never felt more alone in his life.

Mercifully, as he entered the game room at Devil's Den, Teagan found neither Rafe Crandall nor his cronies present. Relieved to be spared the necessity of summoning up a lighthearted banter he was far from feeling, Teagan settled into a quiet round of whist with a rich merchant.

He had amassed a modest stack of winnings when the door opened and the occupants of the room stirred. Teagan looked up to see Jeremy Hartness, Earl of Montford, cross the threshold, his noble lip curled as if in disdain at the assembled patrons, most of whom would never have been allowed to set foot on the stairway leading up to White's.

The wealthy, powerful Earl of Montford. Teagan's first cousin.

For an instant Teagan sucked in a breath and closed his eyes. *Not him, not tonight,* his beleaguered spirit protested.

The earl usually avoided locales in which he might encounter his disreputable cousin, which suited Teagan. When they did chance to meet, normally Teagan was poised and ready to wield his rapier wit, countering the innuendo and outright insult the earl always flung in his direction.

Montford would certainly try to abuse him now, but tonight, Teagan had no heart for a fight.

He bent his head and studied his cards. Perhaps Montford would simply pass by and leave him alone.

Teagan's downcast eyes caught the reflection off the highly polished evening shoes that halted beside his table.

"Well, well, what have we here? It appears the normal level of scum inhabiting this sorry hell has sunk even lower. Unless I'm mistaken, 'tis that infamous Irish Captain Sharp, Teagan Fitzwilliams."

Slowly Teagan looked up. "Why, I believe 'tis my illustrious cousin, the Earl of Montford. Faith, and what would bring you out of your citadel at White's? Surely you don't wish to gain firsthand knowledge of the ills you so love to deplore in the Lords.''

"Still playing the buffoon, I see. Gentlemen, shall we offer this broken-down exile the opportunity to earn a little coin? As a gamester lamentably lacking in skill, he seldom knows where his next meal is coming from. Perhaps we ought to show the lower orders a little compassion.''

The gentlemen accompanying Montford looked at each other uneasily. Among them Teagan recognized several of the earl's boon companions: Rexford, second son of a duke and married to the sister of Montford's wife; Wexley, a wealthy but amusing fribble of good birth; and Albemarle, whose estates marched with Montford's.

"I...I expect we could play a few hands,'' Rexford said, still looking uncertain.

"Nay, Cousin, can you not see they're uncomfortable among such rough company? Faith, and I'd hate to tax the gentlemen's wit or relieve them of their fat purses.''

"Small chance of either,'' Montford replied with a sneer. "Come, gentlemen, have a seat. You, there—out!'' The earl waved a hand at the merchant, who, to Teagan's disgust, scrambled to give up his chair to the new arrivals.

What was Montford up to? Teagan wondered as the earl and his friends called for wine and a fresh deck of cards. Jeremy Hartness had hated him from the moment Teagan's six-year-old foot had touched Montford land twenty-two years ago. It could not be coincidence the mighty earl had appeared at a gaming establishment he'd normally not deign to enter. Montford would never seek Teagan out without a reason, and it wouldn't be a pleasant one.

The earl insisted on piquet, and Teagan drew the obviously nervous Albemarle as a partner. His cousin was reasonably adept, and they split the first two rubbers. The lack of love between the two being well known, word of the match spread, and by the time they began the third rubber quite a crowd had gathered.

Standing at the edge of it, Teagan was surprised to note, was Lord Riverton. Still grateful for the earl's intervention on his behalf at the Insley ball, Teagan gave him a quick nod. Somehow, surrounded by this hostile group, Teagan felt better just knowing Riverton was there.

After the commencement of the third rubber, Teagan's partner began to make a series of such ill-judged plays that they went down heavily, nearly wiping out Teagan's small stack of coins.

So that was the ploy. Well, he'd have none of it.

"Much as I hate to leave so convivial a group, I fear I have a previous engagement. Gentlemen," Teagan said, preparing to gather up his remaining coins.

Montford put a hand out to block Teagan's reach. "What, leaving so soon, and after such a paltry reverse?"

"I've little enough left, and nothing else to stake, as you can see. And I'm expected elsewhere."

"Your penny harlot can wait. Let's have another rubber."

Teagan searched for the proper words to extract himself without slighting his partner. He'd not allow Montford to lead him into a verbal row his cousin could then point to as evidence of Teagan's bad breeding.

"I generally prefer to game on my own, without a partner," he said at last.

"Well, that's easily arranged. We'll make it whist—just you and I. And double the stakes."

Should he lose the first round, doubling the stakes would leave Teagan without a coin to his name. "Another time, perhaps." He started to rise from his chair.

Montford uttered a scornful laugh. "Always knew you were a coward. But then, one couldn't expect proper behavior from a man whose mother betrayed her breeding by running off with her Irish groom like a common strumpet.''

Teagan froze. Someone gasped, and the hubbub of voices in the room dwindled into silence.

Rage filled the icy void he'd wandered in for the past week, rage at the tormentor who'd never lost an opportunity to belittle him since the day a lost, frightened boy had approached the lad introduced to him as his cousin—and got punched in the gut.

Leaning across the table, he slapped the earl's face. ''Name your seconds.''

In the fraught silence that followed, the earl slowly raised his fingers to rub at the red mark Teagan's hand had left. ''Nay, dueling is a custom reserved for gentlemen. I'll not accept the challenge of a worthless guttersnipe. If you want to try to defend the honor of your whore of a mother, sit down and play. And the game's not over until *I* say we're done.''

Icily lucid in his rage, Teagan had to acknowledge his cousin was clever. His own prowess with both sword and pistol were such that fighting his cousin was almost tantamount to the earl's murder. But after the earl had offered him such an insult, Teagan couldn't withdraw, no matter what form was chosen to settle the business.

Teagan sat back down. ''Deal the cards.''

''Very well. Let's make it more interesting and triple the stakes. Ah, have you not sufficient coin?'' the earl interrupted when Teagan started to protest. ''Save your worthless vowels for the tradesmen—I'll have none of them. But you do have one item I'd not mind collecting. Let's add that stallion of yours to the stake.'' Montford turned to his friends with a laugh. ''Horseflesh is the only thing of value the damned Irish have ever produced.''

Ailainn. Ailainn, almost as much friend as mount. Teagan would rather shoot the stallion than see him go to the earl. But truly, he had nothing else.

"So be it," Teagan replied through gritted teeth.

The earl smiled, a curve of the lips that held no warmth. "Done. Now, gather round, friends! Watch me send this blot on the family escutcheon back to the Dublin gutter where he belongs."

Chapter Eleven

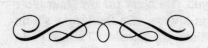

Ruin. His total and irreversible ruin. That was what his cousin intended, Teagan realized.

Having hated him for years, why had Montford chosen this precise moment to strike?

The earl must have been keeping a closer watch on his detested half-Irish cousin than Teagan had imagined, for after the disastrous reverses of last month, his finances were at the lowest ebb they'd been since he'd begun his career as a gambler. Already pledged on the table along with Ailainn was the entire stake he had remaining.

Though his luck had improved of late, he'd curtailed his play the last few weeks, content to quit after only modest winnings, so as to rise early enough to escort Valeria Arnold about London. A small reserve remained back at his rooms, scarcely enough to cover this month's rent, and far less than he'd need to pay his other bills.

Should he lose tonight, word of it would begin to circulate practically before the last card hit the table. By next morning, every merchant to whom he still owed money would be at his door, with the constable on their heels if Teagan couldn't make good on his debts.

Prison. Disgrace.

If he could shake off his anger and play with all the skill he possessed—a skill he knew to be superior to his cousin's—he'd be able to stave off that catastrophe.

As long as capricious Lady Luck did not despise him as much as the earl his cousin.

"Sad as I am to disappoint you, Montford," Teagan said as the earl shuffled the deck, "you'll ne'er be the breaking of me. Should you carry off my blunt—a most improbable event—I can always take the king's shilling."

"About time you should. 'Twould end for good and all your pretensions to being a gentleman. Instead of preventing you, Grandpapa should have assisted your joining the rest of the gutter-born thieves and criminals in the army years ago. Now I, the grandson of his own blood, his heir," the earl continued, his voice growing strident, "he maligned for not wishing to purchase a commission. But his harlot daughter's only son? Oh no, *his* life was too precious to be risked fighting savages in the Americas."

As his cousin's words echoed in Teagan's incredulous ears, he scarcely noted their biting scorn. His thoughts whipped back to his searing final interview with his grandfather after his Oxford debacle. After excoriating him for bringing dishonor on his mother's name, the old man had refused Teagan's plea to purchase him a commission. He'd not inflict upon the army a cowardly Irish beggar's brat, the old earl had railed, adding that if Teagan tried to enlist as a common soldier, even under a false name, Lord Montford would have him found and cashiered out. After which the old man had had him ejected from the house.

Teagan had stalked away, vowing never again to ask his mother's family for anything.

Had his grandfather refused his request—as his cousin's words seemed to suggest—not out of contempt, but from fear of losing his only link to his beloved daughter?

"Why, gentlemen, he's so frozen with terror," Montford's mocking voice recalled him, "he can't even pick up his cards."

Teagan jerked his thoughts back to the present and examined his hand. Inattention now could force him to flee London, perhaps require him to join the army in truth.

Yet despite the dire choice he'd face were he to lose this round, the roiling mix of shock, doubt and disbelief, threaded through with a thin, tentative joy, forced him to voice the question churning in his head.

"You thought Grandpapa favored me? Is that why, though you've always known you would have everything—the title, wealth, power—you've always hated me?"

A sudden rage blazed in his cousin's blue eyes and he leaned close, his clipped, furious words pitched for Teagan's ears alone. "Aye, you. Spawn of a penniless Irish scoundrel. Everyone else knew what you were from the moment you arrived in England—why could Grandpapa never see it? How could he think a few paltry achievements would ever make you superior to me? 'Why can't you ride like Teagan?'" he said, mimicking an old man's tones. "'Why can't you shoot like Teagan?'"

With a growl Montford pushed away and slammed the first card down on the table. "Thank God the old fool died soon after your disgrace, before he was able to recall you. Though I doubt he'd be so proud of you now, were he here watching you be reduced to the stews from which you came. If," the earl added, smiling at Teagan as he took the first trick, "you don't get clapped in debtor's prison first."

Reeling from that second revelation, Teagan struggled to focus on the game. His grandfather had been on the point of recalling him? The old man had possessed a fearsome temper, and though Teagan had never known him to apologize for words or acts uttered in anger, he sometimes quietly attempted to make amends. Had he wished to be reconciled with his only daughter's son?

Perhaps it had been fear of having Teagan restored to the old earl's favor, rather than dislike, that had caused Jeremy Hartness to bar Teagan's entry into the Montvale townhouse that long-ago day. When, having heard his grandfather had been stricken and was not expected to live, he had put aside his pride and come back to see the old man one last time.

The horsewhip his cousin had brandished wouldn't have kept him out. Jeremy's assertion that another confrontation with Teagan would perhaps fatally tax their grandfather's rapidly failing strength had.

Montford smiled again as he won a second trick. *Focus on the present,* Teagan rebuked himself with disgust. If he weren't more careful, the earl would very soon have no need of skill to accomplish Teagan's ruin.

Had that been the purpose of Montford's unprecedented candor? To rattle Teagan out of his customary sangfroid?

The flicker of a glance at his cousin's impassive face told him nothing. Renewed fury settled Teagan's disordered thoughts. *Whatever ploys you use, you've chosen my ground, and you shall not win on it,* he silently vowed.

The room remained quiet, the attention of everyone present riveted on their table. Teagan narrowed his mind to calculating the statistical probability of the cards he needed being still in the deck, and predicting from his cousin's play the cards he held.

Teagan rallied to win the first hand, then lost the second. The earl, he had to admit, had gotten much better at analyzing his opponent.

Still, after Teagan drew for the decisive third hand, the tightness in his chest began to relax. Given what he held, he was reasonably sure of winning at last.

With cool confidence he laid down an ace—only to have his cousin trump it. To his surprise, the earl then led back with another off—from the one suit in which Teagan had

only a single low card. To his growing dismay, with un-
erring accuracy his cousin took control of the game, leading
each play with a superior trump or a higher card in the suit,
as if he had deduced the whole of Teagan's hand.

Teagan was going to lose.

As if from a great distance, he heard his cousin's shout
of triumph as he threw down the last card.

"Done—and done in!" Montford crowed. "Make sure
to send the horse before you slink out of town."

Weighted down by the enormity of the impending disaster, Teagan sat stunned, watching the face card his cousin
had just played spin on its edge.

Like a runaway stallion, his mind raced pell-mell through
the consequences of his impending loss. A lightning-fast,
covert trip to his rooms to recover his few remaining coins
before the news got out and the vultures descended, cutting
off any escape but prison. Shame that he must betray his
landlady's confidence in him by leaving her unpaid. A detached calculation of whether his coins would take him far
enough from London to escape the magistrate. And if he
made it away, whether he'd still retain enough to stake a
renewed round of gaming.

The quixotic conclusion that perhaps he would have to
enlist, after all.

But while those dark thoughts went swirling through his
head, a darker shadow on the edge of the falling pasteboard
suddenly captured his attention. While his cousin accepted
the congratulations of his friends, Teagan leaned forward
to seize it.

Even after he examined it more closely, he had difficulty
believing the stunning conclusion. No wonder his cousin
had been so confident of winning. The cards they'd been
playing with were marked.

His cousin was rising, the other gentlemen slapping him

on the back. Teagan rummaged through the deck, finding on other pasteboard edges the same subtle indentations.

Idiot! He cursed his inattention, for though the marking system was not one he'd seen before, he should have found the earl's unexpected skill in this hand suspect early on, had he not allowed his cousin to rattle him by resurrecting old ghosts.

And then a sense of imminent triumph swelled his chest. 'Twas not Teagan who would be ruined tonight, but his duplicitous cousin.

Much was permitted the favored few who possessed wealth, title and privilege. A man might humiliate his wife by openly flaunting a mistress. Might beat his spouse and children, abuse his servants and retainers, neglect his lands, beggar his estates. But a gentleman never, ever cheated at cards.

To do so would mean expulsion from every club, social ostracism for both the offender and his kin, a shame that would dishonor his name for generations. Even the ignominy of a ruined gamester's suicide was less damaging to his family than the dishonor of his being found a cheat.

All those years of slights, insults, persecution were about to change on the edge of a spinning card.

But even as he opened his lips to proclaim his discovery, Teagan hesitated. His cousin could descend to the fiery pit with Teagan's fervent blessing. But this disgrace would ruin not just Jeremy Hartness, but his entire family.

His wife, a bland society matron of whom Teagan knew no ill except she—or her relations—had displayed the poor judgment to have her wedded to his cousin. Their young son now at Eton where, as Teagan well knew, the boys were even crueler than their elders to one they judged unfit.

And Jeremy Hartness's crime would besmirch the name of the grandfather who had apparently loved Teagan, the name of the mother he still cherished.

What good has being grandson of a Montford ever done you? he asked himself mockingly. But even as he gazed down at the evidence in his hands and chastised himself for being twenty varieties of a fool, his mind was already considering other options.

His cousin's fall would be a mighty one, but few would notice the final ruin of a man clinging to the edges of gentility. How could the ignominy attached to his name be worse? There were compensations, he thought with a bitter twist of the lips, for having no reputation left to lose.

If he could escape with his modest reserve, he could make his way somewhere else. Begin over again. Even join the army, if matters grew too desperate.

Would anyone mourn his disappearance from London? Surely not the brandy-reinforced occupants of such hells as Devil's Den. No one except the landlady he would, he vowed, at some point manage to reimburse.

And perhaps one sweet lady whose grief might be deepened to discover the man she'd insisted on believing a gentleman was in fact only the impecunious gambler everyone had claimed him to be.

Pain twisting in his chest at that thought, Teagan looked up. From across the table, amidst a cacophony of voices, cheers and catcalls, he saw Lord Riverton.

A frown on his brow, the older man met his gaze and jerked his chin toward the cards.

Riverton knew.

Teagan drew in a sharp breath. Before he could speak or move, Riverton reached out to snag the elbow of the earl, who'd just called for his coat and cane.

''Not so quickly, Montford. There's a small matter of the cards...'' Lord Riverton let his words trail off.

Had it been Teagan who'd hailed him, his cousin probably would have brushed him off and walked away. But as a cabinet minister and one of the most highly placed men in England, Lord Riverton could not be ignored.

A cabinet minister renowned for his penetrating intellect, as well. As Montford turned to the older man, the triumph faded from his face, to be replaced by uneasiness. "The…cards, my lord?"

A calm sense of inevitability came over Teagan. *For you, Mama.* Giving Riverton a minute, negative shake of the head, Teagan rose. "The cards fell for you, Cousin."

Riverton returned a sharp look. Teagan met it steadily. Finally the older man nodded. "So it appears."

Relief washed over Montford's face. "Indeed. Good evening, my lord." Giving Riverton a deep bow, Teagan's cousin turned to leave.

"A word with you, Montford, if you please." Lord Riverton's quiet voice cut through the hubbub. While the earl froze in midstep, the cabinet minister turned to the friends who waited near the door. "Go along, gentlemen. Montford will join you later."

The earl looked back at Riverton, hesitating as if he wished to refuse but was unable to devise a sufficient excuse. Finally, summoning up a brittle smile, he faced his friends. "Get a table at White's and order up a bottle, if you please, Wexley. I'll be along shortly." His face paling beneath the smile, he turned to Riverton.

The cabinet minister motioned him to a table in the back corner of the room. "Over there, where we can be private. Fitzwilliams, you will accompany us."

For a few long moments, the earl stood motionless. Teagan had the grim satisfaction of watching a sheen of sweat appear on his cousin's brow. His fingers trembling slightly, the earl reached up to pull at his neckcloth, as if the material had suddenly grown too tight.

Then, carefully avoiding Teagan's gaze, he said, "My pleasure, Lord Riverton."

Teagan followed them to the table and sat where Riverton indicated. Though Teagan himself had chosen not to expose Montford, if Lord Riverton wished to reveal the bastard's perfidy, so be it.

A forced cheeriness in his tone, Montford began, "My lord, how can I be of..." At Riverton's unflinching stare his words trailed off and he swallowed hard.

After a long, tense silence the minister seemed content to prolong, Riverton said quietly, "You miserable little muckworm. Were it not for the respect in which I held your grandfather, I would have ordered that deck to be examined."

As the earl sputtered a protest, Riverton interrupted with icy contempt. "Spare me your excuses. And listen well. You beat your cousin at cards tonight, nothing more. If you or any of your friends spread tales of bankruptcy or ruination, I shall be compelled to reveal what I know. And though Society, hypocritical as it is, might dismiss an allegation coming from Mr. Fitzwilliams, I assure you the ton would take very seriously any such accusation made by me. I trust I've made myself clear?"

The earl moistened his lips. "My lord, I assure you—"

"Good. Remove yourself from my sight. And remain out of it." Riverton waved his hand toward the door.

The minister watched impassively as Teagan's cousin hurried off, then focused his penetrating regard on Teagan. "A costly bit of honor, Mr. Fitzwilliams."

"Ah, milord," Teagan replied, exaggerating the lilt, "as anyone can tell ye, an Irish gambler has no honor."

Riverton lifted his brows, but made no reply. "A fine animal, your stallion. I shall offer to buy him from Montford. Naturally, he will sell the beast to me, so you needn't worry about his welfare."

A small sop, given the enormity of the catastrophe about

to overwhelm him, but Teagan felt perversely comforted. ''Tis most grateful I'd be, milord.''

Amusement flickered in Riverton's eyes, and Teagan had the uncomfortable feeling that the older man knew his feckless gambler's pose for the sham it was. "Given the consequences, I have no doubt your cousin will keep mum about the events of this evening. Which should give you a few days' grace to gather your things and depart London before word of your...pecuniary difficulties gets out.''

The heightened alertness that had sustained Teagan through the game began to ebb, and he felt suddenly weary. ''Aye, my lord. Thank you for that, too.''

Lord Riverton studied him. He seemed about to say more, but after a moment's hesitation, merely nodded. ''Good night, Mr. Fitzwilliams.''

Bidding Riverton goodbye in turn, Teagan rose and made his way into the night. His footsteps on the dark street seemed to echo like the muffled beat of the drums before an execution. Though Riverton was undoubtedly correct about the silence his cousin would maintain concerning the events of the evening, Teagan's long and intimate acquaintance with the less elevated strata of society told him that any one of a dozen other witnesses—waiters, footmen, the doorman—would quickly spread the titillating tale of this verbal duel between their betters.

By tomorrow, every tradesman in town to whom he owed money would be on Mrs. Smith's doorstep, probably followed by the constable. If Teagan wished to avoid the very real possibility of being clapped into debtor's prison, he'd best clear out his things and leave London tonight.

And go where?

Dark memories he normally succeeded in suppressing flashed through his mind. Clutching the fingers of his dying mother long after she'd gasped her last breath, as if his six-year-old hands could keep her from death's icy grip. Fear and blows and desperate hunger, replaced by wretched sickness on the heaving packet that had carried him across the Irish Sea. The kindly face of the clergyman who'd found him starving and half-frozen on the Dublin streets, assuring him the unknown relations to whom he was sending Teagan would welcome him home.

And what a welcome. His hopeful dream of joining a family had not long outlived the moment when the cousin of like age to whom he'd just been introduced—Jeremy, now Earl of Montford—punched him in the stomach.

A more recent memory, even more bitter, replaced that vision. Standing before his grandfather in the late earl's study, the old man's face contorted with rage as he uttered the last words Teagan ever heard him speak: "Get out of my house and take your black Irish arse back to the devil that spawned you!"

He could go there, Teagan thought with macabre humor as he slipped upstairs to his rooms. Fearful that rumors might even now have begun to circulate, by the light of a single candle he quickly packed his few possessions and checked the pockets of all his waistcoats to augment the pitifully small store of coins he'd removed from his desk.

He paused a long moment in front of his books. Then, with a sigh, he mended a quill, pulled a bill from the stack in his drawer and penned a note on the back of it, instructing Mrs. Smith, with his apologies for the inconvenience, to sell the volumes and accept the money thus obtained in lieu of the rent he owed her.

In the bottom of the desk he came across his old dueling pistol. He checked the box and smiled without humor. He had only a few shots left, but if it came to that, one would be enough.

After adding the pistol to his other belongings, Teagan slung the saddlebag over his shoulder. He paused, taking a last look about his room, his eyes lingering on the copies of Homer, Virgil and Plato.

Not all his memories of this London sojourn would be bitter. He'd spent some quiet afternoons recapturing those lazy Oxford days when his life had been lived through the pages of his books, his future seeming securely pledged to the pursuit of scholarship.

And he'd spent some joyous mornings in the company of an intelligent, spirited, inquisitive beauty who'd challenged his mind, tantalized his body and touched his soul. His lovely Lady Mystery, whom he'd once halfheartedly tried to lure to these rooms. One of the very few people he'd met to whom his past and his family background truly seemed to mean nothing, who had taken Teagan as she found him—and seemed to like what she saw.

Desolation settled in his chest. Please God, he prayed, as he crept back down the stairs into the night, let it take several days for word of his ruination to spread to the ton and forever destroy her good opinion of him.

Chapter Twelve

Before quitting London, Teagan made one more stop, at the stables where he boarded Ailainn. The horse lifted his head and whickered as Teagan silently approached.

"It's good ears you have, my beauty," Teagan whispered, stroking the stallion's velvet muzzle. "I must leave you now, but Riverton will make you a good master. A blessing, that, for if I thought you were to go to a rider as ham-fisted as Montford, I might have to use one of my last shots on you, and then where would I be?"

The horse snorted and tossed his head, as if disagreeing.

"Ah, 'tis sorry I am to abandon you, my lovely, but I've no choice. Though Lord Riverton might forgive the theft, you're too striking to pass unnoticed, and the duns would find us too easy to follow."

Giving the stallion one last bit of sugar, Teagan stepped away, resisting the burning in his eyes. *"Taim i' ngra leat,"* he whispered.

Blindly he walked away, forcing his thoughts to the bargain he must strike at a livery stable on the outskirts of the city. He'd need a mount less flashy than Ailainn, and priced accordingly, to get him surreptitiously away.

As he exited the stable, a prickling of apprehension penetrated his depression. Instantly alert, he halted, sensing more than seeing a form in the shadows.

"Don't be reaching for your popper, now." A man's voice came out of the darkness. "I mean ye no harm. In truth, 'tis a proposition to yer benefit I've got for ye."

"Who are you?" Teagan demanded. "Step out where I can see you."

The man moved cautiously closer. In the dim light of a neighboring gas lamp Teagan could just make out the broken-nosed profile of a one-armed man, the buttons of his ragged uniform coat glinting in the gloom. The maimed rifleman he'd seen begging for coins in the meaner neighborhoods by the West India docks.

Teagan relaxed a little. "What do you want, soldier? I'm afraid I've no blunt to spare tonight."

"Boot's on t'other leg, sir! As it happens, I heared ye might be of a mind to earn some yerself."

Teagan smiled without humor. "Ah, how swiftly the news of disaster blows on the wind."

The soldier grinned back, a single tooth gleaming. "Aye, it rightly does. And knowin' how's you might not be wantin' to leave the city, with that purty little lady ye've been squiring about still residin' here and all, there's a gent I knows what thinks ye might be ripe for an occupation to get ye back in the ready."

"Which 'gent'?" Teagan asked, still marveling at the speed with which word had spread from Devil's Den.

"A gent with money in his pockets, and 'tis all ye need to know about him."

A job offered by a gentleman who wished to remain nameless was a dubious prospect, but Teagan wasn't in a position to be overly choosy. "What sort of occupation?"

"Nothin' too hard for an enterprisin' gallant like yerself what knows his way about the streets and the parlors, if ye take my meanin'. Ye've only to drop by the house of a government mort and pick up a case from his stables. If somewhat was to see ye nosin' about, ye can claim to be payin' a visit, which is the beauty of it, ye see. Take the case and fetch a horse from the livery I shows ye, and ride yer bundle to a barkeep in Dover. And keep your trapper shut after. Easy enough, eh? Do it right and quick, with no questions asked, and there'll be a bagful of guineas in it, with a promise of more.''

''And what's in the 'case' I'll be delivering?''

The soldier shrugged. ''No need of you knowin'.''

''Pick up a case—documents, probably—from a government official's house and carry them clandestinely to Dover,'' Teagan mused aloud. ''From which port they'll be smuggled over to France? I'm to be a spy, then?''

The solder pointed to his empty sleeve. ''Done gave me arm for bloody England at Badajoz, and what thanks did I get for it? Me mum was run off the land, me wife and baby starved, and 'tis no one wantin' to hire a one-armed bloke now. Nor has dear ol' England smiled on ye neither, eh?''

What *had* his mother's country—or her countrymen—ever done for Teagan? Why should he feel any loyalty to a land whose inhabitants, since the very day of his arrival on English soil, had despised him as Irish and inferior?

''Well, does ye want the job or no?''

A few midnight rides. The passing on of a handful of anonymous dispatches that would probably never do anyone any harm. And no one would ever know.

He would earn enough to stave off his creditors and stay in the city, build up a stake and resume gaming. Remain in London, where he could devise some way to outflank Lady Farrington and see Valeria Arnold again.

And grasp some small, satisfying revenge on a society that allowed men like his cousin to flourish, while maimed soldiers and honest Irishmen struggled to survive.

But even if no one else ever learned of it, Teagan would

know. And betrayal, even of a nation to whom he owed no loyalty at all, was still dishonor.

It would make him no better than the cousin he despised—make him unworthy of the trust Valeria Arnold had so gallantly and mistakenly placed in his character.

"Tell your 'gent' I'm not his man."

"Is ye sure of it? 'Tis easy blunt to earn for a bruisin' rider like yerself. Iffn' I could ride with this arm, I'd be doin' it meself."

"I'm sure. Now, I'm sorry, but I must be out of London by first light."

To his surprise, the soldier smiled once again. "Aye, if ye be set on the straight 'n narrow, I expects ye must." After giving Teagan a salute with his remaining arm, the soldier melted off into the shadows.

Teagan turned up his collar against the light rain that had started to fall. Already the dense gloom of night was lightening in the east. He wasn't sure how far north his coins would carry him, but if he wished to escape at all, he must get himself to that livery stable forthwith.

A chill rain was spattering the London streets as Lady Winterdale's luxurious traveling carriage bore Valeria away from Grosvernor Square at dawn. A warm brick at her feet and a thick fur wrap across her lap to keep out the damp and chill, Valeria leaned against the padded squabs and numbly watched the now-familiar streets pass by.

So driven had she been to leave by morning, she'd instructed Molly to remain in London to assist Mercy in packing the large barouche with the rest of the belongings the housekeeper had informed her Lady Winterdale always carried when she removed to Winterpark. Hanging on to the shreds of her rapidly disintegrating patience, Valeria had then attempted to soothe the butler's scandalized horror over the fact that she would be traveling without even a maid.

Her early departure also spared her further meeting with Lady Farrington, who had nearly fallen into another spasm when Valeria stopped by last evening to bid her goodbye. Protesting that Valeria was too distraught to make so important a decision wisely, Lady Farrington begged her not to leave. But determined to slip out of town before the ton—and helpful "friends" like Lady Evelyn and the gentlemen from her shopping excursion—learned of her intent, Valeria refused to delay. Her grandmamma's final wish was that she remove to Winterpark, and go she would.

She'd been up late supervising the final packing. But despite her fatigue, after finally reaching the haven of her bed, she'd found sleep eluded her.

It wasn't grief, or nervousness about the challenges awaiting her at Winterpark, that kept her from claiming a few hours' rest before beginning her long and doubtless tiring journey. No, pathetic fool that she was, the watchfulness that had her starting at every small sound, stirring to every servant's muffled footfall, came from the idiotish hope that James had located Teagan Fitzwilliams and was bringing a reply to her note.

Of course, the fitful sleep into which she finally fell was not disturbed by any such event. Mr. Fitzwilliams probably hadn't yet returned to his rooms, if James had indeed managed to locate them. Even had Teagan received her missive, there was no reason to believe he'd feel moved to make immediate reply.

Such foolish behavior only proved, Valeria concluded, watching the drizzle turn to a steady downpour that obscured everything along the road north behind a damp gray veil, that Grandmamma had once again been wise by suggesting she leave the city—and its proximity to the all-too-fascinating Mr. Fitzwilliams. She badly needed the perspective time and distance could provide.

The great wealth that would allow her the freedom to choose her future was now hers—but at the cost, she thought with a renewed ache of sadness, of the one whose sagacity might have guided her in that choice.

What did she want?

The extremely rich Lady Arnold would be forgiven for claiming the escort of Teagan Fitzwilliams on jaunts about the city. Should she arrive at a ton function on his arm, or invite him to her own, however, she would almost certainly subject him to being snubbed, or worse. The great wealth to which she owed her own acceptance would not be sufficient to purchase his social redemption. In fact, her seeming to take up with him now that she *was* rich would confirm, rather than rehabilitate, his reputation.

He would never be thought a respectable suitor, even if he were interested in such a role. 'Twas most unlikely his haphazard youth or his erratic life since leaving Oxford had provided him either experience in or a desire for so permanent a relationship as wedlock. But as a lover…?

The almost tactile tension that simmered between them whenever they were together suggested he would be quite willing to renew the promise of passion they'd forged in the hay barn. Would an undoubtedly glorious but probably fleeting affair with him be enough?

And how would one affect her other choices? A fair-minded gentleman like Sir William might tolerate her friendship with a rogue. Hypocritical as it might be, however, though a widowed *gentleman* might set up a mistress without prejudice to his eventual matrimonial intentions, a matron who took so notorious a lover would likely forfeit any chance of later marrying a man of character. Which would also mean giving up the possibility of an ever-broadening circle of children, friends and grandchildren—

that community of kinship and comfort Valeria forfeited when her parents, her brother and now Lady Winterdale died.

Was a passionate affair, no matter how glorious, worth accepting permanent loneliness for the rest of her life?

Or would she do better to think seriously of accepting the offer Sir William had all but formally made? He'd been a steady, sympathetic presence all through these days of loss and strain. Never once had he intruded upon her grief, nor had he sought to use his privileged position as a close family friend to further his suit.

And she knew beyond doubt *he* was not interested only in her newfound wealth.

If his kisses, thus far untasted, should not stir in her the intensity of reaction of Teagan Fitzwilliams', they would at least have the advantage of permanence. And though no instantaneous, visceral attraction drew her to him, she found his tall, well-made figure attractive, and could easily envision progressing from friendship to a more intimate relationship.

As the miles rolled past in a continued bleak downpour, the same arguments circled around and around until her tired temples ached. Finally, with a burst of anger, she put all such thoughts aside.

Sir William was ensconced in London, and heaven knew when or if she would ever see Mr. Fitzwilliams again. With increased appreciation for Lady Winterdale's perspicacity, Valeria vowed to throw all her energy into mastering her new position as mistress of Winterpark.

Fatigue finally driving the whirling thoughts from her mind, Valeria was dozing in the early dusk of the rainy late afternoon when the coach jerked to a sudden halt, nearly throwing her off the seat.

She righted herself and scrambled to the window, but

could see nothing through the steady rain but a thick stand of trees. "Wilkins, what is it?" she called out.

"An oak be blockin' the road, my lady," came the reply. "The Crown and Kettle's not but a few miles ahead. I've sent Robert to bring back a lad to help us clear it. Don't you worrit none, we'll make the inn afore nightfall."

The coachman doffed his cap and walked over to soothe the restive horses. Valeria settled back on her seat, impatient with the delay and already anxious for the warm fire and hot food awaiting them at the inn.

After a surprisingly short interval, she heard the clatter of approaching hoofbeats. Wilkins appeared by the coach door, his brow creased in a frown.

"Perhaps we be closer to the inn than I thought, for—"

The loud report of a pistol drowned out the rest.

His face a study in dismay, the coachman scrambled for the box. A rough voice shouted, "Reach fer that blunderbuss, laddie, and ye're a dead man."

Wilkins froze.

"Hands over yer heads, now, nice 'n easy."

They were being robbed? Indignation coursed through Valeria, followed by a burst of exasperation. She'd traveled by coach from Bombay to Calcutta with her papa, the pistols he'd taught her to use when she was but twelve years old never far from her hand. But so befuddled had she been while packing last night, she'd neglected to get them from the trunk in which they'd been stored in London.

While she frantically considered how she might turn any of the commonplace objects within the coach into a weapon, a burly man in a frieze coat, his face obscured by a muffler, appeared beside the vehicle. Pointing a nasty-looking pistol at Wilkins, who quickly raised his hands above his head as ordered, he motioned the coachman aside.

"I'm gonna open the door slow, little lady. 'Tis a filthy

night, so don't be botherfyin' Mad Jack aweepin' or afaintin'. Jest hand out yer baubles, and I'll be off.''

In the next instant Valeria heard the report of another pistol, followed by an anguished wail. As she ducked away from the window, a figure hurtled out of the darkness and slammed into the frieze-coated man at knee level, knocking him off balance.

His pistol discharged skyward as he went down. From her position pressed against the door panel, she heard scuffling, gasps of breath and muffled curses, then the crack of bone against bone.

Was the newcomer rescuer or accomplice? Had the cry of a man injured come from her coachman—or another attacker?

Bracing herself in a crouch, hands gripping the only weapon she could devise, Valeria waited.

A second later, the coach door was thrown open to frame a mud-spattered man, his thick hair dripping rain. ''Are you unhurt, ma'am?'' he asked.

Valeria stared into familiar golden eyes whose expression of concern turned to a shock as keen as her own. Her grip slackened on the brick she'd been about to heave.

''Teagan?'' she gasped.

Chapter Thirteen

Wilkins appeared behind Teagan before he could answer. "Cor, didn't recognize ye at first, Mr. Fitzwilliams! Thank the lord ye happened upon us when ye did!"

"You are unharmed, Lady Arnold?" When Valeria nodded, Teagan turned back to the coachman. "'Tis thankful I am as well, Wilkins! Help me immobilize this brigand before he can attempt any more mischief."

As she watched the two men begin to secure the robber with a bit of rope Wilkins produced, Valeria felt suddenly dizzy. With more speed than grace, she sat back on the padded seat. "Allow me to offer my own thanks for your timely intervention, Mr. Fitzwilliams," she called down.

Occupied in knotting ropes about the wrists of her still-unconscious attacker, Teagan nodded. "'Twas my privilege, Lady Arnold."

Her other groom trotted up. "Splendid shot, sir! Winged through the shoulder the one what was guardin' me, and sent the bastard bleating back into the woods—beggin' your pardon, ma'am," he finished, flush-faced.

"I disremember ever seein' a move like how ye took this bounder off his feet, neither," Wilkins chimed in. "A right pretty hook ye dealt 'im!"

"Thank you, gentlemen. The streets sometimes prove a more useful training ground than Gentleman Jackson's. Harness our 'guest' to the back of the coach, please."

While the two servants dragged off the robber, Teagan turned back to Valeria. His eyes widened, and with a wry smile, he extracted from her unresisting fingers the warming brick she still held. "A bit crude, isn't it?"

"Perhaps, but 'twas the best I could contrive, considering I was too totty-headed to bring my pistols."

"Quite enterprising! But since you are safe, let me leave you and help these fellows get your coach underway. Wrap back up, now, before you catch a chill."

He lifted one hand, his eyes warming, and for a moment Valeria thought he meant to touch her cheek. But abruptly the glow faded and he backed away.

"Mr. Fitzwilliams!" she called after him. "When you have finished, please rejoin me! I should like to hear your account of the attack."

Another shouted "halloo" told her Robert must have returned from the inn. Pulling the fur wrap up to her chin against the damp, Valeria settled back on her seat. Her mind busy with speculation, she scarcely heard the distant murmur of voices as the men moved the obstructing tree.

How had Teagan Fitzwilliams ended up on the Great North Road? She'd had no indication he meant to leave London. Of course, she'd not seen him for over a week.

Had he received her note before his departure? Surely...surely he hadn't been following her!

She immediately dismissed so ridiculous a notion. But why had he left, and by what means? She'd seen no horse.

Impatient to learn more, she had to clench her hands in her muff to keep herself from climbing out to check the coachmen's progress. Finally, as the gray afternoon dissolved into black, Mr. Fitzwilliams returned.

"You're now ready to proceed. I'm honored to have been of service." He made her a bow.

Surely he didn't mean to simply…leave! "Please ride with me, Mr. Fitzwilliams. You've not yet relieved my curiosity about the attack and how you came upon it."

For a moment she thought he'd refuse. Then, with a short laugh, he shook his head. "Sure, and any other lady would have fallen into palpitations. Whereas you, Lady Arnold, likely wish to know the make of the pistol the brigand used and just where I wounded his accomplice."

She smiled back. "And how you managed it. Please, do ride with me at least as far as the inn."

He eyed the padded seat dubiously. "'Tis soaked through I be, and muddy besides."

Which meant he must also be chilled to the bone, she realized. He ought to be out of the rain. "My dear sir, had you not fortuitously happened upon us, I would have lost my jewels and my purse, if not much more! I believe I can forgive your leaving a bit of damp in my coach." She patted the seat beside her. "Please."

Still he hesitated. "How could I refuse so gracious a lady?" he said at last.

The words, the smile were as they should be, but the timing and tone of them, the odd hesitations in his speech ever since she'd recognized him, sent a message of alarm to all Valeria's senses. Something was not right with Teagan Fitzwilliams, something beyond the odd coincidence of so unexpectedly encountering him on the road.

As he eased himself into the coach, Valeria noted that under his sodden cloak, he still wore evening dress. She'd lit the coach's lamps while the men moved the tree, and in their light she could see his mud-spattered face was unshaved, his eyes red rimmed, as if he'd not slept in many hours. It appeared he had left London this morning without even having changed his clothes.

He sank back against the squabs and closed his eyes. An air of strained exhaustion surrounded him, as if he had reached the very limits of his physical and mental reserves. She did not think his intervention in the robbery could be the sole reason for it.

What had happened? She opened her lips to ask, then closed them. Tread cautiously, instinct told her.

"Since we can now be private, I shall avail myself of your first name, as we did in London. How did you come to be in this vicinity, Teagan? I did not see your horse."

He opened his eyes. "The animal pulled up lame some miles back, I'm afraid. I was leading him when I heard the first pistol shot."

She noted he did not answer her first question. "Not your fine stallion, I hope!"

"No, I—" He stopped abruptly, and some fleeting emotion passed over his face before he continued. "I left Ailainn back in London. 'Twas a job horse, poor beast."

"You heard the shot, and then…?"

"Grabbed my pistol and crept to the clearing. Downing a tree to block the road is an old robber's trick. Seeing there were but two of them, and the coach door not yet opened, I knew 'twould be safe for me to…interrupt."

"Safe to—" She gasped. "You might have been killed!"

He shook his head. "With the weather so foul, they weren't expecting outside aid, and I was able to approach quite close. Clipping the accomplice was mere target practice, and once I knocked down the brigand at the coach door, I knew with your groom and coachman, it would be three of us against their two."

"I think you're incredibly brave. Most men would have kept to the shadows and hoped to remain unnoticed."

At her fervent tone, he seemed almost to…wince. "I'm no hero, Valeria," he said quietly.

Once more the feeling invaded her that something awful had occurred, and once more she had to restrain herself from asking what. "You have certainly shown yourself one to me. You are...traveling north?"

"To Harrowgate, I expect."

"Then you must be planning to break your journey at the Crown and Kettle, since Wilkins tells me it is the best hostelry for miles. Won't you join me for dinner? 'Tis the least I could offer you, as my rescuer."

She waited for the smile, the polished reply full of teasing innuendo that the charming Mr. Fitzwilliams would normally have returned. Instead, he clenched his jaw and looked away. Her alarm deepened.

"Teagan?"

He looked back, his smile forced. "I suppose I'm in no position to refuse your kind offer."

"I would enjoy your company," she said softly. "I've...missed the chats we shared in London."

He straightened abruptly. "Excuse me! I have not yet expressed my sympathy on your recent grievous loss. That is, I expect you didn't get my note."

He had written? Joy made her heart leap. "No! When did you—"

"No matter. Doubtless you left before it could be delivered. I *am* sorry, Valeria."

"Thank you. I grew to be...very fond of her."

She fell silent, a silence that stretched between them, a silence the always witty, ever entertaining Mr. Fitzwilliams would normally have broken with some clever question or teasing inquiry.

Finally Valeria said, "I...sent you a note as well. Last evening. To tell you I was leaving London for Winterpark, Lady Winterdale's country home. 'Twas her last request that I go there immediately."

He nodded. "I'm sorry, but I did not receive it. I—my landlady—was not in when I last stopped by my rooms."

"Do you make a long visit in Harrowgate?"

"Perhaps. I'm not yet sure." He sighed deeply and ran a hand through his sodden hair. "Ah, Valeria, I might as well confess what you've no doubt already surmised. I lost badly last night, so badly I cannot meet my obligations in London. I had to quit the city forthwith."

Leaving behind even his beloved stallion? "I see," she said, choosing her words with care. "And you go to Harrowgate on a repairing lease?"

"Yes. I really ought not to dine with you this evening. There's certain to be dice or cards in the taproom, and...and I ought to begin that repair immediately."

His funds must be limited indeed if he dare not wait even a single night before attempting to recoup his fortunes. Small wonder she sensed about him such an air of weary desperation.

Suddenly she realized how truly alone he was. Even in her darkest days at Eastwinds after Hugh's death, though bereft of her beloved family, she still had duties to perform, retainers who were also friends, and a home to call her own.

Since he had no family worthy of the name, perhaps a friend could help. Yet because they *were* friends, how it must gall his pride for her to see him in such dire straits. If she wished to assist him, she would have to go about it indirectly.

"Having journeyed all day," she said at last, "I'm both fatigued and famished. Robert will have ordered up rooms and a meal when he stopped at the inn for assistance, so I expect to dine right after arriving. Would you not spare me the fate of eating alone? Since I'll be retiring immediately after, you would still have time for a full evening's...activities."

Once again he made no quick rejoinder, added no flirtatious offer to assist her in retiring. Instead, a slight smile curved his lips. "You are kind, Lady Arnold."

Her concern deepening, she cast about for some means to dispel the grim resignation that clouded his countenance and colored his voice.

"I believe the inn is a several-mile journey. Shall we continue the discussion we began at Tower Green about Mary, Queen of the Scots? Is it true the Irish would have supported her, against Elizabeth?"

"Sure, and the Irish have always rallied round any who oppose England," he replied, a flicker of interest stirring in his exhaustion-glazed eyes. "Though I've no doubt, had that lady been more astute and ended up on the throne, the lads across the sea would have opposed her as well."

For the remainder of the short drive, Valeria engaged him in a discussion of English politics, and Teagan gradually recovered some of his normal, easy manner.

His reserve returned when they reached the inn. As he handed her down from the coach, however, the front door of the establishment opened and the landlord hurried out, followed by a plump, red-faced lady and half a dozen men.

"Welcome, Lady Arnold!" the innkeeper called. "And a hearty welcome also to the gallant gentleman who foiled Mad Jack! Mr.—"

"Teagan Fitzwilliams," that gentleman replied with a bow as the men from the taproom shouted and clapped.

"Joey, my stable boy—he helped move the tree that blocked your carriage, my lady—rode on ahead and told us of the ambush," the landlord said as he advanced toward her. "Lucky ye be that Mr. Fitzwilliams came upon ye, Lady Arnold! Mad Jack's a fearsome customer, and has given the local magistrate the slip for weeks now."

The landlord reached her side and bowed. "Such a frightening experience! My wife has your room and a hot posset ready, if you'd like to retire immediately, and will

send supper up in a trice. Mr. Fitzwilliams, allow me and
the neighborhood to offer you dinner and a round.''

The landlord's expression of sympathy provided Valeria
a perfect opportunity to crystallize the sketchy plan she'd
been formulating. ''Thank you, sir,'' she replied, trying to
sound faint and anxious. ''My nerves are sadly overcome.''

Ignoring Teagan's start of surprise, she continued. ''Although I had intended to remain here until my maid and
baggage catch up to us, this episode has so distressed me
I am most uneasy about the rest of the journey. Mr. Fitzwilliams,'' she said, turning to him, ''I expect you plan to
set out tomorrow. I will advance my own departure, if I
can impose upon you to escort me the rest of the way to
Winterpark. It would greatly ease my mind, and I'm sure
my servants would appreciate your support.''

''Indeed, sir,'' Wilton called down, doffing his cap.
''James done told us you was a right'un. The boys 'n me'd
be honored if ye'd travel on with us.''

The landlord's wife stepped over to pat Valeria's arm.
''You poor, poor dear! 'Tis a wonder you didn't swoon
dead away! I certainly hope the kind gentleman can delay
his journey long enough to assist you.''

Teagan looked over at Valeria, eyebrows raised at this
sudden attack of nerves. She lowered her lashes demurely.

''If it will make the lady easier in her mind, of course I
must do so,'' he replied, subtle irony in his tone.

The assembled crowd murmured their approval.

''Thank you, Mr. Fitzwilliams,'' Valeria replied. ''I am
now even more deeply in your debt. Mrs....''

''Gowan, ma'am,'' the innkeeper's wife answered.

''Mrs. Gowan, will you pack us a basket of victuals and
fetch me in the morning when Mr. Fitzwilliams is ready?''

''Certainly, my lady.''

''Then with thanks to all of you, gentlemen, I shall retire.
Until the morning, Mr. Fitzwilliams?''

For a long moment Teagan fixed her with a quizzical gaze, as if trying to determine just what sort of rig she was running. Then he bowed and took her outstretched fingers to kiss. "Until morning, Lady Arnold."

Amid clapping and cheers from the onlookers, she followed the innkeeper's wife into the building.

Though regretting the loss of Teagan's company during dinner, Valeria was pleased at the success of her stratagem. If she could just keep him occupied on the journey until he lost that frighteningly desperate air...

Perhaps she might even persuade him to remain for a few days at Winterpark. A blast of warmth entirely unrelated to her gratitude for his rescue blazed through her at the thought.

His belly full of the best dinner he'd had in weeks and his head woozy from the drinks raised in his honor, much later that night Teagan walked unsteadily up the stairs to the bedchamber the innkeeper had insisted he take for the evening. To cap off the night, jingling in his pockets was a small stack of coins he'd won off the local magistrate, who'd been happy to lose his blunt to the man who'd relieved him of the problem of Mad Jack.

From its beginning, with Teagan reduced to the most desperate conditions he'd experienced since being cast out of his grandfather's town house ten years ago, this day had improved beyond imagining. When his job horse had pulled up lame, leaving him soaked, stranded and near penniless by the side of the road, he'd tethered the poor beast in the woods, pulled out his pistol case and loaded the weapon, nearly convinced that the Almighty was trying to tell one Irish drifter it was time to return to his celestial home.

Then he'd heard the pistol shot, and the rest had been automatic. In his comings and goings in the meaner neighborhoods, he'd seen too many petty thugs like Mad Jack to stand by and allow him to abuse a lady, even an arrogant English aristocrat who probably deserved whatever punishment the brigand had intended to mete out.

And then to discover the carriage belonged to Valeria! It seemed odd that she would have rushed out of the city, despite the folderol about following Lady Winterdale's last request. Surely it would have made more sense to remain in London, attended by the solicitous Sir William and the hordes of other suitors who would find ways to entertain the newly rich widow, despite her being in deep mourning.

And why had she practically compelled him to escort her to Winterpark? With a humiliation that made his face burn in the darkness, he knew she was too intelligent not to have understood far more about his true circumstances than he'd admitted in his one cryptic utterance. Did she mean to bid him begin his "repairing lease" at Winterpark?

The notion of a few days' respite was all too attractive. He couldn't remember the last time he'd slept a whole night through. The very idea that he must begin gaming again with his reserves so slim that every coin must be counted, every wager carefully calculated in order to avert disaster, made his stomach churn with revulsion.

He remembered only too vividly his original precarious climb out of penury. Endless nights of slowly building a stake, followed by the terror of unexpected reverses that could wipe out a month's worth of gains in an evening. The constant uncertainty, the distasteful necessity of cajoling drunks, deflecting the malicious and forcing himself to win from lads too green and green-faced to be able to count the cards in their hands.

Teagan reached the landing and stumbled into his room, then began pulling off his still-damp garments. One coin from tonight's precious winnings he'd expended to have the innkeeper's wife extract a change of clothes from his soggy saddlebags to air out and press for tomorrow, and another for the hot water to bathe and shave with in the morning. It seemed an eternity since he'd last felt clean and dry.

Stripped down, he dropped wearily onto the softness of the bed. *Mhuire,* but he hated the necessity of beginning again. Ten years ago, the indignity of it had been blunted by rage and heartache over Evangeline's duplicity, the ruin of his career and the unfairness of his exile. Fueled by anger and grief, he'd careened through the first few months almost unaware of what he did.

And made mistakes he now regretted. But that excess of emotion had burned itself to cinders long ago. This time he had no inclination to mask the bitterness of his descent with sweetly false matrons and quantities of strong drink.

What choice did he have but to continue gaming? He leaned back against the headboard, supporting his aching head on his hands. 'Twas amusing, really. Even were he finally ready to concede victory to his cousin by relinquishing his last pretensions to gentility, having been raised as a gentleman, he knew no trade by which he could make a living.

There was gaming, the army—or marrying a rich woman like Valeria Arnold.

Valeria, who'd been both friend and lover. The mere thought of her in the barn at Eastwoods still had the power to speed his pulses and harden his body in an instant.

The blaze of attraction that had ignited in Yorkshire still smoldered between them every time they met. In London Teagan had teased her about it, daydreamed of its fiery potential. Had hoarded the possibility of once again claiming her, with the greedy pleasure of a small child hiding a sweetmeat, delighted by knowing it was his, to devour whenever he chose. With little effort, Teagan knew, he could persuade her to become his lover again, and under the potent spell of passion, probably bewitch her into wedlock.

Thereby solving his financial woes forever.

The idea of using her like that revolted him.

With a bitter bark of laughter, Teagan sat back up. A fine, proper rogue he was. Too proud to enlist in the army, too principled to perform a possibly treasonous task, too squeamish to seize the solution that would set him up for life. Bleating and moaning about having to dirty his hands once again with gaming, the only other option open to him.

Of course, there was always the pistol.

An equally disturbing idea suddenly struck him.

Perhaps Valeria Arnold had a very different reason for coercing his escort.

Since he'd last seen her, the balance between them had shifted. Lady Arnold was no longer owner of a barely profitable sheep farm, a fellow orphan and shabby-genteel outsider tolerated at the edges of the ton. Possessed of great wealth and the influence that accompanied it, she could now command a leading role in Society.

If she invited him to linger, would it be as the friend who had explored London with him? Or as other rich matrons had before her, would she offer him the bounty of her home in exchange for his performance in her parlor and her boudoir, until the novelty of his attractions paled?

Destroying the magic of what they'd shared by turning it into a transaction driven by lust and power?

His mind rebelled at the thought. The honesty, purity and intelligence his Lady Mystery had displayed at every meeting were not a sham. She'd not insisted on seeing him just to spite her chaperone, had not been merely toying with him all those mornings they explored London, sharing ideas and laughter. From initial attraction, they'd come to know and like each other. She respected him—had she not demonstrated that on numerous occasions?

But she'd not then been a rich English matron.

Was it in fact Lady Farrington who'd rebuffed his calls and notes after Lady Winterdale's death? Or, with her position assured, had Lady Arnold decided it was no longer politic to be seen with Teagan...at least not in London?

Not for many years had someone from English society seemed to reach out to a lonely Irish outcast, to solicit his opinions, admire his ideas and value his person. He must not forget how that interlude with Evangeline had ended.

Indeed, every hope he'd ever cherished had turned out to be false: finding a family, winning Evangeline's love, pursuing a career as a scholar. 'Twas idiocy to let himself believe that Valeria Arnold, now that she possessed wealth and position, would treat Teagan Fitzwilliams in the same manner as when she'd been the impecunious Lady Arnold.

Wasn't it?

His eyes burned and his head ached dully. *Mhuire,* he'd think no more on it. Tomorrow he'd escort Lady Arnold to Winterpark as promised.

He only wished his chest didn't ache with apprehension that his beloved image of Lady Mystery, like every other illusion he'd cherished save that of his mother's love, was about be shattered by reality's iron fist.

Chapter Fourteen

Late the following afternoon, Valeria gazed out the window of her coach at the gatehouse beyond the tall iron entry portals of Winterpark. Her new home.

She took a deep breath and tried to stifle the nervousness fluttering in her belly. For the first time, she wished she had waited at the inn for Mercy and her baggage. Through all the many changes in her life she'd had her old nurse at her side. Coming now as mistress to the new household whose respect she must win, she sorely missed the comfort of her friend's presence.

Part of her unease stemmed from her uncertainty over what to do about Teagan Fitzwilliams. The slight relaxation in his manner during their drive yesterday had disappeared once they reached the inn, and his behavior today had been even more distant. He'd declined her offer to accompany her in the coach, preferring instead to hire another mount and ride beside the carriage.

She'd heard him trading quips and conversation with the coachman—and had been ashamed by the pang of envy that provoked in her. Though Teagan had politely accepted a share of the lunch Mrs. Gowan had packed for them, he'd chosen to tie his mount behind the coach and climb up on the box beside Wilkins to eat it.

The remote and silent stranger he'd become was so far removed from the engaging Teagan she'd thought she knew that she was no longer sure whether he needed or would accept anything more from her. However, as she girded herself to take up her new duties, she decided she would still extend to him the hospitality of Winterpark. Good breeding alone dictated that, since he'd been gracious enough to delay his plans in order to escort her home, she should invite him to remain as long as he wished. He could then accept or refuse as he chose.

The idea of him cooly declining and riding out of her life without a backward glance, as he had once before, was so dismaying she thrust it from her mind.

The carriage was now traveling down the wide graveled drive Wilkins had described, which after about a mile circled in a large arc around the front lawns of Winterpark Manor itself. Stilling another anxious tremor, she focused her thoughts on planning how best to greet her new staff.

In the fading light of the late spring day she noted the drive was well kept, the parkland stretching out from it neatly scythed. Of course, she'd expected that Lady Winterdale's favorite property would be perfectly maintained, ready at any moment should that exacting lady pay an unannounced visit. As the carriage began to round a wide curve, Valeria thrust her head out the window to get her first glimpse of the house, and caught her breath.

Centered on a tall rise, the dark bulk of what must be forestland behind it, the building glittered in the distance with a summer firefly twinkling of lights. With its dignified grandeur and the beckoning glow from its myriad of mullioned windows, for an instant it seemed to Valeria as if the spirit of Lady Winterdale herself were present to welcome her. Her chest tightened with a bittersweet mingling of gratitude and grief.

As the carriage halted beside a large brick portico, a liveried footman ran over to let down the steps. "Welcome to Winterpark, my lady," he said, assisting her out.

Valeria murmured her thanks and looked over at the handful of retainers who had trotted up to greet Wilkins, tend the horses and begin unstrapping the baggage.

Teagan dismounted and handed the reins to a waiting groom. "'Tis a lovely new home you have, Lady Arnold."

"Yes," she replied, nerves once again on edge. "Shall we go in?"

He nodded and followed her up the entry stairs. An austere personage in black livery, the butler by his manner and carriage, opened the massive front door to admit them.

"Lady Arnold," he said with a bow as they entered. "On behalf of the staff, may I welcome you to Winterpark. I trust your journey was a pleasant one?" His glance slid to Teagan. "You've brought guests, my lady?"

"Yes. Giddings, is it not? Mr. Fitzwilliams, an acquaintance from London, assisted me after my carriage was attacked yesterday near Dade's Run."

Amid the exclamations of distress from the butler and the two attendant footmen, she continued. "No one was injured, thanks to this gentleman's timely intervention, but my nerves were sorely shaken. Wishing to reach Winterpark as quickly as possible, I prevailed upon Mr. Fitzwilliams to escort me immediately. My maid is following with the rest of the baggage."

Giddings gave Teagan another bow. "Our thanks to you, sir, for rescuing our mistress! The housekeeper, Mrs. Welsh, is supervising the preparation of your bedchambers and will wait upon you shortly, my lady."

"Thank you, Giddings. Given the lateness of the hour

and my fatigue, I should prefer to see only you and Mrs. Welsh today and meet the rest of the staff tomorrow.''

"As you wish. When should you like dinner served?''

Valeria stole a glance at Teagan. He stood silently studying her, a sort of guarded expectancy in his eyes.

Perhaps he was merely exhausted. He could not have had much sleep the last few days, and had been in the saddle since early morning.

"Mr. Fitzwilliams, after your many kindnesses, please forgive my being such a poor hostess, but I should really prefer a tray in my rooms tonight.''

The butler bowed. "Of course, Lady Arnold. Shall I show you both to your chambers?''

"I would like a brandy in the parlor first,'' Teagan said, avoiding Valeria's glance.

"Certainly. Robbin?'' The butler nodded at a footman, who sprang to attention. "Show Mr. Fitzwilliams to the parlor and pour his cognac. Robbin will convey your dinner order to the kitchens whenever you are ready, sir.''

"I shall bid you good evening, then, Mr. Fitzwilliams,'' Valeria said. "I remain greatly in your debt. Although I shall be much occupied the next few days assuming my duties here, please feel free to remain at Winterpark as long as your plans permit. I'm sure Giddings and the staff will extend to you every courtesy.''

He raised an eyebrow, as if doubting her words. "Your offer is most kind. Perhaps I shall take you up on it.''

His tone, too, seemed almost…mocking. Uncertain what to read from it, Valeria hesitated. Finally, conscious of the waiting butler, she said merely, "Good night, Mr. Fitzwilliams.''

"My lady,'' he replied with a deep bow.

Valeria followed Giddings to the stairs, conscious of Teagan's gaze still fixed upon her back. Whether he chose to stay—or leave—was up to him. But after his puzzling behavior of the last two days, she could not help feeling a distressingly acute sense of…loss. Evidently the friendship she thought they'd forged in London had been only an illusion of her overhopeful imagination.

He'd outflanked her first offer, if such it had been, Teagan thought as he fought to hold open his eyes and finish the brandy he'd ordered. With him being shown to his rooms well after she retired, if she had intended to convey, by word or gesture, her willingness to have him join her in her suite, she'd now have no opportunity.

Would she have extended such an invitation?

He still couldn't quite believe she would. But after deliberately keeping his distance all day so as to avoid having her say or infer something that might confirm his worst suspicions, he hadn't been able to prevent himself from ordering the cognac. Thus guaranteeing that his faith in her honesty could remain unbroken at least one more day.

She would be occupied with her new responsibilities, she'd said. He should avail himself of the hospitality of Winterpark for as long as he wished.

Was that truth, or merely polite words meant for the servants' ears?

He'd put it to the test, Teagan decided. He would rest here a few days, continue to avoid her company so she might be free to "assume her new duties." And see how long it took before Valeria Arnold shattered his last illusion by having her unobliging guest evicted.

He was wrapped in a large, warm cocoon, with crisp clean linen beneath his cheek, his head cradled against a softness like eiderdown—or a woman's breasts.

Valeria.

But as he snapped his eyes open, Teagan discovered himself alone in what turned out to be a very large canopied bed with hangings of rich blue satin. He looked around in bewilderment, the sunshine filtering through the lace veiling the tall windows setting dust motes dancing and making him squint against the brightness.

Was he back in his grandfather's chamber at Montford?

Consciousness, and with it, memory, returned with a jolt. No, not Montford. He was at Winterpark. Valeria Arnold's newly inherited manor, where she'd invited him to tarry as long as his "plans permitted."

Plans she must know were nonexistent.

Before he could assemble his still-muddled thoughts and decide whether he would in fact tarry, or call for his horse and ride off without seeing her again, a soft tap sounded at his door. A red-haired, freckle-faced young girl in maid's uniform entered immediately after, a bowl of fresh flowers in her hands.

She halted in surprise as she noticed him staring. "Ah!" she exclaimed. "'Tis awake ye are at last, sir! Mrs. Welsh was after thinking ye'd sleep the week through."

Teagan pulled the sheet to his chin and eased up against the pillows. "How long have I been asleep?"

"Two nights and most of two days, sir," she replied, depositing the arrangement of golden daffodils and pink tulips on a side table. "'Tis afternoon now."

He must have been more exhausted than he'd realized, he thought in shock. At that moment his stomach growled, protesting its long neglect. "No wonder I'm so famished," he said ruefully. "Would there be any chance of getting a cup of ale and some cold victuals from the kitchen?"

"Oh, better than that, sir! Mistress gave orders that we weren't on no account to disturb ye, but to have a hot meal waiting whenever ye awoke. Oh, and I'm to summon Nichols to assist ye when ye're ready to bathe and dress. He's just a footman—our late mistress being a widow so long, we've no gentleman's gentleman about—but Nichols's uncle is valet to some fancy London gent, and he's always wanted to take up the trade… But now me tongue's runnin' on like a fiddlestick, and here ye be, fair starving!''

The maid rushed over to give the bell pull a vigorous tug, then turned to make him a curtsy. ''I'm Sissy, sir, and we be ever so pleased to welcome ye to Winterpark.''

Undisturbed rest. A hot meal. The services of a valet— or almost a valet. If Valeria Arnold were trying to entice him to stay, she was certainly making the terms of whatever bargain she eventually wished to strike attractive.

But after a long rest that left him more energized than he'd felt in months, with sunshine to warm his face in a beautifully appointed room where he was being waited upon with such solicitous attention, Teagan found he was no longer so bitterly suspicious. And it was impossible not to respond to the little maid's loquacious cheerfulness.

''Is that Irish I hear in your voice, Sissy?''

''Aye, sir. Lady Winterdale, God rest her soul, had an estate near Killarny, and after her last visit brought me mum back here. I understand ye're from the fair isle yerself! Which explains how ye come to be so uncommon brave.'' The maid's eyes widened with awe. ''By the saints, 'tis but natural ye were worn to a nub! Wilkins says ye vanquished those robbin' brigands all by yerself!''

So he was being touted a hero, as well. Teagan couldn't help grinning. ''How many of these brigands did I dispatch? 'Twas rather dark, and I couldn't see well.''

''Oh, I disremember—'twas so excitin', the way Wilkins told it! Despite the rain and gloom, he says ye shot one of 'em from long range clean through the shoulder, and disarmed another afore he could move! 'Tis no wonder our new mistress feels so beholdin', ye savin' her baubles and rescuin' her person from—'' the maid halted, her freckled cheeks pinking ''—a-an Awful Fate! 'Tis grateful we all are to ye, sir, for protectin' Lady Arnold. She's not so grand as the old mistress, but she's ever so kind, and—ah, here I go ablatherin' again. I'd best be gettin' back to the kitchen afore me mum takes a birch rod to me. Yer food will be up directly, and ye're to ring for Nichols when ye're ready.''

With another curtsy, the little maid bustled out.

Teagan stretched back in the soft bed and stared at the intricate patterns on the mullioned ceiling. If one were going to have one's illusions shattered, as least it eased the sting to have the carnage take place in such luxurious surroundings.

But perhaps, for once, he had encountered someone who truly was as honorable as she appeared. Even given the beauty of these splendid surroundings, that would be the most wonderful awakening of all.

An hour later, fed, bathed and groomed nearly as well as Ailainn by the eager ministrations of his would-be valet, Teagan left his luxurious chamber.

Lady Arnold, he was told when he inquired of the servant leading him on a tour through the house, had ridden out to inspect some of the tenant farms. In her absence, however, the mistress invited him to avail himself of the fine table here in the billiard room, or select from the assortment of instruments there in the music room, or take out a weapon from the gun room, should he wish to try the hunting in the home woods. When the young man opened the door to display the next grand chamber, however, Teagan knew he need explore no further.

Having been told all his life he was destined for the fiery pit, Teagan had never given much consideration to what heaven would look like. But as he stood on its threshold, the thought suddenly occurred that for him, this room would be its very image. Inhaling sharply with awe and delight, he walked into Winterpark's library.

Except for the fireplace wall and a mullioned window

overlooking what appeared to be a rose garden, the large room was entirely given over to bookcases. A small fire burned in the grate to ward off the afternoon chill, adding a piquant hint of wood smoke to the familiar odors of leather binding and aged vellum.

Excitement swelling his chest, Teagan dismissed the footman and hurried to the nearest bookshelf, which, he soon discovered, housed what appeared to be a complete selection of Shakespeare. From there he wandered around the circumference of the room, trailing his fingers reverently over the best collection of fiction, poetry, philosophy, natural science and ancient literature he'd been privileged to gaze upon since leaving Oxford.

Behind the fretwork doors of a secretary near the window, he found some of his dearest friends: Plato, Horace, Virgil, Homer. Drawing out a volume, he sank down into the leather wing chair beside the secretary, and with the joyous thankfulness of one who, after a long, dangerous journey, at last reaches safe haven, began to read.

Some time later he looked up, startled to note that the daylight by which he'd begun had been replaced by a golden glow of candles he didn't remember lighting. His stomach once again protested his inattention.

He cast a glance at the large clock ticking on the mantel; 'twas nearly time for dinner. He would have to put up the book and return to his rooms to dress. After having abandoned his hostess for two entire days, he should try to be at his most entertaining tonight.

But as he walked to the desk to search for a marker, his hands stilled on the page. Buttressed by unpleasant memory, his suspicions returned with a rush.

Since he was traveling in the same direction, he'd offered to escort home the rich widow who'd befriended him at the house party they'd just attended—and been unexpectedly invited to sojourn there. Having lost heavily that week, he'd gratefully accepted....

Enough, he thought, pushing the degrading images away.

He turned to leave, then halted. Having reached one of his favorite passages, he really did not wish to abandon his book and go to dinner. Perhaps he would request that a tray be brought to him in the library.

If he did, would Lady Arnold come in later, her slender form displayed in a tantalizing cloud of low-cut silk, her dark brows creased in annoyance, her voice subtly shaded with the inference that he owed her his company at table...and elsewhere? As had that other matron in another library, at another needy time in his life?

And should he refuse her unspoken command, would he find himself shown the door, dismissed as precipitously as he'd been that long-ago evening?

Carefully Teagan marked his place and walked to the bell pull. He'd have his dinner here at the desk.

And discover this very night whether Valeria Arnold was indeed a treasure like finest gold—or merely another of the brassy imitations he'd been encountering all his life.

As if from far away, the sound of persistent tapping gradually intruded upon Teagan's consciousness. Someone was knocking at the library door, he realized.

Before he could brace himself for an encounter with a possibly indignant Lady Arnold, Giddings entered.

"Will there be anything else tonight, sir? My mistress instructed you were not to be disturbed, but 'tis late and I wish to retire." A trace of unbutlerlike aggravation altered his normally impassive expression.

Teagan glanced at the mantel clock—and was shocked to find it after midnight. "N-no, nothing, thank you, Giddings. I hadn't realized the time. Please send the footmen to bed, as well. I can find my way unassisted."

"Thank you, sir, and good night. I'll have Robbin bring you additional wine and candles." The butler bowed and turned to leave.

"Giddings!" Teagan called after him.

"Sir?"

"Has...has your mistress retired yet?"

The butler stiffened. "Several hours ago. I should be loath to rouse her, sir, as she begins her duties—"

"No, I didn't mean that you should." The staff seemed properly protective of its new mistress—a testimony to how quickly Lady Arnold had taken over the reins. "I wished to know her...whereabouts, that was all," he finished lamely. "Good night, Giddings."

The butler gave him a wondering look, which Teagan supposed he deserved, and bowed himself out.

Teagan glanced from the mantel clock about to chime the astonishing hour of one, to the remains of his dinner, to the door through which the butler had just disappeared.

The door through which Valeria Arnold had not entered.

His spirits leapt and a smile blossomed on his face.

Perhaps his Lady Mystery wasn't an illusion, after all.

After Robbin brought in his supper tray earlier this evening, Teagan had sat tensed, ears tuned for the sound of footsteps as he ate, only one eye on his book. But as the mantel clock ticked away and no lady in an evening gown and an aggrieved attitude appeared to interrupt him, the words of Homer worked their usual magic. His mind slipped back to the vicissitudes of Odysseus's journey, both his dinner and his dilemma forgotten.

As if summoned by his thoughts, Robbin reappeared with a tray bearing wax tapers and another decanter of wine. Thanking him for both, Teagan bade him good-night.

He listened as the servant walked back down the hall, his muffled footfalls gradually fading into a silence broken only by the occasional creak of several-hundred-year-old

Elizabethan beams and the soft scuffling of the nocturnal creatures in the garden outside the window.

Leaving him once more alone in a dwelling filled with peace and beauty, free to enjoy an activity far different from those transpiring in the overcrowded rooms he would normally occupy at this hour. Where, by rights, he ought to be seated now, stomach churning from too little food and too much cheap liquor, nerves taut as he counted cards and calculated wagers, eyes burning from smoke and liquor fumes, ears assaulted by raucous laughter and loud voices. A seat he *would* be occupying, had he not met Valeria.

Oh yes, she'd realized the full import of his circumstances practically from the moment she recognized him after the attack on her carriage. With the empathy of a kindred soul, and a keen sensitivity for his self-esteem, she'd quietly, generously given him this opportunity to rest and refresh his badly battered spirit.

Teagan tried to remember another place and time he'd been offered shelter, food and diversion, for which some service had not been exacted in return.

His mother's family had begrudged him the very air he occupied and the morsels he consumed, making him pay with slights, insults and blows endured for every day of charity they'd resentfully provided. At the dubious haven of Eton he'd had to beguile his schoolmates with quips and tricks to earn the pennies that kept him from starving between terms. At Oxford...he still could not bring himself to think back on the devastation of Oxford.

And in the years since, the charming rogue's persona he'd perfected in the wake of his banishment had been welcomed at gaming rooms, dinners and house parties only as long as he entertained while plying the cards of his trade.

The last crusty scab of suspicion peeled away, leaving a fragile, tender new skin of faith. Awe welled up in him, as it had at Oxford when he'd discovered that within the world of scholarship, he could not only belong, but excel.

Shame succeeded it.

By doubting her honesty he'd wronged Valeria and shown himself unworthy of the unwavering purity of friendship she'd extended.

The desire to make amends consumed him. Suddenly he couldn't wait to see her again.

Carefully he closed the volumes on the desk and blew out all but one branch of candles. Taking those, he exited the library and took the stairs to his room.

Beginning tomorrow morning, Teagan Fitzwilliams would seek every possible way to demonstrate his appreciation for the truest friend he'd ever had.

Chapter Fifteen

Following directions given by the helpful Nichols, Teagan found his way to the breakfast parlor early the next morning. A rising excitement tempered with no small amount of nervousness tightened his chest and brought a smile, unbidden, to his lips.

He paused on the threshold, still seeking the best words to frame an apology, should Valeria have taken offense at his missing dinner last evening. But as he scanned the chamber, he discovered not the dark-haired Lady Mystery he sought, but a tall, thin older woman who turned to him, a forbidding expression on her shrewd face.

Valeria's nurse Mercy, he recognized from several previous meetings, who appeared to be gathering up her mistress's sewing things.

Damping down a sharp disappointment, he entered.

"Good morning, Mistress Mercy. How was your journey from London? Less distressing than Lady Arnold's, I hope."

"Tolerable."

That response not being amplified by further comment, after a moment's hesitation, Teagan proceeded to the sideboard. Having filled his plate, he tried again.

"You arrived yesterday, Mistress Mercy?"

"Yes."

"With no lingering threat of highwaymen, I trust?"

"Highwaymen?" She sniffed in disdain. "We're here, and you're here, and enough said, young man. I'd suggest you eat your breakfast before it turns cold."

Teagan could not help grinning. "Ah, Mercy-lass, ye know ye're fair bursting to converse with so charming a gentleman as meself."

The maid's glacial look thawed somewhat. "Aye, you're a rogue good and proper! I've seen your like too often in the army, sweet-talking lads with more flash than merit."

Teagan touched his chest with a theatrical gesture, as if wounded. "Upon my word, Miss Mercy, did I not know better, I might believe you don't like me overmuch."

"You're handsome as you can stare, with the devil's own tongue to boot, and you may work your wiles with my blessing—as long as you don't work them on Miss Val."

Teagan sobered abruptly. "Surely you know I'd never bring harm to your mistress."

Mercy raised her eyebrows. "Nor threaten to?"

Half amused, half appalled, Teagan said, "Whist, but ye're not implying *I* set up that ambush at Dade's Run!"

"Perhaps not," Mercy conceded, "but you must admit, 'twas devilish convenient, you popping out of the woods just in time to save her. And thereby making her feel beholden enough to change her plans and invite you for a cozy stay—when you should be going on about your business.

"Nay—" she waved him to silence when he would have protested "—mayhap I do you a disservice with my suspicions. But this I know for truth. Miss Val has a weakness for you, and I'll not have you taking advantage of it. That poor lass lost her whole family, survived a husband too addled to realize the treasure at his feet, then found a grand-mamma only to have her taken almost the moment the lady grew dear to her. She don't need more heartache in the form of a fast-talking rogue who'll try to seduce her for the amusement of it.''

Teagan met Mercy's accusing stare. ''On several occasions, your mistress has stood my staunch friend. I've had few enough of those in my life that I'd risk ruining the relationship by trying to take advantage of her.''

The two of them exchanged glare for glare. Finally, as if satisfied, Mercy gave a short nod. ''See that you do not. I promised the late colonel, her papa, I'd watch after her, and so I will. Remember that.''

''Lady Arnold's welfare is of great concern to me,'' Teagan replied. ''Remember that.''

''Words be easy,'' she retorted. '''Tis deeds win the battle. Good day, sir.'' Clasping the sewing basket to her bosom like a shield, Mercy marched to the door. Just before exiting, she paused to look back at him.

''I'm instructed to tell you there be horses aplenty in the stables that need exercising. You can have your pick.''

''And where is your mistress today?''

The nurse hesitated, as if debating whether she might withhold the information. ''She's driven out to visit more of the tenants,'' she said at last, her tone grudging. ''We don't expect her home before tea.''

''Thank you, ma'am. I'll endeavor to do nothing to earn the hostility you've graciously accorded me,'' he replied, grinning.

With another darkling look, the nurse quit the room.

Despite the residual sting of having to ride a horse other than Ailainn, Teagan decided to avail himself of the stables. He'd enjoy the exercise as much as the beast, and perhaps on his ride he might encounter Valeria.

Some hours later, disappointed at not having met her, he

was returning to the manor along a trail the head groom had recommended—through the open woodland in the hills above Winterpark—when he spotted a small gig driving toward him. He was delighted to discover Valeria at the ribbons, a soberly dressed older gentleman riding a tall gray gelding alongside the vehicle.

As Teagan approached, she pulled up the gig. "Good afternoon, Mr. Fitzwilliams. I see you found a horse to your liking. Are you enjoying your ride?"

"Very much, Lady Arnold. The woodlands about Winterpark are lovely. If the farms are in equally good heart, 'tis a fine estate."

"The farms are very well kept, thanks in large part to this gentleman. Mr. Fitzwilliams, may I present Lady Winterdale's estate manager, Mr. Parker."

The two men exchanged bows. "Can I escort you back to the house, Lady Arnold?" Teagan asked.

With an expression of regret, she shook her head. "No, I have several farms yet to visit. Though I should enjoy your company until our paths diverge."

"Shall I ride on ahead, then, my lady?" Mr. Parker asked. "If I can inspect the equipment I mentioned at the Barrows farm before you arrive, we shall finish our rounds more quickly."

"Of course, Mr. Parker. Left at the next crossroads?"

"Yes, Lady Arnold. The Barrows farm is but half a mile farther. Pleasure to meet you, Mr. Fitzwilliams."

At Valeria's nod of dismissal, the estate manager put spurs to his horse. Valeria set the gig moving, and Teagan motioned his horse to keep pace.

"You are looking rested, Mr. Fitzwilliams."

He grinned over at her. "As well I should be!"

She chuckled softly, and it struck him again how much he'd missed her engaging gurgle of laughter, the warmth of camaraderie they had shared in the city.

"I must apologize once again for being such a neglectful hostess," she said. "No doubt I shall master them in time, but the duties here are more wide-ranging than any I have shouldered before."

Teagan remembered the maid's enthusiasm and the butler's protective concern for his mistress. "From what I've seen, your staff is much taken with their new lady."

She laughed again. "I expect they're relieved to discover I'm not nearly the tyrant their former mistress was! Though she trained them well. The household runs so smoothly, it scarce needs my guiding hand."

"They have certainly been most accommodating. Indeed, 'tis rather I who should beg *your* pardon for being so disobliging a guest! As if sleeping through most of two days was not impolite enough, I became so engrossed in my book last evening that I missed dinner, though I do appreciate the tray Robbin so kindly procured me."

"I had hoped you would enjoy Lady Winterdale's magnificent library. Ah, but here's the turning. The farm isn't far, and the view is much prettier if you continue along straight. Please, don't let me detain you."

Teagan didn't want to leave her, didn't want their too-short conversation to end so abruptly, but her words seemed so clear a dismissal he felt a shaft of dismay. Perhaps she *was* angry with him for neglecting her, after all. "You will be returning for dinner?"

"I'm not sure. There are mills and fences and some sort of mechanical plow I must inspect, apparently. Perhaps I shall see you later."

She signaled the horse to turn at the crossing. Unable to conjure up a reason to make her linger, Teagan was forced to halt his mount and let her pass.

She glanced up and smiled as the gig turned—the same shy, uncertain smile he'd found so irresistible that first morning in her barn.

The thought triggered memories that set his pulses racing. For a crazed instant he thought of seizing the gig's traces to stop the vehicle, carrying Valeria to the nearest croft or shelter where he might once again use his hands and lips and expertise to turn those dark eyes smoky with desire, make her slender body writhe with passion.

Not here, not yet. He gripped the reins so hard their leather bit into his fingers and forced himself to let her go.

And then laughed at his own absurdity. Had he not just last night felt the righteous horror of an outraged virgin at the notion of her as a calculating seductress sweeping into the library to have her way with him?

Whist, but he was an idiot of an Irishman to have resented any opportunity to be once more transported to that heaven.

Anticipation fanned his ever-smoldering hunger into a fire that flashed through his veins. Every sense energized, he spurred the stallion to a gallop.

May the God who watches over fools and gamblers send Lady Arnold to the library tonight, he prayed. Whatever proposal she had a mind to offer, whatever the reason behind it, tonight he had no intention of resisting.

Several hours later, Valeria peeped into the library. The scene within brought a smile of delight to her lips.

Cravat askew, booted ankles crossed, a glass of wine in his hand, Teagan Fitzwilliams reclined in his chair behind the library desk, a book propped on one knee. Before two brilliantly lit, double-branched candelabras, a half-consumed dinner sat neglected on a tray pushed to one side, while the rest of the desk's broad surface was strewn with a haphazard assortment of volumes large and small.

Still smiling, Valeria noted that the doors of the nearby mahogany secretary stood open. Having taken an exhaustive tour of the library her first afternoon at Winterpark, she knew the secretary housed Lady Winterdale's impressive collection of ancient literature. Mr. Fitzwilliams was a lover of the classics, it appeared.

He straightened, and Valeria darted back. But he merely readjusted the volume on his knee, nodding as if in agreement with the long-dead author, and then repeated a sentence she supposed must be Greek. "Ah, yes!" he said, and smiled down at the book.

Valeria's chest tightened. *Yes, indeed,* she thought, taking in his intent but relaxed stance, the vitality his figure conveyed even when motionless, the obvious pleasure evident in that smile. His appearance this afternoon had not been an aberration. Gone entirely was the tense, brooding, exhausted man who'd briefly shared her carriage en route to the Crown and Kettle.

Fierce gladness filled her that, despite her misgivings upon their arrival, she'd persevered to offer him this gift of time and solitude. However temporary a reprieve it might prove from the harsh reality of his circumstances, his three days at Winterpark appeared to have succeeded in revitalizing him, body and spirit.

Although he did seem to be avoiding her, she thought, her delight dimming a little.

Small matter, that. He was a man, after all, and it might be more than a man's pride could suffer to admit he'd needed the respite she'd given him. Too lowering to reaffirm that he must soon depart and remain out from London until he could sufficiently recoup his finances.

But if he did leave with only a short courtesy of a farewell, she would at least know she'd offered a refuge when he'd needed it most. And with absolute conviction, she believed that whether or not he could bring himself to express it, he had recognized and appreciated that gift.

And that, she told herself, squelching the forelorn hope

that now or someday they could share more, might well have to be satisfaction enough.

"Lady Arnold!"

Valeria jumped guiltily, heat pinking her cheeks at the knowledge that he'd caught her spying on him. "M-Mr. Fitzwilliams! Please, don't let me disturb you."

"Have you dined yet?"

"Yes. One of the tenants was kind enough to regale me with an excellent rabbit stew." She smiled wistfully. "The meal reminded me of my campaigning days in India with Papa and my brother Elliot."

Teagan fixed on her those glittering golden eyes she found almost impossible to resist. Her body began to tingle and her willpower to dissolve even before he spoke.

"Will you not join me for a glass of wine? I can assure you it is excellent."

In the suddenly small confines of the library, he radiated a masculine presence that sang a siren's song to every nerve of her body. Even knowing the shoals ahead, she doubted her ability to steer clear if she approached any closer. "It...it is rather late."

His smile faded, increasing her guilt. "Could you not spare a moment? At least long enough for me to thank you."

She didn't pretend to misunderstand. "Friends...assist one another, Teagan. And don't need to be thanked."

"Then would you do something for me—as a friend?"

Agreeing was a bad idea. A very bad idea, when she hungered with the ferocity of a starving beggar invited to a banquet to touch his hair, his body, to feast once more on those lips.

My house. My library. No one need ever know.

"Would you?" he repeated, both a command and an appeal.

She shook her suddenly woozy head. "W-would I what?"

His smile deepened and his eyes fixed on her lips. She could almost feel the warmth of his breath on them. Shivers skittered across her stomach.

"Stay and talk with me." He tapped the volume at his knee. "About this, if you like. A wonderfully written book is a glory in itself, but even better when it's shared. Please." He gestured toward the sofa before the fire.

'Twas embarrassing how intensely he affected her, alarming—as well as arousing—how much those naughty little suggestions darting through her mind magnified his allure.

She should be sensible and go up to bed.

But that would be ungracious, would it not? He might believe that, finding herself now a wealthy woman, she had no more use for his company. Though she thought it unlikely, given his experience with the female sex, that he could be unaware of his potent effect on her.

Still, she ought to be courteous. She could manage sitting by the fire on the sofa while he sat behind the desk and they discussed a common love of literature.

As if bound to him by some unspoken accord beyond her mind's control, her feet had carried her halfway across the library before she realized she'd entered the room.

Teagan smiled at her, wondering if she realized how adorable she looked, her face flushed, her fluttering hands betraying the nervousness that seemed to pull her at once to go and to stay, as it had in the barn at Eastwoods. To his relief, after a long hesitation she walked in and took the place he indicated on the couch.

"I must warn you," she said as she arranged her skirts, "I'm an indifferent scholar. Living in India much of my youth, where both distance and climate argued against

Englishmen maintaining well-stocked libraries, resulted in rather large gaps in my knowledge of literature and philosophy. I see from the selection on the desk that you prefer the ancients. Is that what you studied?''

How had he survived almost two weeks of her absence? It was all he could do not to walk over and draw her into his arms. He was almost positive she would welcome the embrace. Almost.

What had she asked him about? His studies, of course. He felt a bit dizzy, and shaking his head to clear it, he tried to focus on the conversation.

''Y-yes. While most of the lads at Eton struggled with languages, I found I had a gift for them.''

''Dear me, how unfashionable!''

''Aye, but since I could also put a bullet through a wafer at twenty paces and mill down upperclassmen who outweighed me by several stone, I was spared any indignities being attempted on my person.''

Although the intense attraction she exerted over him did not lessen, as the conversation progressed Teagan relaxed a bit. How strange, that he could feel such a strong desire and yet at the same time chat with her so easily, friend to friend.

He looked back up to find her grinning at him. ''You know, you lose that Irish lilt when you speak of your books. Which is a shame. I rather like it.''

''I'll not believe that,'' he replied. ''Surely, like the rest of your countrymen, you despise all things Irish.''

''I met many fine Irishmen with the army. Perhaps some a bit too fond of grog, but good soldiers all—skilled, loyal and ferocious. The kind of ally one would wish at one's back in a battle—or when facing down highwaymen.''

Teagan laughed. ''I hear I've become a legend.''

''Thank Wilkins.'' She rose and walked over to the desk, where he still stood. As the distance between them narrowed, the very air between them grew charged. Once again he had to struggle to focus on her words rather than her nearness.

"Are these works your favorites?" she asked, pointing to the volumes he'd set out on the desk. When he nodded, she continued. "What is so inspiring about them that a young lad would struggle to master an antique tongue, merely for the privilege of reading them?"

"For one, every question of philosophical significance was first posed by Plato and Aristotle, and all analysis since is based on their work. But to read them in the Greek—ah, the precision and clarity of the language, the poetry of its form, make it well worth the mastering."

"A master of Greek? My, you *are* accomplished! I wonder you did not make a career at scholarship, given that—" He must have winced, for she stopped abruptly. "I-I'm sorry. That is none of my affair."

"You needn't apologize." His knew his smile had a harsh edge. "A scandal that was the talk of the ton hardly qualifies as confidential. 'Tis true that playing the gamester wasn't my *original* plan."

"But after...what occurred, you had no other choice," Valeria said quietly. "Life is so often unfair. You forfeited your future, but I've not heard anything to suggest the lady involved suffered accordingly."

She obviously wished to know the whole, and there was no reason not to tell her, Teagan supposed. For the first time, he even felt a willingness to share the bitter truth.

The sympathy in her glance was almost...painful, however, and he looked away. "I'd penned her enough rash testaments of my devotion that, once the affair became known, it was no piece of work to fix the blame. I even wrote one note—by the saints, what a fool I was!—begging her to run away with me. As if any woman with a particle of sense would have eloped with a stripling who possessed barely a shilling and no possible means of support.''

Though he shook his head mockingly, he knew Valeria's discerning ear had probably read in the timbre of his voice how desperately the love-besotted university lad had suffered from an older woman's rejection, more keenly even than from the wreckage of his career.

He looked back at Valeria, a wry smile on his face. ''I can scarcely believe I'm burdening you with sorry details that, I assure you, I've never before revealed.''

''Friends trust each other with their confidences,'' she said softly. ''I am honored you would confide yours to me.''

Warmed by her sympathy, he tried to lighten his voice as he continued. ''She did succeed in recapturing the full attention of her often-neglectful husband, which was perhaps her intent all along. In fact, I later came to suspect she arranged our last meeting so that we *would* be discovered.''

As the full meaning of that revelation penetrated, Valeria's pensive expression turned almost—ferocious.

''That selfish, calculating bitch!'' she cried. ''She *used* you, then!''

At first startled by her vehemence, Teagan began to chuckle. ''My dear innocent, lest you have any doubt, let me assure you I used her, too—thoroughly and often.''

''But to deliberately betray you, with no regard whatsoever to what that must mean to your position at the university! Why, she cannot have cared for you at all!''

Teagan's face sobered. ''No, I don't expect she did.''

''Well, I think she should have been flogged in the main street of town!''

Teagan watched her, so small and fierce, and the teasing reply he'd meant to utter failed him. So fierce—on his behalf. Bristling to right the wrongs done him.

"Whist, such a bold champion ye be," he said unsteadily. "Ready to charge into battle."

"Well, someone should have!" she retorted.

A sparkle of more than ordinary brilliance filled her dark eyes. His throat constricting, he reached out, to catch on his finger one crystalline tear.

She was weeping—with outrage at his pain.

Suddenly, the faint odor of a dimly remembered perfume washed over him, the feel of gentle hands lifting him to his feet, brushing off his knees and hugging him close. The reassuring certainty that whatever distress he'd suffered would be dissipated in the security of that embrace.

He came back to the present to find his fingers still resting on Valeria's cheek. She stared up at him, motionless, as if in thrall to his touch.

Teagan's chest tightened until it was difficult to breathe. A light-headed, falling sensation made him dizzy. To steady himself, he reached out and drew her, unresisting, into his arms.

"Ah, sweet lady," he whispered into the silk of her hair, "don't weep for me."

She moved away, and, panicking at the thought of letting her go, he tightened his grip. But she merely drew back far enough to angle her face up to his.

Gentleness ignited into conflagration at the first brush of their lips.

She made a small, impatient sound deep in her throat and dug her fingers into his shoulders, urging him nearer. Except that he'd already tightened his arms to crush her close, starving for the feel of her against his chest, desperate to taste her lips, her tongue, her teeth, to inhale the essence of her and transport them to a place where separate entities dissolved and they became one.

His blood was boiling through his veins, his pulse frantic to keep pace. Her fingers tugged aside his loosened cravat, stroked the skin beneath, slid lower to scratch at the buttons at his neck.

With the last shred of his rapidly disintegrating sanity, Teagan realized that if she succeeded in wrenching open his shirt and running her greedy, knowing fingertips over the bared skin of his chest, he'd be catapulted beyond control, driven only by the raging need to disrobe and possess her. Here, now, beside the desk or on the sofa, in a public room where at any moment a servant might walk in.

Disengaging from that kiss was the hardest task he'd ever performed. With a mewling sound of protest she resisted his retreat.

"Valeria, don't!" he gasped. "Touch me again, and by the saints, I'll be taking you right this minute, in your own library. You can't want that!"

Her eyes unfocused, her breathing ragged, she stared up at him as if his words made no sense. "I—I can't?"

"No, sweeting." Unable to let her go, he left his hands loosely cupped over the softness of her shoulders, and by a ferocious force of will kept her at arm's length. "You...wanted us to be friends. Just friends."

"Friends?" she repeated, swallowing hard. "D-did I? I seem to be having difficulty remembering."

The entreaty in her passion-glazed eyes made it difficult for him, too, to recall the reasons why they must resist what they both wanted. "So do I," he admitted.

"Teagan, could we not be...closer friends?"

Another wave of heat scalded him at her inference. "*Mo muirnin,* that's what you want?"

"Yes," she whispered faintly, and then louder, "yes."

So be it, he thought, and abandoned the thankless battle to be noble. "You'll let me come to you later?"

"Come now."

With hands that trembled as much as his own, she reached to pull his head down for another fierce kiss. ''Hurry!'' she said, and gathering up her skirts, fled from the room.

Chapter Sixteen

Teagan gave Valeria a half hour to prepare for bed and dismiss her maid, then he blew out the candles and headed for the stairway. He climbed the risers almost without seeing them, his breath coming fast, his heart tripping a rapid beat as if he'd been running rather than maintaining the decorous pace of a guest retiring for the night.

He entered his room and leaned back against the door. How much longer must he wait until he could be reasonably sure of not encountering any servants in the hall? Restless, he fingered the buttons at his waistcoat, then decided not to strip to his shirtsleeves. He wanted Valeria to relieve him of his garments...one by one.

Greedily he envisioned it, the images sending a dizzying rush of heat and need through his already needy body. How he loved her touch, that endearing mix of eagerness and hesitancy as her fumbling fingers struggled to detach a button from its mooring. The catch in her breath when garment gave way to skin; the shuddering inhale as, with the pads of her fingers, she explored the contours of his body, avid, eager, yet reverent.

Cherishing.

His skin grew damp with a moisture she soon would take

on her tongue, giving back of her own. And suddenly he could not wait a moment longer.

Forcing himself to move calmly, like a proper guest on a nocturnal search for wine or candles, he proceeded down the hallway into the master wing. And then he was before her door, the handle turning noiselessly as he grasped it.

He slipped in, and caught his breath. Evidently she'd not heard him enter, for Valeria stood near the window, her back to the door, her hands clasping and unclasping behind her. Pale moonlight silhouetted the dark outline of her figure within a halo of silky golden fabric that reflected the glow of the candles on the bedside table.

"Valeria," he whispered.

With a small exclamation of surprise she whirled to face him. Before she could move, he covered the distance between them, took her hands and kissed them.

"You're trembling! I'm sorry I frightened you."

"No, I'm not frightened." Her wide dark eyes devoured his face, uncertain still. "It's…just that it's been so long—and I want you so badly."

Tenderness invaded his chest and he smiled at her. "I'm here, *mo muirnin.*"

He drew her into his arms. She slid her hands into his hair, tangling them in its strands, and pulled his mouth to hers in a fierce, hard kiss that left him gasping. While her eager tongue danced with his, their bodies bumped at chest, waist, hips in a series of torrid collisions that made him realize she wore nothing beneath the fine silk of her robe.

When at last she broke the kiss, his knees were rubbery. She swayed as well, and he put his hands on her shoulders to brace her. "Ah, sweeting," he said with an unsteady chuckle. "We've no need to rush. I want to carry you to the luxury of that great soft bed and come to know you again one slow inch at a time."

She shook her head vehemently, her eyes pleading. "Not slow! Not this time. Now, Teagan. Please!"

Inhaling a deep breath, she gently pushed away his fingers, loosened her robe and shrugged it off her shoulders. Bereft of speech or movement, Teagan watched as the filmy material drifted to the floor, leaving her naked and vulnerable to his gaze.

"Now," she whispered.

Transported to paradise, where does one start? At the hollow above the smooth curve of her collarbone, which cried out for his tongue? The plump breasts whose erect nipples beckoned him to taste and touch? The satin round of belly he could almost feel skimming beneath his fingertips, gliding under his lips? Or the tight curls below, springy softness concealing velvet folds whose hidden pearl yearned for the completion of his kiss, the caress of his thumb?

The tightness of his breeches approached pain, but he would stave off fulfillment. The first time they'd come together, months ago, had been his. This, the first time they'd lie together after so long a wait, would be hers.

"What do you want, Valeria?"

"What do—?" She broke off, confused. To his delight, comprehension sent a rosy blush to her cheeks. "I...I want you to...take me."

"How shall I take you? Tell me."

"I..." She moistened her lips. He bent to capture her tongue, drawing it between his lips to stroke and tease, but preventing her from pressing her body against his.

He released her mouth. "Say it, Valeria. The very words as you describe it will give me pleasure."

"I...want your hands...on my breasts."

"Like this?" He cupped his hands under them, rubbed his thumbs across the nipples.

Her gasp was his answer.

"What now?" he whispered.

She wobbled, her grip on his arm unsteady. "B-bed."

Hands still caressing, he helped her pliant body recline on the sheets, propped pillows beneath her head.

"Your mouth…" She urged his chin downward.

"At your nipples?"

"Ah, yes," she said, then groaned as he gently raked one taut tip with his teeth.

Eyes closed, for timeless moments she held him there, to pleasure first one breast, then the other.

Finally she moved him away. "Please…I want…you," she said between gasps, "here." One hand flailed toward her slightly parted thighs. "Within me."

Her skin was sheened with dampness, small rivulets of it pooling between her breasts, in the valley of her navel. Teagan knew she could not be far from completion. And much as he yearned to join her in one flesh, he craved even more to relive the dream that had titillated him all these months—the slow torture of his body inflamed, while her fingers freed him from his clothing one agonizing button at a time. He didn't want this to end too soon, in a frantic pop of fasteners, a ripping down of his trouser flap.

Besides, the means of sweet deliverance were so temptingly close. He nudged at her thighs, which she hastened to part wider. Then, before she could realize his intent, he moved a finger within those hot silky folds while he bent to suckle the sensitive nub above.

Her back arched; her nails bit into his shoulders. Moments later she uttered a muffled cry as the waves of pleasure he unleashed washed over her.

Afterward, she lay limp and spent. Still completely clothed, he eased up to recline beside her.

When at last her dazed eyes opened, he leaned to gently kiss her cheek.

"You cheated," she accused.

"I deflected."

A lazy smile grew on her lips, a wicked twinkle in her eye. She traced a finger down his shirtfront, slowing as she descended, inching past his waistband, creeping down the superfine of his breeches, until she stopped with the barest pressure of her fingertip against the pulsating bulge beneath his trouser flap.

He stifled a groan.

"Now," she murmured, "I want slow."

Much later, Teagan awakened against the damp pillows to find Valeria asleep in his arms. A sense of awe filled him as he gazed at her relaxed figure, her head cradled in the hollow of his shoulder, her breasts at his chest, her soft belly and warm thigh pressed against his thoroughly satisfied member, one long sweep of leg entwined with his.

Powerful emotion surged through him. He drew her closer and wrapped his leg more tightly around hers. He'd been wrong about the library, he decided. *This* was heaven.

He couldn't remember ever sleeping close to anyone before. He'd been exiled to the garrets growing up, and for protection's sake had never attempted to lie beside any of the lads while at Eton or university. Even if he'd had the inclination, given the nature of his relationship with the ladies with whom he'd previously trysted, there'd been good reason not to linger once the coupling was done.

He almost shook Valeria, wanting her to wake and share with him this sense of euphoria and peace, then chuckled at his foolishness. She'd be up betimes to care for the Winterpark flock. Not being able to make out the time on the mantel clock above the dying fire, he wasn't sure how much longer before he must leave her.

Though he wished the night might never end. The strength of his will had been nothing against the ferocity of his need, and though they'd avoided torn buttons and ripped clothing, even the second loving had not been slow enough. But the third—ah, that was a sensual ballet of point and counterpoint, arched arms and the curve of leg over leg...hands skimming down a shiver of skin...lips dipping to drink and drink again...the final melding of limbs into a long-delayed, sense-stunning climax.

He was smiling into the darkness, reliving it all over again, when Valeria stirred.

"Teagan?" she breathed.

He kissed her forehead. *"Mo muirnin."*

She smiled. "I hope that means something good."

"My darling."

Her smile softened. "You have made me feel cherished, and I thank—"

He put a finger to her lips. "Whist, and what did ye tell me earlier? No thanks needed between friends. Especially not very close—" he kissed her eyelashes "—very special—" he kissed the tip of her nose "—friends." He claimed her lips.

She parted them for him, met his tongue in a waltz that was long and slow and sweet, until the member he thought totally satisfied began to stir once more.

But there was no more time now, he knew, so best to stop this before it began. He broke the kiss and pulled her up to sit beside him.

"Do you visit tenants again today?"

"Yes. Would...would you like to accompany me?"

"I should be delighted."

"I shall be leaving very early.

"I'll find you."

"I'll have Cook pack a lunch."

He nodded and made himself ease from the bed, to keep himself from blurting that the food didn't matter; he could nourish himself on the sight of her face, drink in the timbre of her voice and the sound of her laughter.

But then he'd sound like the besotted moonling he was.

The fire had died to embers and he shivered a bit in the chill. "'Tis cold. You *could* help me dress."

Her teeth gleamed in the darkness. "No. This friend is better at assisting you to *un*dress."

Suddenly he wasn't so cold. "I shall remember that."

After donning his clothes, a mundane procedure made unexpectedly erotic by knowing that she was naked, watching him, Teagan came back to the bed.

He leaned over to fill his hands with her bare breasts while he nibbled at her lips. "Until later."

"Aye, *mo muirnin.*"

Valeria hugged herself and watched Teagan's silent exit. 'Twas still before dawn, but she had no desire to sleep any longer. Besides, it would be best if she were to make her preparations and depart even earlier than usual. Before her new household she might don her clothes and her respectable widow manners with impunity, but Mercy knew her too well. One look, and the maid would guess everything.

This interlude with Teagan was a madness that could not long endure, but for the few precious days that it lasted, she meant to throw aside caution and enjoy every moment. She did not wish to hear—or heed—the warnings of disaster her old nurse would feel compelled to deliver.

All her life Valeria Arnold had followed instructions, done her duty, made the best of whatever fate dealt her. And when Teagan Fitzwilliams rode out of her life again, as she knew he would, she would doubtless need every bit of her fortitude and endurance to survive.

But for the first time in her life, she was with a man who not only could bring her to a level of pleasure she hadn't dreamed possible, but one who stimulated her mind and evoked her laughter as readily as he stirred her senses. No love she'd before experienced, certainly not for her father or Elliot or even for Hugh, had made her feel so closely bonded to another human soul.

If only to herself, Valeria admitted she had committed the unpardonable sin of falling in love with Teagan Fitzwilliams. She knew the catechism of punishment well enough to realize she would probably soon be suffering the torments of the damned. But for now, she intended to drain every honeyed drop in the wine of this short-lived, unexpected gift. And let the future worry about itself.

She'd managed to keep herself from asking how long Teagan meant to stay, knowing any answer shorter than "forever" would be impossible to bear, knowing she dare not count on her increasingly feeble pride to prevent her begging him to remain longer.

He would be here until he rode away, she thought as she climbed out of bed. And he would not ride away today.

The Lord be praised for Wilkins's busy tongue, Teagan concluded as his brown gelding trotted beside Valeria's gig. He'd feared when he recklessly invited himself along today that his presence might be met with wary hostility or, even worse, give rise to immediate suspicions about their relationship. But the story of his dashing rescue had apparently spread about the countryside, for he was greeted wherever they went with almost as much curiosity and acclaim as Valeria herself.

'Twas quite a novelty, being welcomed as a hero.

His enjoyment of that notoriety did not approach the pleasure of spending a whole day in Valeria's stimulating and knowledgeable company. He'd managed his grandfather's stud farm over several summers, and was impressed by the breadth of her acquaintance with agricultural procedures. As was the estate manager, Mr. Parker, who accompanied them and often sought her opinion.

But what enchanted Teagan most was simply contemplating the contrast between the decorously gowned Lady Arnold conducting estate business with her retainers—and the naked, candlelight-dappled enchantress who only a few hours ago had acted out his most erotic fantasies.

The proper decorum they had to maintain before the estate agent and the various tenants, rather than frustrating him, seemed to enhance the power of their wordless communication. The lingering glances, hands that almost but not quite touched, the brush of his sleeve against her skirts as he helped her down from the gig—each revived a bit of the magic of that midnight interlude. Who would have thought propriety could be so arousing?

As the hour approached noon, Valeria pull up the gig.

"Mr. Fitzwilliams and I will lunch by the river, Mr. Parker. You are welcome to join us, or since we are near your sister's farm, you might wish to visit there."

Mr. Parker's face brightened. "That is most kind, Lady Arnold. If you are perfectly sure you will not need me, I should like to stop at Susan's."

"Please go, then, and give your sister my regards."

"Of course, Lady Arnold. Thank you again."

Teagan's pulses sped as the estate agent departed. "Freeing us from our chaperone, my lady?"

Valeria gave him a demure look from under her lowered lashes. "Mr. Parker fair dotes on his nephews, and never misses an opportunity to see them. And with you to carry the basket, I don't expect I shall need his assistance at luncheon. Unless you would like to recall him?"

"Certainly not. I am here to serve your pleasure," Teagan said, taking the basket she indicated.

"I hope so," she murmured. "Follow me, please?"

Bemused, Teagan followed, not sure what his Lady Mystery had in mind. But after they crossed a field and penetrated beyond a screen of trees, he stopped short. "Ah, 'tis lovely!"

Valeria turned back to him, his awe mirrored on her face. ''Is it not beautiful?''

Down a steep, wooded incline he saw a sun-dappled clearing beside a swiftly flowing, crystalline river, its far bank protected by a thick copse of oaks.

''Mr. Parker showed me the place on my first tour of Winterpark,'' she told him as they picked their way down the trail. '''Tis where all the lads swim in summer, he said.''

Teagan noted the river's shallowness and seclusion. ''It looks ideal for that. And for a picnic.'' He chose a wide oak at the clearing's edge and set down the basket. ''My lady, your banquet awaits.''

She offered her hand, and he eased her to a seat on the blanket she'd spread, then sat beside her, her hand still in his. The afterglow of intimacy shared, the promise of passion to come, shimmered in the air.

Teagan stared at her lips, already thirsting to kiss her. ''This,'' he said, ''is going to be a very long day.''

''And I thought you were enjoying yourself!''

''Your company is a delight. But after last night, I find myself impatient to be your *close* friend once more.''

Her lips curved into a smile. Slowly she lowered her eyes to his neck cloth.

Best redirect this conversation, lest he forget Mr. Parker would soon be rejoining them. Shifting uncomfortably, Teagan released her hand. ''Whist, my naughty sprite, how you set me ablaze with only a glance! But tell me, are *you* enjoying yourself here? Winterpark looks to be a heavy responsibility. Will you stay here to manage it, or leave it in Mr. Parker's capable hands and return to London? If rumors of Lady Winterdale's wealth are correct, you have the freedom to do whichever you like.''

Valeria looked up from the package of cold chicken she was unwrapping. ''Perhaps I shall stay here...I'm not sure as yet. I've never had a settled home. Given Papa's numerous postings, we never stayed long in one location.''

Nor, shuffled from one unwilling relative to the next, had he. He could well understand her uncertainty.

She offered Teagan the meat and cheese, then accepted the glass of wine he'd poured. ''Having experienced the whirlwind of a Season once, I've little desire to return to London and live among Society. Once I have Winterpark settled, perhaps I shall travel.''

''And where would you go, Miss Adventurer?''

''I've always envied gentlemen, who, if they had the funds might journey wherever they wished. Now that *I* have funds, perhaps I shall become one of those eccentric ladies who tour exotic foreign lands. Before I resign myself to a lifetime of Ladies Aid Society meetings and parish charity work, there is so much left to see!''

She made a sweeping gesture toward the river near their feet. ''I'd like to barge the Euphrates and pole down the Nile. Cross the Alps and climb the foothills of the Himalayas. Sleep in the shadows of the Pyramids, and walk barefoot on the sands of Cadiz!''

Her ardent enthusiasm brought a smile to his face. But recalling the wealth that would enable such travels led him to the unpleasant truth that so rich a widow was most unlikely to end up an eccentric explorer. A surge of indignation rose in his chest at the thought of his Lady Mystery being cajoled by some gentleman into giving up control of her estates—and her dreams.

And suddenly he felt compelled to ask, ''Would you take no companion on those adventures?''

She grew still, then looked up at him. ''I might.''

He grew still as well, trapped by the yearning in her gaze. Helpless, he leaned toward her. She met him halfway, just a gentle nuzzle of lips, sweet and impossibly arousing.

"Perhaps we should have kept our chaperone, after all," Teagan murmured unsteadily.

"And why is that?"

"With no maid to attend you and no ironing girl in sight, I cannot proceed where I'd like if we're to emerge from this glen with your reputation intact."

A sparkle danced in her eyes. "A dilemma, but…"

His temperature shot up at that small hesitation.

"'Tis true," she said in a musing tone, as if calculating a problem in mathematics, "that I cannot remove or replace so fashionable a gown without proper assistance—quite an argument against fashion, I must say! Nor is there a way to conceal a neck cloth wrinkled beyond repair. But—" she reached for the top button of his waistcoat "—even if your cravat remains tied, I see…possibilities."

His heartbeat sped to a gallop and his mouth dried. "D-do you?" he stuttered.

"The army teaches one to be very resourceful," she murmured, freeing the two top buttons of his waistcoat and one in the shirt beneath.

"Praise the Lord for army training."

He reached for her, but she batted away his hand. "We've already established that Lady Arnold must remain pristine. You, my dear *close* friend, are easier to tidy."

By the saints, she had learned her lessons well. She pushed him gently back against the tree trunk and slipped one more button free, her fingers dipping beneath the cloth such that the edge of her nail just grazed his nipple.

A moan escaped him. "Valeria, love—"

She shushed him with a finger to his lips, and he abandoned any attempt to speak. One button at a time, she bared his chest from collarbone to waist, all the while watching him, just watching, eyes avid and plump lips pursed. Slower still, she freed the fastenings of his breeches, careful now to touch only fabric.

The soft breeze brought shivers to the intimate skin she exposed, further hardened his aching fullness. Though almost completely clothed, he felt more naked now than he'd ever felt undressed.

"Valeria, torturess, what are you doing?" he groaned, when for long charged moments she neither stroked nor kissed, touching him only with her eyes.

She smiled. "Admiring the…scenery. But I suppose you should find it difficult riding in that state?"

The mere thought dragged from him another strangled moan, which apparently was answer enough, for she nodded. "Then I shall have to correct that. So, *mo muirnin.*" She dropped her voice to a whisper. "What would you have me do?"

The cool air caressing his nakedness seemed to fan, rather than mitigate, the inferno scorching his heavily clad back, legs and shoulders. As did her naughty, knowing look while she awaited his answer. Imagining what she might do with her cool satin fingers and hot velvet mouth nearly brought him to climax.

Not being at all shy, he had no trouble voicing his preferences. And with a hungry intensity that suggested she'd been saving him for dessert, she hurried to comply.

By the time, a heart-stopping interval of supreme bliss later, he had revived sufficiently to recover sight and breath, Valeria was gathering the remnants of the picnic food. She took the last sip of wine and conveyed it from her mouth to his.

"Don't," she ordered when he moved his still-shaking hands to try to rebutton his garments. "I shall attend to those directly."

And so, while he sat there bemused, she proceeded to put up food, glasses, napkins, plates, pausing at intervals to cast lingering, provocative glances at the unclothed portion of his anatomy. After finishing with the picnic things, she knelt beside him, once more making a leisurely exploration of his mouth while refastening his garments with soft, glancing touches, until he was nearly ready to begin all over again.

"That," he pronounced after she'd dismissed with an airy wave of her hand his protest at being informed they must now return to the gig, "was definitely cheating."

She made a little moue of her lips, prim as a nun. "No more so than you were last night."

"Ah, but last night we played more than one hand. Whereas you've just called the game to a halt."

"There's always tonight, isn't there?"

He caught her by the shoulders and pulled her to him, claimed her lips in a quick assault that within seconds splintered her facade of matronly composure.

"Yes, sweeting," he whispered, bracing her shaking body against him, savage satisfaction filling him at the intensity of the response he evoked in her, "you can wager on tonight."

Chapter Seventeen

With a whistle and a spring in his step, Teagan entered the breakfast parlor. Valeria was not present, but he hadn't expected her to be. Given the paucity of rest they'd had last night, he wouldn't be surprised if, her duties requiring her to remain at the manor today, she slept until noon.

However, awakened by the bright sun streaming in his window, despite his scant two hours' slumber Teagan had never felt more alive, more energized. Since, having crept back to his own room in the predawn stillness, he could not doze with Valeria in his arms, he'd decided to rise and dress. He was, he'd realized with a grin, quite famished.

As if she'd been watching for him, a moment later Valeria's nurse Mercy walked in. Even the dour look on the woman's face as she gazed at him could not dent his high spirits.

"And a lovely good day to ye, Mistress Mercy," he sang out, strolling over to fill a plate at the sideboard.

"Mr. Fitzwilliams," the nurse responded.

"Do you bring me a message? Or is it just that, it bein' such a beauteous morning, ye're wishful of conversin' with me today."

"I bring no message...from my mistress."

Grinning, Teagan continued. "Sure, on such a day a stroll in the gardens would be just the thing. Or, as I remember ye're not much for strollin,' perhaps later I could take ye and your mistress for a drive."

"My mistress, having work to do, has departed."

Teagan looked up in surprise. "I thought she wasn't to ride out today."

"Parker summoned her early. An accident at the mill. She went to assist."

Teagan halted in the midst of buttering his toast. How early? he wondered with a spurt of unease. He recalled her bedchamber as he'd left it in the misty predawn—sheets in disarray, her night rail flung on the side chair, the lingering odor of lovemaking potent in the air.

Mercy would have gone to awaken her.

He glanced over to find the nurse staring at him, accusation in her eyes, and felt a flush mount his cheeks.

She watched him steadily while the attending footman poured him coffee, waiting until the servant left the room.

"'Tis I who have a message for you, Mr. Fitzwilliams," Mercy said quietly after the man's exit. "Don't do this to her. 'Tis crime enough that you'll shatter my poor mistress's heart when you go. Winterpark can be a haven for her, with work to help her heal. Go now, before 'tis too late. Don't leave her to deal with the shame of a bastard brat."

Before he could think what to reply, she walked out.

His high spirits vanishing with his appetite, Teagan stared at his chilling toast and cooling coffee.

He knew Mercy had disapproved of their London excursions together. For the first time, he saw his sojourn here through her eyes as well.

A feckless, indigent gamester with no money and few prospects. Valeria's irresponsible lover, taking advantage of her goodwill, living off her largesse.

The image sickened him.

Though he'd never sunk to accepting the hospitality of a lady to whom he was not sincerely attracted, he had on several occasions dallied with women who supplied him with comforts for the duration of their liaison. Those females weren't fit to mention in the same breath as Valeria.

Their time together, from the very first meeting at Eastwoods, had been far more than a meaningless tryst based on lust and mutual convenience. Regardless of how it might appear to Mercy—or any other uninvolved outsider.

Surely Valeria knew the truth of that, didn't she?

For a moment the need overwhelmed him to run to the stables, ride out to find her, assure her...of what?

That he loved her? That a half-breed Irish gambler of no income and dubious reputation begged the honor of the pure, lovely, *rich* Lady Arnold's affection?

What did he know of love, beyond the hazy memory of a six-year-old in his dying mother's embrace? But if it meant the mere sight of her filled him with gladness, her wit and intelligence drew him so strongly he wanted to be nowhere else but at her side, and her touch had the power to melt him where he stood, then love her he did.

Buttressed by the hope of asking for her hand, he could steel himself to a new round of gaming, and having redeemed his debts, could return and ask her to marry him.

But though that would protect her from the dishonor of conceiving a bastard, it would do little to preserve her reputation. In fact, he thought, remembering with humiliation and chagrin the tarnish still clinging to his mother's name, it might well expose her to permanent derision for being, like Lady Gwyneth, foolish—and wanton—enough to cast herself away on an Irish wastrel.

If he truly wished to protect her, the best thing, as Mercy urged, was to leave her. Leave, and never come back.

The very idea of it made him want to howl with anguish.

Only then did he realize how completely Valeria's essence had seeped into every pore of his being, so that the thought of living without her seemed no life at all.

He might as well choose the pistol.

Mercy was right, though; he should leave soon, before the servants began to murmur about his nocturnal wanderings. Before the full significance of the energy flashing between himself and Valeria became apparent to more than her faithful nurse. Before her credit and her credibility suffered in her household and her neighborhood.

How much longer was safe—a day, maybe two? And even that, if he touched her, would risk the possibility of a child. How could he manage to stay without touching her?

The enormity of impending loss sucked the energy from his body, left him too listless even to rise from the table. After Robbin, brow creased in concern, asked him for the third time if he wished more coffee, Teagan forced himself up and drifted down the hall, feeling already like a sacrificial offering about to be stripped of his soul.

Without remembering how he'd gotten there, he found himself in the library. Mechanically he began to reshelve the volumes he'd left strewn on the library desk—a task so reminiscent of his exit in disgrace from Oxford that he had to choke down a bitter laugh at the irony.

But then indefatigable determination of the sort that must have led his mama to escape her relations and set off into the unknown with her Irish lover built back up in him, sparking a new idea rife with possibility.

The solution to this dilemma might be the one he'd rejected ten years ago. Young and hotheaded, at his grandfather's final insult he'd stormed out, vowing never to ask a Montford for anything again. But as ten years without one had demonstrated with painful clarity, all the things he valued most—honor, dignity, the hand of the woman he loved—depended on his occupying a respectable position in society. A position that, by English social code, could be conveyed on him only if he were once again received by his mother's family.

The idea of crawling on his belly to beg his cousin for reconciliation made him gag. But to salvage a life with Valeria, he would crawl and he would beg.

He might not have to abase himself totally, he thought with a grim smile. Should Jeremy prove resistant, a word in Riverton's ear might make the earl more receptive to receiving his disreputable cousin with better grace.

He'd reinstate himself with the family and press them to find him some respectable position—assistant to a government official or secretary to a nobleman. To limit the inevitable gossip among the ton, it would be in the family's interests to find him such a position quickly.

He was quick-witted, hardworking, and as Valeria had said, good at ingratiating himself with people at all levels of society. Once in a position, he would excel.

Having reconciled with the Montfords and taken that post, he could then return, confess his love and beg Valeria to marry him as soon as he'd worked himself to a level in which the world would not consider their union quite so dreadful a misalliance.

Valeria would marry him...wouldn't she?

Mercy, who knew her better than anyone, had said he held her heart. Her fierce, continual concern for him surely demonstrated a deep emotion. And her passionate response to him, as powerful as the response she evoked in him— surely that was love translated into touch.

He smiled a little, thinking of the delicious things she'd done to him and for him in the magical stretches of the night. A fierce satisfaction filled him at knowing he was the only man who had ever touched her thus.

The smile faded. She damned well better marry him. He'd gut any other man who dared touch her as he had.

But a plan to salvage their future did not change the bitter fact that he must still leave her now. And soon.

Though he need no longer worry about the possibility of a child. Should she conceive, he would simply marry her sooner. If not for the distress it might cause her to have to marry in that way, he'd welcome any reason that shortened the time before he could return to claim her.

Would she understand why he must go? She was too intelligent not to comprehend the danger they courted. But if he confessed his love and his hopes for their future, surely any hurt his leaving might cause would be offset by knowing that as soon as he could, he would come back.

Sure, and what did he have to offer her now but fine talk? he thought, frowning. The most derelict drunk in the parish could boast of the grand feats he would perform—tomorrow or next week or next year.

If she did love him, being Valeria, she might well press him to disregard the opinion of Society and marry her immediately. She might not understand his need to prove himself—in his own eyes and the world's—a man worthy of her love. She might even think his plan an excuse to evade marrying her, and doubt the strength of his affection.

Which would surely wound her more than leaving now with his vows of love unspoken.

"Words be easy. 'Tis deeds win the battle," Valeria's nurse had said, and she was right. Teagan would not speak to Valeria until he'd translated plans into action and action into accomplishment.

Which meant when he departed, he might express only his fervent vow to return.

The thought of leaving still too painful to contemplate, he turned his mind to planning, and another prospect flashed in his mind. Perhaps he need not approach the earl, after all. His mother's maternal family included a duke and claimed influence even superior to the Montfords'.

One of the few pleasant interludes he could remember from childhood was visiting Lady Charlotte Darnell, his mama's first cousin. That lady—she'd urged him to call her "Aunt Charlotte"—was now a widow residing in London.

Lady Charlotte it would be, then. But before he figured out how to approach her, he must solve a much more difficult dilemma—finding a way to say goodbye to Valeria.

Perhaps he should simply pen her a note and leave now, before she returned and the magnet of her presence could draw him away from his resolve to depart. But that was the coward's way, and after all she'd given him, she deserved better than a letter left with the butler.

Besides, remaining until tomorrow would mean they'd have tonight. One last night.

Only the last for now. For when he'd built a new life worthy of her, he would come back to reclaim her—and all the other nights of their lives.

Though exceedingly weary, Valeria was not able to return to Winterpark Manor until late afternoon, when the fire at the grain mill had at last been put out, those wounded in the dust explosion that caused it cared for and returned to their families.

A smile curved her lips as she walked up the entry stairs. Ah, what a joyous reason for fatigue! Perhaps she could rest before dinner. Teagan would be departing all too soon, and she had no intention of wasting the few nights she had left with him in slumber.

He must have been watching for her, for he appeared in the hallway immediately after Giddings took her wrap.

"Valeria, welcome back. I trust the situation at the mill is now resolved?"

"Yes. The building shall require repairs, but no one was grievously injured, thank goodness."

"I'm glad to hear it. If you are not too exhausted, would you join me in the library for a moment?"

Ah, the library. Sparkles danced across nerves she'd thought too tired to respond when she recalled what had begun the last time she'd been in that room with him.

"Yes...my very close friend," she murmured, smiling.

A smile he didn't return. Alarm banished fatigue in an instant.

He neither looked at her nor touched her after she followed him in. Her stomach commenced a downward spiral.

He was going to tell her he was leaving. He would smile, and kiss her hand, and express his appreciation for her kind hospitality...then announce his imminent departure.

Out of the whole of a long, bland, passionless lifetime, could she not have just a few more days of bliss?

She took a deep, shuddering breath. If this were the end, let her manage it with dignity. No tears, no argument, no begging him to remain just one more day.

Head held high, she walked to the sofa and seated herself. "What is it, Teagan?"

He paced to the window, then turned to her. His face looked as strained as she knew hers must be.

"There is no easy way to put this, so I'll just say it outright. I must leave Winterpark, Valeria."

Even with her expecting them, the words still struck like a blow. She gripped the sofa arm to steady herself. "When?"

"Tomorrow."

So she had one more night. Or did she? Had the time they'd shared, so unparalleled in splendor for her, been merely one more of any number of similar interludes for him? One which had now lost its luster? No, she could not believe that.

"I see," she managed to reply at last.

"You cannot think I *want* to go!" He strode over to seize

her hands and kiss them. "There is nothing I would love more than to remain here with you, as lost in our own private world as we have been these two days past. But as Mercy pointed out to me this morning, we both know that cannot be. The unusual circumstances of my arrival have allowed us a few days' grace, but if I linger much longer, malicious gossip about the real nature of our relationship is sure to erupt. I will not stay and cause your new staff and neighbors to turn against you."

He paused as if he would say more, then closed his lips. Unable to trust her voice, she merely nodded.

"I will come back, Valeria. 'Tis time for me to get my affairs in order, as I should have done long since. But once I do, nothing under heaven will keep me from you."

"Get...your affairs in order?"

"I mean to approach my mother's family and see if they will permit a reconciliation. Gambling was never to be more than a temporary support, and it's past time for me to find a more respectable occupation."

A wistful smile touched his lips. "I'd like to become a man you can be proud to acknowledge as your friend. A man people will not feel obliged to warn you against."

"I am proud already to call you my friend."

He swallowed. "Ah, lass, 'tis the beauty of ye," he said, his voice rough. "Ye see good where there is none."

"Nay, Teagan. I see what everyone else has overlooked."

His jaw tightened, and as if unable to restrain himself longer, he pulled her up from the sofa and into his arms, crushing her against his chest.

"Ah, *mo muirnin,* I shall miss you every day and every hour. And thank the lord at the end of every night, for it means one less day remains until I see you again."

He would come back.

He sought her lips, and Valeria gave them eagerly. His

kiss, deep, urgent, almost frantic, seemed to say he, too, needed to affirm that this bond they shared would endure the trials of separation to come.

Then he released her, pushed her gently back to a seat. "If I am not to ruin all yet, I shall have to be more discreet than that for the rest of today."

"Surely…we will still have tonight?"

"You'll allow it?"

"Yes! Oh, yes."

"Saints be praised," he said fervently, making the sign of the cross. "I don't think I could face the purgatory of leaving tomorrow if I did not know we still have the heaven of tonight."

With a quick sideways glance, as if afraid someone might oversee them, he kissed Valeria on the forehead. "Go rest, then, *mo muirnin*. We've but one more night, and I promise to make it one you will never forget."

A gentle rain was falling at dawn the next morning as Valeria walked Teagan down the path to the stables. He'd slipped to the kitchen to pack himself some meat and cheese for the journey so he might be off at first light, the better to reach London as soon as possible.

"I'll leave the horse at the posting inn. One of their ostlers will return him."

She nodded, biting her lip to avoid asking if he had sufficient funds for the journey, knowing that, even if he did not, his pride would not allow him to accept any from her.

She waited while he entered the stable, saddled a mount, sent the sleepy groom he'd awakened back to bed.

The drizzle had stopped and the new sun had just begun to peep over the eastern hills as they walked toward the carriageway out of Winterpark, both silenced by the heavy weight of imminent separation.

Out of sight of both house and stable, he wrapped his

mount's reins around a tree and took her in his arms. For a long, precious moment he simply held her, while Valeria memorized the sound of his heartbeat and breathed in the scent of his skin.

The passion they'd shared last night had been rough and frantic, slow and gentle by turns. The kiss he bent to give her now was the latter, long, lingering, tender. Despite her best intentions to be strong, she felt the hot sting of tears behind her closed eyelids.

He broke the kiss and she lowered her head to his shoulder, not wishing to look up so he could say goodbye, hoping with all her strength that he would say instead the words he'd hinted at but never spoken, the three words she so badly wanted to hear. Freeing her to say them, too.

But he said nothing. At last he lifted her head, framing her face in his hands, the golden cat eyes that had enthralled her from the first commanding her gaze.

"On my mother's grave and by all the saints, I swear I will come back, Valeria. Do you believe me?"

"Yes," she replied, disappointment battling with the hope that urged her to trust his words. "I believe you."

"Goodbye, then, *mo muirnin*," he said roughly, brushing his lips against her forehead. "Dream of me."

He pushed her gently away. Without looking back he strode to his horse, untied the reins and leaped into the saddle, kicking the stallion into a trot.

Numbness, like the shock after a mortal injury during which one does not yet feel pain, held her motionless as he rode away. Valeria wasn't sure how long she stood there, the sun of a new day dappling her hair, a soft breeze wafting bird calls to her from the trees beyond the flower border. All the signs of a normal morning, as if half her soul and all her joy had not just been wrenched from her to disappear down the road to London.

She turned toward the house—and found Mercy approaching her. ''Child, child,'' the nurse sighed, her eyes scrutinizing Valeria's face, ''what have you done?''

''What I wanted, Mercy,'' she replied fiercely. ''And I will not regret it.''

''Ah, Miss Val,'' the nurse murmured, holding out her arms and gathering Valeria close. ''I surely hope not.''

Chapter Eighteen

A week later, Teagan presented himself at the Mount Street town house of Lady Charlotte Darnell. Once he'd set out from Winterpark, his entire mind and will focused on what he must accomplish, as often happened with fickle Lady Luck, the cards that had fallen so badly the previous month suddenly realigned themselves in his favor. A few nights' concentrated effort at inns along the road back to London had amassed him sufficient funds to be able to return to his rooms and stave off the threat of the magistrate.

Dressed now in the best Weston and Hoby could offer, trying to keep his nervous fingers from rearranging his cravat, he stood in Lady Charlotte's anteroom while the butler went to determine if his mother's cousin would receive him. If ever Teagan needed the Jester's glib tongue and charming manners, 'twas now.

Please, Mama, he prayed, *let Lady Charlotte remember me with kindness.*

A few moments later the butler returned. "My mistress is in the morning room. If you will follow me?"

He never heard the butler announce his name. A shock pulsed through him the moment he beheld the tall, golden-haired lady who sat on the brocade settee, her clear blue eyes examining him avidly.

In the small study of the rambling manor at the stud farm Teagan had managed for several summers, he'd come upon a miniature that the friendly cook informed him was of Lady Gwyneth—apparently the sole remaining portrait of the earl's disgraced daughter. A portrait that bore so uncanny a resemblance to Lady Charlotte that for an instant he'd wondered if it were his mother come back to life.

"You are the image of Mama!" he blurted. Then, remembering the imperative to make a good impression, he swept her a deep bow. "Excuse me! 'Tis good of you to receive me, Lady Charlotte."

His mother's cousin continued to study him, her serene face impassive. Desperation making sweat pop out on his brow, he held her glance and tried to smile.

She shook her head slightly. "Teagan, Teagan," she said, advancing toward him with both hands outstretched, "why have you stayed away so long? And it's 'Aunt Charlotte,' you will remember."

So dizzy with relief he thought he might faint, Teagan sent a silent prayer of thanks to his mama and all the other saints in heaven before bending to kiss her fingers.

"What a handsome devil you've grown to be! And you are correct—your mama and I looked so alike many thought us sisters rather than cousins. But come, sit with me." She waved him toward the settee. "I'll have Martin bring us tea—or shall we make that champagne? A reunion after so many years demands a celebration!"

While the butler brought wine and refreshments, Lady Charlotte chatted about his mama and their growing up together. Once they'd disposed of the refreshments and sipped the promised champagne, she said, "But enough of ancient days. Tell me how you are and what you've been doing! I can't believe you've committed half the sins gossip lays at your door—no more than I believed the tales the Montfords told about you when you were growing up."

Teagan smiled ruefully. "I expect in both cases much of the talk is deserved. Since I learned early on that Mama's family would attribute blame to me regardless of how I behaved, it seemed only prudent to earn the thrashings I was going to receive anyway."

"And in more recent years?"

He shrugged. "I've been an honest man, if a gambler can be described as such." He paused, his face heating. "The affair with Lady Uxtabridge I regretted almost from the moment it began, but at the time I was still too angry and bitter to heed the harm I caused. After that...despite what rumor claims, my dealings with the ladies have been no more reprehensible than any other bachelor's."

She chuckled. "If Society were to ban every gentleman who committed youthful follies, the ton would be thin of company indeed! I don't know what happened at Oxford— and no, you needn't tell me! But I thought it dreadfully wrong of the family to break with you over it. Of course, Uncle Montford was ever a hot-tempered, harsh disciplinarian. Indeed, I never forgave him for what he did to Gwen, forcing her to choose between her home and the man she loved. And I still blame Uncle Montford for her death."

A fierce expression briefly creased her forehead before she continued. "At the time of the Oxford...incident, my husband agreed with the earl, and absolutely forbade me to interfere. Sometimes when one is handling a forceful gentleman, as with a feisty stallion, 'tis best to let him have his head until he settles down. I hoped you would contact me, send me some word. But you seemed to go off in a different direction altogether, which only confirmed Darnell's view that your grandfather was right, and made it impossible for me to approach you. By the time my husband died last year, I was not sure you would care to be approached, after so long a silence. I am so very glad you decided to seek me out at last.''

She paused and gave him a searching glance. "So, why did you decide to seek me out?"

"Perhaps because I am finally past the period of youthful follies. I have had enough of gaming, Aunt Charlotte, of living on the fringes of decent society. I came to ask if you would be willing to assist me in finding proper employment and...and help me redeem my reputation.''

To his surprise, she leaned over and gathered him into a swift embrace. "Oh, my dear Teagan," she said as she released him, "that has been my fondest wish ever since the dreadful interview with your grandfather turned you against us all! Of course I shall help you. Perhaps, when we have achieved your aims, I shall feel less guilty.''

"Guilty, Aunt Charlotte? Whatever for? You must know I would never have wished to come between you and your husband. You shouldn't take yourself to task for not intervening with Grandfather.''

"It's more than that, Teagan." Her smile faded and a look of grief came over her lovely face. "Your mama was not just my cousin—she was my dearest friend. When she ran off, I felt bereft, and when she died, it was as if I had lost a part of myself. When that clergyman found you in Dublin and sent you home, I felt a merciful God had given something of Gwen back to us. I...I wanted to take you. I *should* have taken you.''

Tears gathered at the corners of her eyes. "Had our situations been reversed, Gwen would have found a way to do that for my son," she asserted, her voice fervent. "No grandfather's contention that he belonged with the Montfords, or husband's insistence that she safeguard her strength for a babe of her own, would have stopped her.''

The lady's distress seemed so deep Teagan felt moved to protest. "You mustn't blame yourself. I'm sure you—"

"I haven't yet told you the whole. Do you remember the one visit you paid me, soon after you came to England?"

"It is one of my most pleasant childhood memories."

She squeezed his hand. "I was in a...delicate condition at last. I begged my husband to let you come, and since he wished to keep me happy, he asked Montford to send you to us. But I became ill, and they returned you to your grandfather. I...lost that child, and took many months to recover. After that episode, Darnell wouldn't hear of your returning. You were too rough and ill-behaved—I would tax my strength. I knew from your short visit how you were being treated, but I put my hopes for a child of my own over the welfare of my dearest friend's s-son."

Lips pressed together, Lady Charlotte fell silent.

She had wanted him, Teagan thought with a sense of wonder. Surely it could make no difference after all these years, yet somehow the knowledge that his mother's cousin would have taken him in, had she been allowed to, still had the power to warm some cold, lonely place in his heart.

And she had suffered from her failure to help him. Teagan put a sympathetic hand on her shoulder.

Wiping her eyes with an impatient gesture, Lady Charlotte turned back to him. "By the time I conceded that my hopes of a child would never be realized, you were nearly grown. Then came Oxford, and once again I let others overrule the judgment of my heart. Again, I failed both you and Gwyneth. I tell you all this not to assuage my guilt by asking for forgiveness—nothing will make amends for the errors of the past—but so you will understand why I assure you there is nothing I will not do now to help secure your future.

So," she patted his hand, then rose and crossed to ring the bell pull, "let me write some notes. Several of Darnell's friends still hold positions of influence. Surely one of them will know just the posting to meet your needs. Shall I ask them to join us for dinner tonight?''

Taken aback by the swiftness of her action, Teagan stuttered, ''I—well—y-yes, tonight would be fine.''

''That is…you do not have any previous engagements?''

''No, my lady. I am entirely at your disposal.''

''Excellent. I must go write the necessary letters.''

Teagan rose and bowed. ''How can I thank you enough, Aunt Charlotte?''

She hesitated. ''There is one thing.''

''If it is within my power to perform, it is yours.''

She smiled, so tentative and uncertain that he was instantly reminded of Valeria, and a pang of longing pierced him, marrow deep.

''Would you consider…staying here with me? I know the offer comes twenty years too late, far too late for you ever to allow me to claim you as the son I never bore, but having the ton know that you are residing with me would advance your cause, and—and I should like it very much.''

Teagan came over to kiss her hand. ''I should be honored to reside here. Honored to be considered a son.''

Once again tears glistened in Lady Charlotte's eyes, and once again she brushed them away. ''T-thank you. That means more than you will ever know. Please excuse me while I prepare the letters, before I turn into a watering-pot like one of those vaporish females I so deplore.''

She linked her arm in Teagan's and walked with him to the parlor door. ''I'll instruct Martin to have a suite of rooms prepared, to be at your disposal whenever you choose to make use of them. Now, bid me goodbye like a dutiful son,'' she ended, smiling as she held out her hands.

Teagan saluted them in the elaborate French manner. ''My very dear Aunt Charlotte, I am forever in your debt.''

''Nonsense. 'Tis rather I who am in yours! Perhaps now,

when I meet her in the hereafter, I shall finally be able to look your mama in the eye.''

Late that afternoon, Teagan returned to Lady Charlotte's town house, the sum total of his earthly possessions bound up in two small trunks and one string-wrapped bundle, the latter given him on his way out of his lodgings by his tearful landlady, Mrs. Smith.

After bidding him wait a moment, she'd scurried off and returned with a parcel in which he recognized the used copies of Herodotus, Plato, Homer and Virgil he'd left with her to pay off his debt. ''Knowin' how much store you put by 'em, I couldn't bring meself to sell 'em,'' she told him. '''Specially with me being right sure you'd be acomin' back. Best of luck to ye, now.'' Depositing the books on top of his other effects, she'd pushed him toward the door.

The sense of awe and excitement he experienced upon crossing the threshold of his new home recurred as Martin, with a deference Teagan thought almost excessive, ushered him into the suite of rooms Lady Charlotte had allotted him. The bedchamber with its Chippendale mahogany furnishings was nearly as grand as Valeria's chamber at Winterpark, and the attached sitting room offered a pair of comfortable leather armchairs and a study desk flanked by bookcases, as well as a large window overlooking the back garden.

Martin informed him that, though the late Lord Darnell's valet had already obtained another position, Martin had a nephew who'd just finished his training as a gentleman's gentleman, whom Martin would be happy to recommend to Mr. Fitzwilliams.

The situation was so reminiscent of Nichols at Winterpark that Teagan had to smother a grin. Informing Martin he would consider it, he dismissed the butler.

His grin returned as he gave the elegant bedchamber a

slower inspection. The only thing that would make this long-delayed homecoming sweeter, he decided, would be if he could look forward to sharing that large canopied bed with Valeria tonight.

Bittersweet longing dimmed his excitement. What would she be doing at this moment? Riding out to meet her tenants? Sitting in the estate office consulting with Mr. Parker? Clipping herbs in the kitchen garden with Mercy?

Missing him, as he was missing her?

He'd just, with another silent thanks to the loyal Mrs. Smith, arranged his meager collection of books on the bare shelves of the nearest bookcase when a tap sounded on the door, followed by the entrance of Lady Charlotte.

She stopped in the center of the chamber and gestured around. "You like the rooms, I hope?"

He walked over to kiss the hand she offered. "They are splendid, Aunt Charlotte. Indeed, they seem to have cast upon me such a reflection of glory that, since the moment I entered them, Martin has been practically begging me to allow him to be of service."

Lady Charlotte laughed. "As well he might. They are the master's rooms, after all."

His teasing smile faded as the significance of her gesture penetrated. "Aunt Charlotte, are you sure—"

"Hush," she said, putting a finger to his lips. "I wished you to have them. After the part Darnell played in keeping you away so long, it only seemed fitting, somehow. But I really came to see if I might steal you away for a time. Rather than writing a reply, one of the gentlemen to whom I directed a note has called in person. He's been a particular friend for years, so I'm delighted he is eager to meet with you. He's waiting below, if you can forgo your settling in long enough to receive him."

Teagan's heartbeat quickened. This, now, was the second test he must pass—convincing a man of sense and breeding that he could fulfill the requirements of whatever position the gentleman wished to offer him.

"Of course. I shall be right down."

"Excellent. I'll tell him you are coming and wait with him below." After a slight hesitation, as if uncertain how he would receive such a familiarity, she leaned up to kiss his cheek.

Teagan watched her walk out, then lifted a hand to his face, warmed by her lips. He couldn't remember the last time he'd received a kiss of affection completely devoid of carnal overtones. It felt odd—and strangely comforting.

So startled had he been by her gesture, he'd neglected to ask the name of the gentleman awaiting him. Well, no matter. Aunt Charlotte would introduce them soon enough.

Taking a deep breath, he strode back to the bedchamber to check his reflection in the pier glass, making sure his cravat was neatly tied, and brushing a nonexistent bit of lint off the dark blue lapels of his coat.

He must be polite, respectful, not too charming. Make a favorable impression and appear to be a credit to his aunt. Uneasily, he wondered just how much the unknown gentleman knew of him and his reputation.

Then, shoulders back and spine ramrod straight, he walked down to meet Lady Charlotte's friend.

Quietly he entered the room where his aunt sat beside her guest, a gentleman whose back looked vaguely familiar. Two steps later Teagan halted in surprise. "Lord Riverton!"

The gentleman turned to him, ironic amusement in his gaze. "Mr. Fitzwilliams."

His aunt looked from one man to the other. "I see there's no need for introductions. I shall leave you two to converse, then. You will return for dinner, my lord?"

"I should be delighted, Lady Charlotte."

Lord Riverton stood and bowed as Lady Charlotte, giving Teagan a quick wink of encouragement, walked out.

"Won't you sit, Fitzwilliams? Although I suppose it is presumptuous of me to invite you to be seated in your own drawing room." Riverton raised an eyebrow. "My compliments. You are more resourceful than I'd thought."

Not sure whether Riverton's comment was sincere or mocking, Teagan replied, "It is Lady Charlotte's drawing room, my lord. I am but her guest."

"And her kinsman as well, are you not?"

Teagan nodded. "Lady Charlotte, out of affection for my late mother, has agreed to help me obtain a responsible position. Do you...have such a post to offer me?"

"Actually, I've had a post in mind for you for some time. Please, sit, and let us discuss it."

Teagan took the chair indicated, spirits quickening at the inference that his next goal might be within reach. He liked and respected Riverton, and whatever the earl had to offer, he'd do his utmost to satisfy his requirements.

"By the way, that stallion of yours is doing well. A bit of a handful when he's fresh, but quite a sweet goer."

"Then you've removed him from Montford's care. Thank you for that, my lord."

Riverton nodded. "As I mentioned, I've been observing you for quite some time. Were you aware of it?"

"N-not exactly, my lord. I did notice you seemed to turn up in locations I would not normally have expected you. And assisted me on several occasions, as well."

Riverton chuckled. "Crandall's doxy fair at the hunting box. An...interesting affair, to be sure. You occupy a rather unique position, Fitzwilliams. Though of the gentry, your need to survive after Oxford forced you to mingle with, and develop a broad acquaintance among, the lower orders. I could use a man with such contacts."

"In what way, my lord?"

"Actually, I've already approached you about it. Through an intermediary, of course." Riverton fell silent, watching Teagan's face.

Teagan scanned his memory, trying to recall a time at which he'd been contacted by anyone on a matter of employment. Then the connection slammed home and he whipped his glance to Riverton.

"That night in the stable after I lost everything to Montford—*you* were the one who sent the soldier?" he demanded, incredulity mingling with horror.

"Yes. But before you draw your pistol, let me assure you that I represent the opposite of what you are now presuming. The world knows me to be a member of the privy council. But only a few—including your aunt, whose late husband previously occupied this post—know that I also hold a hidden portfolio to investigate and pursue men who attempt to subvert the interests of our nation."

"You are...a spy?"

"I prefer to view myself as a protector of the liberties and privileges all Englishmen enjoy. I'm assisted in that aim by a number of men at all levels of society, in and out of government. Such as Sergeant Wilkerson, who approached you that night."

"Then why—" Teagan began, but Riverton waved him to silence.

"I shall explain. You were quite justified in assuming, by the manner in which the job was presented to you, that what you were being offered that night was a treasonous assignment. Particularly after that episode with your cousin, I was reasonably sure what caliber of man you are. But before I could ask you to assist me, I needed to be absolutely convinced of your honor. Given the straits to which you were reduced, I knew if you would not stoop to betrayal then, you were incapable of it."

Teagan sat back in his chair, trying to sort out all the revelations. "I...I'm a bit taken aback."

Riverton laughed softly. "As well you might be. I'd known for some time you must be a man of intelligence. You'd not have survived solely by gaming otherwise. It remained only to determine if the caliber of your character matched that of your wits. Now that I am convinced it does...would you be interested in assisting me?"

A covert fighter protecting English society against treason and corruption. Teagan grinned. Quite an extraordinary position for a half-breed Irishman.

"What would you have me do?"

"Actually, the assignment offered that night was genuine—if the opposite of what you were led to infer. I've been watching a minor government official whom, lamentably, we believe is selling copies of secret documents to the French. We know dispatches are being sent from his home to Dover. We need to know the identity of the person or persons who are receiving them and carrying them to France."

"And I would determine that, under guise of being the runner paid to transport the packets?"

"Yes. We want a full description of the recipient, plus any information you can glean on where he comes from, whether he carries the messages to France personally or turns them over to a different agent, and by what means the messages themselves leave England. Information that might be gleaned from conversation and observation by a gambler flush with a new stake, while he plied his luck at cards in a Dover tavern."

Riverton paused. "I would be remiss if I did not warn that 'tis dangerous work, Fitzwilliams. With the financial rewards so great and the consequences of discovery so dire, men would kill to protect their investments and cover up their involvement."

"'Tis not that part that troubles me, my lord." Teagan frowned, his excitement dimmed. "If I understand you correctly, in the job you envision I would continue to play the Jester? A man living by his wits and the roll of the dice? 'Tis precisely that life I wish to escape."

"I think we might be able to accommodate both our aims. You want to be readmitted to the Polite World. For that, only two things are essential—the correct backing, and money." Riverton gave him a sardonic smile. "Though it pains me to admit how shallow our privileged world can be, once it becomes known you have Lady Charlotte's support, and once you begin spending the funds I will make available to you, I believe you will find Society pleased to accord you a very warm welcome back!"

Teagan took a moment to absorb the import of Riverton's words. "Even if I appeared still to spend my life gaming, among company of rather dubious reputation?"

Riverton shrugged. "I offer you Lord Crandall, Westerley, and any number of similar fribbles."

Teagan laughed without humor. "Point taken. You are sure I would be of more use to you as the Jester than, say, as a respectable secretary or assistant?"

"You would be of nearly irreplaceable value in such a role. Men who can move easily—and when need be, invisibly—among all levels of society are extremely rare. You would be performing an invaluable service for me—and your country. A service that would have to remain unacknowledged, of course. But there would be a handsome monetary reward, quite enough to support rumors of newly acquired wealth. So…will you assist me?"

Teagan sat silent, considering. He would be restored to Society, have an income that forever freed him from fear of want. But…in the eyes of everyone, he would still be the irresponsible Teagan Fitzwilliams, gambler and rogue.

Not the responsible man with a respectable position beside whom Valeria could stand with honor.

"I trust the lady will have you, anyway."

Teagan's gaze jerked back to Riverton. "How did you…"

The minister smiled. "Fine spymaster I'd be if I didn't know where my operatives were at all times, eh, Fitzwilliams? She's lovely, and I wish you the best of luck winning her hand. Though, by what I saw at the Insley ball, and by Wilkerson's news from the docks, I suspect her heart is yours already." His face sobered. "This is not precisely what you envisioned, I realize. But the work of combating England's enemies is constant, and vitally important. Can I count on you?"

I am already proud to call you my friend. Valeria had been ready to stand by him, even as an indigent gamester. Still…Teagan wanted so much for her to know he was now doing something of which she could truly be proud.

"Would I be able to tell her the truth?"

"In vague generalities, perhaps. 'Tis not wise for any of us to divulge specifics to our loved ones. As you can understand, not only would we risk inadvertent disclosure, such knowledge would place them at risk."

Teagan extended his hand. "When do I begin?"

Smiling, Riverton shook it. "Shall we discuss it further tomorrow? When I bring back your stallion. Consider him the first payment on what England owes you."

Chapter Nineteen

A month later, grubby and bone-weary, Teagan rode Ailainn back to his aunt's town house in Mount Street. The report he had just delivered to Riverton, painstakingly gathered over many evenings of gaming and not a few heart-stopping nights trailing a man he'd observed with the barkeep to whom he'd given his packets, should lay the groundwork for breaking up the ring that was marketing the stolen dispatches. Riverton had commended him on his work, Teagan recalled with a novel sense of satisfaction.

Riverton also told him that while he was away, Aunt Charlotte had been staging his reintroduction to the ton. He should expect several months of dinners, balls and receptions, during which Lady Charlotte would manipulate the social connections necessary to guarantee his permanent acceptance. After that, Riverton warned, Teagan's worst problem would be avoiding the schemes of matchmaking mamas who, assured of his restored status, would be almost as devious as their government traitor in attempting to trap the handsome, newly rich Mr. Fitzwilliams into marriage.

Recalling how Lady Insley had nearly fainted at the idea of admitting him to her ball, Teagan had difficulty believing the warning. But he'd gladly run a gauntlet far more dangerous than girlish sighs and matchmaking stratagems in exchange for the stature that would allow him to court Valeria Arnold with honor.

He'd debated penning her a note...but Riverton was correct. 'Twas better not to invite speculation by writing from Dover, nor could he reveal what he was doing there. Instead, he'd concluded, he'd wait until he could journey to Winterpark and speak with her face-to-face...and ask for her hand.

'Twas early evening by the time he'd returned Ailainn to the stables, ordered up hot food and water from the kitchen, and proceeded up the stairs to his rooms.

He sank into one of the leather armchairs, too weary to move, wanting nothing more than a warm bath, a warm meal and sleep. A knock at the door made him look up.

"Aunt Charlotte!"

"Welcome home, Teagan!" She walked over and bent as if to hug him, but he fended her off.

"I'm all over mud and smelling of horse."

She gave him a quick hug nonetheless. "As if I care for that! I'm so relieved you are safely back. I know you cannot tell me where you were or what you were doing, but I do know it was most probably dangerous."

Teagan gazed up at her anxious face, his respect for her rising another notch. Suddenly he remembered Riverton informing him that the late Lord Darnell had formerly held the position Riverton now occupied. She must have lived with similar uncertainty for years.

"No wonder you are so circumspect! And no wonder that your husband did not wish to add to your worries by seeing you saddled with an ill-behaved, half-Irish brat."

A look of sadness dimmed her face. "That was at least part of his reasoning, I suppose. I never managed to convince him it would be a blessing, not an imposition. But," she said, her expression clearing, "I disturbed you only to

ask if, after you've bathed and dined and had a chance to
rest, you feel you could accompany me this evening.
There's a rout hosted by some friends of Lord Riverton at
which I should like to present you.''

Teagan had to laugh. ''Lord Riverton warned me you'd
begun your campaign for my rehabilitation. I suppose we
must begin, then. But would your hostess not be inconven-
ienced by so late an addition to her guest list?''

''Not at all. I told our hosts, the Earl and Countess of
Beaulieu, I would bring you along if you'd returned.''

A niggle of foreboding arose, and Teagan had a vivid
image of walking through a throng of richly dressed aristocrats, all of them with heads averted, pointedly ignoring
his presence. He'd weathered such humiliation before, but
he dreaded having Aunt Charlotte witness—and be grieved
by—such a spectacle.

''Are you certain 'tis a good idea to begin tonight?''

''Are you too fatigued?''

He could hide behind that excuse, but he owed it to her
to express his reservations honestly. ''I am sure your
friends would greet me kindly, but I am…somewhat concerned about the welcome I'll receive from their other
guests. I…I don't want to embarrass you, Aunt Charlotte.''

Lady Darnell took his hand, mud and all. ''Teagan, do
you trust Lord Riverton's strategies and expertise?''

''Absolutely.''

''Then you mustn't doubt mine in my own arena. I possess a great deal of social power, and I've been wielding
all of it on your behalf.'' She gave a self-deprecating smile.
''I've little enough else to show for my life. For weeks
now, I have regaled every person of prominence, from
Prinny on down, with my delight in having persuaded my
dear cousin's son to take up residence with me. They know
I have settled an income on you and named you my heir.
No one who wishes to safeguard a position in the ton will

dare show you less than extreme cordiality, for all London knows any individual foolish enough to incur my displeasure might as well slink back to whatever provincial backwater from which they sprang. In fact, I rather fear you will be flattered and toadied to a most uncomfortable degree.''

His mind still worrying over the prospect of his gracious aunt being wounded by slights directed toward him, it took a moment for the information she'd just delivered to register. "You n-named me your heir?" he echoed.

"Yes. The solicitors completed the paperwork last week. And though I am sure Riverton will see you well compensated for your recent efforts, the income I mentioned is now available for you to draw upon whenever you wish.''

Surprised and moved, Teagan hardly knew what to say. "You are too generous, Aunt Charlotte. I will be well paid for my work—"

"Nonsense. I have a large income in my own right from my grandfather the duke, in addition to the very comfortable legacy Darnell left me. Besides, the family owes you that and more. Uncle Montford should have settled an income upon you when you went to Oxford, if he hadn't been so disagreeably ill-tempered and controlling. You cannot imagine how I regret all those lost years I might have been indulging you in ponies and sweetmeats and all the treasures young lads enjoy.''

"You would have spoiled me outrageously.''

"Indeed I should have. Besides, I understand you may soon be wishing to set up a household of your own. No—I shall not tax you about the lady. I do hope you will bring her to meet me soon, though. So will you not accept the income? It would give me so much pleasure.''

Teagan put his hand to his chin, as if giving her question serious thought. "Now, let me see. Whist, and shall I whistle a fortune down the wind and grieve the heart of a kind lady who's shown me naught but affection since the moment I turned up, like a bad penny, on her doorstep?''

Lady Charlotte burst out laughing. "My, but you sound like your papa when you do that!''

Teagan's merriment vanished. "You...knew my father?''

"Of course! You're his very image. Impossibly handsome he was, magical with horses, and so charming I vow he could coax the birds into song. Quite frankly, I envied your mama." Lady Charlotte's smile faded. "Gwyneth knew what she wanted from the moment she met Michael Fitzwilliams, and he felt the same. 'Tis tragic a love as deep and mutual as theirs ended as it did. But here is Harold with your dinner and your bathwater, so I'll leave you. Can you be ready by nine? Riverton is calling.''

Teagan pushed away a vague sense of unease. "Let the games commence," he said, reaching for the dinner tray.

Lady Charlotte laughed. "Let them commence indeed! And I have no doubt that you will bring home the laurel wreath of social victory!''

After his aunt departed, Teagan began eating while the servant set up the hip bath by the fire. But the meal he'd been so hungry for suddenly seemed tasteless.

Though Lady Charlotte seemed to blame his grandfather for the tragedy that had overcome his parents, Teagan believed a man was accountable for his own actions. Whatever his reasons, Michael Fitzwilliams had abandoned his dying wife and penniless son.

All his youth his Montford relations had drilled into him how much he resembled his irresponsible wastrel of a father. Having Aunt Charlotte, who had actually known the man, confirm the resemblance disturbed him more than he wished to admit.

A few hours later Teagan stood with Lord Riverton at the foot of the stairs, waiting for his aunt to descend. As she appeared on the landing, he heard Riverton's intake of breath and smiled. In her gown of frosted lavender silk, which brought out the blue of her eyes, Lady Charlotte did indeed look magnificent.

With the dignity of a queen, she slowly descended the stairs to take the hand Riverton offered. "Charlotte," the earl said, gazing into her eyes. "How is it you contrive to look younger and more beautiful every time I see you?"

Blushing a little, his aunt laughed. "Really, Mark, were we not such old friends, I would accuse you of flirting. At the least, 'tis bald-faced flattery."

"'Tis the Lord's own truth," Riverton responded. "To me, you still look every inch the beauty who took the ton by storm at her come-out ball."

"Stuff and nonsense," she reproved, tapping him with her fan. "I vow you don't even remember that night."

"Do I not?" Riverton replied. "You wore a gown of celestial blue satin over an open robe of white, with a wreath of white rosebuds in your hair. I thought you the most exquisite creature I'd ever beheld."

The teasing look on his aunt's face faded. "Y-you do remember," she faltered.

"Every moment," Riverton affirmed, his voice intense.

So that is how the land lies, Teagan thought, his smile broadening.

A blush tinging her cheeks, his aunt turned toward Teagan. "I expect we mustn't keep the horses standing. Teagan, you will give me your arm?"

"Of course, Aunt Charlotte." He threw the older man an apologetic glance as his aunt, after according Riverton a rather nervous smile, passed him to take Teagan's hand.

Teagan thought he heard the earl sigh, and then they were descending the stairs to the carriage.

"Are you acquainted with our hosts this evening, Teagan?" Lord Riverton asked as they entered the vehicle.

"Lord Beaulieu," Teagan said, trying to place the name. "Ah, he's the 'Puzzlebreaker' who founded that club devoted to the solution of mathematical problems?"

"Yes. An interesting and intelligent man," Riverton replied. "Also an associate of mine."

Teagan glanced up at Riverton, who gave him a slight nod. Another member of Riverton's network, he surmised.

"His wife is a lovely lady, formerly widow of Viscount Charleton," Lady Charlotte said. "I was particularly glad you were able to join us this evening, for this will be her last public entertainment. She's in a delicate condition and is about to leave London for her confinement."

"First child," Riverton said with a laugh. "Beaulieu is so nervous, you'd think he were about to give birth."

"As well he should be nervous," Lady Charlotte replied sharply. "So many things can go wrong."

She averted her face, and Lord Riverton reached over to touch her hand. "I'm sorry, Charlotte," he said quietly. "That was poorly said."

She shook her head slightly and turned to the window. "Ah, we've arrived. What a crush of carriages!"

Teagan had seldom seen his imperturbable employer so at a loss for words, and felt a sympathetic pang. With a hopeless shrug at Teagan, Riverton turned to help Lady Charlotte descend from the carriage.

Then they were caught up in the throng and borne along to the receiving line. Lady Charlotte again took Teagan's arm, presenting him to her acquaintances as they waited.

Had it not been so bitterly ironic, Teagan might have laughed out loud. His aunt's prediction had been only too correct. Gentlemen who a month previous would scarcely have accorded him a glance, much less a word, lingered to shake his hand, two of them insinuating they would be delighted to introduce his name as a prospective member of their club. Matrons who had shunned his gaze and crossed the street to avoid subjecting their innocent offspring to the contagion of his proximity now flocked around him as if he'd discovered the secret location of the fountain of youth, their blushing daughters in tow. Before he'd met his hosts, he'd been pressed to sign a dozen dance cards.

All this courtesy was being extended, he thought with faint contempt, to a man who had reportedly just returned from a spate of gaming at the spas along the coast. Wealth and sponsorship were indeed splendid launderers of character, it appeared.

After being kindly greeted by the earl and his countess, he was borne off by Lady Charlotte, who insisted on claiming him for the first dance.

As he returned her afterward to Riverton's waiting arm, Holden Insley called a greeting.

"Mr. Fitzwilliams, may I join the multitude—" Insley waved at the eager crowd already pressing up to them "—in congratulating you on your recent good fortune!"

"Thank you, Holden. I must admit I'm finding the change a bit...overwhelming."

"I cannot think of anyone more deserving of good fortune. I had best release you, though," he said with a chuckle, "before some impatient matron with a daughter to present stabs me to death with a quill from her ostrich plume headdress."

He walked off, leaving Teagan to parry the enthusiastic greetings of several such matrons. After signing yet another dance card and extracting himself from the lady's clinging hand, he attempted to head toward the refreshment room, where he'd seen Riverton disappear.

"Well, well, Jester! If you've not landed on your feet like the proverbial tomcat."

Teagan looked up to see Rafe Crandall blocking his path, swaying slightly, the equally inebriated Wexley behind him. "Stap me, if I didn't damn well nearly swallow my teeth t'other day when Winslow—family's all to pieces, y'know, and three daughters to marry off—put up your name for membership at White's!" He raised a champagne glass to Teagan, slopping some of the contents. "I shall try to win some of that new blunt off you, eh? Though I do think it blasted unfair, don't you, Wexley? Doxies already hang over Jester. Now that he's rich, all the hothouse flowers in London'll be rubbin' their petals up against 'im, too."

"Unfair," Wexley echoed, shaking his head and almost losing his balance.

"Watch out. Those virginal buds'll be wantin' to lure you not to pleasurin', but to the parson's mousetrap!"

Had he really spent most of the last ten years in such company as this? Teagan thought with a grimace of distaste. "Thanks for the warning, Rafe. I'll be on my guard."

"See that you are." Crandall wagged a finger in Teagan's face before moving out of his way. "Bad enough t'see you redeemed. If I heard you was to be leg-shackled, 'twould be enough to make a fellow lose his lunch."

As the evening progressed, however, Teagan began to wonder if he might not prefer Rafe's company, after all. He'd lost count of the effusive matrons who'd greeted him and the profusion of tongue-tied maidens who'd been thrust before him, with whom he'd attempted to carry on a stilted, mostly one-sided conversation.

No wonder Valeria wanted no part of this, he thought. For a moment, the urgent desire to gaze on her lovely, intelligent face, hear her musical voice and her witty commentary, filled him with a wave of acute longing.

The strong sense of being watched pulled him from his

reverie. He glanced up to find the Earl of Montford staring at him, a sardonic look on his face.

Teagan stiffened. "Cousin," he said, nodding.

Montford didn't return the courtesy. Before Teagan could summon up a properly piquing comment, yet another eager matron rushed up to introduce her daughter and solicit his signature on her dance card.

Montford watched until the pair walked away. "My, what a spectacle. But I'm not as easy to gull. Blood will out. I'll wager those little fillies making eyes at you wouldn't be so eager to jump into harness if they knew how quickly your dear papa abandoned your mama. You may have induced Lady Charlotte to cover your sins and endow you with funds—or should I say 'seduced'?—but—"

Riverton seemed to materialize out of nowhere, to clamp a hand on the earl's arm. "Montford," he interrupted in a low, steely voice, "if you want to keep all your teeth, I advise you not to complete that sentence."

Montford gave Teagan a resentful glance, but fell silent.

"I expect you to treat your cousin, if not with friendliness, at least with courtesy," Riverton added.

After a long moment, Montford turned to give Teagan the minutest of bows. "Cousin. Since you've brought your watchdog, I suppose I must comply."

"You would be advised to remember what this watchdog watched," Riverton said, his tone still menacing. "Recall also that I possess fewer scruples than your noble cousin. Indeed, I must insist that you stroll with me. There seems to be a small matter of which you need reminding."

Riverton swept a gesture toward the door. After an irresolute moment, Montford nodded. Giving Teagan a look of loathing, he followed the cabinet minister.

While Teagan stood watching them, a heavy woman in

a puce gown, her headdress rising several feet above her elaborate coiffeur, bumped into him.

"Why, Mr. Fitzwilliams," she cried in shrill tones, latching on to his arm. "How nice to meet you again. Lady Amesbury, you'll remember! You must come take tea with us tomorrow, must he not, Marianne?"

She jerked forward a thin, plain brunette with the frightened expression of a cornered rabbit. "Y-yes, Mama," she replied in a barely audible voice.

"Marianne has been in raptures over you, Mr. Fitzwilliams! Now, surely you cannot wish to disappoint a lovely young lady, eh? Do say you will come tomorrow."

A scarlet flush mounted the girl's pale cheeks. "Please, Mama," she said in an urgent undertone.

"Pish-tosh, Marianne, sometimes a girl needs to take the lead—and a gentleman don't mind knowing he's appreciated, does he, Mr. Fitzwilliams? You will be there, won't you?" Her grip on his arm tightened, as if she did not intend to release him until she'd obtained his consent.

Her daughter had turned pale, and she looked as if she were about to expire on the spot from mortification. Vulgar and encroaching as Teagan found the mother, he could not help but feel sorry for the girl.

"Should you like me to call?" he asked Miss Marianne.

She goggled at him, as if astounded he'd actually deigned to address her. "I, ah, y-yes," she stuttered.

Already regretting his momentary chivalry, Teagan could do nothing but bow and agree to present himself the following day. Shaking free of Lady Amesbury's arm, he made his way toward the refreshment room, determined to find his aunt and beg her to let them depart.

As it was, he had to endure several more dances before he at last made his escape. His head pounding more painfully than with the worst of cheap brandy hangovers, he sank thankfully into a corner of the coach.

"Aunt Charlotte," he groaned, "I believe I was mistaken. I don't wish to be reinstated, after all."

Riverton chuckled. "You've only begun, my friend. You do realize you are expected to call tomorrow upon every one of the young ladies with whom you danced tonight."

Teagan groaned again. "Do you not have some urgent assignment for me, sir—preferably to the Outer Hebrides?"

"You'll be wishing it were to the Straits of Magellan once you've taken tea with Lady Amesbury," his aunt said.

"I felt sorry for the daughter," Teagan admitted.

Riverton grinned. "By the time tea is concluded, you will doubtless have confirmed the old adage that no good deed remains unpunished."

The carriage slowed before the Mount Street town house, sparing Teagan a reply. As the hour was late and he'd been in the saddle for nearly the whole of the day, he excused himself from having brandy in the parlor with his aunt and Lord Riverton. Though as he mounted the stairs, he could not help throwing a speculative glance back at Riverton, his dark head bent over Lady Charlotte's blond one.

Fatigue was only partly responsible for Teagan's need for solitude. The degree of attention he'd been accorded was, as he'd told Insley, unsettling, and made him speculate that except for the stain it cast upon his reputation, his banishment had perhaps been more boon than bane. Certainly he'd had more intelligent and stimulating conversation in half an hour with Valeria than in that whole evening with a mansion full of people.

Valeria. His thoughts returned to her like a lodestone to the north, but for the first time since he'd left her, worry clouded the purity of his longing to end their separation.

His aunt's and cousin's words echoed in his head.

His parents' love had been deep and mutual, Aunt Charlotte said. Certainly his mother had believed Michael Fitzwilliams's vows of affection, abandoning her privileged place in English society to run off with him.

And then had been left by him to die alone and destitute in a Dublin hovel.

How could his father have loved Gwyneth Hartness—really loved her, as Teagan loved Valeria—and disappear, leaving her ill and penniless, with a young son to care for? Had time and proximity and poverty degraded that deep emotion? Or had he not been capable of love that endured?

Teagan was his father's image, as even Aunt Charlotte had told him. If he persuaded Valeria to pledge him her love, how could he be sure he too did not possess some flaw deep within his character, a weakness that might lead him to one day leave her as well, heartbroken, if not penniless?

Every instinct protested. He loved Valeria with all the strength his soul possessed, and would gladly lay down his life for her.

But could he *live* a lifetime with her?

What, after all, did he know of love or permanence? His sole previous grand amour had endured a mere matter of weeks, and the casual relationships he'd had with women since weren't worthy of mention.

An excruciating memory, perhaps the most devastating of his life and one therefore that he rigidly suppressed, forced itself into consciousness. The look on the face of his Oxford mentor when he'd walked in to find Teagan in flagrante delicto with his son's wife: horror succeeded by sorrow—and deepest disappointment.

Teagan would rather shoot himself than ever bring such a look to the face of Valeria Arnold.

How could he know for sure he would not? Until he could convince himself he could never subject her to that abomination, he must not return for her.

Chapter Twenty

Valeria sat in the estate office trying to force herself to concentrate on the ledger before her. Sighing, she reached over to sip Mercy's special chamomile tea, beside which reposed a basket containing two of Cook's best jam tarts fresh from the oven. Adding their sweet scent was a vaseful of summer's first roses, just delivered by Sissy.

All the staff were so solicitous, trying to cheer their list-less mistress, that she would have to at least nibble at a tart, although it seemed her appetite had vanished with her enthusiasm weeks ago. One drizzly morning that was turn-ing to sunshine as Teagan Fitzwilliams rode away.

For a fortnight after his departure she had been so ill she could not eat at all. Half defiant, half terrified by her folly, she had shared Mercy's unspoken fears. Yet with the relief that came with her courses had also come an unexpectedly deep sense of disappointment.

She had not conceived his child. She would not carry within her a part of him that would belong to her forever. She did not have reason to call him back.

Though that latter thought had occurred only to be con-temptuously dismissed. Teagan had promised to return, and she would wait for him to honor that pledge. She would never stoop to trapping him with a woman's oldest trick. Once had been more than sufficient to give herself in marriage to a man who didn't really want her.

Would Teagan return? In more than two months, she'd received not the briefest of notes. Though he had not promised to write, somehow she'd expected...something. Some contact that assured her that what they'd shared still meant as much to him as it did to her.

Had he won enough to make it back to London? Was he able to reconcile with his family? Was he seeking a position, or now embarked in a new post, and if so, where in England had that taken him? Was he even now making preparations to return to her, buoyed with confidence at the success of his plans?

Or had his family rejected his overtures, leaving him trapped in a gambler's uncertain life, mired in a role he believed made him unworthy to approach her?

Oh Teagan, why have you not written to me? she thought, suppressing the tears that seemed of late to come so easily. Even the worst news would be easier to bear than this uncertainty.

At a soft tap, she looked up, to see Mercy entering.

"We have visitors, Miss Val. No—not him."

Heat burned in her cheeks, followed by anger. Rage at the foolish hope that still caused her heart to leap every time Giddings came in with a tray that might bear a letter, or when she chanced to hear hoofbeats or the rattle of a carriage approaching up the drive.

Mercy came over to place a sympathetic hand on Valeria's shoulder. "I'm right sorry, chick, but 'tis even worse. Sir Arthur and Lady Hardesty are awaiting you."

"The Hardestys!" she exclaimed with a groan. "Whatever brought them here?"

"Lady Hardesty says they were journeying to London, and Winterpark being but half a day's travel off the main road, she felt she simply must stop to see you.'' Irony colored the nurse's tone.

"How did she even know I resided here?'' Valeria grumbled. "Ah, yes. Maria Edgeworth, the town crier. Which means she must know all about Grandmamma's bequest, and be even more convinced that I should make the perfect wife for her son. I don't suppose you could say I'm out?''

"I could, but 'twould only delay her.'' A grim look came into Mercy's face. "She was hinting that they expected to be avisiting near on a week.''

"A week!'' Valeria said, her voice rising to a squeak. "I shall be ready to do murder within a day!'' An even more unwelcome memory intruded, and she groaned again. "'Tis worse than her ploy to bring me to Hardesty's Castle. I should not be surprised if she intends to remain until she manages to throw Sir Arthur together with me in some 'compromising' situation that, she will insist, requires us to marry in order to preserve my reputation.''

Valeria paced to the window. "I shall see them now. Then, while Lady Hardesty rests later this afternoon, I can figure out some means to detach them from Winterpark.''

Smiling with gritted teeth, Valeria entered the parlor to greet her unwanted guests. "Sir Arthur, Lady Hardesty. How…unexpected to see you.''

"Dear, dear Valeria, how could we be so close and not stop to express our condolences over your grievous loss?'' Lady Hardesty exclaimed, as if they'd come for a morning call instead of from a distance of several hundred miles. "Besides, traveling is so injurious to my delicate health, I must interrupt my journey at frequent intervals.''

Valeria cast a skeptical eye over Lady Hardesty's stout figure and glowing cheeks. Sir Arthur, however, did look pale and uncomfortable. Not entirely, she suspected, from the motion of the carriage.

Taking pity on him, she extended her hand. "Sir Arthur, you appear fatigued."

He kissed her fingers. "But you, Lady Arnold, are, as always, kindness and beauty personified."

"Oh, Arthur is always in perfect health!" his mother said. "Now *I* am feeling rather faint. Perhaps some tea and cakes would restore me. That is, assuming the cook kept here by Lady Winterdale is superior to the creature you employed at Eastwoods. And Valeria, dear, why are your entryway and mirrors not still draped in black?"

"It has been more than three months since Grand-mamma's passing," Valeria replied, ignoring the first remark and trying to rein in her temper.

"Well, one must not be remiss in observing the proprieties! Appearances are important, especially before the servants. At least you are still wearing your black. Although you must tell your maid—I trust you now have someone more skilled than that elderly nurse—to be more careful how she irons the bombazine. I believe I see a shiny spot on your skirt."

"You must excuse me while I go see about refreshments," Valeria said, fearing for her temper—or the nearest china vase—if she did not make an imminent escape.

"Very well, if you cannot trust your butler to make the arrangements. After we've eaten you can take Arthur for a walk in your gardens, which my guidebook tells me are excellent. A walk is so beneficial for the constitution."

Valeria wasn't *that* sorry for Arthur Hardesty. "Then he should escort you, Lady Hardesty. 'Twill help you recover from your journey."

Her smile disintegrating into a grimace, Valeria stalked out of the room and leaned back against the closed door with a sigh.

Giddings approached, concern creasing his brow. "Is something wrong, my lady?"

"N-no, Giddings. My...guests are a bit trying.

"Please send in tea and cakes." A thought occurred, and she added, "Ask Mercy to prepare me a pot of the chamomile, as well."

There was nothing humorous about the Hardestys lingering at Winterpark.

She couldn't endure a week of Lady Hardesty's tactless manipulation. She must find a way to speed their departure, she thought as she reentered the parlor.

She found Lady Hardesty examining the jade figurines on the mantel.

"Antique, are they?" her ladyship inquired, as if inspecting the possessions of one's hostess were part of the normal protocol of an afternoon call.

"Ming dynasty, the registry reports," Valeria replied, her temper once more aflame. "If you would be seated, Lady Hardesty, tea should be here momentarily." Turning to Sir Arthur in an attempt to redirect the conversation away from his mother, she inquired, "How goes the farm work at Hardesty's Castle? Was the shearing successful?"

"It went splendidly," Lady Hardesty replied for him. "Arthur, you must tell dear Valeria about the several days you spent overseeing the shearing at Eastwoods. Arthur takes particular interest in insuring your property is correctly managed."

I'll bet he does, Valeria thought acidly.

"Masters appeared more frail than ever when I visited last week," Lady Hardesty continued. "And your housemaid, Sukey Mae, the one I often recommended you dismiss, has proved herself the trollop everyone knew she was. Ran off with the squire's groom—and no wedding before that trip!"

"Ah, here's the tea," Valeria said, as Giddings came in bearing the massive tray. A merciful space of time was occupied fixing cups and dispensing the jam tarts.

"The small pot contains my herbal brew," Valeria informed Lady Hardesty, who was avidly emptying her plate. "My own health has been indifferent for weeks, and I've had to resort to herbal infusions to settle my stomach. Indeed, my throat has been rather raw and I fear I may be developing a cough. I was...reposing when you arrived."

"Valeria, dear, you work too hard. Managing an estate this size is too arduous a task for a gently bred lady. You need a husband to take the burden from those slender shoulders—don't she, Arthur?" Lady Hardesty cast an arch look at her son, who choked on his tea.

To wrest control of an estate as wealthy as Winterpark, Lady Hardesty was apparently prepared to risk her oft-proclaimed delicate health—which was not so delicate that it prevented that lady from consuming an impressive number of jam tarts, Valeria noted.

"Oh, and speaking of bad breeding...I've just received the most amazing news! It seems that blackguard I warned you about last winter is now running the most astounding rig on another supposedly genteel lady of the ton!"

"Mama, really," Sir Arthur objected. "Lady Charlotte Darnell was first cousin to Teagan Fitzwilliams's mother."

Valeria's heart skipped a beat and she almost dropped her teacup. "T-Teagan Fitzwilliams?" she stuttered.

"So-called 'aunt' she may be, but I still say there's something havey-cavey going on. As unrepentant a gamester as ever, and out of the blue, here he is living in Lady Charlotte's home, being introduced by her to Society and, rumor has it, even named her heir!"

"Perhaps he has finally reconciled with his mother's family," Sir Arthur said. "In that case, we should commend both sides for settling their differences."

"Well, I think a woman of her mature years should know better than to have been taken in by such a rogue!"

"Apparently she's not the only one so taken in," Sir

Arthur persisted, some irritation in his tone. "Your friend Maria said in her letter that not only is Lady Charlotte introducing him about, he is being everywhere received by the first families. She even wrote that several young ladies have already set their caps at him."

"Set their caps at him and the Darnell fortune," Lady Hardesty retorted. "More fools, they! That squabby little Marianne Amesbury he's said to be courting has neither wit nor beauty. Ha! Offspring of a nobleman and a vulgar Cit's daughter! If she does manage to snare Fitzwilliams, I predict she'll end up abandoned just like his mama, Lady Gwyneth."

"You have ever been prejudiced against poor Mr. Fitzwilliams!" her son exclaimed. "As I've often told you, Mama, I knew him well at Eton, and *I* found no vice in him."

For the next few moments mother and son squabbled over the merits of Teagan's character, requiring no comment from Valeria. Which was fortunate, for she did not think she could have managed a coherent word.

By the time an uneasy truce finally brought momentary silence, she had recovered herself enough to quickly insert, "How fatigued you must be, Lady Hardesty. Please, allow Giddings to show you and Sir Arthur to your chambers. I myself intend to seek my bed." She rose and walked swiftly over to yank on the bell pull.

"You do look rather unwell, Lady Arnold," Sir Arthur observed. "Mama, I believe we are tiring our hostess."

Snatching up the last of the jam tarts, Lady Hardesty allowed her son to hoist her to her feet. "You'll be able to change to half-mourning soon, Valeria dear, which will not make you look as haggard as that black. Very well, Arthur, I'm coming. We shall see you for dinner."

Valeria marched over and yanked open the parlor door,

causing Giddings, who'd apparently been leaning into it while he turned the handle, to nearly fall into the room.

"Please convey Sir Arthur and Lady Hardesty to their chambers," she said, wild with impatience to be rid of them so she might sort out her shocked and conflicting emotions.

"This way, Lady Hardesty, Sir Arthur," Giddings intoned, and at long last led them away.

She needed silence and solitude. Without even waiting to find a wrap, Valeria half-ran to the library, jerked open the terrace door, and fled into the gardens.

She should be thrilled for him. Apparently Teagan had succeeded in obtaining a rapprochement with his family, although according to Lady Hardesty's informant he had not given up gaming. His reputation must also be a fair way to being mended if he was being received not just by his own family, but by households with marriageable daughters.

Were the young ladies tossing their caps at him?

Was he in fact courting one in particular?

The pain of that thought cut so deep Valeria's knees were suddenly weak, and she had to sit down abruptly on the nearest garden bench. No, she could not believe the vows of constancy he'd uttered with such fervent conviction could have been forgotten so quickly and completely.

Besides, Maria Edgeworth was the worst sort of gossip, whose tales could not be depended upon to contain more than a modicum of truth.

But if he had reconciled with his family and nearly restored his good name, why had he not come back for her? Or at least written of his progress?

Perhaps he was still arranging employment, though if she could believe the report of his being made the heir of his mother's wealthy cousin, he'd have no need of it.

Or perhaps Valeria was an even greater fool than the Cit's daughter who thought to capture Teagan and the Darnell fortune. Perhaps she, too, was merely another woman he'd bewitched, pleasured well and left behind.

Even as her heart cried out against that painful assessment, the sound of footsteps crunching on the gravel pathway caught her ear. She looked up to see Giddings approaching. ''A letter for you, my lady,'' he said.

He had written, after all! Her bruised spirits rebounding with a joyous leap, Valeria thanked the butler and took the folded paper from his hand. Fingers trembling with eagerness, she unfolded the missive.

And found at the bottom of the page of sloping masculine scrawl the signature ''W. Parham.''

Disappointment struck her like a blow to the chest. She shut her eyes against the tears that threatened, her rigidly clenched fingers crumpling the paper.

She would not weep. She'd vowed over Hugh's grave never to waste another tear on a man, and she had no intention now of breaking that vow.

Some time later, when she felt she could open her eyes without the vista beyond them blurring, she smoothed the paper and read Sir William's letter.

My dear Lady Arnold, I hope this finds you recovering your spirits after the pain of your recent loss. I certainly wish it may, for London seems very dull without you, and I impatiently await your return to the city.

The Season continues much the same, though you will probably be pleased to learn your friend Mr. Fitzwilliams has reconciled with his family and is presently residing with his mother's cousin Lady Charlotte Darnell, a most influential Society hostess. He's become quite the darling of the young ladies, as one might expect of a gentleman of his charm and address.

Please know I stand ready to lend you whatever assistance it is within my power to afford. I should be honored to come to Winterpark and escort you back to London whenever you are feeling sufficiently recovered to undertake the journey. Your friendship has been my most particular joy, and it remains my fervent wish that it might continue to grow and deepen.

In hopes of seeing you again soon, I remain...

Senses dulled to a low throb of agony, Valeria refolded the letter and stared sightlessly at the garden.

So most of what the Hardestys had reported was true. Teagan was restored to favor. She must be glad for that.

But if he had not felt compelled to inform her of so important a development, he could not hold her in the same degree of regard and affection she did him. While she worried and wondered and pined away at Winterpark, he had been disporting himself with the eligible ladies of London. In all likelihood, he was never coming back.

The conclusion cut like a sword slash to the bone. She had to breathe in and out slowly, cautiously, until the pain was bearable.

If Teagan Fitzwilliams was not coming back, what was Valeria Arnold to do with her life?

At least part of Lady Hardesty's assertion was true. Including Winterpark, the London town house, Eastwoods, and several other minor properties she'd not even visited yet, her estates now required more work than she wished to take on alone. And having tasted the delights of passion, she did not wish to live the rest of her life celibate.

After secretly hoarding for several weeks the suspicion that she might be with child, she now found the idea immensely appealing. She would, she concluded, very much like children of her own.

Which all suggested that, as Lady Hardesty would no doubt be delighted to point out, Valeria ought to seriously consider the idea of remarrying.

Not Arthur Hardesty, of course. But Sir William Parham, who'd been her quiet support through the trial of Lady Winterdale's funeral, who'd both generously alleged Teagan Fitzwilliams's honesty and with self-deprecating modesty expressed his own wistful desire to win her affection, might be the very man.

Quiet, dependable, well-respected. A skillful husband of her new estate and a kind husband to her person. A good provider who would be a fond father to her children. Perhaps even a man with whom she could share a mutually enjoyable passion, if not one as mindlessly intoxicating as that which she'd experienced…elsewhere.

It suddenly occurred to her that in Sir William's letter she had the answer to all her dilemmas.

She would not have to outwit or displace the Hardestys. Nor did she need to remain passively waiting for a man who could not even be bothered to pen her a letter. She would simply announce to her erstwhile guests that she'd received an urgent summons to return to London immediately.

Of course, she would assure them, they were welcome to rest at Winterpark until Lady Hardesty recovered fully from the rigors of their previous journey. Since circumstances compelled her to travel at a pace far too fatiguing for one of her ladyship's delicate constitution, Valeria would have to deny herself the pleasure of their company on the road.

Once there, she would see if, from the ashes of heartache and disappointment, she might be able to build a new relationship. One whose virtues of friendship, mutual respect and permanence compensated for its lacking heart-stopping extremes of ecstasy and despair.

Teagan Fitzwilliams is in London, her heart whispered.

London is a large metropolis, answered her head. And she had no desire whatsoever to see him.

* * *

In the late morning ten days later, Teagan reclined in the leather armchair in his sitting room, trying to summon up some enthusiasm for the masquerade ball Aunt Charlotte wished him to escort her to this evening.

The patina of social acceptance had quickly worn thin. 'Twas amusing, Teagan thought, that this former social pariah who'd been banned as a threat to virginal heiresses, was now, as heir to a sizable fortune, in danger from them.

The Marriage Mart of London society must be negotiated by a single gentleman of means with the caution of a Castlereagh, he'd discovered. He must not pay undue attention to any one maiden lest he give rise to expectations he had no intentions of fulfilling. And he must be ever mindful of the circumstances and chaperones attending any maiden with whom he found himself, so as to avoid potentially compromising situations.

Such as had been the case with the Amesbury chit. A moment of compassion had led him to ten days' worth of intricate social ballet in order to extricate himself short of a declaration, but with honor intact.

And though he pitied the poor girl, his sympathies ended well short of offering marriage. The contrast between her painfully young and diffident character—unfortunately all too typical of the tender maidens to whom he'd been introduced—and Valeria Arnold only made the intelligence, wit, independence and passion of that lady more striking.

The lady to whom every night he made love in his dreams, every morning awoke disappointed not to find in his arms. With his social position firmly secured, he ached to return to her.

If only he could banish the doubts that spawned nightmares that woke him, bathed in sweat, wracked by visions of a woman dying alone and abandoned, a woman with his mother's body and Valeria's face.

He had betrayed a trust before, he thought, recalling with a wrench of pain his Oxford mentor's sorrowful face. What made him so sure he would not do so again?

His father's son...cast in his father's image. Flesh of flesh, blood of blood—and heart of deceitful heart?

He slammed his fist down on the table in despair. Somehow he must decide soon...before he lost everything by making Valeria lose faith in his vows to return.

"Teagan, may I come in?"

He started at the sound of his aunt's voice. "Of course, Aunt Charlotte."

She entered a moment later, a small wooden box in her hands. "While up in the attics searching for my costume, I found this. 'Tis something I'd always intended to give you someday, but had forgotten I still possessed."

She held it out. Curious, he took it.

"It contains your mama's letters. The clergyman who found you discovered these at the rooming house in which you'd been living when Gwyneth died. Uncle Montford was going to burn them, but Gwen's old governess, knowing how close we had been, spirited them away and sent them to me. I kept them, thinking one day you might like to have them."

"Have you read them?"

"No. Most of them were written by your father to Gwen, and I felt they were too private for my eyes. But I hoped perhaps they might help you better understand the man your mother loved so much."

Teagan was not so sure he wished to read them, either. "Thank you, Aunt Charlotte. That was very kind."

She smiled. "I must help Charity finish my costume, so I'll leave you to them." Dropping a quick kiss on his forehead, she slipped back out.

Teagan put the box on the table and stared at it.

Why should he wish to read the letters of a man who

had so bewitched his mother that she'd followed him to her death, in heartbreak and penury?

His grandfather was right; they ought to be burned. He carried the box to the hearth.

But as he removed the first letter, the faded, spidery script of the missives written nearly thirty years ago by the man whose blood coursed through his veins, but about whom he knew so little, cast an irresistible spell.

Teagan walked back to his armchair, set the box on the table beside it and began to read.

The notes were arranged in roughly chronological order. Apparently once Lady Gwyneth's parents became aware of her attraction to a totally ineligible Irish groom, the young lady was packed off to her cousin's and the groom banished to the stud farm at Langdon—the same one Teagan had later managed, he realized. The two had then established a clandestine correspondence.

The bulk of the letters expressed their love and longing, their search to find some way to bridge the social chasm that separated them. And when the lady's parents threatened to put an end to her infatuation by marrying her off to a more acceptable suitor, Teagan found a note planning an elopement.

Despite his initial disdain, he was caught up in the drama of his parents' love and separation, which paralleled in some ways his own with Valeria.

But it was the final two letters that riveted his attention. The first, written by his father from the port of Galway, sent love and encouragement to his wife and young son in Dublin, and adjured them to stay at the boardinghouse where he'd left money for them during his journey to the Americas. Once he'd settled and bought property, he would send for them to begin a new life in a land where no one would think twice about an earl's daughter marrying an

Irish groom. A land where a man's character and achievements, not his pedigree, determined his worth.

The last letter, from a shipping company in Galway, dated just a few days before his mama's death, regretted to inform Mrs. Fitzwilliams of the demise of her husband aboard the brigantine the *Merry Alice,* lost with all hands in a violent storm off the Irish coast.

Teagan sat motionless, the letter clutched in his fingers, as the full implications of his father's correspondence gradually filled his mind.

Michael Fitzwilliams had loved his wife and son until the day he died. He'd left them to travel to the Americas where he, a man possessed of sufficient funds to buy both overseas passage and property upon arrival, intended to build a new life for them.

Not a wastrel. Not irresponsible. Not a careless bastard who'd abandoned his own son and the woman who'd loved him to die in penury.

Carefully Teagan refolded the letters and tucked them back in the wooden box. His one legacy from the father who'd loved him.

Then an even more arresting conclusion captured him.

If his father had honored his love and trust until death, then Teagan need no longer fear to go to Valeria.

The box forgotten, he ran to find his aunt.

He tracked her down in the sewing room and begged for a private moment. Obligingly, she dismissed her maid and beckoned him to a chair.

"What is it that has put that starry light in your eyes, my dear?"

"I shall tell you all about it later. But for now I need to inform you I cannot escort you tonight. I must leave London as soon as I can pack a bag."

"In such a rush? May I ask your destination?"

"Winterpark, a country estate that is now home to Lady

Arnold, the late Dowager Countess of Winterdale's grand-daughter.''

His aunt's delighted smile faded. "Lady Arnold?" she repeated, distress in her eyes. "Are you telling me Valeria Arnold is the lady for whom you've been pining?"

"I shall pine no longer," he said, excitement bringing a smile to his lips. "In fact, if I am very lucky, I shall bring her back to introduce to you—as my affianced wife. Give me a kiss, and I'll be off."

He bent down, lips pursed. She ducked her head to avoid his salute. "Lady Arnold is not at Winterpark."

Teagan paused. "You must be mistaken. I know she retired there after Lady Winterdale's death."

"Yes, but she returned to London about a week ago."

Valeria here? Then why had she not contacted him?

"Are you sure?" he demanded.

"Absolutely. She paid me a call yesterday. Oh, Teagan, there were a number of ladies present, and I'm afraid they were gossiping—about you."

Teagan grew very still. "And what were they saying?"

"Lady Jersey and Mrs. Drummond-Burrell and Princess Esterhazy were here, and the princess commended you for your recent exemplary behavior. Then Sally asserted that there is nothing so engaging as an almost-reformed rake. When I protested that assessment of you, she pointed out as proof all the young ladies whose mamas have been pressing invitations on you, and the Amesbury chit everyone says you've been courting. Then...then Lady Arnold asked me if it were true that you were courting her, and I said I wasn't sure, but that you had called there quite often and were not the sort of man to trifle with a girl's affections."

Teagan groaned and closed his eyes.

"Oh, Teagan, I'm so sorry! I had no idea—"

''No, how could you? But I must seek her out at once, before my case is irretrievably lost.''

''Does she have any idea of your true feelings?''

''An idea, but I never confessed my love openly.''

Lady Charlotte gave him a push. ''Then you've not a moment to spare. Sally Jersey told me after Lady Arnold left that Sir William Parham had confided to her he meant to propose this very afternoon!''

Chapter Twenty-One

Valeria sat by the window in a pool of early afternoon sunshine, waiting for Sir William to arrive. He'd begged leave to call upon her at one. She was reasonably sure he meant to make her a proposal of marriage.

She was not at all sure what she would reply.

Deny it as she may, she'd been secretly hoping ever since her arrival a week ago that, some morning or afternoon, Molly would run in to announce that Teagan Fitzwilliams had called. She'd held her breath at each of the evening entertainments she'd attended, usually on Sir William's arm, half hoping, half dreading to meet Teagan.

He hadn't called. She hadn't met him.

Ever since arriving, she'd also debated the wisdom of writing to inform him of her return. But what would she say? ''Dear sir, I have come back to London to see if the passionate love you made to me at Winterpark was indicative of a lasting affection, and to discover if you truly meant your vow to return.''

She'd concluded 'twas impossible. Surely he would soon discover that she had returned. If he wished to make good his vow, he would seek her out.

But when days passed with no word of him, in desperation she'd actually called at his aunt's house, almost expiring with fear that he might be in the parlor with his aunt when she arrived. Mercifully, he hadn't been, but what she'd learned there had been almost as heartbreaking as being treated by him with casual courtesy as an acquaintance with whom he'd once explored the city.

According to the ladies present, including his aunt, Teagan was in fact courting the Amesbury girl. Even more damning, Lady Charlotte had answered all her questions with a cordial openness that made painfully clear she had no notion that Teagan was even acquainted with Valeria.

If he had not so much as mentioned her to the lady who had opened her home to him and made him her heir, Valeria could not fool herself any longer that he'd ever harbored toward her any truly serious intentions.

He'd only promised to come back. She did not doubt the intensity of the passion they'd shared, and was certain if she offered herself, Teagan might oblige her by continuing their affair. But he'd never spoken of love, never offered marriage. Only her imagination had filled in those gaps.

Whereas Sir William was about to pledge her both. Was she ready to abandon her consuming, painful, hopeless infatuation with Teagan Fitzwilliams in exchange for the solid reality of Sir William's care and comfort?

She heard murmuring in the hallway, and a moment later Jennings opened the door to announce Sir William.

He walked toward her smiling, warm affection in his eyes. She allowed him to kiss her hands.

"Valeria, I expect you know why I asked if I might call on you today. It cannot come as any surprise that I—"

"Please, Sir William, go no further!" she exclaimed. "If I am not being too presumptuous in assuming a proposal is your intent, I beg you will not."

Surprise and distress replaced the glow in his eyes. "You find me so distasteful? But I thought—"

"You know I do not! You are everything that is fine and caring and admirable. It's just...I am not sure yet whether I can return your sentiments with the fervency you deserve. For a time, I harbored a...prior attachment, from which I have not yet entirely recovered."

He regarded her gravely. "I see. Does the...object of this attachment not reciprocate your affection?"

"N-no. Oh, you mustn't fault the gentleman—'twas mere foolishness on my part. But I would not insult the purity of the sentiments you've expressed by leaving you in ignorance of my...circumstances."

He smiled wryly. "You haven't yet given me time to express my sentiments," he pointed out.

She felt her cheeks flush. "N-no, I suppose not."

"Valeria, do you think there is a chance you might...recover from this prior attachment?"

She returned his serious regard. "'Tis possible."

"You are correct in assuming that I wish to hold the whole heart and loyalty of the lady I ask to be my wife. But as long as there is still a chance your affections may become as fully engaged as I would wish, I must be content with that." He gently tipped up her chin with his finger. "Not happy, you understand. But willing to wait until you are ready to offer more. Have we a bargain, then?"

"I...suppose so," she murmured, watching a hotter light spark in his eyes before his gaze lowered to her mouth.

And then he swiftly bent to kiss her.

'Twas a mere brush of his lips, which he made no attempt to prolong or deepen. Yet when he straightened, his breathing was uneven and the hand at her chin shaking.

"Yes, I am entirely ready to hope for more," he said.

Valeria wasn't sure what she was ready for. Sir William's kiss had certainly been pleasant enough, but she'd felt—disloyal. As if betraying a trust.

"I brought my traveling carriage," he said, stepping

back, "in hopes that, had I received a favorable reply to the question you prevented my asking, I might have conveyed you to meet my mother. But since you haven't precisely refused, either, I should still like you to accompany me. 'Tis a fine afternoon, the drive is quite pleasant and my mother is an admirable lady with whom I think you would enjoy becoming acquainted. Will you come?"

Would Sir William attempt more liberties in a closed coach? But if she were contemplating marriage, Valeria ought to take this opportunity to know him and his family better—and to learn how she truly felt about his taking liberties.

"Yes, Sir William. I should like that very much."

Two hours later Valeria sat beside Sir William as his coach traveled past the lightly wooded fields just north of London. He had not attempted to take more liberties, engaging her instead in easy conversation, and much of the constraint she had initially felt upon being closeted alone with him in the coach had dissipated.

They had just begun a discussion about poetry when a shout, followed in rapid succession by the loud report of a pistol, brought the carriage to an abrupt, jolting halt.

The incident at Dade's Run coming instantly to mind, Valeria drew in an alarmed breath. But before she could move or speak, the carriage door was flung wide and a one-armed figure in a uniform coat too grimy and tattered for her to be able to identify the regiment pointed a pistol at them. "Stand 'n deliver!" he ordered.

Keeping the pistol trained on them, the soldier angled his head back. "Always wanted to say that," he informed someone behind him.

"Get them out of the coach," a muffled voice said.

"You 'eard the guv'ner—out ye go, me pretties. Arms up and no funny business, neither."

"Please, sir, be calm and stop waving that pistol," Sir William implored. "I'll step out if you wish, but let the lady remain in the coach."

"Don't worrit yerself, we don't mean no harm to the lady. But out 'e says, so out ye goes." The soldier motioned with the pistol. "Now, be quick about it."

Indignation had begun to replace Valeria's initial shock. "You, sir, have taken the king's coin. How dare you disgrace your uniform by becoming a common thief?"

"Feisty one, ain't ye?" the soldier said with a chuckle, waving Valeria past him.

Reluctantly she climbed down. Outside she saw two more armed men, pistols trained on their coachman and groom. Then, as Sir William stepped out, a tall figure dressed all in black, a scarf obscuring his face, came from behind the coach and knocked him to the ground. When she cried out in protest, the one-armed soldier turned his pistol on her, forcing her to stand by helplessly while the highwayman swiftly bound the struggling Sir William's wrists behind his back and gagged him.

After the dark-clad bandit finished trussing up Sir William, he nodded to one of his accomplices, who lay down his pistol and came over to bind her wrists as well.

"You will all hang, you know," she said furiously.

The dark-clad man forced Sir William's strenuously resisting body into the coach and shut the door, then turned to her. "Will we now?" he said in an all-too-familiar lilt before clapping a gag over her mouth.

Incensed, she kicked and struggled as he picked her up. "Drive home, easy," he instructed Sir William's coachman, who hastened to obey. Then, hefting her to his chest, he carried her to a waiting gig.

He deposited her beside it and waved a hand at his accomplices, who lowered their weapons and trotted toward horses tethered in the woods beyond the highway. Before she could attempt to scramble away, an awkward business with no hands to brace herself, the bandit once more clasped her to his chest.

Not until Sir Williams's coach was well away and the horsemen nearly out of sight did her abductor remove the gag. Jerking her head, she managed to nip one of his fingers.

He yelped and waved the injured digit. "Sure, and is that any way to reward me for removing the cloth?"

"Teagan Fitzwilliams, I'm going to murder you!"

Grinning, he pulled the mask from his face. "Ah, 'twas certain I was that I'd fooled ye, lass."

"For a few moments only. But what maggot did you take in your head, abducting me off a public highway? And how dare you tie up Sir William? I expect he shall shortly call you out for that affrontery!"

"Whist, but the man's lucky I only tied him up. I should have gutted him for trying to run off with ye. But he's welcome to go a round with me at Gentleman Jackson's, if 'twill soothe his injured sensibilities."

"He wasn't 'running off' with me. We were making an afternoon visit to his mother."

"He had the effrontery to ask to marry ye, didn't he?"

"I cannot see how that is any of your concern."

"Not my concern! Did I not ask ye to wait for me? Did I not vow on my mother's grave I'd be back for ye?"

"Yes—months ago. And not a single word did I hear from that morning to this. Until my former neighbors happened to stop at Winterpark, I had no idea whether you'd even reached London. And when I did hear of you—accepted by your family, embraced by the ton, pursued by the ladies—what was I to think? Even your aunt believed you to be courting Miss Amesbury."

"Actually, I was doing my very best *not* to court her.

You have no idea how complicated it can be for a gentleman who's turned respectable to avoid marriage.''

"It seems you've been doing quite an admirable job.''

"Ah, Valeria-love, I'm sorry for that. After Aunt Charlotte accepted me, and it become apparent that my reputation could be salvaged, all I wanted to do was come for you. But...but then I began to doubt myself. After all, what had I ever known of constancy? All my life, I've been told I am a wastrel just like my father. The only person besides you who ever offered me acceptance and respect, who seemed to believe I possessed honor and character, I repaid by seducing his daughter-in-law and betraying his trust. I worried that some flaw within me might someday cause me to do the same to you...and I couldn't bear taking that risk.''

"Oh, Teagan, you would never serve me thus.''

"I now believe that, too. I've just read the letters my father wrote to my mother. He didn't desert us, Valeria. He was lost at sea on his way to build a new life for us in America.''

In his expression, in his voice Valeria could read how much that fact meant to him. "I'm glad for you, Teagan. But if you wanted to propose to me—I'm assuming this elaborate charade is a proposal?—why did you not simply call? There was no need to play highwayman. And I would be very obliged if you would remove the ropes binding my hands. They chafe dreadfully.''

"Since you've no place to run now but back into my arms, I suppose it's safe," he agreed, untying the cord and then rubbing solicitously at her wrists.

"The highwaymen was Mercy's idea—well, indirectly,'' he continued. "And I did call. But Molly told me you'd gone off with Sir William, to his mother's. And my aunt had informed me earlier that Lady Jersey knew Sir William intended to propose today. So naturally I assumed—''

"Incorrectly, as it turns out."

"—that he'd proposed, and you'd accepted. I couldn't let you make a mistake like that."

"A mistake? Marrying a good, responsible, upright man who, when he wants to propose, makes a proper call at a proper hour in a proper parlor?"

"You wouldn't be happy living with so stuffy and predictable a husband."

"Oh, would I not?"

"Come now, Valeria-love! You're more a rascal than I ever was. What proper matron would seek out and seduce a known rogue—in her hay barn? Or defy convention to befriend him in London? Or leave her proper suitor dangling and conduct an affair with him under the noses of her new household? Or pleasure him in an open field in broad daylight?"

"Perhaps," she conceded. "But I do want some proper things. A home. Children. A place to settle down."

"Ah, Valeria, your home is here." He put her hand to his chest. "Within the heart of a man who is terrified to promise you forever, but cannot envision life without you. Who couldn't possibly deserve you, but nonetheless wants to cherish you and your children for the rest of our lives with all the passion he possesses."

Before she could stop him, Teagan went down on one knee. "My dearest Valeria, will ye go adventuring with me? Will ye sleep with me in the shadows of the Pyramids, and walk barefoot with me on the sands of Cadiz? By the way, my employer—I'll explain that to you later—tells me there may be trouble brewing in Egypt, and wants to send me to investigate. We could make it our honeymoon trip."

"Egypt, is it?"

"Aye. Mayhap a bit of the Maghreb as well. Anything for my lady's pleasure. Ye like camels, do ye?"

A properly demure look on her face, Valeria rested her

chin on her fist, as if considering carefully. "Well, if you're prepared to offer all that, how can I refuse?"

And then that irredeemable rogue Teagan Fitzwilliams, in a delightful demonstration of some of the passion he possessed, showed Valeria right there on the public roadway just how thrilled he was at her acceptance.

* * * * *

REGENCY
Collection

*Let these sparklingly seductive delights whirl
you away to the ballrooms—and
bedrooms—of Polite Society!*

Volume 1 – 4th February 2011
Regency Pleasures by Louise Allen

Volume 2 – 4th March 2011
Regency Secrets by Julia Justiss

Volume 3 – 1st April 2011
Regency Rumours by Juliet Landon

Volume 4 – 6th May 2011
Regency Redemption by Christine Merrill

Volume 5 – 3rd June 2011
Regency Debutantes by Margaret McPhee

Volume 6 – 1st July 2011
Regency Improprieties by Diane Gaston

12 volumes in all to collect!

MILLS
BOON

www.millsandboon.co.uk

HISTORICAL

Regency

REBELLIOUS RAKE, INNOCENT GOVERNESS
by Elizabeth Beacon

Notorious rake Benedict Shaw can have his pick of *ton* heiresses, but one woman has caught his experienced eye... governess Miss Charlotte Wells! And he isn't used to taking no for an answer...

WANTED IN ALASKA
by Kate Bridges

Outlaw Quinn can't risk doctor's visits—kidnapping a nurse is the only answer. But Autumn MacNeil is only dressed as a nurse for a costume ball, Still, there's no way he can let her go now...

TAMING HER IRISH WARRIOR
by Michelle Willingham

Widow Honora St Leger knows there is little pleasure in the marriage bed, so why should she care that the disturbingly sexy Ewan MacEgan is to wed her sister? Ewan finds himself drawn to the forbidden Honora—one touch and he is longing to awaken her sensuality...

On sale from 1st April 2011
Don't miss out!